BRADLEY BAKER

and the Amulet of Silvermoor

DAVID LAWRENCE JONES

BRADLEY BAKER

and the Amulet of Silvermoor

The Amazing Adventures of Bradley Baker

BOOK TWO

Cover illustrated by Abie Greyvenstein

Author's Official Website: www.bradley-baker.com

ISBN 978-0-9561499-4-7

1

First published in the UK 2011

Avocado Media - Devon TQ1 2BT United Kingdom

www.avocadopublishing.co.uk

This book is dedicated to my father...

Douglas Albert Jones

…in recognition of his 39 years service with the

National Coal Board!

1

The Mauled Miner

The year is 1975 and the coldest Halloween eve you could imagine has been bestowed upon the small mining village of Ravenswood. A young Patrick Baker has not yet met his beautiful wife Margaret and he is currently working as a colliery electrician maintaining the surface plant at Silvermoor in Yorkshire. Many more years will follow before his son Bradley is born, who at the tender age of eleven will become the eternal chosen one. At this point in time the boy hero apparent is just a twinkle in his father's eye.

Silvermoor is a record breaking pit and is producing a million tons of coal per year, which feeds the local power station situated on the outskirts of Sheffield. It is a time of camaraderie, as the union of miners worked together in dirty and treacherous conditions. Coal offers the workforce job security within the local community and it forms the back bone to support local industry.

The black crystalised fossil fuel is being mined with great precision deep beneath Silvermoor's landmark winding wheels. The odourless methane from the freshly cut coal mixed with the sulphur dioxide emitted from the fault lines fill the underground workings with a deadly cocktail of gas, as the constant droning of heavy machinery simulates the sound of the industrial grind. The main colliery fan on the surface circulates the bitter October air through the inter-linking manmade passageways. This helps to disperse the heat that emanates from the heavy operating plant, which requires minute-by-minute maintenance from the perspiring mineworkers. There is constant a hive of activity within the parallel headings, which lead to each coal face. Both the inlet and the outlet headings carry an airborne mixture of stone and coal dust, as the steel toe caps of the miners boots rake up a haze of trodden ground.

Row upon row of razor-sharp tungsten teeth from one of the coal producing cutters tear into the jet-black strata of the Ravenswood seam. The huge drum turns progressively slow, as it moves along the *Number 5* coal face. Hydraulic jets of cooling fluid smash against the grinding picks and the creamy white liquid turns to black slush, as it mixes with the fine airborne dust. Not all the coolant hits its mark and the resulting over-spray covers the machine operator from head to foot with an ebony coat of black sludge.

Patrick Baker's older brother carries the huge responsibility of controlling the main coal-cutter on the *Number 5* district. Henley is guiding the heavy machine and it moves steadily along the metal-linked panzer chain that carries the coal away from the face. The experienced machinist wipes the dust filled coolant from his brow and he watches in amazement, as the spliced chunks of coal tumble onto the steel conveyor unit.

An elite team of chock men operate the hydraulic supports, as the entire coal face setup moves forward in a unified tandem. A series of loud explosions emanate from the cavities behind the supports, as solid rock collapses to fill the void left by the rich vein of black glistening coal. The miners work relentlessly and move around like a warren of burrowers, as the underground activities near the end of the afternoon shift. The dancing rays of light from their cap lamps cross like laser beams, as they ferry back and forth along the hundred metre long coal face.

Barney Huddlestone tapped his work colleague on the shoulder and raised his voice to conquer the noise of the heavy machinery. "Hey… Baker, it's nearly time to finish the cutting – it'll be shift end in five minutes so make sure this is the last run mate!"

Henley turned his head and shouted out his response. "You've got no chance me old cocker… there's still time for this beast to make another run along this line of black firewood!"

"Come on… enough is enough!" pleaded the tired face worker. "The lads have done their bit… it's time to go home!"

Henley laughed and maintained is stubborn authority. "We all need to earn some extra bonus and I'm sure Silvermoor's top brass will appreciate an extra ton of coal in their hopper tonight!"

Barney shook his head and his cap-lamp flickered, as he shouted. "We'll miss the paddy train back to the pit bottom if you don't make this the last one… my missus will kill me if I don't get home in time to mend her washing line – she's been going on at me for three weeks and I promised her I'd fix it ready for the morning!"

"What you going on about Barney… forget the washing line – I'm taking this baby down that face again!" replied Henley, as he pushed the reverse button on the control panel. "Anyhow, your missus won't need a washing line… it's probably still snowing on top - now get back on those chocks and follow me down!"

Barney's request had fallen on deaf ears and he had no choice but to reluctantly agree to Henley's instructions. He shook his head and followed his team leader's order then crouched to return to his chock support position.

Barney turned and gave a thumbs-up, as Henley pushed the metal lever and the coal cutting machine droned into life again. The large drum began to turn with an effortless motion and the grating of metal against coal echoed down the face, as the picks started to embed themselves into the prehistoric strata.

The operation had only moved about twenty metres along the return face when there was a loud bang. "What on earth was that!" shouted Henley, as he instinctively held up his arm to shield his eyes from the stray slithers of coal that flew from the cutter.

"The drum is stuck... I think we've hit some hard rock – there must be a fault line in the coal seam!" replied Barney.

"I'll see if I can release it... here hold this!" shouted Henley, as he pointed to the operating lever.

"What are you doing, Henley?" demanded Barney. "You can't go over the panzer when it's not isolated... it's too dangerous mate!" he warned and took hold of the lever.

"Don't be daft man... I've done it before – I just need to hammer this wooden block under the base and it'll cut free!" replied Henley, as the machine groaned under the pressure of the trapped drum.

"I'm not at all happy about you going behind that machine while it's still running!" insisted Barney, as he pulled at the sweaty grey vest that clung to Henley's back. "Don't be an idiot man... you'll injure yourself – now stop being stupid!"

The machine began to smoke under the immense pressure and Henley grabbed his work colleague's hand to pull it away from his clothing, just as the coal face deputy approached. "Let go of my shirt, Barney... the machine is overheating and the sooner I get in there to release the drum – the sooner you can go home to mend that blooming washing line of yours!"

Barney released his grip and turned to acknowledge the deputy. "Hello Ralph, before you ask... don't worry - Henley says he knows what he's doing and he has things under control!"

The deputy ignored Barney and asked. "What on earth is going on... why has the drum stopped?"

Barney explained that the cutters had bitten into a fault line of solid rock. He then insisted that the deputy tell Henley to turn off the machine.

"You're a bit late Barney... he's gone over the metal conveyor – he's disappeared behind the drum!" declared the deputy. "He's in big trouble... he could get the sack for that!"

"Henley Baker... get back here - Ralph says you'll be in the dog house if you don't get yourself out of there!" shouted Barney, as the colossal coal face machine began to vibrate.

There was no answer from his colleague and the machine let out a huge crunching noise, as the drum began to turn again slowly. Barney pulled the control lever back to stop the cutters from eating further into the coal and shouted out to his friend. "Well I'll be damned... you've done it – well done, Henley!"

Still no answer came from behind the drum and the deputy hit the emergency stop button. The whole coal face operation came to a standstill as machine after machine stopped humming and the metal-sheathed lights beneath the chocks went out one by one. "Let's get over there!" he insisted.

Barney did not hesitate and he followed the deputy over the panzer conveyor belt and witnessed their colleague lying motionless with his face down in the freshly cut coal. "Henley... are you okay mate?"

There was still no movement and Barney knelt down next to Henley. He took hold of his arm and gently turned him over onto his side, as he put his friend into the recovery position. "Henley... please talk to me!"

The deputy knelt down beside Barney and reached out to remove Henley's hard hat. "Turn your cap-lamp down... it's too bright – I can't see anything because you keep shining it in my eyes!" he ordered. "Is he alive?"

Barney reached up to his helmet and turned his lamp down to the dim position. He then focused the light on the back of Henley's head and placed two fingers on his neck. "I don't like this boss... I can't feel a pulse – I think we need to turn him on his back!"

"Okay... after three!" agreed the deputy, as they both took hold of Henley's clothing. "One...two...three - lift!"

"Arrrrrrrrgh!" shouted Barney, as he jolted backwards and landed hard against the panzer side.

"Oh my God!" exclaimed the deputy. "His face...it's gone!"

Barney regained his balance, as he lifted himself away from the metal conveyor belt and re-approached the horrific scene. The two men stared in disbelief at their dead mineworker friend. Henley lay still and his facial features had been removed by the sudden movement of the drum. The sharp cutters that he had so meticulously maintained each and every arduous shift had now gouged out the front of his skull. His featureless face glistened, as the black coal dust clung to the open wounds like iron filings to a magnet.

A chilling rush of air gusted from behind the hydraulic chocks and at that moment every light along the coal face flickered then extinguished again. The rays of light beams that emanated from every miners cap lamp along the chock line were snuffed out too, as the coalface fell in to complete darkness.

Barney reached up to his helmet and attempted to turn on his lamp but to no avail. "What's happening... my cap lamp isn't working?"

"I don't know!" shouted the deputy, as he too tried to turn on his light and tucked up his collar to shield his neck. "That wind... it feels so icy and it sounds so eerie!"

"Yeah and it smells disgusting... like decaying flesh!" exclaimed Barney, as he covered his nose to smoother the stench. "It reeks of death!"

There was a sense of confusion and the noise of frightened voices echoed along the coal face, as all the mineworkers panicked in the still of the clammy darkness. Then suddenly the coal face was illuminated again and all the cap lamps re-lit simultaneously, as the commotion stopped.

There was an empty feeling amongst the ranks and the men stared at each other in amazement, as the deputy let out a shocking cry. "He's gone… his body – it's disappeared!"

A search of the district ensued but Henley Baker's body was never found. The cutting of coal at the *number 5* face was halted prematurely and the area where he perished was shut down soon after his disappearance. Up until the colliery's closure in 1992 the haunting sounds of the *Mauled Miner* could be heard along the old underground passageways following the horrific accident.

Many miners refused to work along the Ravenswood seam and most fled the scene when the cold mid-winter winds blew along the district and the eerie hallowing sounds echoed out from behind the old mine workings.

Barney Huddlestone has since retired and still spends most of his afternoons in a drunken state at the bar of Silvermoor Working Men's Club where he continues to recite his tale to any interested listener. The legend of Henley's ghost has passed the test of time long after the unfortunate event.

Patrick Baker swore never to speak of the incident again and he has hidden the truth about his brother from both his children. Bradley and Frannie have never been told about the way their uncle died on that fateful day back in 1975.

2

Birthday Celebrations

It is late October in the present day and the summer holiday in Sandmouth seemed like a distant memory to Bradley Baker. It was incredible to think that only a few months had passed since he had returned to the village of Ravenswood having just participated in an amazing adventure. The time spent with Aunt Vera in Devon had changed his life forever and he now carried an enormous responsibility on his young shoulders.

Bradley had promised Meltor that the journey into Pathylon would be kept a secret and the trust that had been bestowed on him by the Galetian High Priest was a huge honour. Although the evil curse over Pathylon had been successfully lifted and the King was now free, Bradley's ownership of the sacred *grobite* still carried a huge liability. The ancient gold coin had been gifted to him by Meltor and it was a portal key that empowered him to travel back to the arcane world of Pathylon. Bradley was the *Eternal Chosen One* and he was fully aware that his services could be called upon at any time by the High Priesthood, which governed the faraway kingdom.

Memories of a friendship lost following his incredible journey down the plughole filled him with sadness at the demise of his Krogon friend Grog. However, this was ceded with excitement at the thought of meeting his two new found friends Musgrove and Sereny again. But before they could all be reunited, he was to enjoy a very special day.

It was Bradley's twelfth birthday and he stared at two perfectly wrapped presents, which were stacked adjacent the other gifts he had already opened. These included a new mobile phone from his parents and an old Swiss army knife, which used to belong to Grandpa Penworthy. He focussed on the available space on the small coffee table in the front lounge of 127 Braithwaite Road and recalled an unforgettable time he spent lake fishing in Devon with his grandfather.

Bradley cast his mind back to a sunny day at *Town Park Lakes*, on the outskirts of Sandmouth where Aunt Vera lived. Even back then he was a budding adventurer who had always been fascinated by the multi-functional tool in his grandpa's fishing tackle bag. He was only six at the time when his grandfather promised him that he would be given the Swiss army knife on his twelfth birthday.

It was a shame grandpa wasn't around to see his big day. Grandma had carefully wrapped the knife and she had included an old note that his grandfather had written detailing clear instructions that Bradley must only use it when out fishing with his father.

Bradley's thoughts of his adoring grandfather were interrupted by the urgent sound of his mother's voice. "Come on Bradley... open the rest of your presents," insisted Margaret, as she pushed some of them aside and maneuvered a homemade birthday cake into the empty space on the table. "I don't know why you keep drifting off ... you are supposed to be enjoying your birthday."

Margaret encouraged her son to stop day dreaming and Bradley refocused his attention onto the twelve candles that flickered on the cake. It was his favourite; chocolate sponge with butter-cream filling and smothered in thick dairy milk chocolate. She had predictably positioned two customary plastic footballers and goalposts on top of the traditional masterpiece.

"Where's the football?" asked Bradley, as he made his mother aware that the same opposing footballers who appear every year on each cake had nothing to play with.

"Oh... I'm sure it's in the loft with the rest of your *Subuteo* stuff," replied Margaret, as she pointed at the ceiling. "And I've no intentions of going up there right now... I hate that loft ladder because it always catches my fingers - you'll just have to pretend there's a football on there."

Bradley's father entered the room having overheard his son's request. "Here you go!" said Patrick, as he removed some well-chewed gum from his mouth and rolled it into a ball. "Will this do?"

"Don't you dare!" warned Margaret, as she snatched the sticky sphere of spearmint from her husband's hand. "That's disgusting, Patrick!"

"I was only joking dear!" exclaimed Patrick, shrugging his shoulders and aiming a chilled-out look in Bradley's direction and muttered under his breath. "*Corrrrr... eggshells or what?*"

Margaret heard her husband's comment and gave Patrick a disapproving look. She re-coiled her neck in readiness for the next stage of what appeared to be the start of a slanging match. Bradley ignored his parent's impending spat and picked up his new mobile phone just as Grandma Penworthy intervened. "Stop messing around you two... my gardening programme starts in a bit and I need to get home and I can't miss that lovely *Monty Don* - he's doing a piece on his lettuce today!"

Bradley could not resist. "What's he doing on his lettuce, Gran?" he asked with a raw smile.

Grandma paused for a second and then the realisation of what Bradley had said prompted the expected response. "Don't you start... you cheeky little monkey!"She insisted and continued to clatter her knitting needles together whilst sitting comfortably in one of the fireside chairs. "And you can put that phone down and blow the candles out... don't forget to make a wish Bradley!"

The boy smiled and acknowledged his grandma's request by affording her another innocent look, whilst he continued to explore the menu screen of his new mobile phone. "I seem to be having problems getting a signal, anyway... so I'll have another go at setting up the *Wi-Fi* connections later," he declared. Then to his surprise, the phone started to vibrate and emitted a sharp beeping sound.

"Is that a text coming through?" asked Grandma.

Bradley did not answer. He was intrigued at the blue gemstone that had just appeared on the screen and it started to flash. The network icon in the top right hand section of the screen appeared and displayed a series of five bars. "Ah... I've finally got a signal!" exclaimed the excited boy. "Don't recognise the network though."

Patrick sat down beside his son and took a look at the screen. "*TECO*?" he read. "Never heard of that one... must be a new network from BT - they've been advertising something about their new phone systems on the TV."

Bradley ignored his father's comment and the appearance of the birthday cake disturbed the network observations, as the screen went blank. He pressed the on/off button but nothing happened. "I think the battery needs charging."

Margaret asked her son to put the phone down and repeated Grandma's request. "Come on... it's time to blow out your candles and make a wish," she insisted, as K2 appeared.

The arrival of the cake had aroused the dog's attention, as Grandma continued to knit one pearl one, as Bradley's father formed a tight headlock around the Burmese Mountain Dog's broad neck. The hungry hound readied himself for the kill and Patrick struggled to control the mischievous dog, as the great family pet slobbered at the sight of the chocolate feast.

Bradley's little sister muscled in on the act and echoed their mother's instruction. "Wish for something really nice," insisted Frannie, as she prodded her elder brother in the thigh. "A trip to *Clumber Farm Adventure Park* would be good."

Bradley put down the phone and deliberately ignored his irritating little sister, as he played along with the birthday ritual. He closed his eyes and prepared to complete the task and thought to himself. "Forget the kiddy tractor rides at Clumber Farm... I want some real adventure."

It did not take him long to think of a wish and he succeeded in blowing out all twelve candles in one breath. Applause and cheers echoed around the room, as Bradley's attention to the birthday celebration wandered yet again. The voices of congratulation faded into the distance and his wish for another great adventure took his mind back to the land of Pathylon.

The completion of the ancient ritual conducted by King Luccese had successfully lifted the evil curse that had once shrouded the arcane world. The earthquake that followed the ceremony had partially destroyed the Island of Restak and the Kaikane Idol that had stood so proud. The Vortex of Souls had long since died and the Forbidden Caves had collapsed. There was no way in or out of Pathylon and Bradley thought of his old friend Meltor, as his concentration was disturbed by Frannie's screaming.

"Oh no... K2's got the cake!" shouted the excited girl.

"Quick Patrick... grab him!" exclaimed Margaret, as the dog brushed heavily past Bradley's father.

The naughty hound soon fled the scene with the chocolate cake lodged firmly in his large jowls. Margaret, Patrick and Frannie chased the clumsy dog out of the house into the garden.

As the commotion continued outside, Grandma Penworthy adjusted her knitting needles and caught Bradley's attention by throwing a ball of wool in his direction. "What are you thinking about Bradley?" she asked. "You look like you're somewhere else today... what's the matter?"

"Oh, nothing Grandma... just thinking about stuff - you know," replied Bradley in a nonchalant manner.

"What are you up to young man?" enquired Grandma, as she bent down to pick up a piece of stray chocolate sponge and butter-cream from the carpet.

"Really Gran... its nothing," insisted Bradley, as he walked towards the door. "When Mum comes back in, please tell her I'm just going to the toilet."

"But you've not finished opening your presents yet!" exclaimed the old lady. "There's still a couple left... it's not like you Bradley to leave gifts unopened – what's the matter with you?"

Bradley looked down at the two unopened presents and quickly assessed by their shape what they might be. One was shaped like a box of chocolates; either *Cadbury's Roses* or *Quality Street* and he muttered to himself. "No prizes for guessing that one." He then picked up the other present to test its suppleness. "Socks!" he exclaimed without hesitation.

"Well are you going to open them?" insisted Grandma.

"Later Gran... later – I'll wait for Mum and Dad to come back in," replied Bradley, as he put down the obvious gift and focused his attention back on the new mobile phone that his parents had bought for him.

"Alright then... you go on – I'm sure there'll still be plenty of time before your Dad takes me home," explained Grandma, as her grandson prepared to leave the room.

Bradley made his way upstairs and sought refuge in the bathroom so he could continue to reminisce about the unbelievable summer adventure he had encountered with his new friends.

Meltor had entrusted Bradley with the sacred *grobite* coin. Only Musgrove and Sereny knew it still existed and he was looking forward to a reunion with them over the October half term break. The inquisitive boy could not wait to see if the coin would provide more excitement and adventure for the three heroes.

Bradley stared at the plughole in the bath tub and smiled to himself. He then left the bathroom and entered his bedroom. The frustrated boy proceeded to search through his drawers and then turned his attention to the untidy window sill. "Where's that coin?" he muttered to himself. "I have to find it for when Muzzy and Sereny arrive... I can't remember where I put it."

Bradley started to panic and began to visualise Frannie finding the grobite and possibly taking it to school for *show and tell* in front of her classmates. He was sure he had put the sacred grobite in his sock drawer, but it was not there now.

He made his way to the top of the stairs and leant over the banister. Bradley shouted down to his sister. "Have you been messing around in my bedroom, Frannie?"

There was no answer from the little redhead, as she continued to chase the dog about the garden with their parents. K2 was having lots of fun leading them a merry dance around the ornate fish pond with the chocolate cake still hanging from his slobbering mouth.

3

Message for the King

Meanwhile in the parallel world of Pathylon, an aging Galetian woke suddenly from his alarming deep sleep. Meltor's bed sheets were soaked from the sweat that had perspired from his aching body. The High Priest's heart was racing and he kicked back the heavy bed covers with his trembling feet.

He sat upright then swung his legs round and off the side of the huge ornate bedstead. The exhausted High Priest paused for a few seconds and stared at the bedroom window that overlooked the magnificent City of Kasol at the heart of the Galetis Empire.

The clear blue skies above continued to broadcast a message of calmness across the five regions of Pathylon, since Varuna's capture and imprisonment in the Shallock Tower. King Luccese had regained his throne and was now enjoying a mutually beneficial trading arrangement with the Freytorians. Harg, the disgraced High Priest of Krogonia, had been banished to the Unknown Land and a renewed diplomatic strain ran through the High Priesthood that governed the land. The sorceress Flaglan had been pardoned by the King and continued to lead the Tree Elves that frequented the great Forest of Haldon.

Meltor tried desperately to recall the strange images from his dream. Bradley Baker and the other human visitors from the outside world had played an important part in it. However, there was something troubling the old Priest and his dream had turned into a nightmare, as he recalled terrible dark scenes from his blurred vision. "This is bad," he muttered and placed his head in his hands. "This is very bad indeed... the sacred grobite will have to be activated once more - the boy hero will have come back to Pathylon."

Meltor's thoughts focused on Bradley Baker, who he had heralded as the eternal chosen one. The old Galetian knew he could call upon the brave youngster whenever Pathylon was in danger. He hoped that the boy still possessed the gold coin, which contained the mystical powers necessary to transport him back into the arcane world.

The High Priest had hoped he would not need to call upon Bradley so soon after the last debacle and he reached for a porcelain jug, which was placed on his bedside cabinet. Meltor poured some fresh Klomus water into a nearby goblet and took a long drink. The dark side of his dream became even more apparent, as the hallowed river water passed his lips.

Meltor regained his composure and quickly rose to his feet. "I must alert King Luccese," he murmured, as he made his way to the en-suite bathing chamber.

This was not the first dream of its sort. Meltor had been having the same recurring images flashing in his mind ever since the departure of the Freytorian Iceberg Ship some months ago. He had been harbouring a terrible premonition for some time, but he had not mentioned anything about it to King Luccese or the members of the Royal Congress. The wise Galetian did not want to create any unnecessary panic within the High Priesthood, but this last dream had been visually clear and had confirmed his suspicions.

Meltor made his way over to an ornate writing desk and dipped a writing quill into the ink pot on the dresser. He began to make notes about his dream on a piece of ancient cretyre paper, but his concentration was interrupted by a delicate knock on the bed chamber door. He rose from his seat and moved back towards the bath chamber and lifted a crimson robe from its hook. "Enter!" he ordered, as he pulled on the gown, which was hemmed with gold and jade coloured thread.

The door creaked and a thin strip of light from the hallway spanned across the bedroom floor, as the gap in the doorway widened. A petite Galetian female appeared and gently pushed the heavy door open, as she entered the room with her head lowered.

Meltor continued to scribble on the note paper and the young girl approached him tentatively. "My lord... breakfast is now being served in your study," explained the pretty maid. "I have collected your copy of the *Empire Times*... it has been neatly ironed and is ready for your perusal," continued the nervous servant and she maintained a courteous rapport, whilst her master completed his written note. "Is there anything you would like me to take downstairs for you, sir?"

"No... no – that's fine, thank you my dear," replied Meltor, as he finished tying the braid around his muscular torso. "Oh... there is one thing you can do for me – please take this letter to the city mail room and ask the *Galetian Bird Whistler* to send it to the Royal City of Trad for the urgent attention of King Luccese."

Meltor picked up the quill again and signed the letter then walked towards a burning oil lamp that adorned his carved dressing table. The High Priest pulled out a taper from a small glass vase and held it in the flame for a few seconds until it started to glow. He proceeded to light a nearby candle and poured the hot wax onto a fold in the letter. Meltor then slowly turned his hand and positioned the huge gold ring that coveted his middle finger above the melted wax. With meticulous precision, he rolled the Galetian seal onto the red wax to authenticate the importance of the message.

"There you are my dear... please make sure this reaches the King by first light tomorrow," instructed the High Priest, as he blew over the hot wax to aid the cooling process.

"Yes... of course my lord – I'll take it over straight away," she replied, taking care not to smudge the perfect seal, as Meltor maintained his hold on the letter. "I'll make sure the bird whistler attaches it to the finest raven in his aviary, my lord."

"Thank you, that's very kind of you young miss," replied Meltor. "And by the way that scent you are wearing... it suits you - you smell really nice my dear." The bashful maid tugged softly on the note, as the Galetian's strong hand finally released its grip and he spoke once more. "Please inform the kitchen staff that I will be down to eat my breakfast shortly."

"Yes sir... and thank you for your generous comments, my lord," replied the timid servant, as she turned towards the door.

The maid finally left the room and a final whiff of scent reached Meltor's nose, as the troubled Galetian walked over to the window. He stared out and within a few minutes witnessed the young female running across the courtyard in the direction of the city mail room.

Within minutes a large black raven was released from the roof top chamber of the post room. The elegant bird flew towards Meltor's window and swooped down to gain eye contact with the High Priest. It was as though the raven knew how important the message was and it wanted to reassure him that the note would reach its destination safely.

"Fly strong and direct my friend!" encouraged the High Priest, as he touched the window pane to acknowledge the hovering bird's gesture.

The raven instinctively blinked its eye lids then turned in mid-flight and flew upwards out of sight. Within seconds the bird swooped back down and returned to Meltor's window, where it majestically hovered again circling its wings in slow motion. With a final gesture of assurance to the Galetian High Priest, the strong feathered creature cast its large wingspan backwards and thrust itself downwards to gain the momentum it needed to embark upon its arduous journey to the royal city.

4

The Old Blue Light

Back in Ravenswood, it was a bitterly cold and windy Saturday afternoon during the October half term holiday. Bradley's low key birthday celebrations had filled the morning and he had managed to un-wrap the chocolates and the socks before Grandma Penworthy departed the Baker household in time to catch her gardening programme.

Bradley was still worried about the disappearance of the sacred grobite coin and he had struggled to concentrate on his father's affections during their morning walk.

Patrick Baker stopped to catch his breath and he looked back down the hillside to witness his twelve year old son tumbling in the long grass with K2. The unplanned walk had been taken so the greedy hound could carry out its business following the consumption of the rich chocolate cake but K2 was more interested in antagonising the boy. The playful dog had pinned the boy's slight figure to the floor and proceeded to wrap his affectionate wet tongue around Bradley's cold face.

The northern chilled air bit aggressively into Patrick's cheeks, as he cupped his gloved hands. Bradley's father attempted to exhale a warm gust of air from his blue lips into the thermal knitwear that protected his numb fingers. "Come on, Son!" he shouted and made a final effort to reach the peak of the steep hill. "Hey Bradley... come and take a look at this fantastic view!"

"I'll be right with you, Dad!" replied Bradley, as he forced the over-excited canine from his upper body by pushing his boot soles into K2's midriff. "Just as soon as I can get this stupid dog off me!"

Patrick started to laugh and shouted some commanding words of encouragement to persuade the persistent hound to leave his frustrated son alone. Bradley finally broke free and continued his ascent up the hill, as K2 bounded in hot pursuit of his young master.

Once at the top, Bradley stood at his father's side and gazed out over the valley. The trees were bare and the top branches still bore remnants of the early snow that had bizarrely fallen a few days before. The skies were full of grey clouds and the wind whistled around the ears of the two ramblers, as they continued to take in the pre-winter setting. K2 had now lost interest in Bradley and sought pleasure in sniffing at every clump of grass, as he carried out a systematic marking of scent on the surrounding foliage by continuously cocking his hind leg.

"Look over there, Bradley," observed Patrick, as he pointed to a dip in the valley. "You can just make out the roof of our house."

"Oh yeah... I can see one of the vent pipes from the old mining shaft," replied Bradley. "And look, Dad... there's the old blue light you used to look after."

Bradley was referring to the cenotaph memorial, which now stood in the middle of the small housing estate and still commemorated the soldiers that fought and lost their lives during the two great world wars. Patrick used to maintain the mercury vapour lamp that was positioned behind the blue glass lens at the top of the war memorial. The changing of the lamp formed part of the weekly maintenance checks, which was part of his duties as an electrician when he worked at Silvermoor Colliery.

The tree-lined valley, which they now overlooked, used to accommodate the site of the coalmine's surface power plant and shaft winding gear pit heads. All the old colliery buildings and winding wheels were gone and the black coal slag heaps were now covered in a blanket of rich green grass. All that remained of Patrick's old work place was the cenotaph and the two vent pipes, which stood vertical like ship's masts and marked the location of the sealed-off shafts.

"It's a shame it all had to be levelled," remarked Patrick, as he wiped his nose with his sleeve. "Blimey it's cold!"

"Do you miss working at Silvermoor Colliery?" asked Bradley.

"Not at all... since my brother passed away – the closure of the pit has been a godsend!" replied Patrick.

"You don't talk about Uncle Henley very much... do you Dad?" asked Bradley.

"Nothing to talk about," replied Patrick in a protective tone, as he attempted to avoid his son's inevitable question. "He died long before you were born... I hadn't even met your Mum – so she never got to know him either!"

"How did he die?" asked Bradley.

Patrick paused for a moment. "That's a conversation for another time Bradley... when you're a bit older."

Bradley's father turned away and the inquisitive boy realised that this particular line of questioning was over, so he picked out the vent pipe above the old East Pit Shaft again. The tall column jutted out of the ground like a giant periscope. It was adjacent his house, which was built only a few years ago. The new Silvermoor housing estate extended westward from the village of Ravenswood to accommodate the growing population in the area.

"Dad?" asked the inquisitive boy, as he pointed towards the housing estate.

"Yes," replied Patrick, peering down at the puzzled look on Bradley's face.

"You know our house?" continued Bradley. "…is it safe for us to live in?"

"Of course it is, Son," laughed Patrick. "How many times have I got to tell you… both the old East & West Pit shafts were sealed off over ten years ago with some thirty metres of reinforced concrete?"

"Yeah, but…" continued Bradley.

"No buts, Son… trust me it's as safe as houses - get it, safe as houses?" replied Patrick, attempting a humorous jibe at his son's expense with a typical *dad-joke.*

"Not impressed Father," replied Bradley. "I'm being serious… it's important!"

"Sorry Bradley… I didn't mean to make fun - I know the precarious position of our house concerns you," replied Patrick, as he patted his son's back. "Let me reassure you once and for all… we're not about to be swallowed up into the depths of the old mine workings of Silvermoor - just yet!"

"Just yet!" replied Bradley, as he gave his father a disapproving look.

"Oh Bradley… leave it will you!" insisted Patrick, who was now starting to lose patience with his son's paranoia.

"But, Dad…"

Patrick tried to change the subject, as Bradley refused to back down and attempted to interrogate him again. "Are your hands warm enough, Son?" asked Patrick. "Where are your gloves?"

"I forgot to bring them with me," replied Bradley, as he sought warm sanctuary in the large pockets of his camouflaged canvass jeans.

Now that his father had pointed it out, Bradley started to feel the cold in the tips of his fingers. He forced his hands deeper into the side pockets of his trousers and pushed passed his new mobile phone to find an even colder object. Bradley smiled immediately and turned to look at his father. "I'm really looking forward to seeing Muzzy and Sereny again, tomorrow," he enthused and held tightly to the metal coin.

"What made you say that?" asked Patrick.

"Oh, nothing," smiled Bradley, as he wrapped his fingers around the sacred *grobite*, which had reminded the boy of the recent adventure in Pathylon.

Bradley's mind wandered for a moment and he thought back to the time he had spent with his new friends during the summer holiday in Devon. The time spent at Aunt Vera's cottage and the mystical experience down the drainpipe still felt as though it had all happened yesterday.

Bradley thought back to his journey into Pathylon and how he had been heralded the *Eternal Chosen One*. Meltor had entrusted him to keep the magical coin, which had enabled him to travel to the arcane world of Pathylon via the plughole in Aunt Vera's hot tub.

Musgrove Chilcott and Sereny Ugbrooke would be travelling by train in the morning and arrangements had been made between the children's parents that the two friends would be staying at Bradley's house over the half term. Since their memorable time spent together in Sandmouth, the three of them had kept in touch by email and had made some exciting plans for the Halloween celebrations, which would take place during their week's holiday together.

Patrick interrupted Bradley's thoughts and proceeded to explain some of the workings associated with the old Silvermoor coalmine. "It's hard to imagine that this is the exact spot where the old *slag heap* conveyor belt motor used to sit," explained Patrick, as he recollected his time with the National Coal Board. "I used to sit here for hours on the nightshift looking out towards the city lights of Sheffield… thinking what it would be like to work away from a dump like Silvermoor Colliery."

"Well you did get away didn't you, Dad?" exclaimed Bradley, as he held onto his father's arm. "I know it took the closure of the pit to help you get a new job, but at least you're doing what you want to do now."

"Yes... I suppose you're right, Son - I just don't want you to make the same mistake and end up working in some mucky industrial work place that makes you unhappy," said Patrick, as he gently pulled Bradley's head into his side. "I want you to look for some adventure in your life."

"Oh you don't have to worry about that, Dad!" exclaimed Bradley, as he grinned broadly. "I've already tasted a bit of adventure."

"What are you talking about?" asked Patrick.

"Err... nothing, Dad?" replied Bradley.

Bradley had to keep reminding himself that although his father had taken part in the amazing events during the summer holidays, Patrick was one of the adults who now mysteriously knew nothing about it all. Bradley's father had played a significant part in the release of King Luccese and the demise of Varuna, but the magic coin had somehow erased the memories of everyone who had taken part in the search for Bradley and his friend Musgrove Chilcott. Only Bradley, Sereny and Musgrove had been entrusted with the ability to recall the amazing adventure set in the arcane world of Pathylon.

Bradley diverted his thoughts away from the summer activities and he now focused his attention back to the present situation. The young adventurer was feeling very uncomfortable up on the windy hillside and he turned to his father. "Can we go back home?" he shivered, as K2 came bounding back towards them. "I'm getting really cold now, Dad."

"Yes... we had better get back - your Mum and Frannie will be wondering where we've got to," replied Patrick, as he bent down to attach the lead to K2's collar. "We'd better put this on you old fella... it's starting to get dark and we don't want you wandering off again."

5

An Urgent Meeting

Back in the medieval world of Pathylon, the exhausted raven had flown determinedly throughout the day without stopping for a respite. The gentle winds that blew northerly from beyond the Peronto Alps had carried the exhausted bird through the darkness of the following night. The long arduous journey had taken the great black messenger over the Galetis Empire and across the Forest of Haldon. The intelligent feathered creature had then followed the River Klomus and eventually reached Trad's city mail-room, as the dawn broke over the capital.

The High Priest of Devonia was informed of the bird's arrival and he made his way hastily across the main square to the mail-room. The Devonian bird whistler was waiting and he carefully handed the letter to Pavsik. "Ah, the seal of the Galetis Empire... this must be from the wise Meltor - it must be important," he stated and broke the crest embedded in the crimson wax.

Pavsik quickly read the contents of the note and rushed out of the building in the direction of the Royal Palace. The square was now heaving with traders' busy setting up their stalls in readiness for the morning fruit market. The High Priest patiently made his way through the maze of brightly coloured canvasses and eventually reached the tall ornate gates that formed the entrance to the palace grounds. The guards on duty acknowledged his arrival and recognised the urgent look on his face, as they pulled on the heavy gold bars. Pavsik squeezed through the opening and quickened his pace, as he made his way down the long driveway that led to the main entrance of the palace. Another pair of guards saluted, as he entered the magnificent building and continued through the winding passageways that led to the royal chamber.

More palace guards stood to attention and uncrossed their long battle sabres, as Pavsik pushed open the heavy wooden doors that secured the King's private quarters. He scanned the huge room and noticed the King lounging quietly near an open fire. Luccese was relaxing on a crimson couch and he talked softly to his beautiful wife, who was sat at his feet. Queen Vash had been crying and she stared lovingly into her husband's eyes, as the startled King rose to his feet and reached for his sheathed sword.

Pavsik bowed his head and fell to one knee and pleaded forgiveness, as Luccese pulled out the steel blade. "Sire... please do not raise your sword - I did not mean to disturb you!"

"What is the meaning of this, Pavsik!" demanded Luccese, as he retracted the sword back into its sheath. "Have you no sense of privacy?"

"My lord, I am so sorry to barge in like this... it's just, well – err..." The Devonian High Priest hesitated. "Here, my lord... it will all make sense if I give you this message - it is addressed for your urgent attention!"

King Luccese took the broken sealed letter from Pavsik's nervous hand and looked at the Galetian imprint in the wax. "Please get to your feet Pavsik... I didn't mean to shout at you," endeared the King, as his wife left the chamber. "It's just that Queen Vash has received sad news that her mother is not well... it was a delicate moment – you understand?"

"Sire... I am so sorry!" replied Pavsik, as he regained an upright position. "I just got so carried away with the urgency of delivering the message to you, your majesty."

"Never mind dear Pavsik," insisted Luccese, as he handed the letter back to his trusted High Priest. "Please read it to me... I do not have my reading lenses to hand."

Pavsik unfolded the letter and immediately made Luccese aware of Meltor's words. A brief conversation followed and without hesitation they agreed that a date must be set for a gathering of the High Priesthood.

Luccese walked back towards the great marble fireplace and paused for a moment, as he watched the flames dancing off the cretyre logs. He then turned to Pavsik and suggested. "All five regions must be represented and all the leaders must attend this meeting, Pavsik... I don't want any excuses - even Flaglan from the Forest of Haldon," he insisted. "I fear for the safety of Pathylon... especially with it being so soon after Varuna's evil deed - he upset the harmony within the kingdom and the populous are still feeling uneasy about the recent curse that cast a dark shadow over our land."

Pavsik reminded his King. "Don't forget my lord... we only have four elected leaders at this time since you banished Harg to the Unknown Land - we have not yet had time to elect a new High Priest for Krogonia."

"Yes... yes of course, I am aware of that – this is something we will also have to address at the meeting," acknowledged Luccese, as he strode back and forth within the royal quarters. "It is important the Krogons across the Satorc Bridge have our support and I fully understand that they cannot continue indefinitely without a regional High Priest... so much to do and so little time - anyhow, at least we can set the date." He stated and returned to the fireplace, as he reached up to the mantelpiece to retrieve a half filled glass of wine. "We'll hold the meeting the day after tomorrow... this should give everyone time to get organised - now, please make the necessary arrangements, Pavsik?"

"I'll put it on the royal calendar immediately, Sire... and I'll send out the invitations for the meeting within the hour," replied Pavsik. "Where shall we hold the gathering, your Highness?"

"Here... in the royal capital - the top chamber of the Shallock Tower would be very appropriate," replied Luccese. "Especially as Varuna still languishes in one of the cells just beneath the meeting room... but make sure no word of this is leaked to the palace guards - I don't want that obnoxious Hartopian getting wind of the meeting."

"What difference would it make, my lord?" asked Pavsik, as he turned to leave the chamber.

"None!" replied the King. "I just can't stand the thought of that cowardly thug gloating inside his cell... the less that evil Hartopian knows the better!"

"Very well, your majesty," smiled Pavsik, as he left the room and gently closed the doors behind him.

The next few days leading up to the meeting passed quickly and the High Priests started to arrive for the important gathering in Trad. Flaglan, the beautiful High Priestess who represented the Forest of Haldon, was unexpectedly the first to arrive in the royal city. She was joined by Pavsik who escorted the sorceress to the meeting room inside the Shallock Tower. It was not long before Meltor arrived from the Galetis Empire, followed by a young Hartopian called Guan-yin the newly appointed female High Priest for the Blacklands.

The conversation between the regional leaders was minimal, as they sat patiently inside the Shallock Tower chamber and waited for King Luccese to arrive. It was not long before an announcement bellowed from one of the tower guards. "All rise!" he instructed, as the King entered the chamber and everyone rose to their feet.

"Thank you guard... now please leave us," said Luccese calmly. "And please be seated everyone."

"Good to see you again… my beloved and forgiving King," commented Flaglan, as the curvature of her chest heaved within the delicate scantily clad clothing that adorned the slim figure of the beautiful temptress.

"Nice to see you have dressed appropriately for the occasion, my dear Flaglan," replied Luccese, as he trained his eyes away from the buxom chest of the flirtatious High Priestess.

"You do not approve, my lord?" smiled Flaglan, as she revelled in her sultry beauty.

"I feel it would be more appropriate my dear Flaglan if you could adjust your attire slightly to adhere to the professional standards I expect when the High Priesthood meet on occasions like this," suggested Luccese, calmly.

"Occasions like what?" enquired the sorceress.

"I will discuss the agenda with everyone here present in due course, Flaglan," replied Luccese. "Now, if you would please tend to your costume… as I politely asked."

"Oh… of course my lord," replied Flaglan, as she adjusted her robed voiles to suit her King's request. "What would your beautiful Queen think if I did not honour your wishes in her absence?"

Luccese frowned and fought to hold back his reply. Queen Vash was still upset by her mother's illness but he was not going to let Flaglan's provocative comments and demeanor draw him into referring to a private matter.

Pavsik could see by the look on the King's face that he was beginning to look uncomfortable with the affected manner of the gorgeous High Priestess and he decided to deflect the conversation. "Err… th - thank you Flaglan!" He interrupted. "Now, shall we move on to the reason why we are all here today – the agenda for the meeting Sire?"

"Yes, Pavsik… thank you – now let's get down to business," agreed Luccese, as he gave his Devonian High Priest a grateful glance. "It is good to see you all again… but I regret to say - under grave circumstances."

"If I may now ask, your majesty... why have you summoned us here?" asked Guan-yin nervously.

"Well my dear High Priestess... it's a shame that the first invitation you accept, as the new leader of the Blacklands – is one with such a negative influence," explained the King. "I think the best way to start this meeting would be for Meltor to tell us of his recent premonition," suggested Luccese and he offered an open hand for the Galetian to continue. "I request that you take the chair, my old friend."

The ailing High Priest politely covered his mouth with a tight fist, as he coughed and stood to thank the King for calling the meeting. "Before we move to the main item on the agenda... I would first like to make a recommendation," requested Meltor. "As you are all aware, we currently have no designated leader for the region of Krogonia and I would like to propose someone to take on that responsibility... even if it is on a short term basis - the region needs some stability and there is no obvious Krogon choice to succeed Harg."

"I'm intrigued... who do you have in mind, Meltor?" asked King Luccese.

"Well... Grog would have been the obvious choice but as you are all aware he bravely lost his life in defense of the kingdom - therefore, I am proposing someone else who is very dear to us all," Meltor continued. "My lord, I propose that we recommend a true friend and ally to the royal congress for consideration..."

"A true friend and ally... who do you speak of?" demanded Flaglan, as she adjusted her delicate costume to suit the King's request.

"If I might finish," insisted Meltor, as he cast his female peer a disapproving glare. "I propose we recommend..."

Before Meltor could finish his sentence, there was a loud thud against one of the chamber windows. The assembly of delegates all turned their heads in the direction of the leaded stone-framed glass. The disturbance had coincided with a very important announcement from Meltor and everyone was holding their midriffs in reaction to the sudden noise.

"What was that?" asked Guan-yin shakily, as her weasel-like snout quivered. "I don't know about the rest of you… but that made me jump!"

The timing was impeccable and Meltor made his way over to the window and opened the sash. He looked outside to check what had caused the noise and saw a stunned feathered creature lying on the stone sill. The amused Galetian let out a huge sigh and a good-humoured laugh, as he turned to the astonished group. "It's okay my friends… it's just a poor moola bird – it must have be blinded by the sun," assumed Meltor, as he closed the sash and refastened the iron closure. "It did hit the window with a fair old bang… the little thing is recovering on the sill – I think it will be okay!"

"Never mind if the moola is alive… I agree with Guan-yin - that made me jump out of my skin." stated Pavsik in a light-hearted tone, as he looked around at the faces of the delegates. "Is everyone okay and are you all ready to resume?"

Everyone nodded and the meeting room inside the Shallock Tower soon filled with laughter, as the condition of the moola bird took precedence over more serious matters. Meltor recomposed himself and addressed the group again. "My lord and fellow High Priests… I shall continue," announced the Galetian, as the noise of hilarity faded into a serious anticipation of his imminent announcement. "As I was just about to say… I propose Turpol the Gatekeeper to lead the Krogon populous."

There was an instant groan of murmuring from the delegates and Flaglan was quick to offer her opinion. "Ha, ha… you must be joking?" she exclaimed and burst into uncontrollable laughter. "That moola bird must have known you were going to announce something ridiculous… you can't be serious about that ugly little dwarf leading a bunch of eight foot lizards?"

"Silence!" shouted King Luccese. "That's quite enough, Flaglan… now hold your tongue and have some respect for Turpol and our Krogon friends - if you have nothing constructive to say, please say nothing and keep your petty opinions to yourself!"

"But Sire..." The High Priestess squirmed. "Meltor is talking out of his..."

"I said be quiet Flaglan... your comments are not constructive," ordered Luccese, as he calmly turned to Meltor again. "Your suggestion has credibility... I believe we can trust the Gatekeeper and your proposal should be put to the vote - those in favour of Turpol raise your right hand."

Pavsik supported Meltor's proposal and although Guan-yin had not met Turpol, she put her trust in the decision of her two senior peers and followed their actions by also raising her hand. The sheer audacity of Flaglan's blatant disrespect for Meltor's choice of candidate was enough for the Hartopian to overrule her unprofessional behaviour. The vote was made unanimous by the King's right hand also being raised.

Flaglan stayed silent and had no alternative but to accept Turpol as the recommended candidate of the High Priesthood for Krogonia, albeit on a temporary basis. The mumblings inside the chamber were interrupted by the Galetian High Priest's dulcet tones. "Thank you for your support... I'm sure you will agree this is a just reward for Turpol's efforts in helping to lift the evil curse that was cast over Pathylon recently," proclaimed Meltor in a proud manner. "Now that matter is put to bed and out of the way... let me explain the main reason why we are assembled here today."

Meltor went on to describe the details of his premonition and his most recent dream to the assembled hierarchy. "I fear we have little time," he said, with an urgent pace in the tone of his voice. "The power of telepathy has afforded me knowledge of a great danger to Pathylon... this has been compounded with images from a dream I had a few days ago."

"What is it Meltor?" asked Guan-yin, as she placed her elbows on the large wood-carved table. "It is well known that your premonitions have never been wrong before… so please inform us of your concerns."

Meltor sat back in his chair and composed himself. The wise Galetian could sense a feeling of uncertainty around the table so he spoke calmly. "My dear friends… I fear Pathylon is in great danger from an evil strain that escaped us during the recent uprising."

Flaglan spoke. "Is it the Freytorians again… have they taken up their pillaging ways and returned to inflict more damage to our regions?"

"No… our relationship with the Freytorians is very good and we continue to trade well with them," replied Meltor, as he rose from his chair again and pushed back his cloak. "The danger emanates from within our own world."

"Then who or what endangers our lands?" asked Pavsik.

"It concerns the missing Amulet!" exclaimed Meltor, as he placed his hands on his hips.

The Galetian started to pace around the back of each chair, placing his large hand on the shoulders of each delegate. He arrived at the King's throne and paused before touching his friend's royal cloak.

"Are you referring to the Amulet of Silvermoor?" asked King Luccese, as he moved his eyes to follow Meltor's hand clasping his robe.

"Yes, your royal highness… I indeed speak of the Amulet," replied the Galetian, as he acknowledged the King's reaction and lifted his strong hand from Luccese shoulder.

Pavsik interrupted briefly. "But I thought the Amulet was lost during the quake that partially destroyed the Island of Restak."

"It was indeed lost… the clasp that secured King's royal necklace did break amid the chaos that followed the ancient ritual but it has been found and has now fallen into unscrupulous hands – or should I say paws," replied Meltor, as he moved back from Luccese. "I have seen the Amulet in my dream and…" He paused for a moment and made his way back to his seat then stood in front of his chair and placed his clenched fists on the table. "Basjoo Ma-otz has the amulet!" he exclaimed.

The stunned audience gasped in horror and then a mumbling chorus of concerned voices erupted inside the chamber. Basjoo Ma-otz had not been seen since he fled from the Shallock Tower following a confrontation with Meltor after he had witnessed the Krogon army converging on the city of Trad. The cowardly Hartopian half-breed was appointed the High Priest of the Blacklands during Varuna's illegal reign but had since vanished without a trace. He mirrored Varuna's appetite for evil and was the Hartopian that had played a major part in Meltor's recent nightmares. The old Galetian knew the reason why Basjoo Ma-otz had not been found to date and he was keen to inform the delegates of his whereabouts. The weasel-like creature could tragically influence the future of Pathylon and he must be stopped.

Meltor interrupted the mutterings and suggested to the delegates that they stay calm. "As I said… the Amulet is now in the hands of Ma-otz," continued Meltor. "Now as you know he's a very bitter and twisted Hartopian and he will go to any lengths to seek revenge against our government – especially me."

"Why would he want revenge against you?" asked the young and inexperienced Guan-yin.

"I'm sorry Guan-yin… I know you are a Hartopian too - but I forget that you are so young," apologised Meltor. "You will not have experienced the old rivalry between the Hartopians and the Galetians."

The High Priest for the Galetis Empire continued to explain about a certain event in Pathylian history. He informed Guan-yin about an unsuccessful invasion by the Hartopians and how a young Basjoo Ma-otz kidnapped Meltor's granddaughter and beheaded her during a vengeful ritual.

"You are all aware of my personal hatred for Basjoo Ma-otz," stated Meltor, as he held on to the tethered handle of his sword. "The Staff of Evil that he gloatingly displays… bears the small skull from the sacrificial slaughter of my granddaughter - and I can assure you that this continues to fire a raging revenge inside me!"

"That is terrible, Meltor… it makes me ashamed to be a Hartopian," declared the young female leader of the Blacklands.

"Please do not feel that way, Guan-yin… for this happened a long time ago – you should be proud to lead your Hartopian people," assured Meltor. "Anyhow, Ma-otz is not of pure Hartopian blood… he is a half breed and the primitive flax that makes up his being should not be allowed to tarnish the reputation of the fine citizens of the Blacklands – your people are not to be associated with the wrongdoings of this evil scum."

The King intervened. "To this day… the rage inside you is still very evident and we all sympathise with your feelings towards Ma-otz," assured Luccese, as he afforded his friend a caring glance. "Nothing we say today will dispel your hatred of him and what he did to your granddaughter is unforgivable… I feel sure you will get the opportunity to strike your anger on the fiendish creature in due course - but please tell us was affect his acquisition of the Amulet will have on our kingdom."

Before Meltor could answer, Guan-yin echoed the King's sentiments and then she asked. "Do you know the whereabouts of… I hate to say - my fellow Hartopian?"

"In my last dream I witnessed Basjoo Ma-otz crossing the Peronto Alps… I can only assume he is heading for the Unknown Land," replied Meltor. "And, your highness… this is what concerns me most – the effect of Ma-otz's acquisition of the Amulet depends upon him finding a sacred location deep inside the Unknown Land."

Flaglan had now calmed down and spoke softly. "Surely he cannot hurt us from such a remote location."

44

King Luccese interrupted Meltor's chairing of the meeting and he stood to address the High Priesthood. "Thank you Meltor... you may now relinquish the chair – I have an idea where you are going with this," he explained and replicated Meltor's stance by leaning forward and placing his clenched knuckles on the table. "Correct me if I'm wrong... but I believe there is a secret time portal, which was built many centuries ago by an ancient race that originated from another world beyond the Unknown Land.

"That is correct King Luccese," confirmed the wise old Galetian. "Sorry to interrupt... please continue, your highness."

The King thanked Meltor and continued to address the attentive audience, as he described the strange beings that had built the time portal. Pavsik, Guan-yin and Flaglan were totally engrossed in the King's disclosure and they sat spellbound by the revelations that followed.

Luccese continued. "The strange beings were flax-like in appearance... but they were much taller and they were able to walk on their hind legs – we do not know much more about these mythical creatures, but we do have evidence that they did once exist."

"If I may interrupt again, your highness?" requested Meltor.

"Certainly my friend... if you have more information on the strange creatures – please continue," agreed Luccese, as he sat back and sought the comfort of his throne.

"Not I... but I know someone who will inspire us all on this subject," replied Meltor.

"Who do you speak of Meltor?" enquired Pavsik.

"Our newly appointed leader of Krogonia of course... Turpol the Gatekeeper has studied the ancient scrolls in greater detail," replied Meltor. "I suggest we call him to the meeting... he will have great knowledge of the creatures."

"Very well... Turpol must join us – I feel this would be a good time to take a short break," suggested Luccese. "Please arrange for our friend to join us!"

"Thank you Sire, I will make the necessary arrangements immediately," agreed Meltor, as he made his way to the chamber door.

The Galetian High Priest held the door ajar in readiness for King Luccese to retire from the meeting room that was now engulfed with a hum of exciting revelations. This prompted Luccese to rise to his feet and address the congregation of High Priests once more. "We will reconvene in an hour," he instructed. "But remember... not a word to anyone outside this chamber."

The delegates agreed then swore allegiance to their King and the meeting was adjourned. Meltor held out his arm to invite Luccese through the exit from the chamber. He then followed his King out of the room and they both descended the winding staircase that spiraled down the Shallock Tower. "I hope you have a plan Meltor," stated Luccese, as the pair hurried in parallel down the staircase.

"Let's see what Turpol has to offer," replied Meltor, as they finally reached the bottom of the tower. "I'll see you in an hour, my lord."

King Luccese shook his friend's hand and headed off in the direction of the Royal Palace, whilst Meltor strode in the opposite direction towards the city mail room.

It did not take long for Meltor to reach his destination and he entered the communication depot with great assurance. The chief bird-whistler stood up and acknowledged the High Priest. "Meltor... to what do we owe this honour of your presence?"

"We need to dispatch a raven quickly," he instructed. "An urgent message is to be sent Turpol the Gatekeeper." The old Galetian continued to make the necessary arrangements for word to be sent out to invite the dwarf to join the delegation and within minutes a jet black raven was released out of the mail depot and into the Devonian skyline. Meltor watched the bird fly away into the distance. "Hurry little creature... we have no time to waste!"

6

The Old Photograph

Bradley and his father were still looking out over the landscape where the old Silvermoor Colliery site used to stand. They took a final look at the splendid view and then started to descend back down the hillside towards the valley. K2 displayed a final show of defiance, as he jumped up at Patrick's hand in an attempt to bite at the leash that was preventing his escape. The over-excited dog's attempts were to no avail and the clumsy hound settled into a gentle cantor, as they walked at a fast pace down the grassy slope. K2 sniffed the ground at every opportunity, as Patrick extended the lead to allow the inquisitive dog the slack to lag some ten metres behind.

The wind speed was increasing and they hurried their pace and the bottom of the valley levelled out. Patrick and Bradley headed back in the direction of the Silvermoor housing estate and as they neared the end of Braithwaite Road, Patrick tugged on Bradley's arm. "Come with me," he insisted and guided his puzzled son over to an old red brick building situated on the corner of the road.

"Why are we here, Dad?" enquired Bradley, as they stood in front of the boarded-up entrance.

"This is one of the original pit surface buildings that was spared by the demolition company... it used to be the old lamp room at Silvermoor Colliery - it was turned into a grocery shop but it closed down when the new supermarket opened in Bramley." explained Patrick, as he cupped his hands and peered through a gap in the boarded glass frontage. "I know it's always been here... we pass it every day, but I thought we'd take a look inside."

"So why have you pointed it out to me today?" asked Bradley, in an inquisitive tone.

"Well... as we were talking about Silvermoor up on the hill - it got me thinking about the chap who used to run the shop," explained Patrick. "I remembered he had some old photographs of the colliery that hung on the shop wall and it made me wonder whether they were still here," he concluded and attempted to turn the door handle.

"You can't just go in there without permission!" exclaimed Bradley. "It's private property!"

"It says *to let* on the sign up there," replied Patrick, as he pointed the sign on the boarded window and turned the handle again. "There's no harm in looking... come on - we could be prospective tenants just taking a look!"

"Mum will kill you!" stated Bradley, with a mischievous grin on his face.

"Well, she won't if she doesn't know about it... will she?" laughed Patrick, as the latch clicked and door opened. "Brilliant... it's not locked!"

Bradley was intrigued and he followed his father into the dimly lit retail unit. The crackling and crunching of broken glass could be felt beneath their boots, as they entered the premises and their eyes adjusted to the surroundings.

The ex-colliery electrician's assumption had proved to be correct and he held out his arm to encourage his son. "Look Bradley... up there," said Patrick, as he pointed to a photograph on the wall, which was hung next to a coil of hemp rope. "That's the *East Pit* winding gear... we used to call it the pit head."

"Wow, that's amazing… it looks really old fashioned and scary," replied Bradley, as Patrick lifted the picture down to get a closer look.

"This picture was taken in the 1940's… you tell because the tops of the winding gear had more metal girders fitted to protect them when I worked at Silvermoor – look Bradley, do you see that building?" asked Patrick, as he pointed to the base of the pit head winding gear. "That's where our house is now… right where the East Pit head used to be."

Bradley looked at the photograph in amazement. "It's hard to believe that all that ironwork and those big wheels used to stand on the same plot as our house!"

"It sure is… and it was a sad day when they pulled it all down," replied his father, as he stared at the picture and started to reminisce. "Many mineworkers lost their jobs when they closed Silvermoor Colliery… and the mining community was split apart."

"Is that why you went to work for *EMMCO*?" enquired Bradley.

"Yes… I had no choice," replied Patrick. "I had to go where the work was... I know I go on about how bad it was working at Silvermoor - but I do miss the old colliery," he continued and placed the picture back on the wall. "I can still hear those winding wheels turning and the chants of the workers being lifted out of the mine."

"You really miss it… don't you Dad?" confirmed Bradley, as he placed his arm around his father's waist.

"Yeah I do… I remember a time when I was travelling out of the mine up the 746 yard long shaft in the mucky old lift cage," said Patrick. "The cage had two decks to it and on this particular occasion I was in the lower one… then some idiot in the upper deck decided to empty his water bottle and we all got drenched - the silly sod made us all think he was having a pee."

"That's funny!" laughed Bradley, as he imagined the water seeping through the cage floor onto the dirty faces of the mineworkers.

"It wasn't funny at the time I can tell you… the poor fella was nearly lynched!" replied Patrick. "You wouldn't put it past someone to do that sought of thing you know!"

"That's disgusting Dad… I still can't believe you actually worked down there in those dark mucky tunnels!" exclaimed Bradley. "It must have been so far down underground and really hot."

"Oh Bradley, there is so much I could tell you… it's hard to describe it, Son - you'd have experience it to fully appreciate just how bad it was down there!" replied his father, as he stared at the picture again. "Working down a coal mine… I wouldn't wish it on anyone - there were no toilets you know and…!"

"Okay… far too much information, Dad!" he interrupted. "I'll take your word for it!"

Patrick laughed and turned his attention back to the picture on the wall. Bradley could tell by the deep look on his father's face that he wanted to keep the picture. "Why don't you keep it?" he encouraged. "I'm sure no one will notice it's gone… go on, take it – you can hang up it in your workshop when we get home."

Patrick felt some kind of ownership of the old picture and afforded his rebellious son an endearing look. "I suppose you're right... your Mum hardly ever goes in my workshop - except when she needs something from the chest freezer," he replied and carefully removed the framed photograph from the wall again.

Patrick took a step back to direct the beams of light form the doorway onto the picture. Just then there was a loud crack, as a wooden board gave way under his foot. In an instant, he keeled over and his left leg disappeared beneath him. The startled man was helpless, as he fell backwards with a loud crash and air was filled with a cloud of dust. Within seconds, another floorboard gave way and his right leg disappeared through the rotten timbers, as Bradley failed in a vain attempt to grab his father's sleeve.

"Oh no... Dad!" shouted Bradley, as he witnessed the unfortunate accident unfold before his helpless eyes. The worried boy tried to focus through the dust-filled air but he could not see his father. He waited for the dust to settle before approaching the gaping hole in the floor. He peered into the abyss and called out in a nervous tone. "Dad... are you okay?"

There was no answer and Bradley called out again. "Please answer me, Dad... are you alright?" pleaded the distraught boy, as he listened for the faintest of replies.

The reply never came because Patrick was unconscious and Bradley could now see he was lying on his back about five metres down. The frightened boy trod carefully on the fragile timbers and looked more closely at the floor. He realised that they were actually a pair of old wooden doors that were covering the opening to a cellar beneath the old lamp room. The old doors had finally given way after all these years.

Bradley felt powerless to help his ailing father, as he peered into the hole and muttered to himself. "I am supposed to be the eternal chosen one... some hero I've turned out to be - I can't even save my own Dad from falling through a floor!"

7

Letter from the Admiral

Meanwhile inside the Shallock Tower a disgruntled Hartopian languished inside a cold cell just a few floors below the King's chosen meeting room. Varuna did not look so ruthless without his skulled headdress and long robes. His demeanor was sullen and portrayed that of a beaten adversary. Without his splendid attire and only a discoloured white smock wrapped around his skinny form, his appearance was scrawny and unthreatening.

He sat quietly in a dark corner and concentrated his attention on a small insect that was scurrying across the floor of the straw strewn chamber. The defeated traitor held a small stone in his right paw and with a casual flicking movement cast the object in the direction of the tiny creature.

The stone moved effortlessly through the air and landed on top of the insect, killing it instantly. Varuna let out a faint croak of satisfaction, as he glanced at the crack in the wall where the ant-like creature had come from. The disgraced Hartopian then broke the silence inside the prison cell and exclaimed. "Come on out you little beauties… how many more of you want to die today?"

A tower guard appeared at the small barred opening in the cell door. "What's going on in there?"

Varuna replied. "Just a little blood sport… nothing to concern you!"

The guard raised his eyebrow and sighed in a condescending tone, as he walked away from the door. "Crazy Hartopian!"

Varuna heard the guard's response but before he had chance to retort his reply, his attention was taken by a feathered creature that had perched on the ledge of his cell window.

"My… my – what have we here?" Varuna muttered, as he stood up from his cold stone seat and stared at the pure white bird. "Now if I'm not mistaken you look like an *Arctic Hawk*… and you are very far from your native land - it's very unusual to see a bird like you flying around *this* part of the world at *this* time of the year!"

The bird of prey from Freytor blinked occasionally but it did not move as the prisoner approached. Varuna looked at one of the bird's claws and noticed a small scroll of paper clutched between its talons. "Now what have you got there?" he commented, as he steadied himself against the wall with the severed stub where once his left paw attached. "Must get myself a hook or something for this thing one day," he thought, as he glanced at the stub and the memories of the incident inside the Royal Palace flooded back.

The comments made by Flaglan still haunted him and he recalled the embarrassment of being bundled out of the ballroom by the palace guards. The Hartopian spoke in a vindictive tone and recited the High Priestesses words. "Let me give you a hand… she said – I'll make her pay for that remark," he muttered and shook his head to dispel the unpleasant thought and concentrated on the hawk. "Anyhow, let's see what you've brought for me little fella!"

The disgraced Hartopian reached out to retrieve the note with his good paw and the bird instinctively pecked it. "Ouch... you vicious *moula* - that hurt!" he roared and his reaction alerted the guard, as the clanking of keys could be heard in the keyhole of the cell door.

In an instant, the door flung open and the guard stood defiantly in the doorway with the sharp blade of his axe firmly fixed in Varuna's sights. "What's all the commotion about... what are you doing with that bird, prisoner?" demanded the guard, as the great white hawk dropped the note and fluttered its black-tipped wing span, as it launched itself away from the window ledge.

The Hartopian caught the piece of rolled paper without the steadfast guard noticing. He then moved towards him and threatened. "How dare you enter my chamber without authority?"

The guard laughed and replied. "Just listen to yourself... you pathetic weasel – you no longer rule over this land Varuna!" he taunted. "Now step back before I cut off your other paw... just sit down and stay quiet – the King specifically asked me to ensure you don't make any noise today."

"So why has Luccese told you I have to be quiet?" replied Varuna, as he took a step nearer the agitated guard.

"Can't say," replied the Guard. "Now get back I said and be quiet!"

"No, I won't... it was okay for me to rant and rave yesterday – so why not today?" insisted Varuna, as he poked his snout nearer the blade of the guard's axe.

The guard pushed the edge of the blade against the Hartopian's nose. "Never you mind... just sit down and stay out of trouble!"

The blade penetrated the soft tissue like a scalpel and a small cut appeared. Varuna reeled back and wiped the spot of yellow blood from the wound on his snout. "You'll regret you did that... I'll be out of here soon and you will definitely pay for that!"

The guarded laughed, as he tilted his head backwards and replied. "As you can see... I'm quivering in my boots - you are a hundred metres from the ground and this door is guarded round the clock," he confirmed. "Get it into your pathetic little mind, Varuna... you're never leaving this tower - now shut it and do as you're told Hartopian scum!"

The guard edged back towards the cell door keeping his axe in front and his eyes transfixed to Varuna's evil stare. He made his way back outside the chamber then hooked the cell door and slammed it shut with a swift movement of his axe. The lock clunked into place, as he turned the key and peered through the bars on the door. "Remember... be quiet!"

The guard disappeared from view and Varuna placed the edge of the note in his mouth and used his good paw to unravel the fragile piece of paper. He placed it by his side on the stone slab and started to read the message;

'Varuna,

You do not know of me, but you have met my twin brother, Eidar. I am Norsk, another military leader from Freytor – an Admiral of the Freytorian Navy. I sit on the Freytorian Senate but I do not agree with the way the leaders of Freytor have changed our ways. I am a pirate at heart and I believe my people should continue to pillage other lands. I have heard of your plight and I invite you to join me in my quest. If you agree I will ensure you regain the Pathylian throne. All I ask in return is access to Krogonia to extract the rich vein of kratennium from the Flaclom Straits.

If you agree to help me then I will free you within a matter of days. All you need to do is tie some cloth to the bars of your window and let it fly like a flag. If you decide not to help me then I will pillage all of Pathylon anyway and destroy the Shallock Tower... with you in it!

Make your choice,

Admiral Norsk'

Varuna was stunned, as he crumpled the piece of paper in his paw and then sat back against the cold stone wall. He started to shake with excitement at the thought of controlling Pathylon again. Admiral Norsk sounded like some kind of mad fool but what had the Hartopian to lose. He got to his feet and pulled the tatty blanket that covered his stone slab bed. "This should be good enough to use as a flag!"

It did not take him long to push the cloth through the bars and secure it with his paw and teeth. "There... let's see what happens next – I'm not only intrigued how I will escape this place?" uttered Varuna, as he looked out and beyond the River Klomus. "I'm also curious as to why Luccese wants me to be quiet... something must be happening inside the tower and intend to find out!" He concluded and moved away from the window to return to his bed slab. Varuna lay back and thought out loud. "What would Norsk want with *kratennium*... it is only used as a means of creating drinking water when it's charged with electricity – a strange request but if that's all he wants in exchange for me taking control of Pathylon again then he can have all the kratennium he wants!"

A few floors above Varuna's cell, the meeting between the Royal Congress inside the Shallock Tower was due to resume in a few minutes. The raven had succeeded in finding the location of Turpol and the dwarf had now arrived safely inside the chamber.

There was a mumbling of mutterings from the delegates, as Meltor congratulated the dwarf on his immediate appointment. The Gatekeeper had just received the news of his promotion to the High Priesthood and he embraced the old Galetian's legs. "Thank you so much for proposing me for the High Priesthood... albeit temporary - it is a great honour my friend," said Turpol, as he released his tiny grip on Meltor's robes. "I feel very proud to represent Pathylon... as you know it has been a dream of mine."

"It is my utmost pleasure… I can't think of anyone better to lead the region of Krogonia," replied Meltor, as he looked down at the excited dwarf. "The Krogons know you well and are fully aware of your old friendship with our dear departed Grog… I think it is fitting that you lead his people."

"Who would have thought it… all those years as the Gatekeeper of Pathylon and now I have the opportunity to represent Grog's people – I will do our brave friend and his region proud," replied Turpol.

"Of that I have no doubts, my friend," agreed Meltor.

"Well, I suppose I must ask… why I was summoned here?" asked Turpol.

Meltor told the wise Gatekeeper about Basjoo Ma-otz and the missing Amulet. The Galetian briefed him about his recent dreams and Turpol was now up to speed on the proceedings. Their conversation was interrupted by the arrival of Flaglan. Guan-yin was the next to arrive closely followed by Pavsik.

The room fell silent and everyone bowed as the King finally entered the chamber. Luccese took his seat at the head of the table. "Thank you everyone… please be seated and a very warm welcome to you Turpol - you must be pleased with your appointment to the High Priesthood!" exclaimed Luccese. "Meltor tells us that you have more information about the strange creatures that frequent the Unknown Land."

"Thank you King Luccese… Meltor has informed me of the dangers confronting Pathylon and I sincerely hope I can be of help to our threatened kingdom," replied Turpol and jumped up to take his seat at the meeting table. As the dwarf sat down, Flaglan burst into uncontrollable laughter. Turpol was so small that his narrow eyelids blinked at slab level and his long pointy nose rubbed on the side of the large table.

"Silence Flaglan!" shouted Luccese, as he pointed at some cushions in the window seat. "Now bring those over for our friend!"

"Sorry, my lord... I couldn't help it," replied Flaglan, as she rose out of her seat sheepishly and ventured in a sultrily manner over to the window to collect the cushions. "Here you are little Turpol... sorry I laughed at you – these should get you up to my level."

"That's enough Flaglan... this is serious – now take your seat and let him continue," ordered the King, as the dwarf scowled at the High Priestess from the great forest. "Please carry on Turpol... when you are ready, my friend."

The dwarf recomposed himself, as he stood up and placed the cushions on his seat to heighten his ability to present to the group. He climbed back into position and cast a wicked look in the direction of the sarcastic sorceress. Turpol then began to address the delegates. "The creatures that Luccese speaks of dwell in the deep mines that are situated at the far edges of the Unknown Land," stated the Gatekeeper. "Please don't take this the wrong way, Guan-yin... but they look a little like Hartopians because their heads have pointed snouts and very prominent teeth - however their fur is as white as the ice-caps of Freytor."

"No offence taken," replied Guan-yin, as all the delegates uttered a mute sound of laughter.

"According to the ancient scrolls, it has taken the best part of a century for the weird looking creatures to evolve into their present form," continued Turpol. "As a result of cross-breeding with men who ventured through the time portal, they can only be described as Mece!"

"You speak of men... do you mean humans?" asked Pavsik.

"Yes... the same race as the *Eternal Chosen One* and his family," replied Turpol. "Our dear friend... Bradley Baker!"

"Ah, Bradley Baker... I hope our young hero is well – let us hope we do not have to call on him for help on this occasion," endeared Luccese.

"I do hope you are right, Sire," agreed Meltor. "However, something haunts me and I feel young Bradley may still have an important part to play in all of this impending chaos!"

The conversion quickly returned to the subject at hand and Guan-yin raised another question. "So why are they called Mece?" she asked.

"Simple... the word is formulated because they are cross-breeds of men and mice - *Mece*," replied the dwarf. "When the humans first entered the Unknown Land through the time portal they thought the weird creatures resembled a rodent species from their own world!"

"How did they manage to cross-breed?" asked Flaglan.

"Trust you to ask that question!" retorted King Luccese, as he scowled at the troublesome High Priestess.

"It's alright, your majesty... I am more than happy to answer the question asked by the High Priestess," insisted Turpol. "Like Flaglan here, the weird creatures were led by strong females of their species... they captured and seduced the men that trespassed on their territory – the offspring were reared and subsequently mated again," he continued. "The resulting species are now known as the Mece."

"Why have we never heard of the Mece before this meeting?" asked Pavsik.

King Luccese intervened. "I have to admit I have heard of these Mece creatures, but I also have to confess... I never thought they would pose a threat to our world." He continued. "Whilst the Amulet of Silvermoor was in our possession... no-one from the Unknown Land could harm us, so the name of the strange species was never uttered - until now that is!"

"So what has the Amulet got to do with the Mece?" asked Flaglan, as she fluttered her long eyelashes at the King.

Turpol shuffled some papers in front of him to attract attention. Whilst Luccese had been talking, the dwarf had found some vital information in one of the ancient scrolls he had brought along to the meeting. "Sorry to interrupt my lord... but I think this might answer Flaglan's question," said Turpol, as he handed the scroll to the King.

Luccese uncurled the delicate document and started to read the paragraph that the Gatekeeper had marked;

"...The precious sapphire that adorns the centre of the Amulet was originally found by the Mece inside on old cavern at the base of Mount Pero, the largest mountain in the Peronto Alps. The sapphire was forged into the centre of a metal sheath containing four chain links. The pendant was thereafter known as the Amulet of Silvermoor, named after the deep mine workings at the other side of the time portal from where the species called Men evolved. The Amulet was worshipped by the Mece and they placed in on a high ledge on Mount Pero to overlook and protect their small township..."

Luccese closed the scroll and handed it back to Turpol, as Guan-yin touched the end of her slender snout with a delicate touch of claw. "How did the Amulet form part of your inaugural necklace, Sire?" she asked.

The King replied without hesitation. "The Amulet was taken from the ledge on Mount Pero by one of my ancestors... an ancient Pathylian King called *Makel* - during a dangerous expedition into the treacherous Peronto Alps," explained Luccese. "Unfortunately, Makel and all but of the exhibition party were killed by the Mece... an injured mountain guide survived to tell the tale – only to die days later through shear exhaustion."

Turpol raised his short grey hairy arm and waved it to attract the King's attention. "Perhaps, my Lord... if I may speak?"

"Of course, Turpol," replied Luccese, as he noticed the dwarf looking intensely at one of the scrolls. "Is there something else in the ancient documents that we should know of?"

"Yes, my lord... I have found an entry in one of the scrolls that relates to King Makel's death," stated the excited Gatekeeper. "It describes how the mountain guide returned to the Pathylian capital and before he died he hid the Amulet somewhere inside the dungeons, beneath the royal palace." Turpol concluded. "I have checked all the documents from the archives and there doesn't appear to be any more entries about the Amulet in the ancient scrolls."

"What about that one?" noticed Guan-yin, as the young Hartopian High Priestess pointed at one of the old documents.

"Are you referring to this?" asked the Gatekeeper, as he held the torn scroll in front of his wrinkled face. "The bottom part of it has been torn off... there's no mention of the Amulet on it – I've already checked."

A hush of silence fell within the chamber, as the group of high ranking delegates stared at the incomplete scroll. No one decided to fill the silence and Turpol's hand trembled slightly in anticipation of a voice that would explain their next move.

8

Green Ember Glow

Meanwhile back in Ravenswood, Bradley Baker was still inside the old lamp room and he looked down into the abyss through the old cellar doors. The dust was obscuring his vision and he felt a vibration inside his trouser pocket. At first he thought it was his mobile phone so he reached inside to pull it out. The phone was silent and it had no signal anyway. The vibration against his leg continued and Bradley reached inside his pocket again. This time he pulled out the sacred grobite and it was emitting a warm energy, which was making it feel quite hot.

Smoke started to emanate from the coin and it began to shine brightly with a green ember glow. The light from the doorway revealed the moving dust in the air and the beams cast precious light onto the active grobite. Bradley was fascinated by the coin's reactivation and he noticed the inscription had changed around the outside of the grobite. Now there was a new message.

Still aware of his father's perilous situation, Bradley read out the inscription;

'Seek out the Mece and find the Amulet of Silvermoor!'

As soon as he had finished reciting the message, the coin began to glow even brighter and it became too hot to handle. Bradley screamed quietly, as he dropped the grobite and it rolled towards the opening in the floor. He lunged forward in an attempt to grab the coin before it disappeared through the splintered timbers. He was too late and it plummeted down to where his father lay motionless on the stone floor below.

Bradley leant over the opening and witnessed the cellar become strewn with light, as the coin emanated an intense array of colour. More green smoke swirled from the centre of the grobite, as the whole building began to shake. Bradley was covered with more dust, as the old lamp room started to vibrate violently. He managed to retain his balance and focused his attention on his father, as the cellar filled with a dark green cloud of dense smoke.

The old lamp room was now engulfed with a plume of emerald mist and the startled boy watched in amazement, as the coin reappeared in front of him out of the green smoke. Now the sacred grobite had grown in size; just like it had done before when Bradley and his two friends from Sandmouth had witnessed the coins antics in Amley's Cove upon their safe return from Pathylon.

The grobite was now the size of a dustbin lid and it was hovering over the broken entrance to the cellar like a huge spinning wheel. Bradley's thoughts immediately turned to the picture of the pit head winding gear because the huge gold coin was simulating the same action.

Bradley started to hatch a plan to save his father and remembered the coil of hemp rope, which was hanging on the wall. He tried to focus on the place where the old photograph had been hanging. At last he could just make out the rope and he launched himself to retrieve it. Without even thinking about the dangers involved, he unravelled the coil of hemp and tossed the rope over the spinning edge of the weightless grobite.

The rope secured itself around the edge of the coin and the grobite stopped spinning momentarily, as it hung magically in mid air. With no hesitation, Bradley took a brave leap and held on to the dangling rope. Suddenly the giant coin began to turn slowly and the faint noise of the colliery's pit head gear started to fill the old lamp room with an industrial echo.

Bradley was safely lowered into the cellar and when his feet touched the basement floor, the coin stopped turning and the grinding sound of the head gear halted. He quickly tied the rope around his father's waist and instinctively tugged on the coarse hemp. The noise of the pit head wheels restarted like the sound of a steam- powered engine and the coin began to turn slowly again. Bradley supported his father's head and then took hold of the rope. Together they were both lifted safely out from the depths of the smoke-filled cellar.

Once clear of danger, Bradley swung away from the hole and jumped to one side still holding on to the rope. He summoned all his strength and pulled on the hemp, as he guided his father away from the perilous gap to safety above the lamp room floor. There was a screeching sound of metal brakes and the sacred grobite reversed its turning action, as it lowered Patrick safely to the ground. The brave boy calmly removed the rope from his father's waist and then threw it to one side.

Bradley covered his mouth and shielded Patrick's face, as the room was now filled with more choking dark green smoke. The gold coin glowed more intensely before crashing to the floor with a loud chink and Bradley again watched in amazement, as the sacred grobite span on its edge before shrinking back to its original size.

The coin finally stopped glowing and Patrick lay very still. Bradley continued to support his head, as the green smoke faded into a whisper of grey dust. The grobite rolled back towards Bradley and span a few more times until it finally came to rest by his side. The excited boy picked up the metal disc, examined the inscription again and placed it safely back in his trouser pocket.

Amazingly, Patrick was still clinging on to the old photograph and at last he opened his eyes to stare at the dirty ceiling tiles above his son's head. "What on earth happened, Bradley... where am I?" he asked in a confused manner, as he felt his throbbing thigh. "...and why are my trousers ripped?"

"Try to be quiet, Dad... you took a pretty bad hit," said Bradley calmly.

"Ouch... my leg really hurts!" exclaimed Patrick. "What happened to me... why am I injured?"

Bradley replied. "Stay still Dad, you fell backwards and..." The cautious boy hesitated. Bradley knew the coin had been activated again and there was no way he was going to explain it to his injured father. Patrick would never believe him and so instead he quickly changed his explanation. "...you fell backwards and bumped your head," Bradley procrastinated, as he helped Patrick to his feet. "Look... you nearly fell down there!"

Patrick regained his composure and held on to his energetic son, as he pointed to the hole in the floor and stated. "That will teach me to get all emotional about Silvermoor Colliery... come on let's get out of here, Bradley - your Mum will be getting worried."

Bradley helped Patrick to his feet and escorted his emotional father out of the old building. He closed the door and played down what had just happened to them both. The boy continued to think on his feet and averted his father's attention to his reminiscing of the old pit head. "I feel I ought to learn more about the old colliery." He suggested to his father. "I'd like to hear more stories about your time down the coal mine."

"I'd be happy to tell you lots of things that happened at Silvermoor Colliery," insisted Patrick and he put his arm around Bradley's shoulder, as he limped along the pavement. "But for now... let's get this picture back home without your Mother seeing it!"

"I'm glad you took it, Dad," insisted Bradley, as he continued to support his father's weight. "It would only have been thrown away if it had been left in that old building."

"I suppose you're right, Son… but as I said - not a word to your Mum!" replied Patrick. "…and don't mention we went in the old lamp room – I don't want your Mother thinking I'm turning you into some kind of criminal!"

"Oh Dad… if only you knew the half of it!" replied Bradley.

"New the half of what?" asked Patrick.

"Oh nothing… anyhow, we didn't break in… the door was open – remember?" replied Bradley.

Patrick gave Bradley an adoring hug and smiled affectionately at his witty son. The two petty-burglars had now reached the end of Braithwaite Road and turned to head in the direction of the east pit vent pipe and the warm confines of number 127.

As they approached the house, Bradley checked his pocket for the coin and he cast his thoughts back to the new inscription he had read in the old lamp room. He was intrigued to find out why *Silvermoor* had appeared on it and what did the word *Mece* represent. One thing he was sure of; when Musgrove and Sereny arrive in Ravenswood during the half term holiday, there will be plenty to talk about.

9

The Missing Piece

A long Pathylian standard flapped in the breeze atop the Shallock Tower, which stood tall and majestic in the distance. The injured Moula bird flew back towards the top window, as the habitual creature recovered from its earlier spat with the leaded glass. It had innocently returned to spy inquisitively through the window at the important delegates inside the elevated meeting room.

The King had finally broken the silence inside the chamber and thanked Turpol for his input, as he continued to address the group. "Well... I do know that the Amulet was eventually discovered by one of my forefathers and it was placed in the inaugural necklace when my Grandfather was crowned King of Pathylon."

"How interesting?" responded Meltor, who had purposely kept quite whilst Turpol and Luccese explained the history of the Amulet. "Now... your highness - if will reveal the mystery and true importance of the *Amulet of Silvermoor*?"

The expected questioning from the delegates inside the chamber was withheld. Instead they adopted a deathly silence in anticipation of Meltor's announcement, as the old Galetian pulled a torn piece of paper from inside his robe. "I apologise for keeping this from you, Turpol... but this is the missing section of the scroll and it describes how the Amulet acts as a mystical device to ward off evil," he smiled and cast a glance at the blinking Moula bird. The High Priest refocused his attention to the entranced group and continued to explain, as he held up the small section of parchment. "When my premonitions began, I took it upon myself to hide this piece... I couldn't risk this information falling into the wrong hands - it was never my intention to mislead any of you, but simply to keep the information safe until I was sure."

"You did the right thing Meltor... but I wish you had confided in me sooner," stated Luccese.

"I apologise, my lord... but as I explained - I had to be sure," replied the humble Galetian High Priest. "I did not want to cause any unnecessary unrest within the royal congress... especially so soon after the recent turmoil created by Varuna and General Eidar."

"I appreciate your caution, Meltor," acknowledged Luccese. "The Amulet that once secured our kingdom has now turned out to be a very dangerous weapon... if placed in the wrong hands it will cause untold havoc -Basjoo Ma-otz has it and we simply must get it back!"

Flaglan asked. "If the Amulet wards off evil... why didn't it stop the recent curse that the Freytorian General cast over Pathylon?"

"Good question Flaglan... I thought one of you might bring that up," replied Meltor. "Well... it's because the Freytorians were not from our world – they journeyed to our mainland across the Red Ocean from Freytor."

"What's the significance of that?" asked Pavsik.

"The magic powers contained inside the sacred Amulet are only able to protect Pathylon from evil that threatens it by land – not by sea," explained Meltor. "The Amulet has protected Pathylon for centuries from the Mece because they dwell on land – their only route of attack is across the Peronto Alps and into the Galetis Empire."

Guan-yin summarised, intelligently. "So what you are saying is... now that the Amulet has gone, the Mece could attack us?"

"I wish it was that simple, my young High Priestess" replied the Galetian. "Certain conditions would have to be met."

"And what might they be?" asked Luccese.

Meltor energetically replied. "Over the past two hundred years, Pathylon has relied on the Amulet to protect it from land based enemies... if Basjoo Ma-otz reaches the Mece and they reposition the Amulet on the mountain ledge from where it was stolen by King Makel – then the force of power emitted from within the sapphire would equate to the amount of time passed since it was first removed."

"So what you're saying is... the Amulet will become a bomb!" exclaimed Guan-yin.

"Yes my friend... a bomb with enough force to obliterate all five regions of Pathylon and any other world that borders the Unknown Land," replied Meltor.

A feeling of disbelief filled the chamber, as Meltor's words were unwontedly absorbed by the delegates. Everyone stayed silent for a few minutes as the reality of the situation sank in. Then Pavsik broke the silence. "Ma-otz has had a huge head start... is there anything we can do to stop him?"

Meltor offered a glimpse of hope. "The Hartopian half-breed traitor must be nearing Mount Pero... for I have foreseen this in my last dream." The wise High Priest continued. "He will find it difficult to locate the correct ledge to place the Amulet, so he will have to seek out the Mece to help him find it."

"Well that should buy us some time," interrupted Turpol. "The Unknown Land is vast... it will take Basjoo Ma-otz quite a while to locate the Mece township."

"That's right," agreed Meltor, affording the dwarf an approving nod. "We must hope that Ma-otz loses his way and this will buy us the time needed to invoke my plan."

"Thank goodness my old friend… you have a plan!" exclaimed King Luccese, as he clasped his crown with both hands. "Go on Meltor… please explain your plan to us."

"Well, it's a long shot… but it could work providing all the right people are involved," replied Meltor, as he unravelled an ancient chart onto the table top and used his dagger to aid his presentation. "This is Mount Pero and here I believe is the approximate location of the time portal."

"Surely you're not suggesting we find the time portal to evacuate our people… that would be impossible!" stated Luccese. "We do not have the time… many of our people would die crossing those snow covered mountains - it's too dangerous, Meltor!"

"No Sire… on the contrary," replied the Galetian calmly. "I was going to suggest that we send a messenger to the outside world… we must seek help from the *Eternal Chosen One*."

"Bradley Baker!" exclaimed Luccese. "Oh Meltor, I admire your confidence in the young boy but that's out of the question… not even he could get us out of this predicament – we must concentrate our efforts on catching Basjoo Ma-otz."

"But your Highness, Meltor may be right," suggested Guan-yin. "The outside world may be our only hope… if we can get a message to Bradley, he may be able to access the time portal – it would be much quicker to reach Ma-otz that way, rather than us trekking over the Peronto Alps."

"Guan-yin has read into my plan well," stated Meltor. "We can still deploy our own search party, but by sending a message to Bradley Baker… it affords us a second chance in case we fail."

"But even if we do get a message to the Baker boy… how will he find the entrance to the time portal on the other side?" asked Pavsik. "Anyhow… all the exits to the outside world are blocked – the Vortex of Souls has long since died and the

70

entrance to the forbidden caves has collapsed… so we'll never be able to get a message to our young hero."

Whilst Pavsik had been talking, Meltor had thought of an idea to relay the message to the outside world. He informed the group of his plan to contact the Freytorians. "The great iceberg ship had made the journey to Bradley's world before so there was no reason why it couldn't do it again."

"That's a brilliant idea!" exclaimed Pavsik. "But you still haven't assured us that Bradley will find the entrance to the time portal."

"That's the easy bit," smiled the Galetian, as he patted Pavsik's shoulder. "Bradley still has the sacred *grobite*… the magical powers of the coin will guide him to the entrance."

King Luccese had heard enough and he stood to conclude the meeting. "Meltor, your plan seems both credible and logical… dangerous, but achievable – it appears to be our only hope of catching Ma-otz before he reaches the Mece people," retorted the King. "However, I would feel more comfortable if you assisted young Bradley in his search for the time portal."

"You mean you want me to travel aboard the Freytorians glacial ship… to the outside world again?" summarised Meltor.

"We cannot rely on the Freytorians to relay this important message… so much depends on this," explained Luccese. "I would prefer it if you delivered the message personally… just as you did before when you disguised yourself as Old Mac the fisherman." The King continued, as Meltor chuckled at the thought of Bradley's Aunt Vera and the missing halibut incident.

"So my days as Old Mac aren't quite finished then… my lord?" replied a relieved Meltor, as he found it difficult to control his laughter.

"No, my friend… I ask you to make one last journey to the outside world, but not as Old Mac - this time you won't need your disguise," explained Luccese. "Bradley Baker will need to recognise you immediately," he continued. "I know the journey threatens your health my old friend, but I need you to do this... Pathylon needs you to do this!"

Flaglan approached Meltor, as he returned to his seat to contemplate the arduous task ahead of him. The sorceress sat down close beside the wise old High Priest and offered him a supportive embrace, as her firm bosom pressed against the Galetian's arm. "Bradley will need you on the other side, Meltor," insisted Flaglan. "If you are successful in locating the entrance to the time portal... he will also need your guidance once inside the Unknown Land."

Usually, Flaglan's words made little sense but on this occasion Meltor rose to his feet to face King Luccese. "I appreciate that the Unknown Land will be a daunting place for our young human friend and it will be very dangerous not only for him but anyone who ventures there." The room fell silent, as the delegates waited for Meltor's reply. "Very well sire... I'll do it!" exclaimed the frail High Priest. "I have no choice... I would lay down my life for Pathylon – you know that!"

"Meltor, you are a brave Galetian... and a true Pathylian patron - your decision to journey to Freytor and beyond is fraught with many dangers," acknowledged King Luccese, as he lifted the back of his hand towards his royal forehead. "I offer you this gesture, in the manner of Bradley Baker's royal marine friends... and I salute you Meltor!"

Luccese had welcomed Meltor's response and the meeting was quickly adjourned. The King's attempt to simulate a human salute had lifted the intenseness of the meeting and everyone started to relax a little.

Meltor had laid down a great plan, however all the delegates were now fully aware of the imminent danger to Pathylon and they could only wait in hope that the Galetian would cross over to the outside world safely to locate the Eternal Chosen One before it was too late.

Meanwhile inside a dormant volcano on the island of Freytor, a ferocious white bear creature was preparing to

72

launch a new type of ice-ship. This was not the typical seaworthy iceberg that the Freytorians used to journey across the oceans. This particular craft had been designed by Admiral Norsk and it was constructed from reinforced diamond-ice located deep below the northern ice-caps of Freytor. The submersible vessel was capable of speeds five times that of the standard Freytorian iceberg ship.

Norsk stood tall on the viewing bridge that towered above the brilliant-white submarine and delivered his final orders to the first officer. "This is a great feat of engineering and we must use this underwater craft to great effect."

The officer replied. "Admiral... I have set the co-ordinates and we will reach Pathylon in less than two days."

"Good... my Brother is due to arrive there by ice-ship tomorrow and we will have a clear advantage to reach Pathylon before him – apparently he has a meeting with King Luccese, however Varuna must be freed so his evil tyranny can be let loose again on the pathetic inhabitants of his homeland – then we will be able to extract the valuable *kratennium* from Krogonia and finish our quest to take over the Freytorian Senate."

"What will be the fate of your Brother, Sir?" replied the officer. "Does it not bother you that he must be removed from the senate?"

Norsk took a firm grip on the ice-railings that surrounded the bridge. He revealed his razor-sharp yellow teeth and replied. "That does not concern you... I will do everything to ensure that piracy is re-established and anyone who stands in my way will be dealt with accordingly – including my twin brother Eidar!"

The two Freytorians made their way down into the submarine and the first officer closed the hatch. "What will you do with the kratennium, Sir?" he enquired.

"An ice-cloud," replied Norsk, as he unveiled a set of blue prints on to the command desk.

"Ughh... I don't get it, Sir – why an ice-cloud?" replied the officer.

"Hah!" laughed Norsk. "You still haven't got it... have you?"

The first officer looked at the blue prints of the ice-cloud. "No Sir... I must be missing something!"

"Just a moment," insisted the Admiral, as he turned to the second lieutenant. "Move out... the co-ordinates are set – we need to leave, now!"

"Aye... aye – Sir!" replied the Freytorian sailor, as he pulled back the main throttle leaver and pressed a number of illuminated buttons on the control panel.

Norsk turned back to face his first officer again. "Now, where were we?"

"I'm still not sure why you want to build an ice-cloud, Sir," exclaimed the puzzled officer.

Norsk placed his huge white paw on the first officer's shoulder. "Imagine what would happen if two thousand tons of pure kratennium was mixed with enough electricity to power a hundred Freytorian cities..."

"Well Sir, you would create a huge amount of water!" replied the bemused officer.

"Exactly... a huge amount of fresh pure Pathylian water!" replied Norsk in a very excited manner.

"I still don't get it!" replied the officer.

"Okay... I'll stop playing games with you – let me make it more obvious," bantered the Admiral. "What would happen if you mixed pure fresh water with the Freytorian Ice-Caps?"

"They would melt!" replied the first officer.

"Bingo... I think we are finally getting through!" gloated Norsk, as he smashed his paw onto the control desk.

"Brilliant, Sir... absolutely brilliant – you are a genius!" admired the officer. "The ice-cloud will be filled with kratennium and you intend to convert it to fresh water to pour onto the ice-caps of Freytor!"

"Go to the top of the class, sailor!" replied Norsk, as he picked up the blue prints and pointed to the design. "You see this hole in the cloud... all I will need to do is summon a bolt of lightning to penetrate the opening and the kratennium will

74

rain down on the senate and destroy the idiotic regime that governs our land!"

The first officer looked at his commander in awe. "With the magical powers bestowed upon you... will be able to summon the lightning bolt."

"That's right... as a Freytorian Admiral I also have the power to launch an evil curse – I will do as my Brother did when he cast the curse over Pathylon," explained Norsk. "The Kaikane Idol that once stood on the Island of Restak will emit the necessary lightning bolts and then all we have to do is direct the cloud back to Freytor!"

"But the statue was destroyed when the island broke up following Luccese release of our fellow Freytorians!" explained the crewman.

Norsk replied. "Why do you think we have built this underwater ice-vessel you idiot – we will retrieve the statue from the bottom of the Red Ocean and restore it back to it's original glory on the Island of Restak!"

"Very clever, Sir... you appear to have thought of everything!" applauded the first officer.

"Thank you... I know – now let's get a move on!" roared Norsk and he wiped away the saliva from his white beard, which had dripped from his razor-sharp teeth.

The first officer had finally understood Norsk's plans and he pledged his allegiance to the intelligent ice-bear Admiral. He took his position at the control desk and ordered the submarine's crew to increase speed, as the bullet-shaped glacial craft tilted and pierced through the watery depths of the Red Ocean at great speed on course for the arcane world of Pathylon.

10

A New Companion

The quest to find the Amulet had now officially begun and the King tasked his Devonian High Priest to make the necessary preparations to set up a meeting with members of the Freytorian senate. Pavsik was in luck, he had received news of General Eidar's imminent arrival in the Blacklands region the later that day. The Freytorian commander was being sent to Pathylon by the hierarchy of Freytor on a new mission to secure a trading agreement with the Hartopians for their rare Black Forrest Truffles.

It was ironic that General Eidar was the Freytorian who would be asked to help the Pathylian population in their hour of need. Following his recent casting of the evil curse it could prove difficult to gain his trust and help to dispatch Meltor to the outside world.

Eidar's casting of the evil curse was always going to pose an uncomfortable hurdle to overcome and the High Priest of Devonia knew it was going to be a hard task to persuade the Freytorian to help the Pathylian people following such an embarrassing situation. The impending conversation could prove too embarrassing for the proud General and both parties would have to put their differences aside to consider the new implications relating to Basjoo Ma-otz's possession of the Amulet. However, Pavsik was confident the unpredictable arctic bear would co-operate with him under these extreme circumstances.

Within minutes the hoffen drawn chariots were gathered and the royal entourage moved out of Trad in convoy, as King Luccese led the negotiation party northward. Eidar had finally arrived on Pathylian soil and the King had already received word that the General had agreed to meet the royal party in the region's capital Hartopia.

The arduous journey to the Blacklands had taken the royal party along an elevated terrain through the Mountains of Hartopia. However, they had planned the route well and managed to avoid the haunted Black Forrest. Meltor and Pavsik were travelling in the second carriage and as they approached Hartopia the large ice-sail that powered the Freytorians vessel could be seen standing tall in the distant harbour.

Pavsik's prediction was proved to be correct and following some very tough negotiations between the two governing councils of Pathylon and Freytor, it was agreed that the Black Forest Truffles would be traded and more importantly Meltor would be transported to the outside world again. The agreement was helped to a mutually beneficial conclusion, as soon as Luccese mentioned a substantial increase to the present trading quota between the two governments. The Freytorians would now be able to enjoy an increase in timber produce, as well as the benefit of a generous Black Forrest Truffle export contract upon the safe return of the Amulet.

The new Hartopian High Priestess for the Blacklands stood to address the delegates. Guan-yin held her glass aloft and proposed a toast. "Your Majesty... and our friend's from across The Red Ocean - to a successful trading agreement and a safe journey to the outside world!" she stated, in a

77

confident tone and everyone raised their glasses to reciprocate acknowledgement of the negotiations.

Luccese applauded the young Hartopian's gesture. "Thank you for those words, Guan -yin... I am sure the General appreciates your toast."

Eidar rose from his seat and touched his glass against the Pathylian King's jewelled goblet. "You drive a hard bargain, Luccese... but then it must be difficult for you to agree to anything following my recent actions."

"I am sure everyone here will agree, we have to put that incident behind us General... it was a misunderstanding and I am sure many lessons have been learnt," replied the King. "Unfortunately, Basjoo Ma-otz has taken advantage of the situation and we must act fast... together - as United Nations."

The Freytorian General turned to face the quiet Galetian High Priest. "Meltor... you have been quiet during these very important negotiations and I fully understand that you must feel great trepidation at the thought of venturing back to the outside world again... I wish you well and I would be honoured if you would travel back to Freytor with me on my ice-ship."

"Thank you General Eidar... your words are received with honour and I accept your offer, but we must leave today – as each minute passes Ma-otz gains more of an advantage," replied Meltor, as he placed his glass on the table.

With the discussions and brief celebrations now seemingly exhausted, the necessary arrangements were put in place in preparation for Meltor's impending journey to the Island of Freytor.

Old age was taking its toll on Meltor and unbeknown to everyone else the ailing High Priest was feeling very nervous about his imminent transportation to the outside world. In the past, he had only ever used the familiar Vortex of Souls to travel in and out of Pathylon and the old Galetian knew from previous experience that the more he travelled through any time barrier between the two worlds, the greater the risk to his health.

Luccese and the royal entourage assembled in readiness for their return to Trad. The King met with General Eidar to sign the trading agreement and Pavsik spoke with Meltor to discuss his final preparations for travel.

"My dear friend, Pavsik... I am glad we have managed to secure passage to the outside world - however, I must inform you that I am not feeling well," explained Meltor. "But I do not want you to worry our King."

"Why didn't you mention it before?" replied Pavsik, as he placed a concerned hand on the Galetian's shoulder. "Your thoughts are now totally focused on the task in hand but yet you grow weary my friend!"

Meltor attempted to contain his emotions. "My nightmares are now being realised," he stated, as his thoughts deepened. "The possible destruction of Pathylon draws closer and the merciless and vengeful actions of Basjoo Ma-otz fill me with utter distaste... I have to stay strong for this journey, Pavsik!"

"Meltor... please don't take this the wrong way – but with due respect you are an aging High Priest and it is admirable what you do now," stated Pavsik. "Your adrenalin spurs you on to fight this new strain of evil... but all the efforts to retain your pride is obviously contributing to your illness, my old friend."

"I would never take anything you say the wrong way, Pavsik... I know your words are genuine and are orated with concern for my health, but I cannot allow Ma-otz to threaten the arcane world of Pathylon," confirmed the Galetian, as he reciprocated his friend's gesture by placing his large hand on Pavsik's arm.

Meltor knew the devastating implications of the Amulet's power when placed in the wrong hands. The Mece must not be allowed to return the Amulet to the sacred ledge on the slopes of Mount Pero and Meltor's health had to hold out so he could travel through the time barrier once more in order to help his young friend on the outside world. Bradley Baker was the *Eternal Chosen One* and he must be guided to the secret entrance, which led to Silvermoor's external time portal. Meltor knew that Bradley was the only one who could intercept Basjoo Ma-otz in time and the High Priest was determined to deliver the important news to the young adventurer.

"Meltor… you have to endure the sea-bound journey to Freytor and even as we speak, I recognise some serious signs of your ill health," observed Pavsik, as he consoled the ailing High Priest from the Galetis Empire. "I must insist that one of my Devonian noblemen accompanies you to Freytor."

"I'll be fine… arrrrgh!" groaned Meltor, as he held his chest tightly.

"Well that just proves that you are *not* okay!" exclaimed Pavsik, as he helped Meltor to sit down. "Now… I insist that Rathek travels with you!"

"Alright, Pavsik… I will let your young nobleman accompany me - but only as far as Freytor," insisted Meltor. "I accept it is a long journey to the ice-bound island."

"That's an understatement, Meltor… the trip across the great expanse of water will be very choppy," replied Pavsik, as he touched Meltor's shoulder again. "Your health has seriously deteriorated my old friend and I will feel much happier knowing that Rathek is with you."

"I know you mean well, dear Pavsik… but please be assured there is still plenty of life left in this old body and I intend to serve my King to the end," stated Meltor. "Anyhow… Rathek will be good company for me during the voyage and if his accompaniment of me is going to make you happy - then so be it."

The two old friends concluded their goodbyes and Pavsik waved to Meltor, as he boarded the Freytorian sailing vessel with Rathek, who had now joined the Galetian at his side.

King Luccese joined Pavsik and also waved to his friend. "Good luck, Meltor… I speak for Pathylon and I wish you great courage!"

The great iceberg ship suffered an arduous journey across the Red Ocean. It was, as predicted, a very rough trip and the affects of the journey had weakened Meltor's health even further. It had taken the ice-craft many hours to reach Freytor and the two Pathylians finally disembarked from the Freytorian vessel.

Meltor and Rathek made their way across the snow-covered port yard towards the harbour-master's office. "You cannot possibly travel through the time barrier like this, Meltor," declared Rathek, as he steadied the old Galetian to sit on a nearby bench in front of the ice-carved port buildings. "I fear you may not survive the journey ahead," he added.

"Don't worry, my young friend... I will be fine," replied Meltor, as he looked around. "It is imperative that we report to the Freytorian hierarchy... so we can arrange for my transportation to the outside world," he continued and attempted to stand up from the bench. "Arrgh!" shouted the High Priest, as he held is hand over his chest again and gripped tightly to ease the sharp pain.

"Meltor... are you alright?" asked Rathek, as he grabbed the Galetian's arm to stop him falling. "Please sit down and rest... you are not well."

Meltor sat with his head forward for quite a while, still clutching at the pain that emanated from his rib cage. Rathek stood on his tip-toes and looked inside the harbour-master's quarters. He was relieved to see a group of Freytorian Sea Commanders inside the building. "I'll call for some help... we need to get you to a healer!" expressed Rathek, as he knocked on the ice covered window.

One of the arctic bear creatures opened the harbour-master's door to establish who the two strangers were. Once their identity had been confirmed it was not long before Meltor was taken inside and then transported to a nearby health pod for further observation. A telepathic message was sent to the Royal Palace for the attention of King Luccese by the Freytorian Emperor to inform him of Meltor's medical condition. It was obvious that the Galetian High Priest was not fit enough to make the journey to the outside world.

King Luccese called a hurried meeting with Pavsik and Turpol and it was agreed that Rathek would be the one that they would have to send across the time barrier to relay the important message to Bradley Baker. The inexperienced and youthful Devonian errant would now be responsible for ensuring the safety of Bradley and to guide the young adventurer to the entrance of the Silvermoor time portal. Rathek did not know the precise location of the entrance, but as Meltor had already explained; the mystical powers from the sacred grobite in Bradley's possession should guide him to the hidden gateway, which would ultimately lead to the secret vortex.

The interception of Basjoo Ma-otz was of paramount importance and it was going to prove an arduous task. Meltor was growing weaker and all hope now rested on Rathek's young shoulders.

11

The Steam Powered Time Machine

Meanwhile in the Unknown Land, a rich vein of evil caught the cold wind that spiralled its way through the snow-topped mountains, which bordered the Galetis Empire. On the downward slopes of the Peronto Alps, Meltor's dream was becoming a reality and a nervous Hartopian half-breed clambered to the top of a large boulder to get a clear view of the valley below.

The air was much warmer now and Basjoo Ma-otz extended his right arm to displace the sweat that streamed down his inner sleeve. He retracted his yellow claws and placed his furry paw above his brow to shield the burning sun from his weasel-like eyes. The *Staff of Evil* remained firmly clenched in his left paw, as the elongated shadows from the Peronto Alps cast ahead of his temporary look-out position.

The sun was starting to set behind Mount Pero and Ma-otz stared out over the barren landscape, as a wide evil grin appeared below his weather-beaten snout. Since his self-exile from Pathylon, the weasel-like creature had so much hatred running through his veins. He had been promised great powers, whilst Varuna held control of the Pathylian throne. But now the Hartopian had lost his High Priesthood status and was forced to abort his short-lived rule over the Blacklands region of Pathylon.

A very bitter Ma-otz was feeling weak following his long trek through the mountain pass and he reached down into his side pack to retrieve a handful of wanjol beans to refresh his pallet. The Hartopian felt a large object inside the bag and he pulled it out to inspect it. It was the missing Amulet and he held the sparkling blue gem up to the sunlight, as the sapphire cast a cold haze over his face. He snarled and gritted his razor-sharp teeth, as he placed the Amulet safely back in the leather bag at his side. "Prepare to die, Meltor!" he roared and continued to stand on top of the rock to assess the valley below. "The end is near my old comrade!" he shouted and began to laugh uncontrollably, as the sun finally disappeared behind the backdrop of Mount Pero.

The Hartopian completed his assessment of the vast expanse of dessert in front of him and then jumped down from the large boulder, which had afforded him an adequate viewpoint to scan the infinite landscape. Ma-otz was desperate to find the race of mice-creatures, so he could wreak his revenge on Luccese and Meltor.

The hunched appearance of the armour-clad creature from the Blacklands was menacing, as he expressed his anger once more and tilted back his skull-clad headdress. "Grrrrrggggghhhhh!" roared the Hartopian, as he took pleasure in the sound of his anger filtering through the mountain landscape. He then placed the base of the staff into the rocky floor, as he positioned his footsteps carefully and continued forward on his trek in search of the Mece people that dwelled somewhere within the Unknown Land.

Meanwhile back in Freytor, preparation to launch the iceberg-ship had halted. A perfect storm was brewing out in the Red Ocean and the extreme weather conditions were making it impossible for the Freytorian vessel to make the arduous journey to the outside world.

Rathek was temporarily stranded on the island and he was unaware of the problem. The Devonian nobleman waited patiently whilst the Freytorian leaders gathered in the capital of Frey. Unbeknown to him, they were in constant telepathic contact with King Luccese and were locked in negotiations to find a solution to the problem.

Freytorian scientists worked tirelessly and at last an alternative mode of transportation was suggested, which should allow Rathek to rendezvous with Bradley Baker on the outside world. He was summoned to the Freytorians headquarters and subsequently invited into a large dome-shaped control room, which was constructed from solid blocks of solid ice.

Rathek gazed in amazement at the multitude of arched doorways connected by crystallised passageways, which led to smaller igloo-type buildings. Each symmetrical room was either a laboratory or some kind of workshop that contained white bear-like technicians in matching cloaks, who were busy at work.

Within the main control room, an array of Freytorian technology was brilliantly displayed, as the sound of electronics filled Rathek's head. The tapping of electrical relays and a multitude of LED's flashed, as they changed colour. The technicians scurried around delivering messages to various computer desks and switch panels, as they checked status charts on various monitors.

"You must be Rathek!" roared a huge muscular Freytorian, as he placed a large white paw on the shoulder of the nervous Devonian.

Rathek's eyes focussed on the shiny metal straps, which adorned the ice-bear's shoulders. "Yes, Sir... and you must be the famous General Eidar – a pleasure to meet you at last," he replied in a nervous tone and held out his hand. "It's a pleasure to me you at last."

"Ah... my reputation precedes me," replied Eidar, as he shook the open hand of the nobleman. "I'm sure you are not best pleased about my recent actions against your world... but please let me assure you my friend that King Luccese and I have healed our differences - we Freytorians are now more than happy to assist you in your quest to find the missing Amulet!"

"We are very grateful for your assistance General and I am confident that our alliance will prove strong enough to last way beyond the immediate threat to our world," assured Rathek. "And... I'm sure by now that you have heard that Meltor is not well enough to travel," explained the Devonian. "So I will be the one travelling to the outside world aboard your iceberg-ship."

"My dear friend, Rathek... thanks for your words of reassurance and I am sorry to hear about Meltor's deteriorating health - but I'm afraid it is not that simple," replied Eidar. "The seas are too rough for the great vessel... the iceberg's sail would not be able to withstand the pressure of such fierce winds - please come with me to the steam hanger."

"Steam hanger?" queried Rathek.

"You'll soon find out... this way - I have something to show you!" replied Eidar, as he summoned the attention of three arctic bear technicians to accompany them.

Rathek followed the General and the technicians out of the control room, as they passed through a series of arched metal-studded passageways. Brass riveted portholes adorned the side of the stainless steel corridors and Rathek noticed a large round door about ten metres ahead.

"The success of your journey to the outside world lies behind this great door," revealed Eidar, as two of the technicians struggled to turn the heavy round pulley handle. "Just because the iceberg ship is rendered useless... it doesn't stop you progressing further - wait till you see this!"

A loud clunking noise vibrated through the icy floor of the passageway, as the lock released inside the large metal door. General Eidar led the way through the doorway and Rathek followed close behind the technicians.

It was very dark inside the next chamber and Rathek did not know what to expect, as he smelt a strange industrial dampness that filled the air. The room felt quite large and the atmosphere expelled on odour of burning coal, as Eidar's voice echoed. "Turn on the lights!" he instructed.

One of the technicians heeded the General's order and pulled a large lever, as a huge ark of electricity sparked across the contacts of the switch. The curved ironwork in the roof of the chamber was strewn with domed mercury lamps, which illuminated bright blue beams of light below.

A large railway platform was revealed and Rathek commented immediately. "I can see why you call this the steam hanger!" he exclaimed, as he stared at the huge black locomotive that filled the large chamber with a majestic-like prowess.

The General replied. "This is the last locomotive we have on Freytor and it has remained in this hanger for many centuries... it is the last of its kind - all the other disused steam engines have been destroyed."

"Why get rid of such magnificent specimens like this beauty!" exclaimed Rathek, as he stroked the side of the engine and felt the cold metal numb his finger tips.

"Many of these were used in the old days to transport mineral fuels from the island's port to Freytor's main cities," explained Eidar. "However, since the island became completely covered in ice, we no longer have use for the conventional railway system... we use telepods now," explained the General. "But I have to admit... these engines were ground-breaking technology in their day - this one we kept as a museum piece and it would seem our scientists have found a way to convert it into a makeshift time machine."

"How is that possible?" asked Rathek.

General Eidar asked one of the technicians to step forward and explain how they proposed to convert the locomotive, in order for Rathek to travel safely to the outside world.

The technician cleared his throat and adjusted his white coat, as he readjusted the round lens spectacles that bridged the end of his snout. "Well... it's quite simple really - the Freytorian time travel technology can be used in much the same way," explained the nervous scientist. "Normal practice would be to use ice-ships... on this occasion your journey to the outside world will be by rail rather than by sea - same technology just a different means of transportation!"

Rathek acknowledged the technicians explanation and turned to look at the old black engine, which was made of cast iron and had a large fanned frontage to clear anything that obstructed its path. Two enormous red funnels stood tall and proud above the engine's boilers and the large spoke wheels stood hauntingly still.

The technicians were now joined by a group of senior Freytorian scientists. They quickly boarded the engine and within minutes the sound of metal against metal screeched, as the wheels started to turn very slowly against the rusty railway tracks. Steam poured out of the funnels, as the train moved forward slightly.

Rathek covered his eyes, as a pair of large doors opened at the end of the ice-passage to reveal the Freytorian sunlight and the engine was shunted out of the corrugated hanger. More scientists appeared and set to work to install the necessary components, which would convert the steam train's workings in readiness for time travel. The co-ordinates were set and at last the engine was ready for the important journey.

"It is now time for you to go," announced General Eidar. "Up you go, Rathek."

"Wait!" shouted a weakened voice from the far end of the snow covered platform.

"Meltor!" exclaimed Rathek, as he clambered back down the steel ladder. "You should be resting!"

Rathek ran past General Eidar and down the platform to where Meltor was sitting in his wheelchair.

"I could not let you go without saying goodbye," explained the Galetian High Priest. "Be brave young Rathek and send Bradley Baker my kindest regards... I am not sure if I will ever see you or him again."

"Don't speak that way, Meltor... you will be fine – now please go back to the health pod and rest!" insisted Rathek, as he held the old Galetian's dry wrinkled hand. "I promise you that I will find Bradley and hopefully the Amulet of Silvermoor!"

"There is something else you should aware of young Rathek... when you arrive in the outside world your appearance will be much older," explained Meltor. "Usually it is the other way round... when I used to travel through the Vortex of Souls, I would grow younger."

"So why has this changed?" asked Rathek.

"The Amulet of Silvermoor is in evil hands... this will have an adverse affect on the time travel out of our world," replied Meltor, as he awarded the young Devonian a reassuring look and smiled. "Don't be alarmed... you will resume your good looks when you return my friend!"

Rathek laughed and thanked Meltor for his advice and assurances. "That's a relief!"

"Thank goodness you came with me, Rathek... now go on my young friend – time is not on our side, please do not let me delay you any longer," concluded the Galetian High Priest, as his voice weakened again.

"I am pleased you came to see me, my lord... it has given me the confidence I needed - I am no longer afraid," confirmed Rathek, as he turned to head back to the engine. "Goodbye Meltor... and keep Pathylon safe until I return!"

Meltor waved, as the medical officer wheeled him back towards the entrance of the metal passageway. As soon as the Galetian was out of sight, Rathek boarded the engine again. He turned and acknowledged General Eidar once more. "Thank you for your help General... I hope this lump of metal works!" exclaimed Rathek. "And please send a message to King Luccese to tell him that I'm about to depart... and General, I fear for Meltor - please make sure his health is monitored whilst I am away."

"Your King is already fully aware of your imminent departure," replied Eidar. "Do not worry about Meltor... and please have faith in Freytorian technology - this engine will take you where you need to go... my technicians have set the correct co-ordinates."

Rathek boarded the train and the sound of the platform controller's whistle blew, as more steam emerged from the bright red funnels. Further grinding of metal ensued, as the engine's wheels began to move again over the tracks.

At last Rathek was on his way and the Freytorian train driver sounded the hooter, as the engine picked up speed. A dense mist soon engulfed the train, as it sped faster and faster towards its destination. Rathek could not contain his excitement, as he stared out of the window. He closed his eyes and held his breath, as the great railway engine lifted from the tracks and climbed up high into the thick fog.

The train driver instructed Rathek to take hold, as he pressed a large red button on the engine's control panel. There was a loud droning noise then a blast of turbo sound and the engine thrust forward at lightning speed, as the Devonian clung tightly to the hand rail above.

The flip of another switch on the controls and a bright beam of yellow light burst out from the headlamp at the front of the steam engine, as the train snaked and disappeared upwards into the dense grey mist.

12

Friends Reunited

The 8:52 train to Sheffield had left Sandmouth station on time and it had been travelling for just over four hours, as it journeyed northward to its Yorkshire destination.

Two very excited teenagers were busy munching on prawn cocktail crisps and toasting their imminent arrival in Sheffield with bottles of cherry flavoured Coke. Musgrove Chilcott and Sereny Ugbrooke had just about finished the last of their packed lunches and were busy planning their Halloween liaison with their new friend Bradley Baker. The memory of their parents waving them off on the station platform in Devon was long forgotten and they continued to chat about their new found freedom away from the prying eyes of over protective adults.

Their travel arrangements had changed from the original car journey, which had been planned to coincide with a business trip to Yorkshire. Sereny's father had cancelled some weeks prior, due to a slight illness and he was unable to travel. So to avoid disappointment, it was agreed that his daughter and her teenage friend would travel by train to stay with the Baker family.

"I can't wait to see Bradley again, Muzzy," said Sereny, as she stared out of the carriage window at some black and white cows grazing in the fast moving Nottinghamshire countryside. "I have a good feeling that we're all going to have a great time in Ravenswood."

"Yeah, it will be great to see Brad again," said Musgrove, as he afforded Sereny an admiring glance.

Sereny was still staring out of the window, but she noticed her friend's look of affection through the reflection in the glass and smiled. She knew Muzzy fancied her but his feelings were not reciprocated. The young Bradley Baker held a fondness in Sereny's heart and she was looking forward to seeing her younger friend, especially now he had just turned twelve. The age gap didn't seem quite so drastic now – seeing as she was still thirteen years old.

Nottinghamshire was soon negotiated by the 125mph train, which was now travelling at great speed through the county of South Yorkshire and this prompted an announcement over the intercom; *'Next stop is Sheffield Station… those travelling to Manchester, please change at Sheffield!'*

"That's our stop Muzzy," exclaimed Sereny, in an excited tone.

Musgrove was still staring at Sereny and quickly looked away, as he felt his face warming with embarrassment.

Sereny smiled again and pinched Musgrove's arm. "Are you okay, Muzzy?"

"Err, yeah… we'd better get our things together," stuttered Musgrove, as he pretended to fumble for some imaginary item in his rucksack.

Another announcement echoed from the intercom; *'This train is now arriving at Sheffield Station, please ensure you have all your belongings… please wait for the train to stop before you disembark and be careful as you alight!'*

As the train neared the station, the two children collected their belongings and sat quietly for a short while until the train came to a complete stop. They both stared at their rucksacks, which were perched on the table in front of them, as they contemplated their long awaited reunion with Bradley Baker.

"Come on then... let's go," said Sereny, as she looked through the carriage window one last time and scanned the platform for any sign of the Eternal Chosen One.

Unbeknown to Sereny and Musgrove, Bradley was waiting with his mother on the wrong platform. It was typical of Margaret to misinterpret situations like this one because when she wrote down her fours they tend to look like sixes. Following her telephone call to the station that morning, she had written down the correct platform number, however on this particular occasion Margaret had read the six as a four.

Bradley's suspicions were further supported by the train arrival times, currently being broadcast on the platform information screens and over the station intercom. The television monitor above the boy's head indicated very clearly that the train from Sandmouth had been running three minutes late and would be arriving at platform six. Even as he tried to point it out, the intercom had already announced the arrival of the Sandmouth Train at the correct platform. Bradley tugged at his mother's arm. "Are you sure we're on the right platform, Mum?" he asked, as he tried to guide his determined mother's attention towards the TV monitor. "It's just announced it... didn't you hear?"

"Bradley... you know I'm deaf in one ear – I didn't hear a thing because you were talking at the same time!" exclaimed Margaret, as the intercom announced the Sandmouth train's arrival once again whilst she was shouting.

The boy grew even more frustrated, as he looked across the railway track to the far side of the station. "Mum... look over there - a train has just pulled in at platform six and it definitely said over the loud hailer that the train from Sandmouth had now arrived," insisted Bradley. "Please look up at the screen... it definitely states platform six!"

"No, it definitely says platform four on my bit of paper," insisted Margaret, as she unravelled the creased post-it note. "Now stop fretting Bradley... you're giving me a headache."

"Oh mother... you just sound just like Aunt Vera!" exclaimed Bradley.

"Hey... that will do, young man," replied Margaret, in a stern voice. "I don't sound anything like your Aunt Vera!"

Bradley was now becoming very irritated by his mother's stance on this matter and he was particularly unimpressed with the way she was treating him. "Mum... I'm now twelve years old... stop treating me like a child," insisted Bradley, as he distanced himself from his mother by about three feet.

"Come here Bradley and stop answering me back... your showing off in front of all these people," replied Margaret, as she reached out to her disgruntled son.

Bradley then let out a short burst of affectionate laughter.

"What are you laughing at, Son?" asked Margaret, as she turned to face Bradley with her hands on her slender hips.

"Oh it's nothing... it's just that you - oh, never mind Mum" said Bradley, as he considered the implications of deepening the hole he was currently digging for himself.

"You know I don't like it when you do that," stated Margaret.

"Do what?" asked Bradley in a teasing manner.

"Stopping what you're talking about in mid-sentence like that," replied his mother. "Now, come on... what was it you were about to say?"

"Oh it's just that you looked and sounded like Aunt Vera again," replied Bradley, as he continued to chuckle.

"Cheeky beggar," replied Margaret, as she started to see the funny side of Bradley's wit. She cast a raw smile at her attractive son and Bradley continued to stand by her on platform four, as she stared down the track in search of the train that had already arrived at platform six.

At that moment, Bradley felt a hand touch his shoulder. He turned around quickly in a startled manner, only to be confronted with a beautiful and very familiar face. "Hello, Bradley Baker," said the girl, in a gentle tone.

"Sereny!" shouted Bradley, as he flung his arms around his friend. "It's great to see you again!"

"And you too… and *Happy Birthday,* Bradley," replied Sereny as she gently kissed him on the cheek. "I'm sure you've grown a little since I last saw you in Sandmouth… you definitely seem taller."

Bradley coloured up a little as Sereny turned her attention to Margaret and thanked Bradley's mum for meeting her.

"Glad you have got here safely…. now where's your other friend… err - Musgrove isn't it?" asked Margaret.

"Here he is!" shouted Bradley, as he caught sight of the boy descending the steps of the footbridge that spanned the two platforms. "Hi there Muzzy!" he shouted.

Musgrove boldly jumped the final few steps and ran over to where Bradley and the others were standing. He straightened the creases in his VW camper van emblazoned t-shirt and hunched his rucksack back on to his shoulder. "Hi there old buddy," replied the out-of-breath surfing fanatic, as he put his arm around Bradley's shoulder. "You may be twelve now but you haven't grown much, Brad."

"That's not what Sereny's just said… anyhow, it's better than being a tall lanky fourteen year old like you!" replied Bradley, as he simulated a playful punch into Musgrove's stomach.

"Hey… watch the new shirt, mate… anyhow, I'll be fifteen at Christmas - so less of the cheek you little Yorkshire pudding," replied Musgrove, as he mimicked Bradley's punch and performed a gentle strangulation movement by wrapping his arm around his friend's neck.

"Stop winding each other up you two," demanded Sereny.

"Oh, take no notice and don't let them bother you Sereny… boys will be boys you know," stated Margaret, as she held out her hand to welcome the energetic teenager. "Hello Musgrove… it's nice to meet you again," she added.

Musgrove released his grip from Bradley and gently shook Margaret's hand. "Good to see you too, Mrs. Baker," he replied. "And thanks very much for letting Sereny and me come and stay with you for the week."

"You're both very welcome... I hope you enjoy your time in Ravenswood," replied Margaret, as she turned to face the station exit. "Well, I think we had better get back to the car... the parking ticket will have nearly run out by now," she added. "I'll see you three in the car park... give you all a chance to say your hellos properly without a boring adult like me hanging around!" joked Margaret, in a humorous tone.

"Yeah, see you back at the car, Mum," agreed Bradley, as his mother turned and headed off in the direction of the car park.

Bradley helped Musgrove and Sereny with their luggage and they all started to walk slowly along the platform.

"Have you still got it, Brad?" enquired Musgrove, as he simulated the shape of a round object by circling his thumb and forefinger.

Bradley laughed and nodded. "Yes, don't worry... Muzzy - it's safe and sound in my bedroom back home."

"Have you tried it out since the summer?" asked Sereny. "Have you been on any more adventures yet?"

"Well, as I wrote in my emails to Muzzy... I've been too scared to use it - just in case something bad was to happen to me," replied Bradley. "I was waiting for you guys to come up before I try it out again... but then something really strange happened yesterday."

"What happened Bradley... have you really been on an adventure already?" asked Sereny.

Bradley gave his friends a brief explanation about what occurred in the old lamp room and the details of the new inscription that appeared around the coin.

"The Amulet of Silvermoor... that sounds awesome Brad, I can't wait to see what happens next,' said Musgrove, in an excited tone. "I think we are in for another great adventure."

"Does your Dad remember anything about the fall?" asked Sereny.

"No... he doesn't remember a thing – he was more interested in the old photograph of Silvermoor Colliery that we found on the wall of the old lamp room!" replied Bradley.

Just at that moment the friend's conversation was interrupted by a loud noise, which bellowed like a clap of thunder through Sheffield Station. The vibration beneath the platform was accompanied by the sound of screeching brakes and Bradley felt a cold sensation running through his body. He noticed Sereny's facial expression turn to that of shock, as if she had seen a huge accident. Bradley turned suddenly and looked down the platform to witness a huge cloud of purple smoke that was spreading like a thick fog across the station. A strange haunting sound echoed across the platform, as the expressions on the three children's faces turned to wide grins and they stared simultaneously at each other. The thought of another amazing adventure was evident in their minds, as the friends conveyed a reciprocal message through their excited eyes.

13

The Valley of Sardan

Basjoo Ma-otz had now travelled a fair distance across the Unknown Land and he was struggling for breath, as the hot rays of the desert sun beamed down from the cloudless skies. His water supply was diminishing fast and he sought some divine inspiration from the powerful Staff of Evil, which he carried as a continuous reminder of his arch enemy, Meltor.

The revenge-seeking Hartopian was feeling vulnerable, lonely and very exhausted. Ma-otz stood deathly still, as he perched himself on top of a nearby cretyre tree stump. This slightly elevated position enabled him a better view of the barren landscape that spread out like a blanket of sand. "Wherever you are Meltor... soon you will feel the wrath of my hatred towards you and your pathetic Pathylian scum friends will suffer the consequences of your actions!" he scolded and held the staff aloft to shield his eyes from the piercing sunlight. "Gods of the Unknown Land... give me the power I desire to continue with my quest to find the Mece," continued the Hartopian.

Basjoo Ma-otz slowly closed his red piercing eyes and waived the *Staff of Evil* in a circular motion above the bespoke scull headdress that adorned his weasel-like head. Dark clouds suddenly started to fill the sky and a grim darkness appeared from nowhere, as the storm-filled nebulas gathered above the spot where he was standing. As the sun disappeared, the Hartopian opened his eyes and concentrated on the skull of Meltor's granddaughter, which adorned the top of the staff. Loud claps of thunder rumbled in the sky above and flashes of bright green lighting began to strike the tip of the staff.

Ma-otz prayers had been answered and it was not long before the dry sand around the base of the tree stump started to crack. Water started to seep through the cracks in the ground and the Hartopian let out a roar of excitement, as the trickles soon became a torrent. Within a few minutes a small stream was created and the water level reached his hairy clawed-feet, as the cretyre stump disappeared beneath the fast-flowing current.

The water was rising at such a fast pace that the valley soon became flooded and the flowing rapids crashed against the rocks, which were now mere islands in a fast flowing river. Basjoo Ma-otz needed to find a better platform on which to stand, as the water continued to rise above his scrawny waistline. It was not long before the valley had become totally engulfed by the raging torrent and the Hartopian reached out for a floating branch, as the water level lapped around his metal chest-plate.

Ma-otz took a firm grip on the dead driftwood and launched himself on top of the twisted branch. He grinned with satisfaction and lifted the staff skyward once more, as the branch drifted along at a faster pace.

Eventually the dark clouds began to disperse and the water level steadied, as the sun reappeared above the newly established river. The water line twisted and stretched ahead into the distance like a newly born snake. The current continued to carry Basjoo Ma-otz along crashing into the occasional rock, as the Hartopian held on tight to his temporary raft.

Ma-otz continued to struggle to maintain his grip, as the water lashed around his face. The Hartopian was growing weaker and his claws began to loosen from the slippery branch, as he let out a frustrating roar. "Damn you Meltor!" Fearing his evil spell was beginning to backfire, he struggled to shout out further obscenities towards his bitter rival, as the water filled his snout.

At that moment a sharp change in the current caused a freak rapid to launch the branch together with the Hartopian into the air. Basjoo Ma-otz was suddenly catapulted out of the water and he landed awkwardly back on top of the driftwood. The bruised renegade spluttered out any unwelcome water and breathed heavily, as he gave out a huge sigh of relief. The startled Hartopian gasped in disbelief, as he lifted his head and looked up at the enormous structure ahead.

Two towering twin peaks stood tall and formed an impressive gateway either side of the newly formed river. The huge needle-like rocks marked the entrance to a notoriously evil area of the Unknown Land and Ma-otz gripped even more tightly to the branch in readiness for his journey into the remote *Valley of Sardan*.

The Hartopian had heard many stories, which had filtered back to Pathylon from petrified guides who had accompanied numerous unsuccessful explorers to the gateway of the fated twin peaks. All those that had journeyed past the two parallel rocks and into the valley had never returned.

The river's current steadied to a gentle flow and Basjoo Ma-otz sat upright on the battered branch. He opened the leather pouch attached to his belt and checked the contents. The Amulet of Silvermoor was safe and he quickly retied the pouch to secure the sacred object, as he guided the branch around another rock by pushing it away with the base of his staff.

Basjoo Ma-otz was totally unaware of what lay ahead of the twin peaks, but the stories of unsuccessful voyages would not deter the fearless Hartopian and he braced himself for the unknown journey further down river in search of the Mece.

Meanwhile, Bradley and his two friends were still standing on the platform at Sheffield Station. The ground had stopped shuddering from the thunderous noise and they gazed in amazement at the purple fog that crept closer towards them.

"What on earth was that noise?" exclaimed Musgrove, as Bradley and Sereny watched in disbelief. "And what's that?" he asked, as the smoke started to disperse and reveal the bright yellow beam of light emanating from the front of the black Freytorian steam engine.

"I think we're about to find out," replied Bradley, as the strange haunting figure of a man alighted the train and made his way towards them.

The three children looked around the platform to assess everyone else's reaction. To their surprise, no one else took a blind bit of notice of the strange occurrence and Bradley started to feel a little nervous as the lonely figure approached them.

"Who on earth are you!" exclaimed Bradley, as he stepped back a few paces to the safety of his two friends. "I'll call for the police if you come any closer!" he threatened.

"Stay away from us you freak!" shouted Musgrove, as he took one pace forward and stood protectively in front of Bradley. "Come one step closer if you dare!"

The tall bearded man stopped walking towards them. He heeded the boy's warning then smiled at all three children and spoke to them very calmly. "I did not mean to startle you all... and I mean you no harm."

"You did more than startle us... now - tell us who you are and what do you want?" replied Sereny sternly, as she too took a step forward to shield the other side of Bradley.

The calming affect of the man's voice seemed to cast a spell over the three children and they started to relax. "My name is Rathek and I have a message for Bradley Baker," explained the Devonian nobleman.

Just as Meltor had predicted, Rathek's appearance was that of an older man. His clothes were greyish in colour and he was dressed in some sort of faded Victorian uniform. Rathek's peaked cap was dirty, his boots had holes in them and the fabric of his suit was extremely worn.

The journey from Freytor had indeed aged Rathek considerably and the nobleman's face was very wrinkled and haggard, yet his smile was very assuring and the children started to feel even more relaxed in his presence.

Bradley looked around the platform and couldn't understand why passers-by were not staring at the strange man.

Rathek took notice of the boy's puzzled look. "They can't see me," he stated. "Only you three children can see me... everyone else in this railway station is completely oblivious to what has just happened - I am completely invisible to them so please act like you are speaking to each other to avoid suspicion."

"Nothing surprises me anymore... after what we all experienced during the summer holidays - I don't disbelieve you," stated Bradley, as he gently pushed past Musgrove and Sereny to confront the stranger. "So what is this important message you have for me?"

Rathek confirmed. "Ah... so you are the famous Bradley Baker!" he stated and respectfully removed his cap to reveal a pair of Devonian horns. "Well... Bradley, I am here to ask you for your help," replied Rathek, as he pointed to the ground, widened his eyes and raised his voice.

"Wait!" replied Bradley, as he pointed at the stranger's head. "They are like... like Devonian horns – you really are from Pathylon!"

"I've been sent by King Luccese... and I am sorry to be the bearer of bad news – but Meltor is very ill and Pathylon is in great danger!" added Rathek and lifted his head.

"Did you say Meltor?" shouted Bradley. "What do you mean he is ill... what is wrong with him?" continued the boy, as he turned to Sereny for support.

Rathek's voice fell quiet again. "Do not worry about Meltor, he has a very weak heart but he is in good hands," he replied, as the children became reassured of the old Galetian's health.

"But what about Pathylon?" asked Musgrove. "You mentioned Pathylon is in danger."

"Basjoo Ma-otz has stolen the Amulet of Silvermoor and we need to get it back before it's too late," replied Rathek. "We must stop him reaching the *Mece*... they must not be allowed to repossess the amulet!"

"Who or what are the Mece?" asked Musgrove, as Rathek shifted his blood shot eyes and stared at the ground again.

Bradley answered. "You remember I told you about the coins new message?"

"What was it again?" asked Sereny.

Bradley recited the inscription again. "*Seek out the Mece and find the Amulet of Silvermoor!*"

The children looked to the stranger for a response to the coin's message but the old Devonian nobleman just stood still, as if he was in a trance. Rathek was transfixed to the spot and was still staring at the ground, as a thick cloud of purple mist began to move across the platform again and the Freytorian train started to move slowly down the railway line.

"Hello... is there anybody home?" asked Bradley, as he clicked his fingers in front of the Rathek's face. "Excuse me... you mentioned the Amulet of Silvermoor!" he added, as the sound of hissing steam filled the air.

"This bloke is either mad or ignorant," interrupted Sereny, as she pulled at Bradley's sleeve. "Let's get out of here... your Mum will be waiting for us."

"We can't just leave him here," said Bradley, as he wafted away the purple smoke around his head. "This man knows of

Meltor and Pathylon... we need to find out more information."

"Let's go, Bradley," insisted Musgrove. "Your Mum is going to *be-none-too-pleased* and I don't like the look of all this smoke - anything could happen!"

"I need to know why the coin has a different message on it and this man has the answers!" exclaimed Bradley, as he held on to Rathek's arms and shook him. "Owning the coin will always involve danger and I'm not leaving till this man tells me what I need to know... now, what does the message mean and what's happened to Meltor?"

Musgrove pulled Bradley away and insisted that they leave. Bradley shrugged his shoulders and eventually released his hold on the Rathek's sleeve. He was not happy to leave the situation, but acknowledged his friend's advice. With that, the three stunned friends turned away from the aged nobleman, then quickened their pace and headed off in the direction of the station car park.

There was another loud clap of thunder and a purple flash of light struck the platform. All three children stopped suddenly and turned back to see if Rathek was still staring at the floor.

"He's gone!" exclaimed Musgrove.

"Come on, let's get a move on you guys," insisted Sereny. "We'll talk about this when we get in the car."

The three friends had only been in Yorkshire together for about twenty minutes and already something weird had happened to them. They chatted intermittently on the way to the car park and debated whether or not this was actually the start of some new adventure or just a false alarm.

Their priority at the moment was not to upset Bradley's mum, especially as Margaret was heading off to Leeds with Frannie and Grandma Penworthy for a two day break the following morning. They wasted no more time and made haste for the car.

Margaret pitched her hand above her brow in a form of salute to shield the glare from the station's roof, as she

104

looked out across the car park in search of her son and his two friends. She was so pleased that Bradley was able to spend some quality time with his friends. However she was becoming a little frustrated at his lack of urgency in following her to the car. She was keen to get back to the house to make a start on the suitcase packing for the brief shopping trip, which had been planned following grandpa Penworthy's death last year.

Margaret felt it would be a great idea to take her mother along to try and take her mind off the sad loss of her father. Patrick had to work so he would be staying at home to look after Bradley and his friends, whilst the departure of Margaret, Grandma and Frannie would allow Musgrove and Sereny the necessary room to sleep comfortably in the Baker household. Sereny would sleep in Frannie's bedroom and Musgrove would sleep in Bradley's bedroom on the bottom bunk of his metal framed bed.

At last the children appeared from behind the car, puffing and panting with exhaustion. Bradley apologised. "Sorry we're late Mum... we got held up by some strange bloke in fancy dress."

"Yeah some tramp in a Victorian railway costume was trying to frighten us," added Musgrove and he looked towards Sereny for confirmation.

"I don't know about trying to frighten us... he certainly scared the pants off me," declared Sereny.

Margaret had no idea what they were going on about and offered them a totally bemused look, whilst she held open the rear door of the estate car. Musgrove and Sereny decided not to explain any more about their meeting with the stranger and started to load their luggage into the boot. With the rear door now slammed securely shut, they all clambered into the car and fastened their seatbelts.

Bradley's mother was very keen to get back home to start her packing and she gave no thought at all to the strange things the children had just been talking about. She started the engine and drove the car out of the car park and onto the main road that led back to the quaint village of Ravenswood.

Bradley looked round to make sure there was a clear gap between Sereny and Musgrove, as he positioned himself in a sideways seating position. "It's really is great to have you guys visiting me in Yorkshire... I'm so excited about what we're going to find out this week – that incident on the platform has certainly set things up well."

Margaret looked in the rear view mirror to monitor the reaction from her son's friends. "What's Bradley going on about, Sereny?"

The girl blushed slightly and replied. "Don't know Mrs. Baker... I think he's having one his adventure moments!"

Musgrove laughed and Bradley turned his head to acknowledge Sereny's comment, as he pulled a funny face. "Yeah... something like that!"

Margaret shrugged her shoulders and tuttered, as she tuned the car radio in to the local station and concentrated on the road ahead.

14

Demise of the Tower

Meanwhile deep beneath the surface of the Red Ocean, the ice-submarine commanded by Admiral Norsk moved slowly through the clear water, as it approached the coastline of Devonia. The crew were busying themselves in preparation for the next stage of their mission. An order sounded out from the vessel's internal communication system and the great torpedo-shaped crystal hull was slowed to an effortless crawl. The propellers at the rear of great ice-submarine were controlled effectively to maneuver the vessel towards a large stone object on the sea bed. The Freytorian Admiral ordered one of his crewmen to halt the vessel, as it hovered over the ancient statue.

An illuminated red button on the command bridge control panel was depressed and a metal hoisting device appeared from a portal at the front of the ice-submarine. The ship's commander stared intensely at a display monitor on the control panel and continued to deliver orders to one of his attendants. "That's it... you've nearly got it – three degrees to the right and grab!" instructed Norsk.

"I nearly have it, Sir," replied the attendant, as he pushed another button to close the clamping device at the end of the mechanical arm. "There... it's secure!"

"Well done!" congratulated the Admiral, as he smashed his clenched white paw on the command desk. "At last we have the Kaikane Idol... now let's head for the surface and mount this thing back where it belongs – on what remains of the Island of Restak."

The ice-submarine's crew maneuvered the vessel towards the surface and the order was given to raise the periscope. A scan of the surrounding waterline revealed the familiar shape of the Island of Restak, as the submarine steadied its speed and glided effortlessly in the direction of the sacred rock.

"Okay... that's far enough!" commanded Norsk, as he pressed the periscope handles back into the column.

The submarine's position was made stable at the far side of the island. The attendant started to operate the mechanical arm, in the knowledge that he was out of view from the mainland shores of Devonia and Krogonia. Only the Black Forest of the Blacklands region was in view, as he gently moved the Kaikane Idol towards a conveyor belt that had appeared out of another portal at the front of the vessel. With very little effort the precise maneuver was complete and the ancient statue lay on its side on top of the conveyor.

Admiral Norsk made his way to the ladder that led up to the viewing gallery. "Come with me, quartermaster... I want to make sure the statue is mounted in the right place – I won't be able to extract the rich vein of power that I need if it is positioned incorrectly."

A series of metal scaffold poles were inter-connected above the statue and they created a rail system, which led all the way to the top of the small island. The Freytorian sailors worked with great precision as they strapped the Kaikane Idol to another hoist, which was attached to the scaffolding.

The Admiral gave the order to start winching the ancient monument up the side of the island and it did not take long before the statue was reinstalled in its rightful spot. "At last...

108

we can begin the ritual - take down the rigging and clear the island of any debris!" shouted Norsk. "The island must be made pure before we summon can the ice-cloud... we cannot afford for it to be contaminated in any way!"

Another twenty crewmen left the confines of the submarine and started to dismantle the hoist and scaffolding. As soon as the site was clear, the Admiral collected the blue prints of the ice-cloud and left the confines of the viewing gallery, as he stepped onto dry land. He ordered everyone to leave the island and he followed in the paw prints of his twin bother Eidar.

Norsk made his way up the side of the great rock to prepare for the first part of the ritual that would release another curse over Pathylon. This time the curse would be cast in three carefully orchestrated stages. Firstly the Admiral would use his special powers to feed the blue print designs of the enormous ice-cloud into the ancient statue. This would generate threads of electrical current into the sky to produce the cloud and send it to Krogonia to extract a rich vein of kratennium. Then once the cloud was full it would be summoned back to the Island of Restak, where Norsk would extract more powerful bolts of lightning from the statue to start the chemical reaction. Once charged, the cloud would be programmed to reach its final destination of Frey and during the journey the kratennium would have been transformed into pure Pathylian water. As soon as the kratennium had reached boiling point, the cloud would expel its contents and melt the great ice city.

The Admiral rubbed his paws together and snarled in anticipation. "It won't be long now... the Freytorian senate will be destroyed and I will be the ruler of Freytor - pillaging and piracy will be reintroduced into the Freytorian ways!" he roared. "And I will return to Pathylon with a fleet of ice-submarines to wreak havoc on this pathetic kingdom!"

Norsk stood in front of the Kaikane Idol and began to recite the words that would start the process, as the crewmen on the ice-submarine watched from the viewing gallery on board the ship.

A loud cracking sound ripped though the air and the first flash of lightning was emitted from the statue, as the blue print details were entered. There was no turning back now and the Admiral completed the task, as a shadow started to appear in the skies above. The mass of dark cloud swirled, as it formed above their heads and bolts of lightning shot out in all directions. Some of the strikes connected the nebula to the statue, as Norsk cowered to avoid the flow of electrical current.

A chorus of cheers erupted from the ship's deck, as the Admiral stood upright and roared into the thunderous atmosphere. He watched in admiration, as the ice-cloud reached its full capacity and started to move in the direction of Krogonia. "Go my beauty... find the kratennium and return here to be recharged - Grrrrrggghh!"

The shadow that had covered Restak moved hauntingly away with the cloud, as it drifted slowly towards the island of the lizard men. Sunlight replaced the shadow and spread over the great rock, as the light enveloped the Kaikane Idol again. The Admiral made his way back to the ice-submarine and boarded the ship, as he immediately addressed the crew. "We must submerge and sail out to sea before the sun melts our vessel... we will return later to complete the task!"

Another loud collective cheer echoed around the viewing gallery and the bear-like creatures raised their arms in unison to salute their commander, as Norsk led his crew back inside the vessel.

The Admiral ordered the hatch closed but quickly remembered the letter he had sent to Varuna. "I nearly forgot... before we set sail - we need to release the evil Hartopian that languishes in the Shallock Tower!"

"What shall we do?" asked the quartermaster.

Norsk replied. "I sent the ice-owl to deliver my message as we left Freytor... so Varuna must have read it by know," surmised the Admiral. "If he is willing to help us... he would have done as I asked and hung something from his cell window."

The quartermaster suggested that the ship's periscope be raised. "We should be able to see the Shallock Tower from here, Sir!"

"Good thinking," replied Norsk, as he made his way over to the control bridge and pulled out the handles to raise the periscope.

"Can you see anything yet, Sir?" asked the excited crewman.

The Admiral roared. "Patience you fool... I'm still focussing the lens!" Explained Norsk and then let out a smirk of satisfaction. "He's taken the bait... I can see some kind of cloth flying from the window bars - Varuna is with us!"

The quartermaster waited for his commander to reinstate the periscope. "What do we do now, Sir?"

The great white bear paused for a moment. "I didn't think the Hartopian coward would go for it... I should have known better though - now send two of your best crewmen over to the mainland with plenty of explosives!" instructed the Admiral. "The infamous Shallock Tower is going to fall and Varuna will be free to suppress the Krogon army... this will ensure the cloud is not disturbed whilst it extracts the rich kratennium!"

As the ice-ship submerged, word had spread across the Blacklands. The High Priestess in Hartopia received a message detailing the sighting of the Freytorian vessel by a family of Hartopians, who had been picnicking at the edge of the Black Forest. They had witnessed the Kaikane Idol being restored and reported the ice-cloud drifting away from the Island of Restak towards Krogonia.

The message relayed to Guan-yin was taken seriously and the inexperienced Hartopian leader acted quickly. She took a decision to inform the King of Pathylon personally and made the necessary arrangements to travel back to the royal city of Trad. The High Priestess did not want to rely on messages

111

being sent by the bird whistler, the events that had taken place on the Island of Restak were far too important.

Guan-yin summoned one of her stablemen to saddle up her Hoffen and she mounted its back as soon as the straps were fastened. "It would appear that Basjoo Ma-otz isn't the only threat to Pathylon... I must inform King Luccese of the Freytorians activities - it shouldn't take me more than an hour to get there!" she declared and kicked her heels into the Hoffen's rear. "Meltor is in Frey and he may be in danger... it look's like the Freytorians could be double-crossing us."

The Hoffen reacted to the High Priestesses command and reared up onto its hind legs, as Guan-yin shouted out an excited cry for the animal to gallop ahead and set off on her journey to Trad.

Meanwhile, the two Freytorian crewmen deployed by Norsk to free Varuna approached the base of the Shallock Tower. They were careful not to be seen by the tower guards and made their way down some stone steps that led to the basement.

They forced the old iron padlock that secured the basement door and slipped quietly into the dark chamber. The explosives were carefully placed at the river side of the basement and the charges were set to blow in ten minutes. By setting the charges in one place, once detonated the tower's foundations would be weakened to ensure the great monument fell directly into the river.

One of the tower guards heard a noise coming from the basement and investigated. As he opened the door, the two crewmen came bursting out and knocked him over. Before the guard to get to his feet, the Freytorians had run across the courtyard and disappeared in to some nearby trees on the edge of the forest.

"Get a message to the King... two ice-bears were in the tower basement - I'll go and check to see what they were up to!" instructed the guard, as his colleague ran off in the direction of the royal palace.

Before the guard could check the basement there was a loud explosion and the ground shook. The cracking of stone and wood filled the air, as the basement wall blew outwards and the tower started to sway. The stone debris from the blast flew in all directions and the guard approaching the basement was hit full in the face, as he collapsed to the floor.

At the top of the Shallock Tower, Varuna rushed to his cell window to check out the disturbance below. "What was that?" he muttered to himself, as the structure started to lean towards the River Klomus. "This must be Norsk's doing... I'd better prepare myself for a crash landing," surmised the Hartopian and he ran to the far side of his cell in preparation for contact with the water. "I hope Norsk knows what he's doing and this great lump of stone lands in the river... that's if doesn't break up on impact!"

The tower broke free from its foundations and collapsed sideways. The tall structure stayed in tact, as it groaned and creaked. Varuna braced himself for impact and a torrent of cold water entered his cell window, as the tower hit the river with a loud splash.

Hundreds of Devonians started to run across the courtyard, as a combination of dust and water camouflaged the explosion. The crowd gathered and the dust subsided with the devastation apparent, as the Shallock Tower lay in crumbled sections. The landscape had been changed forever and a makeshift bridge had been formed across the river by the debris from the fallen monument.

Varuna had managed to climb under his bunk and survived the collision. He removed the wooden lattes from the bed and pushed them to one side, as water gushed around his neck. The Hartopian kicked away some stones to make an exit route from the broken cell. He did not want to wait for any rescue teams to arrive and used the makeshift bridge to escape across into the dense Forest of Haldon.

No-one witnessed his escape and he made his way deeper into the forest until he came to Grog's old cabin. The Hartopian sought temporary lodgings in the deceased

Krogons home, which still had plenty of food and provisions to last him a few days. This made his decision to stay put easy and he secured the front door so he could hide there till the shock of the towers collapsed had been investigated.

A few hours later, Guan-yin arrived in Trad to find total chaos around the demolished tower. She dismounted her Hoffen and walked over to what was left of the basement. The tower guard that had confronted the two Freytorian saboteurs was lying on the ground covered in blood and dust.

The Hartopian High Priestess spotted a group of Devonians lifting away stones in search of survivors. She recognised Pavsik and ran across the fallen debris to speak with him. "What happened, Pavsik - have you found anybody alive?"

Pavsik lifted a stone and threw it to one side, as he spoke with an exhausted tone. "Oh hello, Guan-yin... there was an explosion and the tower came down within seconds - we haven't found anyone alive yet!" he exclaimed. "Varuna was in the tower but there's no way he could have survived this... we are still looking for his body - but so far, nothing!"

Guan-yin commented on the torrent of rapids crashing through the gaps in the stonework, which had been caused by the dam effect of the tower's structure in the river. "Looking at the force of the water passing through, there's a good chance that his body could have been washed away down river... not the best way to die - but I think we can agree it's probably for the best," she assumed. "He was always a danger to Pathylon... even locked away inside a secure cell - but it's not Varuna I'm worried about!"

"Ah... so have other concerns?" asked Pavsik. "I thought it was a coincidence that you happened to be in Trad... so why are you here, Guan-yin?"

"To tell the King about another threat to our great kingdom... it's not just Basjoo Ma-otz and the stolen Amulet we have to worry about - a Freytorian ice-ship was spotted near the Island of Restak!" explained the High Priestess. "And it wasn't sight seeing!"

Pavsik guided Guan-yin off the stones and they walked across the courtyard towards the palace. "Are you sure that wasn't General Eidar's ship?"

"I'm positive, Pavsik... this was no ordinary ice-berg vessel - it was some kind of submarine!" replied Guan-yin. "And its crew remounted the Kaikane Idol on to the island... a Freytorian commander was seen in front of the statue - carrying out some kind of ritual!"

"I saw the thunder and lightning in the distance but I thought it was just a storm out at sea... I know the Freytorians were working on a new ship - but I wasn't aware they had finished the project," replied the Devonian High Priest. "The Admiral in charge of the project is called Norsk... he is Eidar's twin bother."

Guan-yin exclaimed. "Do you think Eidar has betrayed us again... and maybe sent his brother to cast another curse over Pathylon?"

"It's possible... but I can't believe that General Eidar would do such a thing," continued Pavsik. "I am aware that his brother doesn't agree with the way the Freytorian Senate has cleaned up its politics... Norsk is very much still a pirate at heart - maybe he has an agenda of his own."

The two High Priests continued their debate, as they left the disaster zone and agreed that it would be best for King Luccese to receive an update. They entered the grounds of the Royal Palace and made there way along the parade area towards the King's chambers. A palace guard saluted their arrival, as Pavsik and Guan-yin walked through a ceremonial arch that led into Luccese private garden.

The King had already been informed of the two High Priests arrival and met them, as they marched through the main flower boarded pathway. Luccese was shocked to see his High Priestess from the Blacklands. "Guan-yin... this is pleasant surprise - what brings you to Trad?"

The Hartopian repeated her account of what happened on the Island of Restak and Pavsik confirmed that no survivors had been pulled from the ruined tower.

"So many bad things are happening," retorted the King. "We need to regroup and make sure all threats to our kingdom are thwarted," insisted Luccese, as he encouraged the two High Priests to leave the royal garden. "Guan-yin, I know you must be exhausted but please return to the Blacklands and ensure there is no breach of your region from the North." he insisted, as he turned to Pavsik. "Please find Turpol and inform him that the ice-cloud is heading his way... the Krogon army must be ready for any attack - heaven knows what Norsk is up to!"

"Yes, Sire!" replied Pavsik and Guan-yin together, as they headed off immediately.

Luccese looked very concerned, as he witnessed the two High Priests pass through the ceremonial arch. The King shouted to them. "Although Meltor is unwell, I'll get word to him to inform Rathek on the outside world of what has happened here today!" He then concluded. "Rathek will have to hasten his search for Bradley Baker... and Meltor will need to question General Eidar about his brother - I just pray that this is an isolated incident and that Admiral Norsk is acting independently from the Freytorian Senate!"

Pavsik raised his arm to acknowledge the worried King. "Very well, Sire... good luck and please do not worry - the people and armies of Pathylon will unite against this latest act of evil!"

15

The Plot Thickens

As the Baker family's estate car entered the Silvermoor housing estate, it passed the memorial cenotaph before sweeping onto the front driveway of number 14 Silvermoor Close.

Bradley turned round and pointed out of the window to a large metal column. "See that, Muzzy?" he asked, as Musgrove stared up at the vertical vent pipe, which stood about five metres taller than the adjacent street light. "That's one of the air vents from the old coal mine shafts," he declared.

"What is it for?" asked Musgrove, as he continued to stare at the pipe, which was poorly disguised by a tall poplar tree.

"Our house is built above the old East Pit shaft of Silvermoor Colliery and that pipe allows any excess methane gas to escape... if you look over there – that's the other vent pipe sited over the old West Pit shaft," informed Bradley, as he pointed to a second metal column about twenty metres down the street. "You don't have to worry though... there are no toxic gases coming out of them nowadays – they've just been left there I suppose."

"How long have they been there?" asked Musgrove.

"Since the colliery closed back in 1994... my Dad has got a photograph in the house," explained Bradley in an excited tone. "We found it in the old lamp room... when *you-know-what* happened - I'll show it to you when we get inside if you like."

The first vent pipe was positioned in front of the Baker's conifer hedgerow bordering the neighbour's front garden and Margaret maneuvered the car passed it, as she pulled onto the driveway.

"Spooky... fancy living above an old mine shaft," added Sereny, as she joined in the boy's conversation.

"I wouldn't go there if I were you, Sereny," laughed Margaret, as she turned off the car's engine. "Our Bradley gets a little paranoid about the whole idea... anyhow - what's that you said about the old lamp room?"

"Oh nothing, Mum!" replied Bradley, in an attempt to cover up the fact that he and his father had both trespassed when they found the photograph.

"Well... we'll see what your Dad has to say about that!" replied Margaret.

Unbeknown to Margaret, Bradley scowled at his mother and Sereny offered him an affectionate smile. "I'm sorry if I offended you, Bradley," said Sereny, in a soft voice. "I hope I didn't upset you talking about living on top of a mine shaft."

Bradley's face coloured up yet again. "Err, no – no, you err, didn't... it doesn't bother me really," he replied. "Can't blame you for commenting... it is a bit bizarre!"

Margaret's thoughts were of the shopping trip to Leeds and she passed over the lamp room incident, as she caught sight of her son's eyes. She gently smiled at him and could tell Bradley liked Sereny a lot. The adoring mother figure elected to not pursue the matter any further in case of further embarrassment to her love-struck offspring.

"Come on then, you lot... let's go inside!" suggested Margaret, as she removed the keys from the ignition and pressed the boot release.

All the passengers got out of the stationary vehicle and walked to the back of the car to retrieve their luggage. Sereny stared down the street and pointed out the cenotaph, standing about thirty metres away in the centre of a small green.

"What's that for?" she asked. "And why has it got a blue coloured light at the top of it?"

"It's the old war memorial... the local villager's lay poppy wreaths each year on remembrance Sunday," replied Bradley, as he lifted Musgrove's hold-all out of the car. "My Dad used to change the light bulbs in it when he worked at Silvermoor Colliery... but I'm not sure why it has a blue light at the top – do you know why, Mum?"

"No... but obviously your Father will know," said Margaret, as she helped Sereny with her bags. "Why don't you all go inside while I sort out the luggage and then you can ask him about it," she added, looking at her watch. "There's a rugby match just starting on the television... so I assume he'll be in the front room getting ready to watch it."

"Let me help you, Mrs. Baker," offered Sereny, as the two boys walked ahead.

"Thank you Sereny... that's very kind of you," replied Margaret in a kind tone, as the boys made their way up the short driveway.

"Bradley... did you say Silvermoor Colliery?" asked Musgrove, as he opened a luggage cover and pulled out the handle from his bag

"Yes... that's right – Silvermoor!" replied Bradley. "I know what you're thinking Muzzy... *the Amulet of Silvermoor* – there has to be a link!"

"Damn right there has to be a link!" agreed Musgrove. "This gets better... what a week we're in for – the plot thickens!"

Sereny finished helping Bradley's mother with unloading the rest of the luggage and closed the boot of the car. She caught up with boys before they entered the house. "What are you two talking about?"

"Tell you inside!" replied Musgrove.

Bradley led his friends into the house and they followed him through the inner hallway and headed for the front lounge. Margaret was right, Patrick had just settled into his favourite armchair with both feet on a footstool, his left hand securing the remote control and a glass of cold beer in his right hand. The television volume was very loud and he did not hear them enter the room. Bradley popped his head over the armchair and grabbed his father's shoulder. "Hi there, Dad!" he shouted. "Match started yet?"

Bradley's enthusiasm was a little too much for the startled rugby fan and Patrick jumped upwards. The remote control fell to the floor soon followed by a similar action, as the contents of the beer glass saturated his lap.

"What the eck!" shouted Patrick, as he looked down at his wet groin. "Well done, Bradley… nice one, mate!"

Patrick turned quickly in readiness to scold Bradley, but then realised his son's Devon friends were stood in total shock behind the armchair.

"Oh, err… hello you two – how are you both?" said Patrick, as he corrected his vocal tone and wiped his hands over the wet patches on his trousers. "It's great to see you both again… did you, err - have a good journey up on the train?"

Patrick picked up the daily newspaper and covered the tops of his legs and made light of the situation. Bradley, Musgrove and Sereny still stood gob-smacked and looked to each other to see who would speak first.

Sereny giggled and finally broke the silence. "We had a lovely journey, thanks Mr. Baker… it's good to see you again too."

"Please call me Patrick… I can't be doing with all this Mr. Baker business," enthused Bradley's father, as he bent down to pick up the empty glass and recover the beer-drenched remote control device.

"Sorry to interrupt your rugby match, Mr... err, Patrick – Sir," added Musgrove.

"Ah, that's okay... it's only just started, I - err, was just getting up to get another beer from the kitchen," insisted Patrick, as he looked down at his empty glass. "Why don't you all sit down whilst I top-up my glass... make your friends feel at home, Bradley - that's a good lad."

A red-faced Patrick made his way past the three children, as the British National Anthem chorused around the room from the surround-sound speakers. The state-of-the-art plasma screen portrayed the England Rugby Union team in full glory, as the TV camera panned across to reveal the proud faces of the players. Bradley's father turned and paid a final glance at the television set, before departing the living room and heading off in the direction of the kitchen to replace his alcoholic beverage.

Musgrove and Sereny looked slightly bemused by Patrick's actions and looked to Bradley for some kind of reassurance. None were forthcoming and instead Bradley made a suggestion. "Come on you guys... let's get out of here," he insisted and headed for the door. "I'll show you where you're going to be sleeping for the next few days while Mum is away on her shopaholic trip."

"That sounds like a good idea," replied Sereny, as she displayed a sincere look of relief. "I wasn't really that bothered about watching the rugby," she added.

"No, me neither," said Musgrove. "Lead the way then Brad!"

Bradley shouted in the direction of the kitchen to inform his father that he was showing his friends to their rooms. There was no reply from Patrick, so Bradley continued up the stairs in front of his fellow adventurers and then made his way towards Frannie's bedroom.

"This will be your room, Sereny... Frannie will be sleeping in with my Mum and Dad tonight," said Bradley, as he opened the door to his younger sister's bedroom. "Anyhow, I'm hoping tonight will be the only time you'll need to stay in here... this time tomorrow I'd like to think we'll have started another amazing adventure - who knows where we might end up!"

"Let's hope you're right, Bradley... after all, its adventure we came here for," agreed Sereny, as she brushed passed the excited boy and entered his younger sister's room. The sweet scent of Sereny's pigtails caught Bradley's nose, as she moved forward to place her bag on the bed. The besotted boy stood in a dazed state, as he observed the pretty girl look around the poster covered walls. "This is lovely!" exclaimed the observant girl, as she studied a cartoon picture of *Bob the Builder* above the single framed bed-head." How cute!"

The noise of the toilet flushing at the end of the landing disturbed Bradley's dream-like state and Musgrove soon entered the room with a spring in his heel. He collided with a set of drawers and accidently nudged his friend out of the trance.

Bradley coloured up a little and afforded Sereny an adoring glance, as he rubbed his nose and composed himself. "Come on in why don't you, Muzzy!" he quipped in a sarcastic tone.

"Yeah... nice entrance - you clumsy lump!" laughed Sereny, as Musgrove reacted to her jibe by pulling a funny face.

Bradley quickly defused the potential spat. "I'll show you my room now, Muzzy!" he said, excitedly. "We'll be in there together if that's okay?"

"Sure Brad… cool!" replied Musgrove, as he turned to leave Frannie's room and took another opportunity to smirk at Sereny. "Are you coming, gorgeous?"

Sereny smiled and followed the two boys along the landing into Bradley's bedroom. It was much larger than Frannie's and had built-in bunk beds that were constructed like a den.

Musgrove placed his rucksack on the top bunk. "Cool bed, Brad... did your Dad make these for you?"

"Err, yes... err, but not that one," said Bradley, as he pointed at Musgrove's bag. "You'll be sleeping on the bottom bunk, Muzzy," he insisted.

Musgrove replied, "Sorry Brad... I just assumed because I was the oldest – I would be..."

Sereny interrupted, "Well you know what they say when you assume... don't you?"

"No... please enlighten us!" replied Musgrove in a sarcastic tone.

"My Dad always told me that when you assume – you make an *ass* out of *u* and *me*," laughed Sereny, as she wrapped her arms around Musgrove's waist so he could not move.

"Get off me... you sarcastic little minx," laughed Musgrove, as Bradley watched in amusement and with a predictable sense of jealousy.

"Come on you two... I'll show you the most important room in the house," suggested Bradley, in an attempt to separate his squabbling friends.

"Which room is that?" asked Sereny, as she finally released her grip from Musgrove.

Bradley reached under his pillow and pulled out the sacred grobite. He flicked the coin into the air and announced. "The *bath* room of course!"

The three young adventurers all burst out laughing and simultaneously rekindled their enthusiasm at the thought of another possible adventure through the plughole and into the unknown abyss of yet another stinking drainpipe. They soon became embroiled in an exciting conversation about their railway station encounter with Rathek and how it would be possible to find a way of helping Meltor. Their discussions soon expanded into a recollection of their last adventure into Pathylon and how the lost Amulet of Silvermoor had now become the focus of their attention.

Following a brief inspection of the Baker family bathroom, the three children returned to Bradley's bedroom. The host reached over and picked up a note pad and pen, as Sereny and Musgrove settled down beside him. They started to plan their activity for the following day and Bradley began to write down a list of suggested tasks.

The children carried on their debate and time seemed to pass by very quickly, as daylight merged into a wintery cold evening. Sereny suggested that they all go to bed soon. "I'm shattered after that long train journey...I need my beauty sleep – anyhow, we all need to be up early in the morning to make a start on this list.

Musgrove nodded and watched Bradley, as he finished writing on the pad. "So, go on then... remind us, Brad - what's the first item on the agenda for tomorrow?"

Bradley turned the note pad around and showed it to his friends to get their agreement. "Well, I'd say that has to be our first task," he suggested and pointed to the top of the list. "Get back in contact with Rathek and find out what the heck he was going on about at the train station!" He then held out his hand to invite a show of unity.

Musgrove and Sereny nodded, as they placed their right hands on top of Bradley's. The eternal chosen one smiled and stated in a confident tone. "Here's to the sacred grobite and another amazing adventure!"

16

Recruiting the Tree Elves

Back on the Island of Freytor, the medical staff had been working throughout the night to assist Meltor and they had finally managed to steady the irregular heartbeat of the aging High Priest. The departure of Rathek had caused Meltor's heart to fail, as he was wheeled through the Freytorian headquarters. Since then, he had been heavily sedated and lay motionless in his health pod at the medical centre in Frey.

King Luccese had failed to get a message to Meltor to inform him of Admiral Norsk's antics, so he had decided to travel to Freytor with Queen Vash and Pavsik. The trio had arrived on the Island a few hours earlier and they were quickly escorted to Meltor's bedside. The High Priest was still unconscious and was unaware of their presence.

The trip to Freytor was sanctioned by the Pathylian Royal Congress, as they felt it necessary that the royal couple should be escorted to a safe place away from their threatened kingdom, at least until the imminent danger had passed. The populous had voted en mass, throughout all the five regions, for the King and Queen to seek safety - such was their loyalty to the throne and to the saviours of their beloved land.

The royal couple had taken the opportunity to travel to Freytor to be at Meltor's side and to question the integrity of General Eidar. The King needed to know if the Freytorian was colluding with his brother. They feared for their dear champion and ally and if the old Galetian were to die, at least he would be amongst friends.

A vigil was set up next to his health-pod and numerous attempts to send telepathic communications to the outside world failed. King Luccese made a final attempt to get the message about the ice-cloud to Rathek but he had no choice but to give up. "We don't seem to be able to get through to the Freytorians time travelling locomotive... there must be some distortion in the portal's frequency," declared the King, as Queen Vash comforted her husband. "The only other explanation is that Rathek has departed from the train and is looking for Bradley Baker... he won't be able to pick up our signal - so they are going to have find their way back through the Vortex of Silvermoor with no knowledge of yet another threat to Pathylon."

The Queen sympathised with Luccese. "My dear King... Rathek and Bradley will deal with whatever is   put before them - all we can do now is let events take their course."

The King moved towards the health- pod window and stared out over the barren ice caps that surrounded the Freytorian capital. "I just hope that by us being here, it does not jeopardise things back home... I need to be near to Meltor - but our people are in grave danger and I feel we are betraying them by hiding away on this frozen land."

"Don't worry, my dear," replied Queen Vash, as she put her slim arms around the King's muscular body. "I am confident that Turpol, Guan-yin and Flaglan will ensure the ice-cloud is dealt with."

The King turned to face his Queen and held her tiny hands in his. "You're right, Vash... although I still do have my

126

doubts about Flaglan - she can't be trusted," countered Luccese. "But I have to put my faith in all members of the High Priesthood and pray that they destroy Norsk's ice-cloud... I also have to rely on Bradley Baker and Rathek intercepting Basjoo Ma-otz before he reaches Mount Pero with the Amulet."

"Please try to relax, my dear Luccese," insisted Vash, as she interlocked her hands and squeezed the King's fingers. "They will all do you proud... you can't ask for any more than that - the destiny of Pathylon is already set and there's nothing more you can do now!"

"I know, my love... but there's one other thing that haunts me - Varuna has still not been recovered after the collapse of the Shallock Tower and just I hope the evil Hartopian drowned because until we find his body, I will not rest!"

Queen Vash continued to speak with a calm tone to her voice. "Why not put your mind at rest, my dear... let's assume the worse case scenario possible, that means Varuna is at large - why not dispatch a Klomus Hawk to fly to the Unknown Land to intercept Bradley Baker and inform him of the dangers that threaten our kingdom."

Luccese nodded. "That's a good idea, it won't hurt to send one of the royal birds to meet young Bradley... just in case we don't get a message to Rathek - I'll ask Pavsik to send word to the bird whistler in Trad."

The King and Queen debated a little more about the possibilities and scenarios that threatened Pathylon. They held each other tightly and cast another glance out onto the snowy landscape, as the sun started to descend over the distant mountains.

Meanwhile in the Forest of Haldon, the day was also coming to an end and a group of Devonian noblemen passed by the wooden shack at the edge of the River Klomus. An order had been sent by Luccese from Freytor for the search party to seek out Varuna. The Hartopian's body had still not been discovered inside the ruins and the King wanted to be sure

127

that his body was found to dispel any rumours that he had survived the demolition of the Shallock Tower.

Unbeknown to Luccese, Varuna had indeed escaped and he stared through a small crack in the window shutter that secured a small log framed window inside Grog's cabin. He muttered to himself. "I must find Flaglan... she will help me seek revenge on Luccese - I know she still hates me for how I treated her but she still retains a strong desire to rise against the King."

Varuna was keen to find the leader of the Tree Elves and he took another look through the gap in the window. "All clear... I don't think those Devonian's will pass this way again for some time - it's time to leave this pathetic little house and find that gullible High Priestess."

The Hartopian left the confines of Grog's cabin and headed deep into the Forest of Haldon. It wasn't long before he reached an opening in the dense tree bound region. Varuna stopped in his tracks and looked up into the tree tops. He spotted some movement and shouted. "I am Varuna... take me to your leader!"

Within seconds a group of pointy-eared tree elves surrounded the Hartopian and drew back their bows with arrows poised to fire into the weary renegade. One of the tree elves spoke. "The King is looking for you... a group of Devonian noblemen passed through here earlier - give us one good reason why we shouldn't turn you in!"

Varuna replied in a calm tone. "With respect... you should address me with a little more concern for your safety - now take me to Flaglan and I will convey my reasons direct to your High Priestess."

The Tree Elf responded to the Hartopian's outlandish statement with a show of distain. "Who do you think you are, you stupid weasel?" questioned the senior elf. "You forget what you have become... a weak and embarrassing specimen of a failed King - your power has been taken away and you dare to threaten us?"

The group of Tree Elves pointed their outstretched bows at Varuna and their chants erupted into a chorus of intimidating laughter. The Hartopian was surrounded by twenty armed forest dwellers waiting for the order to release their arrows.

"Wait!" roared Varuna, as he raised his arms in the air. "I am unarmed and as you can see... I still carry the wound that reminds me of my previous failings!" he declared and waved his stub at the senior elf.

The distrusting Tree Elf also raised his arm in readiness to command his archers to fire at the escaped prisoner. "My people have waited a long time for this opportunity and I take great pleasure in ordering you execution, Varuna."

As the senior Tree Elf started to lower his arm, all the archer's bowstrings tensioned under pressure, as the Hartopian closed his eyes and feared the worse.

"Stop!" shouted a female voice, as the clambering of hooves echoed through the opening in the forest. "Lay down your weapons!"

Varuna opened his red glinting eyes and witnessed the sultry sorceress dismount the Hoffen, as her delicate clothing caressed the forest breeze. The archer's bows were lowered as Flaglan marched over to the senior elf. There was a brief conversation and then the High Priestess turned to face the waiting Hartopian.

Flaglan walked over to Varuna and her eyes looked down at his severed limb. "I have to *hand* it to you," she laughed. "You just don't know when to give up... do you?"

Varuna's pointed snout quivered, as he replied. "Still using the old *hand* jokes, Flaglan... they are getting a bit boring now - you need to get some new material."

"I'll never get bored of taunting you about it, Varuna... the thought of your paw being cut off inside the Royal Palace ballroom still fills me with satisfaction - it signalled the downfall of your failed attempt at ruling this kingdom and I vowed never to let you or your kind into my great forest again."

Varuna approached the pretty leader of the Tree Elves and gently caressed her chin with the back of his paw. "Then tell me... why did you stop your archers from killing me?"

Flaglan jolted her head backwards to avoid the Hartopian's sleazy touch and pushed his paw away. "Don't touch me you Blacklands scum... I don't want you dead - that would be too good for you!" she expressed. "I want to see you back behind bars where you belong... and where you can rot and die!"

Varuna smirked and let out a crackling cry of laughter. "So tell me my beautiful sorceress... where will you imprison me?" He provoked. "The Shallock Tower has been destroyed and there was a very good reason why."

"What are you talking about?" asked Flaglan. "The tower was sabotaged... probably your old friend Basjoo Ma-otz that did it as part of his quest to destroy Pathylon with the Amulet of Silvermoor!"

Varuna's face lit up with the news of his old High Priest's revenge tactics. "So that's what the meeting was about in the tower... you lot were planning to capture Basjoo Ma-otz - that's very interesting."

Flaglan realised what she had done. The meeting with the King and the other High Priests in the Shallock Tower had meant to have been kept a secret. Now Varuna knew the whole situation and was quick to take advantage. He raised the back of his paw again and stroked the trembling High Priestesses mouth. "You've told me some important tales out of school... my pretty young Flaglan and I'm sure Luccese won't look too kindly on your lack of control of your blabbering mouth," he jibed, as he outstretched a claw and followed the contours of her lips with one of his sharp talons. "Under these revealing circumstances... I think you will be interested in what I have to say."

The High Priestess moved her head sideways and caught the eye of her senior elf. "Lieutenant... take your squad of archers and meet me back at Tree City... Varuna and I need to talk."

"But, my lady... we can't leave you here with him!" replied the Tree Elf.

"Varuna means me no harm... he needs us and I intend to find out what he has to say - now go!" insisted Flaglan, as Varuna moved away and sat down on a nearby cretyre stump.

The archers heeded their leaders request and moved back into the trees. Their metallic armour glinted from the sun beams that danced through the swaying treetops, as they turned to head back to the forest's capital.

Varuna asked Flaglan to sit beside him. "Please be seated my dear... I need to bargain with you."

"You have nothing to bargain with, Varuna... you lost everything when you failed to defeat Luccese," replied the High Priestess, as she reluctantly obeyed the Hartopian's request and sat elegantly on another tree stump.

Varuna revealed his bargaining power. "That's where you are wrong my dear... I have regained an advantage but I need your help - and I have been given another opportunity to dethrone Luccese and you have another chance be Queen of this magnificent kingdom."

Flaglan pulled a disapproving face and responded. "I told you before... I'd rather eat flax excrement than be your Queen - anyhow what's the opportunity you speak of?"

"Ah... so you are interested in being Queen of Pathylon?" probed Varuna.

"I didn't say that... well not in so many words - I would be Queen, but not your Queen!" she retorted.

"Come on, Flaglan... let's agree to take the throne together - I'm not asking for you to fall in love with me," insisted the Hartopian, as he stood and strode across the forest opening. "I just want your support... and control of your army!"

"Never... my Tree Elves are master archers - I'm not letting you take control of them!" shouted Flaglan and she joined Varuna in the centre of the open ground. "If you insist on taking control of this kingdom... then I will be the one to lead my people - now tell me of your plan!"

Varuna and Flaglan agreed to sit and discuss his idea to march against Turpol's lizard men. He explained about Admiral Norsk, the ice-cloud and the kratennium. "We have to make sure the Krogons don't stop the ice-cloud form extracting the kratennium," explained the Hartopian. "After we have defeated the Krogon armies and the ice-cloud heads for Freytor... Norsk will leave us to march into the other regions - the stupid polar bear wants to destroy the Freytorian Senate so he can come back here and pillage."

Flaglan paused momentarily and then made an observation. "Surely, if we are successful in defeating the Krogons and Norsk gets his ice-cloud full of kratennium... that will weaken the Pathylian defense - when Norsk returns to pillage he will be able to end our reign over the kingdom."

"That won't happen... he assured me in writing that all he wants is access to Krogonia to extract the kratennium," assured Varuna. "Anyhow, he can have the Krogon region... their army will have been defeated and we can destroy the Satorc Bridge to stop any Freytorians reaching the rest of the kingdom - I'll settle for four regions as long as I can rule over them!"

Flaglan laughed and twitched her nose. "It would seem that you do have a plan... let's make our way to Tree City so we can brief my army of archers!"

Varuna watched the sorceress as she remounted her Hoffen and snarled to himself. "As soon as her army defeats the Krogons... she will feel the coldness of a blade in her slender back - she will regret her remarks about my severed paw."

"What was that you said, Varuna?" asked Flaglan, as she struggled with the reins of her excited Hoffen.

"Nothing my dear... nothing!" sniggered the scheming Hartopian. "I was just saying to myself... it's good to be working with you again!"

"Oh... right - yes," replied Flaglan, as she held her arm out to the Hartopian to invite him onto the rear of the Hoffen. "Give me your *hand*... sorry that wasn't a dig at you!" she laughed.

Varuna held out his paw and pulled himself awkwardly onto the mount. He lay on his belly, as the Hoffen reared onto its hind legs before lurching forward into a canter. He managed to pull himself around and sat upright, as he pulled the High Priestess into his midriff. Flaglan elbowed the Hartopian in the stomach and they disappeared into the dense forest, as the Hoffen gathered pace and galloped in the direction of Tree City.

Luccese doubts about Flaglan's loyalty to him were about to be realised and the King's fears had become reality, as Varuna roamed menacingly free through the land once again.

17

Light of Mount Pero

Rathek made his way out of the small woodland area located on the outskirts of Ravenswood village. He had found himself on the side of a road next to a sign directing him back into Silvermoor Woods. "Interesting... that has confirmed I'm heading in the right direction," he muttered to himself. "There can't be more than one Silvermoor in this neck of the woods... I don't believe I just said that."

The Devonian Nobleman had a little chuckle at the joke he had just made to himself. He brushed down his ragged cloths and started to follow the tarmac road, which led into the Silvermoor housing estate.

Rathek quickened his pace and hurried ahead, passing the small tower with the blue light atop. He could not stop himself smiling. "This must be the place... thank goodness the *Light of Mount Pero* is still dead," he stated out loud and he looked up at the cenotaph towards the crystal glass panels that protected the blue beacon. "If that light was to shine, whilst I am in this world... it would mean that Basjoo Ma-otz had placed the Amulet back on the sacred ledge of Mount Pero - thank goodness the lamp is distinguished."

The Devonian stopped delaying his advance to find the eternal chosen one and diverted his attention away from the cenotaph. He headed over to the row of detached houses opposite. "Now, which homestead does our young hero reside at?" he muttered and then noticed a uniformed figure next to a red four wheeled vehicle.

A postman had parked his van across the street and he was preparing to deliver some letters. Rathek spotted an opportunity but he did not want to rouse suspicion, so he approached the mail man cautiously. "Excuse me... I wondered if you could help me."

The postman looked surprised to see someone so early in the morning, especially dressed in such an unusual costume. "Home a little late aren't you... or should I say early?" he joked. "Or have you just escaped from a care home?"

"Sorry... I'm not sure what you mean," replied Rathek, as he attempted to read some of the names on the letters in the postman's hand. "You must be doing the job of a raven... err, we have bird whistlers where I come from that carry out your duties - delivering messages."

The postman looked puzzled. "Been drinking have you, Sir?"

Rathek tried to retract his comment, as he realised what he had just said and remembered he must avoid arousing any suspicion. The stuttering Devonian diverted the subject of the conversion back to his clothing. "Oh, I see what you mean... these old rags - I went to a special event last night and it was fancy dress!"

"So you must be feeling a little worse for wear this morning... now - I'm really busy so how can I help you?" asked the postman, as he continued to shuffle the letters into order of house numbers. "Are you lost?"

Rathek spotted the name *Patrick Baker* on one of the envelopes and memorised the house number. "Fourteen," he muttered under his breath.

"What was that you said?" asked the postman.

"Oh nothing... it's, err, been *fourteen* hours since my last drink and I think I must be on the wrong street - thanks for your help anyway," replied Rathek, as he patted the mail man on his back and started to walk back towards the cenotaph.

"No problem... hope you find where it is you are supposed to be!" shouted the bemused postal worker and uttered to himself. "What a *Weirdo*!"

"Thanks!" replied Rathek and he disappeared behind the cenotaph to wait for the uniformed delivery man to finish his rounds. "And give my regards to your Bird Whistler!"

The mail man shook his head and carried on with his post round, as he muttered to himself again. "Definitely a hundred percent *wacko jacko* that one."

Meanwhile, back inside the Baker household Bradley was in the kitchen and had already read the note left by his mother informing him that she had left for the shopping trip with Frannie and Grandma Penworthy. The note also informed him that his father had left early for work so it was his responsibility to sort out breakfast for his two friends.

Musgrove and Sereny were still sleeping so Bradley put the note to one side and helped himself to a bowl of cornflakes. He picked up the milk carton and sat down at the large kitchen table. He had just started to pour the milk over his cereal when the doorbell rang. His concentration was broken and he accidentally spilt the milk over the edge of the bowl. "Oh blast it," he said to himself. "Who on earth could that be at this time in the morning," he moaned, as he mopped up the milk and subsequently discarded the wet dishcloth into the flip bin.

Bradley immediately realised his mistake, so he re-opened the flip bin and plunged his arm in to explore its slimy depths. He moved the contents around a little and retrieved the cloth together with some mixed vegetable peelings and a slice of soggy burnt toast. It was a chore that had to be carried out because he knew his mum would go ballistic if another dishcloth disappeared. He was always being blamed for the loss of dishcloths, which made him even more determined to retrieve this particular one.

Bradley muttered to himself again, as he picked the potato peelings from his fingers. "Suppose if I leave this one in the bin... the price of Mum's shares in *Vileda* would shoot through the roof!" He chuckled and then tossed the dirty cloth into the washing up bowl, which also contained the previous night's crockery and to make matters worse, the cloth hit the bowl dead centre and splashed dirty water in every direction across the work surface. Bradley conceded defeat and decided he could not win this particular battle. The powers bestowed on him as the *Eternal Chosen One* were certainly not working in this instance so he turned away and wiped his sticky hand on the leg of his pajama bottoms.

The doorbell rang again and he finally left the confines of the kitchen war zone that he had created in a matter of minutes. As Bradley made his way down the hallway to the front door, he could just make out the slight figure of a man standing on the other side of the glass-panels. The flustered boy held up his hand to turn the Yale lock and noticed that the chain was not in its slot. He abandoned the release of the latch and quickly replaced the chain then proceeded to open the door slightly.

A cool swirl of grey smoke crept in between the door and frame, as Bradley peered out. He caught sight of a cloaked figure standing on the step and quickly slammed the door shut again causing the smoke to twirl in tight circles like a small tornado.

The doorbell rang again but this time Bradley ran straight upstairs and back into his bedroom. He made his way over to the window, which overlooked the front door. He opened the window and looked down at the canopy that protected the entrance to the house, which obscured his sight of the strange figure. He decided to shout down to the visitor. "Who are you and what do you want?"

The figure stepped back, pulled back his hood and looked up at Bradley, who was now dangerously stretching out to catch a glimpse of the stranger.

Rathek spoke back to the defensive boy in a calm tone of voice. "Please do not be alarmed, my young friend... now - pull yourself back inside before you fall."

"Oh, it's you again," replied Bradley, as he cantilevered back towards the safety of the window frame. "You've got to stop scaring me like this... what is it that you want?"

"I need to speak with you urgently Bradley... after all, you are the *Eternal Chosen One* and I desperately need your help," requested Rathek.

"Wait there... I'll come down - let me get dressed first though," insisted Bradley, as he clambered down from the window sill.

As Rathek waited at the front door, Bradley reappeared at the bedroom window and shouted down to the stranger again. "Are you still there?"

Rathek stepped back into view again to acknowledge the boy. "Yes... I'm still waiting for you, Bradley!"

"Listen... I've had second thoughts - I don't think it's a good idea you coming into my house," insisted Bradley. "I don't know you and besides I think it would be best if we meet somewhere more public... I'll feel much safer that way!"

"That's not a problem... when and where do you suggest?" asked Rathek.

"There's a cafe on Silvermoor Road... next to the newsagents - I'll meet you there in about half an hour!" shouted Bradley. "And I'd lose the cloak if I were you... you look a bit weird - I'll see you in a bit!"

Rathek was shocked at the response he had received from Bradley. He genuinely believed that this so-called boy hero would be more hospitable. The Devonian Nobleman turned to make his way down the garden path and noticed a plastic toy soldier on the ground. He bent down to pick up the green figure and carefully examined it.

Bradley had made his way downstairs and opened the front door. The curious boy watched the stranger pick up the plastic army figure. "Hey... give that to me - he's been on an incredible journey and he'd have lot's to talk about if he were real!"

"Ah, you've changed your mind again... you now want to speak to me, Bradley," acknowledged the Devonian and walked back towards the house.

Bradley stood nervously in the doorway and offered an invitation to the stranger. "Come inside... its cold out there."

"Thank you," replied Rathek. "My initial impression of you was wrong and Meltor was right about you... you are a very trusting individual - thank you for finally allowing me into your home." He handed the toy soldier to Bradley and followed him into the house. "So this must be the soldier that followed you in to Pathylon?"

"It sure is... I wondered where it was - K2 must have taken it outside," replied Bradley, as they entered the lounge.

"K2 was also one of the *chosen ones* I believe," remarked Rathek.

"Yes, he was... but like the others - he probably doesn't remember anything about his adventure down the plughole!" replied Bradley, as he showed Rathek into the lounge. "But then he's hardly likely to tell me... is he - I'd probably get a few friendly growls and a big sloppy lick!"

"Where is K2?" asked Rathek.

"In the back garden, I guess... he's probably digging up stones - he does that quite a lot and Dad gets a bit annoyed," replied Bradley nervously, as he acknowledged that the stranger was making conversation to make him feel more relaxed.

Rathek noticed that Bradley was feeling a little uncomfortable and asked. "Is your Father around?"

"No... he's at work," replied Bradley and then realised that he had just announced that the adult of the house wasn't at home. "But he might be back in ten minutes!"

"Right!" replied Rathek in a disbelieving tone.

Bradley thought of a quick retort to inform the stranger that he wasn't alone and concluded. "Please take a seat and I'll go and wake my friends."

"Thank you, Bradley... that's very kind," replied Rathek and he sat on the sofa.

Bradley disappeared out of the lounge, as he made his way upstairs and knocked on his sister's bedroom door. "Sereny... are you awake?"

There was no reply but Bradley could here water running in the bathroom. He walked along the landing and tapped on the door. "Sereny... it's Bradley - are you going to be long?"

Water from the shower was running and a boy's voice replied from inside the bathroom. "Morning Brad... it's Muzzy - I'm in the shower but I think Sereny's still soundo!"

"Sorry mate... I'll go and knock a little harder - by the way, my Dad's gone to work and we have the house to ourselves!" shouted Bradley. "Well, almost... there is someone downstairs waiting for us - so hurry up and get dressed!"

"Who is it?" shouted Musgrove, as he quickly turned off the water supply.

"You're not going to believe it, Muzzy... it's Rathek - the strange man from Pathylon that we spoke to on the platform," replied Bradley, relieved that he didn't have to shout above the noise of the water any more.

"Oh, right... that's a turn up for the books - at least we don't have to go searching for him," stated Musgrove, as he turned the lock and opened the door.

Bradley was quite impressed with his friend's physique. Musgrove was quite toned with all the surfing he did in Sandmouth. "Come on... get dressed and stop showing off your six-pack."

"I thought Sereny might be up and about," teased Musgrove, as he looked towards her bedroom door.

"Yeah... right!" replied Bradley in a jealous tone. "I'm going to get washed and dressed... be quick Muzzy and wake Sereny - when you've put some clothes on!"

"Okay... no worries mate," laughed Musgrove, as he closed Bradley's bedroom door.

Bradley was just about to close the bathroom door and Sereny appeared in the hallway. "Hi, Bradley... didn't mean to lie in for so long - that train journey yesterday really tired me out."

"Oh... errr, that's okay Sereny." replied Bradley, as he hid behind the door with just his head poking round to acknowledge the pretty girl. Bradley couldn't help but notice that even with her hair scrunched up after a night's sleep, Sereny looked as gorgeous as ever. "Anyway, you did have an early start so it's not surprising that you slept so long... errr - did you sleep well?"

"Like a log... you?"

"I didn't sleep well at all... I couldn't stop thinking of what Rathek told us - speaking of which, he's downstairs in the lounge waiting for us," declared Bradley.

"You're joking... really?" exclaimed Sereny. "I better get ready... are you going to be long in there?"

Bradley showed some chivalry and offered his friend the bathroom. "You have this one... I'll use the sink in the downstairs toilet - I only need a quick wash."

"Thanks Bradley... you are very kind," replied Sereny and she brushed past him. "See you downstairs in a bit."

Bradley could feel his face colouring up again. This girl had the knack of making him feel all mushy and he showed his feelings every time she displayed any sign of affection towards him. He tried to ignore his feelings for her, as he made is way back downstairs and popped his head round the lounge door. "Hi Rathek... sorry to keep you waiting, we'll be with you in a jiffy - can I get you a drink or something?"

"No... I'm fine thanks, Bradley - just need to talk to you about Pathylon," reiterated the Devonian, in a patient tone. "I have some very important things to tell you."

"Okay... won't be long now - back in a bit," replied Bradley and he headed for the downstairs toilet.

At last, all three children assembled in the lounge and sat like three little monkeys on the opposite sofa across from the stranger, as they waited for Rathek to speak.

Bradley decided to break the deadlock. "So, Rathek... at the station, you started to tell us why you had been sent by King Luccese and you mentioned Meltor is very ill."

Sereny added. "You also said that Pathylon is in great danger!"

Rathek remained silent and the children watched as the Devonian stared at the floor. Musgrove commented. "He's doing it again... he's gone all quiet on us!"

Then Rathek lifted his head and spoke softly. "Do not worry about Meltor, he is in good hands."

Bradley replied. "Rathek... you've already told us that - but what about Pathylon, at the station you mentioned Pathylon is in danger."

Rathek replied. "Basjoo Ma-otz has stolen the Amulet of Silvermoor and we need to get it back before it's too late... we must stop him reaching the Mece - they must not be allowed to repossess the amulet!"

"This is crazy!" stated Musgrove, as he stood up and walked across the lounge. "He's just repeating what he said on the platform!"

Bradley interrupted his impatient friend and focussed his attention back on the Devonian. "Rathek... on the platform, I told you about the sacred coin's new message - *Seek out the Mece and find the Amulet of Silvermoor!*"

Rathek's trance-like state continued and his eyes flickered, as another thick cloud of purple mist began to fill the room. "Quickly, the coin... where is the grobite, Bradley?" He asked.

Bradley put his hand in his jeans pocket and pulled out the sacred grobite. "Here, Rathek... it's here!"

The Devonian's head remained still whilst his eyes moved to focus on the grobite. He reached out and grabbed the coin, as it started to glow inside his clenched hand. "Put your hand on mine Bradley and hold onto my arm... now both your

142

friends - all hold onto me!" shouted Rathek, as the room completely filled with the dense violet cloud.

The room started to spin round and round, as everyone's feet lifted off the ground. They started to move through the mist and the spinning motion became faster and faster, Musgrove shouted out. "What's happening to us... where is the coin taking us?"

"Hold on tight my friend," instructed Rathek, as the spiralling motion began to subside. "It won't be long now."

At last the spinning finally stopped and their feet touch solid ground again. The mist began to disperse and their location was revealed.

"Where are we?" asked Sereny, as she and the others scanned the circular-shaped chamber that they had found themselves transported into. "Are we back in Pathylon again?"

"No," replied Rathek." And if the coin has done its job properly we should be no further than the twenty metres I'd estimated from Bradley's house."

Bradley held out his hand, as the Devonian passed the coin back. "Twenty metres... Dad's blue light - the cenotaph?" He exclaimed. "We're beneath the old blue light!"

"Correct... well done, Bradley - the *Light of Mount Pero*," retorted Rathek, as he proudly patted the *eternal chosen one* on the shoulder.

"Why are you calling it that?" asked Sereny.

Rathek replied graciously. "Because it is made from the same cut of sapphire that adorns the centre of the Amulet of Silvermoor... while ever Basjoo Ma-otz has the Amulet, the light will stay extinguished."

Bradley changed the subject. "That's all well and good, but please explain why you went all quiet on us back in the house - that's the second time you've done that to us!"

"Yeah!" exclaimed Musgrove."It's getting a bit spooky and with Halloween approaching and all that... we'd appreciate it if could give us some notice before you do it again!"

Rathek laughed. "The reason I froze on the platform and again in your lounge is because I was concentrating really hard... I was using my telepathic powers to find the entrance to the Vortex of Silvermoor."

"Is this it?" asked Musgrove.

"I'm afraid not... however, I do believe we are on the right track," he surmised. "Look at Bradley's hand... the coin is still glowing - there must be some other door or portal in this chamber, which should lead us to the vortex."

The glow from the coin illuminated the chamber slightly but it was still quite dark and the dust filled beams of sunlight streamed through the old floor boards above their heads. Through the sunbeams, Sereny noticed a triangular shaped rock that stuck out of the chamber wall. She walked over to the extruding stone and reached out her hand. "Look at this, guys!" she exclaimed and pushed gently against the stone.

Rathek shouted. "No... not yet, Sereny!"

The Devonian's warning came too late. A trap door opened beneath the girl and she fell through before any of them could reach her. The trap door recoiled immediately, as Bradley reached for the stone and pushed it again.

"Nothings happening... I keep pressing it and nothing's happening!" exclaimed Bradley in a frustrated tone. "Sereny's disappeared... where has she gone - what shall we do?"

18

Disturbing the Sacred Tomb

Unbeknown to those on the outside world and King Luccese in Freytor, Varuna had now amassed a huge army of Tree Elves with the support of Flaglan. The Hartopian struck a confident pose, as he sat on his Hoffen mount at the edge of the great Forest of Haldon.

Slotted between the trees behind and as far as the eye could see, there were tens of thousands of Tree Elves standing patiently with their long bows strapped to their backs. The army simulated a continuous sea of green, as the foliage from the surrounding trees reflected in their shiny armoured chest plates. The Tree Elves were dressed in their full battle attire and a familiar thin strip of metal on their helmets ran parallel with their noses to protect their elfin faces. The shiny metal on their rounded helmets matched their immaculately fashioned chest plates. Their arrows were tipped with the finest iron that had been forged in Galetian furnaces by the blacksmiths of Castan.

The galloping of a single Hoffen's hoofs could be heard in the distance and Flaglan appeared with her satin laced attire floating in the breeze. The High Priestess rode side saddle past the thousands of loyal archers and saluted them all, as they bowed their heads one by one. She pulled on the reins to slow her lively Hoffen and controlled the beast into a canter, as she continued to negotiate the tall cretyre trees. At last she appeared next to Varuna's mount and the sorceress nodded at her new partner in crime.

Varuna cast his red slit eyes up and down the High Priestesses body. "My dear, you look ravishing!"

Flaglan acknowledged the Hartopian's compliment. The arrogant sorceress knew she looked good in her battle costume and puffed out her heaving chest to attract more attention from her admirer. "You'll never change, Varuna... your mind is always on the same thing - it continues to be your weakness and it will be your downfall one day!"

"My dear Haldon Princess... your beauty will always captivate me - but be assured my mind is definitely focussed on the battle ahead," smirked the evil Hartopian, as he turned his head away from the High Priestess and looked towards the twin towers of the Satorc Bridge in the distance.

The ice-cloud had now settled above the Flaclom Straits and cut a striking image in the distant skies. Flaglan made an observation. "The Krogons will not be expecting an attack... they will probably be wondering why the dark cloud hangs above their region - our surprise assault will catch them off guard and most of their warriors will be unarmed."

Varuna agreed, as he kicked his heels into the Hoffen and it move forward slowly out of the forest into open territory. "We must move ahead quickly... can you give the order for your archers to advance?"

Flaglan nodded and shouted the command to her foot soldiers."Forward and attack the Krogon scum!"

The army of Tree Elves chorused a cheer that echoed eerily through the forest, as the first soldiers emerged from their woodland sanctuary. They all lifted their bows back over their heads and with military precision pulled an arrow from their back pouches in one swift action to load their weapons, as they surged forward in unison towards the Satorc Bridge.

Flaglan and Varuna rode ahead of the foot soldiers and reached the bridge first. They halted their Hoffen and waited for the squadron of archers to catch up. The two Pathylian traitors then crossed over into Krogon territory followed by the mass of charging Tree Elves who narrowed their formation, as they approached the bridge like liquid being poured through a funnel.

The metal bridge frame that supported the wooden slats of the bridge creaked under the weight of the hoarding army, as a relentless stamping of feet pounded the rafters. The invasion of Krogonia had begun.

Meanwhile, the ice-submarine resurfaced in the shallow waters off the coast of Krogonia and Admiral Norsk emerged onto the viewing gallery. The Freytorian commander snarled, as he saw the army of Tree Elves advancing into Krogon territory.

The Admiral roared. "Varuna has done it... the army from the great forest look impressive - now it's time to extract the kratennium whilst our friend's over there distract the Krogons!"

Norsk turned to face the Island of Restak and held out his arms again. He closed his eyes and muttered the lines from an ancient curse. Sparks started to shoot from the tips of his long talons, as a continuous trail of crimson lighting tracked out from the Admiral's claws and hit the distant Kaikane Idol. This started a chain reaction and more lightning bolts rebounded off the sacred monument in the direction of the ice-cloud.

Norsk lifted his arms apart and started to thread the electrical storm into a swirling motion. A deafening clap of thunder filled the dark nebula and a spiralling vortex in the shape of a tornado broke out from the centre of the ice-cloud. The exhausted Freytorian collapsed, as the tip of the tornado drilled into the surface of the Flaclom Straits to start the extraction process of the rich kratennium.

The quartermaster rushed over to his Admiral and supported the white-bearded bear's head. "Sir... the cloud is starting to extract the kratennium - you have done well commander!"

Norsk opened his eyes and stared up at his first officer. "Help me to my feet... the task is not yet complete - I have to make sure that the tornado does not rip too deep into the strata below."

The quartermaster assisted the heavy Freytorian to his feet. "Look Sir, the tornado is cutting through the Flaclom Straits... it has a will of its own and shows no mercy!"

"That's what I was afraid of... we only need the kratennium - any other impurities will contaminate the ice-cloud!" replied Norsk, as he outstretched his arms again to direct the swirling torrent of wind away from the site. "There... that should be enough kratennium - the cloud has lightened in colour and the yellow glow from its epicentre indicates that it is full."

The tornado disappeared upwards into the vibrant nebula and the cloud started to move away from the mainland, as the Admiral held his telescope to spy on Varuna's battle with the Krogons. He quickly put down the lens and directed his arms above his head to guide the cloud towards the Red Ocean. "I have set the co-ordinates for Freytor... the ice-cloud is due to arrive over the City of Frey by midday tomorrow - Varuna seems to have things under control over in Krogonia so our job here is done," stated Norsk, as he picked up the telescope and retracted the lens. "Now let's submerge and head to Freytor... we will need to be there in good time before the ice-cloud arrives," ordered the Admiral and paused for a few seconds. "Ah... wait - first I will need to extract more power from the Kaikane Idol before we leave Pathylon so let's sail back to the Island of Restak."

Most of the crew went below decks but Norsk stayed with his first officer on the viewing gallery, as the ice-submarine moved slowly back towards the Island of Restak along the surface of the water. The ship cut cleanly through the calm

148

sea and the Admiral roared out another order. "Prepare one of the ship's capacitors... I need to fill it with the statue's energy - this power will be used to fire at the hole in the centre of the ice-cloud when we reach the coastline of Freytor."

"Aye-aye, commander!" replied the first officer and disappeared below deck.

Admiral Norsk prepared himself for his next ritual performance and as the ice-submarine neared the island he boarded a landing craft. The quartermaster signalled from the ship that the capacitor was ready and the Freytorian made his way back up to the Kaikane Idol to extract the power he needed.

Meanwhile, Varuna and Flaglan had split ranks. They each led a battalion of Tree Elves to outflank the unprepared Krogon Warriors. Not a single archer was killed and the fighting was over very quickly, as shower upon shower of arrows poured down onto the scurrying lizard men.

Many Krogons were slaughtered during the unlawful rampage and those that survived were rounded up and secured in makeshift enclosures, as Varuna dispatched a dozen archers to seek out and retrieve Turpol. The new Krogon High Priest had failed to defend his region and would now face the wrath of the jubilant Hartopian.

It didn't take long to find the old Gatekeeper and the dwarf was escorted out of the main entrance to the Krogon headquarters. Turpol struggled, as he kicked his short legs and two Tree Elves held the dwarf aloft by his arms. They carried him over to where Varuna and Flaglan had regrouped.

The sorceress laughed uncontrollably at the sight of the dwarf kicking out at both archers. "Ha... ha, look who we have here - the failed High Priest of the moment!" She teased. "Your short-lived stint as leader of this region didn't go too well!"

Varuna calmed the excited High Priestess and ordered the archers to release Turpol. "Are you pleased to see me Gatekeeper?"

Turpol rubbed his arms where the Tree Elves had grasped him. "I should have known you'd be involved in all this... I thought the ice-cloud had been sent by the Freytorians!"

"Oh it was... and an Admiral called Norsk did all that - apparently he is the twin brother of General Eidar," revealed Varuna. "Anyhow, that cloud was nothing to do with me... I'm just helping Norsk in return for his kind gesture - he released me from the Shallock Tower and I am now free to rule Pathylon again!"

Flaglan cast the Hartopian a frowned glare and cleared her throat. "Err-ermm!" she interrupted and reinforced the statement. "What Varuna meant to say is that *we* are going to rule Pathylon together as King and Queen!"

The Hartopian did not want to upset his new adversary and mirrored the sorceress by clearing his throat, as he quickly corrected his last statement. "My apologies... dear Flaglan - yes of course, *we* are going to rule over this kingdom now that Luccese has fled to Freytor."

"Luccese did not flee Pathylon... the populous voted to keep our great ruler safe from the ice-cloud and the meddling Ma-otz - our true King did not want to leave," disagreed Turpol. "You are a fool, Varuna... Pathylon will be destroyed unless the ice- cloud is destroyed and Basjoo Ma-otz is stopped - there won't be any kingdom left to rule unless you stop *you're* meddling!"

"Quiet, Gatekeeper!" roared Varuna. "I am aware of what Ma-otz is up to... but Flaglan has told me of the King's plans and I'm sure our friend Bradley Baker will deal with *Basjoo the Bold*!" he laughed sarcastically and turned to Flaglan. "So... what shall we do with the dwarf, my beautiful sorceress?"

"Do you really need to ask me that question?" retorted the high Priestess. "Kill him of course... he can be buried in that tomb over their with this region's beloved Grog!" she exclaimed and pointed to the large stone monument on the Flaclom Straits that had been erected in honour of the brave Krogon Warrior.

"Very well," replied Varuna, as he ordered the Tree Elves to carry the dwarf over to Grog's tomb. "Turpol the Gatekeeper will be shot in front of a firing squad... arrange your archers in a line and prepare for the sacrifice!"

Turpol was marched over to the monument and blindfolded, as two of the archers pushed the helpless dwarf against the wall of the tomb. The remaining Tree Elves tensioned their bow string, as Flaglan insisted on giving the order to fire. Just as she prepared to carry out the command, there was a loud rumbling from beneath the tomb.

Unbeknown to Varuna and Flaglan, the tornado had penetrated the strata below the seam of kratennium and this had disturbed a secret entrance to another a time portal located below the burial chamber.

Turpol smiled. "You're wondering what that noise is... aren't you?" he asked. "The tornado must have disturbed the entrance to a vortex."

"What are you talking about?" asked Flaglan, as the archers readied for her command. "Fire your arrows at this pathetic creature!"

Varuna intervened. "No... release the tension on your bow strings and put down your weapons - something is wrong!" Commanded the Hartopian, as the firing squad looked to Flaglan for her approval.

The sultry High Priestess reluctantly agreed and nodded her head to indicate to her Tree Elves to lower their weapons. "Turpol must know something... and unfortunately he has an annoying knack of knowing everything!" She shouted and the ground beneath her feet shuddered violently, as cracks started to appear in the dry sand.

Turpol recognised the strange sensation beneath his hairy feet and moved away from the tomb, as the base of the monument started to glow. A continuous flow of bright light flowed through the gaps between the wall carvings like volcanic larva, as a door appeared to open from the side of the crypt. The Gatekeeper suggested they all move back and array of shooting stars were emitted from the open doorway, as the vibration underground increased.

A crimson cloud of smoke escaped from the tomb and Varuna ordered a group of archers to aim their arrows at the glowing gap created by the doorway. The sound of creaking bowstrings being tensioned to their limit supplied a chorus of anxiety, as a small slender figure appeared out of the light. "Get ready to fire!" ordered the Hartopian.

A slender female form walked calmly through the doorway and appeared from the smoke. Turpol let out a loud cry of recognition. "Sereny Ugbrooke... what a pleasant surprise!"

"Hello Turpol... how are you - have you seen Bradley?" replied Sereny, as she brushed down her clothing to remove the dust collected during her incredible journey from Ravenswood.

Before the dwarf had chance to reply, Varuna stepped in front of the girl. "I recognise you... you are one of Bradley Baker's rebel friends - where have you come from and what do you want?"

Sereny trembled and spoke defiantly in a quiet tone, as she recognised the evil Hartopian by his severed limb."The last person I expected to see was you, Varuna... it's a good job we've come back - evil creatures like you should be locked away forever!"

"Silence... you insolent child!" roared Varuna. "I take it that the young Bradley Baker has journeyed with you then?"

"Bradley is not with me... the last thing I remember was disappearing through a trapdoor underneath the blue light," she replied. "Then I found myself tumbling through a spiralling tunnel full of lights... and here I am - but Bradley is coming though and he will sort you out!"

"Ha-ha!" roared the Hartopian in a hilarious tone. "Bradley Baker is just a boy... you lot just got lucky before - this time I will crush him if he dares to challenge me again!"

Turpol moved over to Sereny, who was now shaking. "Come along my dear... ignore him - I'm sure Bradley's arrival in Pathylon will trouble Varuna," assured the Gatekeeper and teased the Hartopian. "Look at him... he's looking worried already... the mere mention of Bradley's name and he's sweating!"

Varuna reacted angrily, as he wiped his brow. "Silence, dwarf... you are talking rubbish - I am not afraid of the Baker boy!" he declared and focussed his attention back on the trembling girl. "Anyhow, what is this blue light you speak of?" he asked.

Turpol could see that Sereny was too frightened to deal with the raging Hartopian and he intercepted Varuna's line of questioning. "The girl speaks of the *Light of Mount Pero*... it sits atop a war memorial near to Bradley Baker's home - it acts as a time portal."

Varuna diverted his attention to the knowledgeable dwarf. "So why has this girl here ended up here?"

Turpol replied. "It would appear that the tornado created by Norsk's ice-cloud has ripped too deep into the strata below the Flaclom Straits... so the entrance to the vortex has been opened and Grog's tomb must have been acting as a doorway to the time portal."

Whilst the dwarf continued his theory, the light in the gap created by the doorway dimmed and finally stopped glowing. Flaglan had been waiting patiently for Varuna to stop ranting and as Turpol concluded she walked into the base of the tomb. The sorceress looked around and noticed that the stone carved statue lid securing Grog's burial chamber was slightly ajar. The curious High Priestess called some of her Tree Elves into the tomb and ordered the heavy cover to be moved aside so she could look inside.

Varuna pushed past the little Gatekeeper, as he followed Flaglan in to the tomb. Turpol regained his balance and caught up with Sereny to check out what the sorceress was up to, as the young girl screamed. "Stop... you can't look in there - that tomb is sacred and you must respect Grog's resting place!

Sereny knew something that the others didn't and as the heavy cover was pushed aside they all peered into the empty tomb. Flaglan gasped. "Where is the dead Krogons body?"

Turpol offered Sereny a quick glance and the girl returned the dwarfs puzzled look with the wink of an eye. The Gatekeeper smiled and he believed he knew what had happened.

Varuna interrupted the commotion inside the tomb and let out another aggressive roar. "Grrrrrgghhhh... everyone out - all of you must leave this tomb, now!" He insisted, as they all scuttled towards the doorway.

Flaglan held back and witnessed Sereny put her arm around Turpol, as the girl whispered in his pointy ear. They passed through the doorway and the dwarf smiled again then nodded, as Sereny confirmed his thoughts. The sorceress pondered a stare at the girl's action and muttered to herself. "What secret are you holding, little girl... what is it that you know that I don't?" she asked herself and uttered again under her breath. "I'll find out what you're up to, don't you worry little *Miss Perfect*... Sereny Ugbrooke thinks she's smart does she - well we'll see about that?"

19

The Hidden Map

Beneath the cenotaph in Ravenswood, Rathek pulled Bradley's hand away from the extruding stone. "We only had one chance to enter Silvermoor through that portal and Sereny took it." He explained, calmly. "We will have to find another way into the underground workings."

Bradley noticed that the coin had stopped glowing. "We have to find Sereny... I hope she's okay - and how will we know where to look for another way in to Pathylon?"

Rathek afforded Bradley man encouraging glance and called over to Musgrove. "Come over here, Muzzy... I'm going to lift you up to that beam - then you can push against the boards," he ordered. "We have to get out of here... the coin will let us know if and where there is another way in."

"But what about Sereny?" asked Bradley, as Rathek lifted Musgrove above his broad shoulders.

"Push, Muzzy... push harder!" instructed Rathek, as the boards finally gave way and a blue ray of light streamed into the chamber. "We'll find her, Bradley... don't worry my friend!"

Rathek squeezed through the floor boards and reached down to help the boys into the base of the cenotaph. The

Devonian forced open a small door to the outside that led out onto a small chained enclosure around the monument and checked to make sure none of the neighbours had witnessed their exit.

"The coast is clear," whispered Rathek, as he ushered the boys across the street and back to the Baker household.

Bradley was first to the front door and turned the handle. "It's unlocked."

Without hesitation, he pushed the door open and they entered the house. Rathek took the lead and guided the boys straight upstairs into the family bathroom. "Do you have the coin, Bradley?" he asked, as the excited boy reached into his pocket to reveal the grobite.

"Here it is... shall I throw it in the bath tub?"

"Not yet," replied Rathek calmly. "Muzzy... can you engage the plug and start running the water please?"

"No problem!" declared Musgrove, as he brushed past Bradley and carried out the Devonian's instruction.

Rathek detailed the next stage of the procedure. "It's important we follow the next steps in the correct order," he explained. "If we don't... we may find ourselves travelling through the wrong time dimension."

"Can't we just throw the coin into the water?" asked Musgrove.

"I'm afraid not," replied Rathek, as he started to remove his cloak and made his way towards the bathroom door. "Now... both of you start getting undressed - I'll be back in a few minutes and keep an eye on the water level."

"Where are you going?" asked Musgrove.

"To find my hold-all... I left it in the front lounge - there is some equipment in it that we will need for our journey," replied the Devonian. "Don't worry... everything will become clearer when I get back!"

Rathek made his way back downstairs and into the front lounge. He looked around the room and spotted the hessian bag by the side of the sofa. As he moved towards the hold-all, he noticed the framed photograph of the pit head gear that Patrick had found in the old lamp room. "I wonder..." he muttered to himself, as he lifted the picture from the sideboard.

Rathek picked up the hold-all then made his way back upstairs to find the boys standing in the bathroom with their hands crossed in front. They looked rather embarrassed and were wearing just their underpants.

Bradley's face was crimson colour and he broke the silence. "Well... you did say get undressed - but we're not getting in naked!" He retorted and proceeded to turn off the running water.

The steam-filled bathroom fell silent, with the noise of the running water having now subsided. Rathek chuckled to himself and reached into the hold-all. "Here... put these on!"

Two pairs of orange overalls were cast in the direction of the two boys. They quickly got dressed into the bright coloured clothing, as Rathek passed them two pairs of thick socks and steel toe-capped boots. It was not long before Bradley commented on their attire. "These are just like what my Dad used to wear when he worked at Silvermoor Colliery for *British Coal*!"

"That's right... I found them in the basement of that old lamp room along the road and took the liberty of dressing us appropriately for our journey - as well as taking into consideration the health and safety issues!" replied Rathek, as he pulled out some important pieces of equipment form his hold-all.

"What are those for?" asked Musgrove, as the Devonian held out a tangled bunch of long cables, which were attached to some square containers. He also lifted out some shiny metal canisters with red clips on the top.

Bradley answered. "They look like cap-lamp cables and batteries... and they are self rescuers - my Dad used to collect his from the lamp room before making his way over to the pit head."

Rathek confirmed Bradley's assessment of the objects, as he picked up a cap lamp in one hand and demonstrated a self rescuer device with the other by holding them both out in front. "We are going to need these when we get down there... it will be dark and we may need this one in case of fire." He stated, as he lifted his arm and held the self rescuer device in the air.

"How do they work... they're just metal cans with clips on them?" asked Musgrove, as Rathek handed the devices to the boys.

"It's what's inside the container that matters... don't worry Muzzy - I'll quickly demonstrate," replied Rathek. "Here is your belt... now push it through the slots on the back of the lamp's battery and also the one on the self rescuer unit - now fasten the belt around your waste," he explained. "You too, Bradley... here's your belt."

"Okay, done that," replied Musgrove, as he waited for Bradley to buckle his belt.

Rathek explained how to release the clip from the self rescuer should they come across any outbreak of fire or smoke underground. He told Bradley and Musgrove that the unit contained a mask that would help them to breathe should they experience any dangerous situations. "These devices will prevent any smoke inhalation and they will protect you

158

from poisonous gases," he explained and then proceeded to show them both how to use the cap lamp, which had three settings. "You see this yellow switch on the cap lamp... you can turn it off or can choose to have the light on full or dipped beam - it's best to have the lamp on dipped beam when we're talking to each other," explained Rathek.

"Why's that?" asked Musgrove.

Bradley turned his cap lamp to full beam and shone it in his friend's face. "That's why!"

"Arrrgh... you're blinding me!" shouted Musgrove, as he shielded his face from the bright light.

"Exactly!" stated Bradley.

"Point taken... clever clogs!" replied Musgrove, as Rathek laughed at the boy's antics.

"Come on you two... let's get on - I have something else to show you," insisted Rathek, as he picked up the framed photograph. "Here, Bradley... please remove the back from this picture frame."

Bradley took the frame and turned it over to reveal a series of metal clips that were holding the hardboard backing in place. "This is the picture that my Dad found in the old lamp room a few days ago... he'll go mad if he finds it missing."

"We don't need the photograph... we can put the frame back in a minute," assured Rathek. "Take the back off the frame, Bradley... there is something inside - behind the photograph," revealed the Devonian, as he handed Musgrove a white pit helmet. "Here Muzzy... you'll need this as well - this will protect your head and you can attach your cap lamp to front of it."

Musgrove started to attach his cap lamp to the helmet, as Bradley carefully pulled back the metal clips and removed the back of the picture frame. Rathek was right and a delicately folded piece of paper fell onto the bathroom floor. Musgrove picked it up and handed it back to his friend, then finished attaching his cap lamp to the hard hat.

Bradley looked at Musgrove in his full attire and chuckled. "You look like you've been tangoed, mate!"

Rathek looked puzzled and Musgrove played down

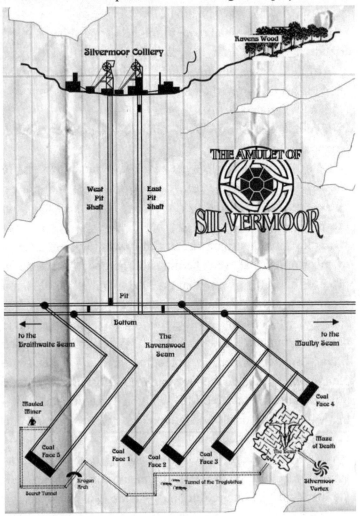

Bradley's comment. "Oh... don't worry - he's just taking the *Mickey*!" He stated. "Anyhow... let's see what's on the note, Brad."

Bradley carefully unfolded the delicate piece of paper and his eyes widened with excitement, as the contents of the page were revealed. "It's a map... a map of Silvermoor!"

Rathek pointed to the symbol on the map. "This is a map with *The Amulet of Silvermoor* embossed on it and there is the vortex that we need to find to get into Pathylon... looks like we're going to come across some dangerous obstacles and we'll have to negotiate some difficult tasks - it looks like the vortex is located beyond the Maze of Death."

Musgrove pointed to another icon of an old mineworker on the map. "Never mind the maze... who or what is that - it says *Mauled Miner* next to it?"

Bradley spoke out. "I think I know the answer to that... I was doing some research for my school Halloween project and I found an article on the internet about a ghost that used to wander through the underground passageways of Silvermoor following a freak accident on the coal face - apparently the mineworker's face was ripped off by a coal cutting machine and he just disappeared."

Rathek commented. "Legend has it that the Mauled Miner still roams the disused mine workings."

"Well every time I used to mention it to my Dad... he used to go quite and told me he didn't want to talk about it," concluded Bradley, as he passed the map to Rathek. "Here... you had better keep hold of this - I might lose it when we go down the plughole."

Rathek put on his orange overalls and placed the map carefully into one of the chest pockets then clipped the metal press stud to secure the precious note. The three adventurers were now ready for their journey and they all climbed into the bath tub. Bradley took the front position near the taps with Musgrove behind him. They interlocked their legs in front and Bradley crossed his to allow more room at the back for Rathek. They looked like a three man bob sleigh team ready to race for Olympic gold, as the Devonian nobleman completed the trio by squeezing in behind Musgrove.

"Wait!" shouted Bradley, as he stood up and climbed back out of the tub. "I need to get a few things... they may come in useful!"

Musgrove turned round and shrugged his shoulders at Rathek, as the water splashed up the side of the bath tub. "It must be something important."

Before Rathek could answer, Bradley reappeared. He jumped back in front of his friend and another series of mini tidal waves lapped up his colleague's clothing as a result of his crashing entry into the water. "Got them!" he declared.

"Got what, mate?" asked Musgrove, as he spluttered an inquisitive reply.

"These!" confirmed Bradley, as he held aloft the *Swiss Army Knife* that his late grandfather had bequeathed him and his new mobile phone. "We don't know what dangers lie ahead of us... the knife was given to me only to use when I go fishing with Dad - although I'm sure Grandfather Penworthy would have approved."

"Why are you taking the phone with you?" asked Musgrove, as Rathek sat patiently with his arms folded at the back of the bath tub.

Bradley offered his best friend a bemused look. "What do you think... I'm going to brush my hair with it?"

"Ha, ha... very funny!" responded Musgrove. "I meant... you won't get a signal where we're going and in any case it will get ruined in the water!"

Rathek nodded and interrupted the boy's conversation. "Muzzy is right... you won't have much use for that where we're going."

Both Musgrove and Rathek's words fell on deaf ears, as Bradley reached over and grabbed one of his mother's plastic bath caps. He insisted on taking both the knife tool and his mobile phone, as he wrapped the phone in the cap then secured both items in his overall pockets.

Rathek shook his head and asked both boys if there was anything else they needed before they embarked on their incredible journey. "The kitchens sink, maybe?" he asked sarcastically, as Bradley and Musgrove kept their heads facing forward and shook their heads simultaneously. The water level was now level within a few centimetres of the top of the bath tub and their clothes were completely soaked, as the Devonian gave the order to release the plug from the plughole. "Is the coin glowing yet, Bradley?"

Bradley held the grobite in the palm of his hand and watched in amazement as the coin vibrated and started to glow. "Yep... it's starting to get really hot and the message around the edge is more prominent than before - I guess it's time!"

"Then read out the message once more!" exclaimed Rathek.

Bradley struggled to hold the hot metal, as he recited the message. "*Seek out the Mece and find the Amulet of Silvermoor!*"

"Now, throw the coin into the water, Bradley!" exclaimed Rathek. "It's definitely time to proceed!"

The coin was cast into the water and the plug finally released from its vacuum, as it shot out of the plughole. The experience in Aunt Vera's bathroom was being re-enacted and a parallel line of bubbles followed the plug to the surface. Again, this prompted the coin to mysteriously rise out of the water into the air. Bradley, Musgrove and Rathek stared in amazement, as the coin hovered and rotated with great speed over the bathtub. Then the coin suddenly stopped spinning and it plummeted back into the depths of the bath's soapy water.

This time Bradley was not frightened but he was still intrigued at the sight of the airborne object falling into the bath again. An eerie sound echoed around the tub, as the coin clinked on the bottom. A gap appeared in the bubbles on the surface of the water and Bradley had a feeling of *déjà vu*, as he peered below the surface to witness the coin tilt upright onto its edge and roll towards the plughole.

The usual array of sparkling yellow stars filled the room, as all three were pulled simultaneously under the water and a multitude of air bubbles chased to the surface.

The gold coin reached its destination and the disk sat snuggly in the plughole. The water in the bathtub changed to a bright green colour and the seal was complete, as the hole in the centre of the coin started to open wider and wider. Bradley felt himself being drawn towards the green hole and the current beneath the surface quickened, as the rapids became taller and faster. Musgrove and Rathek followed Bradley, as they emerged above the surface of the water again.

"I guess this is it... hold on tight everyone!" declared Bradley, in preparation for the roller coaster ride ahead.

"See you at the other side, mate!" shouted Musgrove, as he struggled to keep his balance and crashed below the surface of the raging rapids.

Musgrove emerged again gasping for breath and he could feel the bathroom taking on a different dimension. He looked behind him to see Rathek tossing and turning. Bradley had already disappeared down the plughole, as the bathtub seemed to increase in size but really he was following his friend's lead and shrinking. His thoughts of the latter were confirmed, as he swirled round and round with Rathek in close pursuit within the parallel vortex. Their cap lamp cables became entwined, as they grabbed each others clothing and then they started to spin in different directions.

It was an amazing achievement that they managed to detangle their cables, as the water continued to splurge around their bodies. Then the inevitable happened, as they followed Bradley's path and were both sucked through the centre of the gold coin.

Another adventure through the plughole and down the drainpipe had begun, as Rathek flowed past Musgrove. It wasn't long before both of them caught up with Bradley and their wish for a safe journey looked like it had been realised.

Bradley was still being carried along by the torrent of bath water and he looked up to witness Rathek approaching at a fast pace. He twisted and turned, as the smiling Devonian went past him falling deeper and deeper into the darkness below. Musgrove soon followed and he grabbed Bradley's arm to pull him along. As they fell, they both looked up at the green light that emanated through the centre of the coin which was getting further and further away, as they spiraled around the u-bend and onwards infinitely along the smelly waste system.

A successful navigation ensued along and around more curves in the pipe and finally to the abyss in the form of a vertical pipe linking the first floor bathroom to the ground floor level of the Baker's house. The three adventurers plummeted deeper and deeper into the unknown, as a loud fanfare of mystical sounds and an aura of flashing multi-coloured lights filled the drainpipe. The inside of the pipe became a vortex of spiraling images and the falling water gushed around their helpless bodies.

Bradley remembered his previous journey down the drainpipe back in Sandmouth and looked down towards his feet again, as he readied himself for the end of this eventful trip. He could make out the ground getting nearer and nearer, as he braced himself for impact. A loud squelching sound emanated from his boots, as he landed in the soft sandy bed. He quickly rolled to one side and noticed that Rathek had already landed safely, as the imminent arrival of Musgrove soon followed.

Bradley checked his pockets to make sure all his valuables were still in tact and then let out a cry of delight. "Yesssssss... brilliant - there's no adventure park back in our world that can beat that ride!"

"Nice one, Brad... couldn't have put it better myself!" agreed Musgrove, as he placed one foot after the other into the soggy bed of putrid waste.

20

Meeting of Old Allies

Word quickly spread of Varuna's escape from the Shallock Tower and the fall of Krogonia. Flaglan's Tree Elves had caused absolute chaos within the lizard men's region and as the news reached Luccese in Frey, the King was helpless to react to Varuna's uprising.

Following a meeting with Pavsik and General Eidar, it was decided that it would be best to stay on the island of Freytor and defend Frey from the ice-cloud rather than return to Pathylon at this stage. The King was confident that Rathek would find Bradley Baker and escort him through the Vortex of Silvermoor to intercept Basjoo Ma-otz. With this in mind he could do nothing but wait for Eidar's brother to attack Freytor and planned a strategic defense with the bewildered Freytorian General. "I cannot believe that Norsk would do such a thing... this has put me in a very difficult situation," stressed Eidar, as he paced back and forth down the corridor outside Meltor's health pod. "What must you think of the Freytorians, your majesty?"

The King sympathised with the embarrassed General. "Pleased do not be ashamed... blood is thicker than water and I completely understand your predicament - I am confident that you will make the right decisions do to protect Freytor from attack and I know you will do everything you can to save your brother from his treacherous deeds."

Eidar assured the King. "If we all survive this perilous situation... I give you my word, Luccese that I will do all I can to ensure my brother complies with Freytorian law - we cannot have renegades like Norsk thinking that they can jeapardise our peaceful relations and return to our old pillaging ways."

The King asked the Freytorian not to be too concerned about Freytor's relations with Pathylon and suggested that they go inside Meltor's health pod. The General agreed and they joined Queen Vash and Pavsik, who were still by the Galetian's bedside.

The two worried leaders entered the room and Luccese immediately asked after Meltor's wellbeing. "How is he... has he improved?"

"Still no change," replied Pavsik, as Queen Vash wiped Meltor's brow with a damp cloth.

General Eidar moved to the side of the bed and looked down at the High Priest's ashen face, as the life support machine bleeped intermittently. "He is looking weak and his heart patterns are abnormal... I fear for his life."

Queen Vash mopped the Galetian's brow again and the King bent down, as he spoke gently in Meltor's ear. "Stay with us, my old friend - I will need your guidance and support after all these conflicts have been dealt with."

Meltor's eyelids flickered slightly, as if he had acknowledged the King's words but his body lay motionless and the bedside vigil continued.

Meanwhile deep inside the Unknown Land, Basjoo Ma-otz was exhausted following his long journey down the newly formed river. The temporary raft had broken and had been abandoned. The weary Hartopian had managed to negotiate the rest of the way through the Valley of Sardan on foot. He had now arrived at yet another mountain range, which was located deep inside the Unknown Land.

The half-breed found a smooth boulder to sit on and rested for a while in preparation for the next stage of his search for the Mece. He placed his *Staff of Evil* against the rocks and lay back, as the clouds moved effortlessly in the sky above. The weasel-like creature relaxed and watched them shift, as they changed shape in the swirling breeze. Basjoo Ma-otz closed his narrow red eyes and pictured the demise of Pathylon in his mind.

A raw smile shaped his lower jaw but his thoughts were disturbed by a shadow that cast over his face. He opened his eyes again and the brightness of the sky was now hidden by the silhouette of a very large shaped head. The Hartopian was startled and he sat upright sharply, avoiding a collision of foreheads with the strange lizard-like creature. "Harg!" exclaimed Ma-otz, as he reached for his staff.

The disgraced Krogon, who had been banished to the Unknown Land by King Luccese, had taken the Hartopian's weapon and stood back to question his presence. "What brings you here, Ma-otz?" he asked and held the staff out of arms way.

"Grrrrrrrghhh... hand over my staff, Krogon!" growled the frustrated Hartopian. "Give it back to me and I'll explain why I am here... I promise I will not harm you if you hand it over - without delay!"

Harg hesitated. "You could never be trusted before... so why should I believe you now?" he asked. "You fled Pathylon like a coward... leaving me and Flaglan to suffer the consequences of Varuna's failed bid to seize control over the cursed kingdom!"

"I had no choice... Meltor and the Baker boy, together with the rest of their alliance made it impossible for us to carry on under Varuna's rule - I would have either ended up in the Shallock Tower or most likely banished to this god forsaken place with you." explained Ma-otz. "Now, please give me back my *Staff of Evil*... it's all I have left - hand it over and I will share my plan with you to destroy Pathylon for good."

Harg was still unsure of Basjoo Ma-otz's intentions and held on to the staff with some trepidation. "Here's the deal, Ma-otz... I'll listen to what you have to say - then, and only then, will I consider returning this blasted thing back to you."

Basjoo Ma-otz growled. "Grrrrrrgggghhh... very well, Krogon - but you had better keep your word!"

"Ma-otz... as you so clearly pointed out - I am a Krogon and we are honourable creatures," replied Harg, calmly. "Now proceed... tell me your plans to destroy Pathylon."

"Krogons... honorable?" replied the Hartopian. "I think not... stupid and gullible more like - you lizard men are so archaic it's unbelievable!"

Harg did not fluster under the barrage of insults from the scrawny weasel-like creature. "You sound like a bitter and twisted idiot, Ma-otz... maybe I should break this staff in half and take away what little powers you have left."

Basjoo Ma-otz recognised that he was pushing is luck with the ageing Krogon. He could not risk the staff being broken, as he would need it to extract the necessary power from the Amulet. He calmed his demeanour and quickly changed his tone of voice. "I do apologise, my friend... I did not intend to insult your amphibian race - let's put aside our differences and talk about my plans," he said in a persuasive manner by encouraging Harg to sit his large frame down. "But... please be careful not to break my staff with your fat behind!"

Harg afforded him another distasteful look. "Ma-otz, you're pushing my patience!"

"Apologies, Harg!"

"Stop apologising... I am not offended by you and your kind," replied Harg, as he placed his huge leathery bottom on a nearby rock. "I am interested in sharing your plans to destroy Pathylon though... so come on - get on with it."

Basjoo Ma-otz proceeded to tell Harg of his plan and how he had found the Amulet when the Island of Restak was partially destroyed. He explained to the Krogon about the conditions that would have to be met in order for his plan of destruction to become affective.

170

Harg questioned the power of the Amulet, as Ma-otz pulled the jewelled necklace from the pouch attached to his robes. "So what exactly can that thing do?"

Basjoo Ma-otz laughed and held the Amulet above his head to allow the sunlight to pierce the splendid blue stone at its epicentre. "For many years, Pathylon has relied on this Amulet to protect it from threats that dwell on lands that border the kingdom… all I need to do is locate the Mece and find out from them where to reposition the Amulet. Apparently, there is a sacred ledge located somewhere on the summit of Mount Pero from where it was stolen by a Pathylian King called Makel," he continued. "Once the Amulet is back in position… the power emitted from within the sapphire that you see here shining so elegantly would equate to the amount of time passed since it was first removed - I'll put it more simply for you, the Amulet will become a bomb with the power of a thousand curses that would have a capability to obliterate all five regions of Pathylon and any other world that borders the Unknown Land."

"Interesting… so in effect - the Unknown Land would become an island of its own with nothing surviving around it," replied Harg. "I like the sound of that… we could rule our own land and set up profitable trading agreements with other lands!"

Ma-otz smiled and displayed his yellow teeth. "I'd not really thought that far ahead… it's a very good idea a d one we can pursue - but all that concerns me for the moment is the destruction of Pathylon and anything related to the Galetian Meltor," exclaimed the Hartopian. "But now you've mentioned it… it would be nice to take control over a whole new world created by the destruction of Luccese empire - imagine that, you and me working together to create a powerful new state."

"That does sound very appealing," replied Harg. "Well… based on what you have told me - I do believe I can help you."

"How?" insisted the Hartopian, as he placed the Amulet back in the pouch.

Harg sat smugly, still holding Ma-otz's staff upright. "Because I know where you can find the Mece... or what's left of them!"

"Good... now pass me the Staff of Evil!" insisted Ma-otz, as his stood in front of the smug Krogon. "I kept my part of the bargain... now, give it to me!"

Harg threw the weapon and the Hartopian caught it confidently. The Krogon asked. "So what do you need the staff for?"

Ma-otz held the skull-tipped shaft aloft and roared. "Once the Amulet is placed on the sacred ledge... it will need to be primed with an electrical current - my *Staff of Evil* will attract a lightning bolt from the skies to inject a strain of power to detonate the sequence of destruction!"

Harg shuffled his heavy frame from side to side, as he utilised his huge flabby arms to lever his body and stood up from the rocky seat. His large belly hung down over his clothing and wobbled like a jelly mould, as he patted Ma-otz's armoured shoulder plate to acknowledge his agreement to the plan. The Hartopian buckled slightly under the Krogons heavy slap of approval and disguised the effect of the heavy blow with a slight groan.

As Ma-otz recovered from the Krogons harmless gesture, Harg shared his thoughts. "I didn't expect to find out about such a unique opportunity to seek revenge upon our old regime... my existence here inside the Unknown Land as been very uneventful so far - except of course my discovery of the Mece."

Basjoo Ma-otz slipped his claw beneath his armour and rubbed his shoulder to ease the dull pain inflicted by the Krogon. His pointy ears pricked up at the mention of the word Mece and he enquired of the mythical creatures. "What did you mean, when you said... what's left of them?"

"The Mece appear to be a depleted race... when I visited their village - there were only a hand full of them," replied

172

Harg. "They seemed a timid bunch... but quite friendly - their leader explained to me that they have lost many of the older villagers to preying Troglobites."

"What are Troglobites?" asked the Hartopian.

"Not sure... I haven't come across any since I arrived in the Unknown Land," replied Harg. "The Mece leader described them as giant insects... a much larger version of those!" indicated the Krogon, as he pointed to a line of red ants scurrying through the sand.

Basjoo Ma-otz stamped on the insects and growled. "We will have move quickly then... we don't want the creepy-crawlers wiping out the few Mece that are left - now let's seek out this village you speak of!"

Harg led Basjoo Ma-otz to a narrow gap in the side of the rock and he forced his broad frame through the opening, as his scaly skin left marks on the stone. The gap spread upright with a parallel split in the mountain's vertical strata and they shuffled sideways along the route until they reached another opening.

The Krogon pointed to a rock face, which had a large skull carved into it. Directly below the stone image, a tall arch-shaped opening formed the entrance to a cave. "We can reach the Mece village through there... but we have to tread carefully - they have placed deathly obstacles within the cave to stop intruders getting through."

"You lead the way then!" insisted Basjoo Ma-otz, as he prodded Hargs blubbery backside with the end of the staff.

"You'll never change, Ma-otz... forever the coward!" laughed Harg, as he shook his horned crown and headed for the cave entrance.

Basjoo Ma-otz followed the cumbersome Krogon and muttered under his breath. "I'm not a coward you fool... I'm just using you - you're the stupid idiot leading the way."

As they entered the dark cave, the sound of running water could be heard cascading down the side of the walls. The air was damp and as they ventured deeper into the darkness, Harg held out a torch stick that was tethered to his belt. He

173

struck a piece of flint against the cave side and the sparks flew onto the dry cloth wrapped around the end of the stick. Flames shot into the air and the cave was illuminated, as the reflective torch caused shadows from the surrounding rock formations to dance on the walls.

The Krogon warned, as his croaky voice echoed around the cave. "Don't go beyond those loose stones on the floor... I put them there to mark a hazard - if you were to walk a few steps further on, there is a sheer drop into a deep ravine."

Basjoo Ma-otz heeded Hargs advice and was careful not to wander too far from his footsteps. "You seem to be very familiar with the layout of this cave, my friend... I am pleased you are leading the way."

"I have only passed through here a few times... so we still need to be very vigilant - there still may be some hazards that I haven't marked," confirmed Harg, as he continued further into the cave. "There is an area up ahead, which has many tunnels leading off in different directions... I have not been down them all but I know they all lead to the same chamber," he explained. "They all look the same and the markers I laid down before have gone... someone else must have passed through here since I last visited the Mece."

Basjoo Ma-otz spoke with an air of caution in his voice. "Can you try and remember which tunnel you took last time?"

"No... as I said, they all look the same - I'm trying to remember the route I took," replied the nervous lizard man, as he tentatively edged nearer the junction, which offered a choice of three entrances. "I'm sure it's the middle one... two of the tunnels have trapdoors disguised under the stone dust floors, which are difficult to see - even with a torch light!"

The Hartopian stayed close behind Harg, as the Krogon moved towards the second entrance. "Are there any more dangers after this one?"

"No... when we get through here, it's a clear passage to the other side of the mountain - we'll be able to see the Mece village straight away." replied Harg. "There's a wooden

174

footbridge that spans a gorge and all we have to do is cross that and we'll be there!"

"I'm not sure about this... is it wise for both of us to take a risk?" asked the Hartopian, as his voice stuttered. "Wouldn't it be better if one of us went first... I mean - if you went first?"

Harg laughed and his thunderous tones echoed through all three tunnels. A chorus of combined bellowing laughter filled the cavern at the far end of the tunnels then reverberated back as an eerie echo. "You've got a nerve, Ma-otz... expecting me to risk my life for your stupid plan to blow up Pathylon - forget it!" shouted the Krogon and pushed the petrified Hartopian out of the way.

Basjoo Ma-oz was incensed by the Krogons outburst and threatened. "Stop you fool... take another step and I will emit a fatal stream of lightning from my Staff of Evil - that deep pit we passed earlier will become your grave if you do not obey my command!"

Harg stopped in his tracks and turned slowly to face the trembling Hartopian. "Go ahead, Ma-otz... use your pathetic glow stick if you dare - a single strike from that thing and this whole cave system will collapse!"

The Hartopian did not answer and pointed the skull of Meltor's granddaughter at Harg. Beads of sweat started to appear on the forehead of triple-horned Krogon, as he waited for Basjoo Ma-otz to speak. The lizard man edged his way backwards feeling the water soaked cave walls to guide himself down the passage.

The Hartopian kept the Staff of Evil straight and aimed it at Hargs chest plate, as he lifted his other arm in the air to summon the power he needed. A bright red bolt of lightning pierced through the roof of the cave and hit the skull on the end of the staff. Harg turned to run, as the lightning bolt ricocheted off the staff and hit him between his shoulder blades. The force of the jolt stunned the fleeing Krogon and knocked the clumsy reptile to the floor.

Basjoo Ma-otz lifted the staff in the air and roared. "Grrrrrrrgggghhhh... did you think I would summon enough power to risk my own life, Krogon scum - now you will ensure my safety and take the middle tunnel!"

Harg struggled to move and his body lay like a dead weight on the cave floor. He managed to raise his head and turned to face the demented Hartopian. "You will go to any lengths to destroy Pathylon and your old foe Meltor... you are mad," he stated, as his head hit the floor hard.

The Hartopian moved towards the motionless Krogon. "Harg?" he shouted, as he prodded the lifeless amphibian with his staff. "Harg... don't you dare die on me - you old decrepit lizard!"

Basjoo Ma-otz had underestimated the strength of the old Krogons weak heart. The bolt of lightning was enough to give Harg a coronary. Now the Hartopian had to make a choice; does he give up is quest to destroy Pathylon or does he risk his life and choose one of the three tunnels, which would lead him to the Mece village.

21

Off the Rails

Following an applauded review of their incredible journey, Bradley sniffed the air in an exaggerating manner, as he recognised the smell inside the dark chamber. Just as before when he had travelled down the drainpipe in Sandmouth, the air upon arrival was disgustingly stale and smelt like rotten eggs. He fought to free himself from the slimy foliage, which was up to his waist following his safe landing. Musgrove also struggled, as he rolled over to more solid ground and clambered to his feet. Both boys amused each other and picked at the pieces of green slime hanging from their overalls, as the gung stuck to their fingers like chewing gum.

Rathek ignored the friend's playful banter, as he reached up to turn on his cap lamp and then flicked his head slightly to strain his ear. He looked around the dark chamber in search of the noise and the strong beam from his cap lamp followed the sound of running water. He could just make out a small trickle of water in the corner of the room, which was cascading through the wall like the spray from a shower head. "Over here fellas... I don't know where that water is coming from but let's use it to get cleaned up!"

Bradley and Musgrove made their way over to the running water and joined Rathek, as they cleaned the waste from their clothes.

"Where's your helmet, Muzzy?" asked Rathek, as he checked his top pocket for the map.

Musgrove looked back to where he had landed and noticed the tip of the white hard hat sticking out of the slime. "I see it... suppose I'd better make use of this water and give it a wash as well - don't want my hair smelling of dung!"

Bradley turned on his cap lamp and shone the beam around the chamber, as he trailed his fingers along a wooden unit. "It looks like we have landed in some kind of workshop... look - there are tools hanging from the walls and these look like old work benches," he surmised and twisted the metal handle on a vice, which was secured to the bench top.

Musgrove place the helmet on his head and contributed to the light in the room by attaching his lamp, as he turned on the beam before walking over to join his friend. "Look Brad... there are some notices on the walls - they look like drawings."

"Oh my god!" declared Bradley, as he moved his head to focus his lamp. "These are electrical circuit drawings... we are in the underground electricians workshop - this is where my Dad would have worked!"

Bradley continued to track the beam of his lamp around the storage cupboards below the benches. He stopped and let out a cry of delight, as he read the name plate on the cupboard. "Patrick Baker!"

Musgrove commented on Bradley's find. "Wow, that's amazing... your Dad actually used that cupboard - it's incredible to think we are so deep below the surface."

"It's difficult to believe that this place was a living working environment... and my Dad spent time in here - let's see if the cupboard is unlocked," declared Bradley, as he bent down and twisted the padlock. "Damn... it's locked and the padlock is covered in grease - yuck!" Bradley picked up a piece of cloth from one of the work benches to clean his hands and noticed Rathek was reading something. He turned his attention to the Devonian, who was inspecting the map that he had removed from his overalls. "Have you worked out which way we go from here?"

"Well, we travelled directly from your house, which is located at the top of the East Pit shaft... so that means we should be near the bottom of the same shaft - according to the map we have to find the air doors that lead to coal face number five," replied Rathek.

Musgrove commented in a distressed tone. "Isn't that where the *Mauled Miner* hangs out?"

"Sure is!" replied Rathek, as he folded the map and handed it to Bradley. "Here you go... it's all yours now - you can lead the way, Bradley!"

Bradley acknowledged the Devonian's trust in him but insisted that Rathek kept hold of the map for the time being and nodded his intentions to his best friend. Musgrove rechecked that his cap lamp was adequately secured into the holder on his helmet and they headed off in the direction of the air doors.

Bradley, Musgrove and Rathek left the confines of the workshop and walked through the main pit bottom area, where the West Pit on-setting area was located. Before the colliery was closed, this is where the mineworkers would board and depart the cage to lift them in and out of the mine.

They all continued to make their way through the darkness of the pit bottom and the glow from their cap lamps generated parallel beams of light that danced in different directions, as they moved along. Bradley walked past the old cage lift, as the light beams continued to jump in and out of the steel arched girders that supported the tall roadway. He imagined what it must have been like back when his grandfather and uncle worked down the Silvermoor mine. His father had told him stories about his visits to the pit bottom and the well shaft, but hadn't gone into any great detail about the day to day activities.

"Hey, Brad... come and have a look at this!" shouted Musgrove, who had climbed onto the decking where the men would have boarded the cage lift. "Look at the size of this boulder in here!"

Bradley made is way over to where his friend was standing and looked up, as he moved his head to direct his light through the cage bars. "Wow, that's a huge rock... looks like it's fallen down the mineshaft and probably happened when the contractors sealed the top of the shaft - when the pit was closed!"

"Well... there's one thing for sure - we won't be leaving that way!" declared Musgrove, as he climbed back down to the main pit bottom roadway and moved his head around, as he focussed his lamp on the looping cables that hung in huge down from metal carriers. "This place is absolutely enormous... you would never have imagined how high the passageways were down here."

Bradley remembered what Rathek had told them and courteously dipped the beam of his cap lamp, then nodded.

"My Dad used to describe to me how much space there was down here but it's amazing to see it... now let's find out what Rathek is up to - we have to locate the air doors that are marked on the map," he suggested and held up his hand up to protect his eyes. "Muzzy... you've got to stop pointing your light in my eyes - please turn your beam to dip!"

"Sorry Brad, I keep forgetting... my apologies!" replied Musgrove, as he adjusted his lamp again. "I'm gonna get fed up with turning this blumming thing on and off... it's driving me mad!"

"Okay, Muzzy... don't get too wound up by it," assured Bradley and then attracted his friend's attention to the Devonian nobleman. "Muzzy, stop fiddling with that thing... look, Rathek's over there - by that big machine!" he shouted. "I think he's found something... and it looks like he's got some kind of metal bar in his hand - come on, let's see what he's doing."

The boys made their way over to where Rathek was standing and Bradley asked him what he was holding. The Devonian did not answer. He was totally oblivious to them and appeared to be in deep thought. He was examining the control panel of the machine, which was a haulage locomotive that was used to carry supplies and materials around the pit bottom area. Rathek had the starter handle for the loco in his hand and he was flipping some switches on the dashboard.

"What are you doing?" asked Bradley, as Rathek proceeded to turn a large gauge. "Rathek!" he shouted.

At last the Devonian looked at Bradley. "No need to shout... I heard you the first time," he replied calmly. "Just give me a few more seconds... and I think I'll have this beauty working." He explained and turned another button.

Rathek flicked a few more switches and inserted the starter handle into the front of the machine. He then used all his strength to crank the engine. With just a single turn, the locomotive roared into life and the pit bottom was echoing with the sound of industrial grind, as the air thickened with diesel fumes.

Musgrove shouted above the noise of the engine. "What are we going to use this for?"

Bradley noticed Rathek's eyes focus on the air doors at the end of the roadway. "Very clever, Rathek!" he congratulated. "I take it the air doors are locked?"

Rathek smiled and held out a welcoming arm.   "Come on... jump on board you two - it's time to smash our way through!"

Once the boys were safely on board, Rathek pulled the brake handle and pushed his foot on the accelerator pedal. The locomotive's engine hesitated at first and misfired three times before lurching forward, as it spluttered into full revs. "Hold on tight, fellas!"

The engine built up speed and the air doors grew larger, as the locomotive approached at top speed. Bradley held onto the back of the Rathek's metal seat and braced himself for impact. He closed his eyes as the front of the engine smashed through the first set of doors. Fragments of wood and metal flew into the air, as the heavy machine moved forward slicing through everything in its path like a hot knife through butter.

Bradley opened his eyes, as the second set of doors was effortlessly carved into by the locomotive. The engine failed to stay straight on the rails and it started to lean to one side, as the wheels on one side of the runaway machine lifted off the tracks. "Jump, Muzzy... this things going to turn over!" shouted Bradley and he pulled at his friends cap lamp cable.

Musgrove held out his hand and used Bradley's arm as leverage to hoist himself on top of the engine. Impact with the side of the roadway was imminent and he jumped off the locomotive hitting the stone dust floor with a hard impact.

Bradley did not hesitate and followed Musgrove's trajectory, as he fell sideways onto the rails. "Arrrghhh!" he shouted, as his elbow struck the metal track. He tumbled over and looked up at the troubled Devonian, who was still trying to steer the veering locomotive back on to the rails. "Rathek... jump!"

It was too late for Rathek to escape and he stayed in his seat to ensure the boys alighted before the locomotive ploughed into the side of the arched roadway. There was a huge explosion and a giant fireball erupted from the leaking diesel oil that spewed from the ruptured engine.

Debris from the machine was flying in all directions and the fire intensified, Bradley recognised the immediate danger to his friend. He held his injured arm firmly and ignored the throbbing pain, as he shouted over to Musgrove. "Get into that man-hole and put on your self rescuer!"

Musgrove put his thumb in the air, as he scrambled to his feet and headed towards one of the small niches carved out in the side of the passageway. Both boys arrived at the man-hole at the same time just as the fire ball passed the entrance. The man hole had done its job, as they each released the clips from their self rescuers and attached the masks to their faces.

They waited inside their protective cocoon until the flames diminished and a swirl of black smoke filled the roadway. The stone dust thrown up by the force of the explosion started to settle and the boys decided to leave the safety of the man-hole to seek out their brave driver. They immerged from the man-hole and began to walk tentatively through the decimated remains of the diesel engine. Bradley shouted a muffled cry through his mask. "Rathek... are you okay?"

The density of the mask prevented his voice from projecting beyond the filters within its plastic casing so he pulled the device from his face. The smoke made Bradley choke but he continued to shout Rathek's name into the black smog.

No answer came from the rubble strewn across the road way and the two boys continued to search through the debris. The smoke began to disperse and Musgrove removed his mask to speak to his injured friend, who was still holding his elbow. "It's not looking good, Brad... I think Rathek must have perished in the flames - and you don't look so good, mate!"

"Don't worry about me, Muzzy... keep searching - we have to lift every piece of rock and metal to be sure," insisted Bradley, as he noticed a limb sticking out from beneath a large sheet. "That looks like the side of the loco's engine cover and there's a leg... and it's moving!"

They jumped over the engine's charred remains and moved quickly to take hold of the metal cover. Bradley relayed the lifting instructions to his friend. "Gently does it, Muzzy... the slightest movement could crush him."

The boys used all their strength and gently lifted the cover to one side, revealing the injured Devonian beneath. Musgrove was stronger than Bradley and he took the weight of the cover and pushed it away, whilst the eternal chosen one took hold of Rathek's head and placed a small block of wood beneath it for support.

They both crouched down either side of their groaning colleague and offered words of encouragement. Rathek opened his eyes and smiled at the boys. He tried to lift his head but quickly placed it back onto the temporary pillow. "That worked then!" he joked. "You two look like you survived the crash, okay... but I don't seem to be able to feel my legs!"

Bradley reassured the ailing nobleman. "Stay still Rathek... there is a girder across your lower body - it's probably stopping the blood supply from reaching your legs and why you can't feel anything."

"We have to try and move it, Brad!" exclaimed Musgrove, as Rathek drifted into unconsciousness. "We don't want to risk hurting him further... but he's closed his eyes again so we better act fast!"

Bradley agreed. "We don't have any choice... the roof of this roadway has been damaged by the fire - it could cave in at any moment," he replied and looked up at the gaping hole in the corrugated sheeting above their heads. "You support that end and I'll wedge a block under it to take the weight."

Musgrove positioned himself at one end of the girder and took hold. "Okay, Brad... get ready - I'm going to lift now!" he instructed, as Bradley pushed the block under the metal beam.

Rathek groaned as the pressure was released from his legs. He opened his eyes again. "That's better... I can feel my toes again." he revealed and moved both his feet.

Bradley and Musgrove were satisfied that no bones were broken, as they pulled Rathek out of the rubble and helped him to his feet. The Devonian brushed down his clothing and reached into his top pocket to pull out the map. He handed it to Bradley. "You better look after this from now on... we would have been in big trouble if this had gone up in flames!"

This time Bradley accepted the map and responded the Devonian's comment. "You're alive... that's all that matters - now, do you think you can walk?"

"Yes, I'm fine... lets move on - we've wasted too much time," replied Rathek, as took a few steps forward. "We need to find coal face number five... it's this way - are you boys ready?"

Bradley looked at Musgrove and smiled. "Let's go... this is the bit you've been dreading, Muzzy - you might finally get to meet the Mauled Miner!"

"Ha... ha - just make sure you have that Swiss army knife at the ready!" requested Musgrove, as he picked up the starter handle from the crippled locomotive. "I'm taking this with me... just in case!"

22

Attack on Aedis

Turpol and Sereny were secured in a crudely constructed cage attached to the back of a Krogon mineral transport vehicle. Two Tree Elves sat at the helm of the cart just in front of the cage and pulled the reigns gently to calm the impatient Hoffen. The soldiers were waiting for their orders to depart and held tightly to the shackled animals in readiness for the journey to Trad.

Varuna had claimed Grog's mount Shatar and the Koezard twisted its head and pulled at the reigns. The determined Hartopian fought against the lizard creature's reluctance to his ride and Shatar finally gave in to Varuna's forceful handling. The faithful mount had sensed that Sereny knew something about his old master and he decided to obey the Hartopian's commands.

Varuna looked out over the open land that made up the Flaclom Straits. It was covered like a blanket with Flaglan's army, as they amassed in battalion formation. Over twenty thousand Tree Elves stood in organised lines as far as the eye could see, as the archers waited for their leader's signal. Flaglan mounted her Koezard. and the sorceress held the colours of Haldon at the end of a long pole, as she lifted the emblazoned flag into an upright position. The banner flapped in the gentle breeze and the Tree Elves cheered in unison, as the High Priestess kicked her heels into her heavy breathing mount. Streams of hot air puffed out from the Koezard's nostrils and it moved ahead, soon developing a canter as the army took their first steps back towards the Satorc Bridge.

The wheels of the cart carrying Sereny and Turpol creaked, as they turned slowly over the chalky roadway. Flaglan maneuvered her Koezard to ride next to the cart and shouted over to the girl. "You know something... don't you?"

Sereny moved closer to the dwarf to seek protection and she answered quietly. "I don't know what you mean."

"Speak up!" demanded Flaglan, as her mount reared up. The High Priestess controlled the Koezard and readjusted the flag pole in her hand to retain a grip on the heavy standard. "You do know what I mean... tell me what happened to the Krogons body - where is Grog?" she shouted, as the flag continued to flutter loudly above her head.

Turpol held Sereny against his small frame to offer her the assurance she needed, as the girl spoke in a more confident tone. "When I escaped from Grog's crypt... his body wasn't in there - that's the truth, I swear!"

"I don't believe you!" replied Flaglan. "Before we get to Trad... you will tell me what you know or I will kill you - for now think about the consequences if you don't!" she threatened, as the disgruntled sorceress kicked hard into her Koezard to guide it away from the cart and galloped ahead to join Varuna at the front of the entourage.

Varuna matched the gallop of his accomplice's mount and asked what all the fuss was about. "Why are you so angry with the girl... doe's her presence in Pathylon threaten you, my dear?"

"Of course not... anyway, it's not the girl I'm worried about!" replied Flaglan.

The Hartopian laughed and offered little response to assure the flustered High Priestess. "Grog's body has gone missing... so what?"

"The missing Krogons body intrigues me... it doesn't feel right - the girl knows something!" replied Flaglan.

"Oh leave her be... we have much more important things to be concentrating on - when we get to Trad, we will be glorious in victory over the pathetic Devonian noblemen who guard the capital!" bragged the Hartopian. "Now let us revel in our power and guide your splendid archers to Trad."

The cart wheels juddered, as the prisoner's vehicle crossed the wooden slats on Satorc Bridge and Sereny and Turpol huddled together in the cage. Varuna led the entourage into Devonian region and encouraged the elfish army to move at pace, as they marched on towards the royal capital.

It did not take long to reach the City of Aedis and the archers massacred all that challenged their charge. Hail upon hail of arrows poured onto the city like a deadly rainstorm and everyone wandering the streets were cruelly slain. Every building was rampaged and all those that apposed their onslaught were executed. Varuna and Flaglan met little resistance and the element of surprise employed to attack the small city meant that Aedis was taken within minutes. However, word reached Trad of the impending threat and the Devonian noblemen prepared for the imminent attack on the royal capital.

Varuna addressed Flaglan's archers. "This is just the beginning... we will march on Trad and take the Royal Palace - I will be your new King and Flaglan will be your Queen!" he shouted, as the archers raised their bows and cheered at the couple. "Together, we will rule over Pathylon!"

Flaglan mounted her Koezard and let Varuna finish his speech. As Varuna steadied his mount in preparation for the march on Trad, she leant over and offered some stern advice. "Don't be too confident in victory yet, my hasty Hartopian... we have to beat the Devonian noblemen and they are highly trained - and in future, ask for my permission before you address my people!"

"We *will* defeat the Devonian noblemen... and as for asking for *your* permission to speak to *your* people - look around you my dear, they are *my* people know!"

Flaglan had no chance to reply, as Varuna kicked his Koezard and moved away. The sorceress snarled a frustrating response to the Hartopian's words and had no choice but to follow his lead.

All the Devonians that survived the onslaught of Aedis were gathered together and secured inside the city's council buildings, as a regiment of Tree Elves were left to guard the prisoners. All the other battalions of archers followed Varuna's entourage, as it moved out of the city in a precise formation. The Hartopian ordered the cart carrying Sereny and Turpol to join their march on to the capital of Pathylon.

Meanwhile deep underground in the Silvermoor mine, Rathek's aching legs grew stronger with every step he took along the main passage that led to the intake roadway for coal face number five. Bradley and Musgrove shone their cap lamps ahead and signalled that it was alright to proceed.

Bradley referred to the map to ascertain how far it was to the coal face. "Once we reach the face, we need to look out for a secret entrance... according to the map this will lead us to the Krogon Arch, which is here," he explained and pointed to the drawing.

"Isn't that where the Mauled Miner hangs out?" asked Musgrove.

"Well, the icon of the ghost appears before the Krogon Arch on the map... so yep - brace yourself, Muzzy," teased Bradley, as he bent down and picked up a leather strung pouch. "This could be useful," he declared, then folded the map carefully and placed it in the small wallet, as he pulled on the drawstring.

"It must have belonged to an old mineworker," surmised Rathek, as Bradley tied the pouch to his belt.

"Well... it's mine now - it will keep the map safe and clean," said Bradley assertively, as he turned his cap lamp to full beam. "Let's move on... the secret entrance is about a hundred metres ahead and there should be a right dog-leg about fifty metres ahead - look out for any strange markings on the roadway when we get near to the coal face."

Musgrove tentatively trailed the others by a few metres and he clenched tightly to the starter handle, as his knuckles whitened. "Not looking forward to this," he muttered to himself.

It did not take long for them to reach the dog-leg in the roadway and Bradley waved his arm to indicate that they should move quickly ahead. Rathek was now fully mobile and he acknowledged the eternal chosen one's instruction by encouraging Musgrove to keep up.

About forty metres ahead Bradley stopped and shone his lamp up and down the side of the roadway. He had noticed an arrow painted on one of the arched girders that formed the shape of the intake. The corrugated sheeting behind two girders looked slightly displaced so he approached it and held out his hand. "Pass me that starter handle, Muzzy."

"Not a chance mate... this is going to say hello to the Mauled Miner - thank you very much!" exclaimed Musgrove, as he maneuvered the metal rod behind his back.

Bradley assured his friend. "You can have it back when I've finished with it... I need to use it as a crowbar - I think the secret entrance is behind this sheeting."

Musgrove reluctantly handed the starter handle to Rathek, who was nearest to him. "Please make sure he gives it back to me!"

"Don't worry Muzzy... I'll make sure Bradley returns it to you - just as soon as we get through," promised Rathek and passed the metal bar to Bradley. "Here you go... and please be careful - you don't know what danger lies behind there!"

Bradley placed the starter handle behind the edge of the corrugated sheet and pulled back sharply. The sound of falling debris could be heard clattering against the metal sheeting and he stepped back to let the small rock fall subside.

Musgrove and Rathek aimed their cap lamp beams at the opening created by Bradley's first attempt, as the make-shift crow bar was inserted again. A second act of leveraging dislodged the sheet and it collapsed on to the stone dust floor. Bradley shot backwards to avoid the falling metal and Rathek steadied the boy's balance. The corrugated sheet flipped back up towards them like a springboard and they both turned away to shield their faces, as the sheet recoiled.

The sharp object finally came to rest a few metres away and Bradley gasped. "That was close... thanks Rathek - that thing could have taken us both out!"

"I was sent here to guide and protect you, Bradley," replied the loyal Devonian. "I will die for you if I have to."

Musgrove commended them both and pointed to the newly formed gap in the curved wall. "Well done, you two... now look through there - I think you've found what we've been looking for!" He confirmed and directed the beam of his cap lamp at the opening. "The dust is still settling but it looks like there's another passageway behind there."

Bradley handed the starter handle back to Musgrove and approached the gap. He removed the cap lamp from his helmet and stretched the cable, as he placed the lamp through the hole to reveal a solid stone-carved corridor.

"Be careful, Brad," warned Musgrove, as Bradley put his head through the opening. "You don't know what's lurking behind there!"

Bradley was conscious of the lever marks left by the crowbar and he made sure he did not catch his face on the sharp metal edges. He slowly turned and moved his upper body through the hole, as he shone his lamp around. "All I can see is a long stone tunnel... by the look of the marks on the walls, it looks like it's been hand-made using pick axes - it must be quite old because there doesn't appear to be any machine markings on the sides of the passageway."

"Is it safe to go through?" asked Rathek.

"Yes, I think soooooooooooo...."

Bradley did not get the chance to finish his sentence and he was pulled through the gap so quickly his voice culminated in such a high pitch that the rock strata about the roadway rattled against the corrugated sheets.

Musgrove leapt forward and put his head through the hole and witnessed Bradley being dragged down the stone tunnel by a strange figure. "Hey... put him down - come back here."

Rathek rushed up to the back of Musgrove, who was trying to squeeze through the hole. "What is it Muzzy... what's happened to Bradley?"

"Something's taken him... it looked like a man - but I'm not sure," replied Musgrove, as he forced his body into the secret tunnel. "I'm going after him!"

"Wait for me, Muzzy... and don't worry - he won't hurt Bradley!" shouted Rathek, as he pushed his upper body through the gap. "Help me, Muzzy... I'm stuck!"

Musgrove took hold of Rathek's collar, as the Devonian forced his waist past the sharp metal edges of the sheeting. He caught his belt on a jagged piece of steel but Musgrove summoned all his strength and pulled him free, as the sound of tearing cloth cut an unwanted seam in Rathek's clothing.

At last they were both safely inside the tunnel, as Musgrove aimed his lamp in the direction taken by Bradley and his abductor. "You said *he* wouldn't hurt Brad... how do you know that thing was a he - it could have been a female chimpanzee for all you know?"

"Trust me, Muzzy... there's things I know - let's find them and I'll explain later," insisted Rathek.

"Was it the Mauled Miner?" asked Musgrove, as he grabbed hold of Rathek's overalls with both hands. "Has the ghost of Silvermoor taken Brad?"

Rathek gently pulled Musgrove's hand away from his clothing. "Please calm down Muzzy... yes - I have every reason to believe it's the Mauled Miner, but he won't hurt Bradley."

"How can you be so sure?" demanded Musgrove.

"I just am... it's too complicated to explain right now - you're going to have to trust me," replied Rathek, as he readjusted his clothing and turned his lamp on to full beam. "Come on... let's find them - I promise I will explain everything later."

Musgrove reluctantly agreed and followed Rathek's lead, as they made their way along the tunnel. They successfully negotiated a series of twists and turns through the narrow passageways and arrived some twenty metres away from a stone-carved archway, which was majestically carved into the rock.

Musgrove carried on walking, as Rathek stopped to catch his breath. The boy looked inquisitively at the images that had been scribed into stonework. "This must be the Krogon Arch described on the map," he stated. "I recognise some of the carvings... some of them look a bit Grog-like - they must be images of lizard men from Krogonia."

Rathek caught up with Musgrove and they stood side by side beneath the magnificent monument. "Good observation, Muzzy... you're right, the carvings are depicting a confrontation between Krogon Warriors and the Mece - it must have been erected here to commemorate a battle that took place many years ago."

"But who built it?" asked Musgrove. "It's a long way from Krogonia!"

Rathek explained. "Don't forget about the Vortex of Silvermoor... we're not as far away from Krogonia as you might think - the Unknown Land is at the other side of the portal so the Krogons would have had easy access to Silvermoor."

Musgrove paused for a moment. "It's difficult to believe that all this was going on right under our noses!"

"Come on Muzzy, there's been lots of things going on for centuries that you don't know about... but we don't have time to talk about them now - let's move on."

"You don't seem to have time to explain anything... do you, Rathek?" acknowledged Musgrove.

As they passed through the archway, they were welcomed by a familiar friend. Bradley came running towards them. "Get back!" he shouted, as the Mauled Miner followed close behind him.

Musgrove lifted the starter handle above his head in readiness to strike down the ghost and Bradley shouted over to his friend. "Not him, Muzzy... he's on our side - it's them we've got to worry about!" he exclaimed, as a colony of ferocious giant ants appeared in the distance.

"Oh my god... what the eck are those things?" shouted Musgrove, as he turned to run with Rathek.

"Not now, Muzzy!" replied the Devonian. "And don't say I haven't any time to explain - just run!"

Musgrove did not argue, as they chased Bradley and the Mauled Miner through a crack in the tunnel wall adjacent the Krogon Arch. Once through, they all kept running down an even narrower passageway until they came to a dead end.

"Now what do we do?" shouted Musgrove, as he pointed at the ghost. "And what are we going to do with him?"

"Calm down, Muzzy," replied Bradley. "The Mauled Miner means us no harm... this situation was meant to be and he's part of all this - he is here to guide us to the Vortex of Silvermoor."

"That's if we get that far!" replied Musgrove. "Are you saying we were meant to find him?" he asked.

Rathek was the furthest up the passageway and he had his back to the opening. He intervened in the conversation.

196

"Muzzy, I told you there was more to this than you could have imagined... you must understand that whatever happens from now on - it will have an impact on whether or not Basjoo Ma-otz destroys Pathylon."

At that moment, Bradley noticed a shadow appear and it was closing behind the nobleman. "Rathek... watch out!"

23

The Maze of Death

Rathek was in immediate danger from one of the huge black insects. The creature moved so fast that the Devonian was taken by surprise, as it wrapped a leg around his waist and lifted him helplessly off the ground. He pulled at the insect's painful grip and shouted out to Bradley, as if to convey his last words. "When you get inside the vortex... remember to take the right fork - I think this thing is about to kill me!"

"Rathek... no!" shouted Musgrove, as he swung the starter handle in front of the giant ant. "Let him go you stupid bug!"

"Urrrgghhhhh!" exclaimed Rathek, as the creature's two large pincers clamped his throat and closed savagely around the circumference of his neck.

The cable that fed the power supply from the battery on Rathek's belt was severed by the creature's cutting action and the light from the lamp on top of the Devonian's helmet distinguished to simulate the impending termination of his life. Rathek called out with his final breath and choked. "Bradley... I cannot escape this... you must act bravely and take out my heart when I am dead!" He called. "You must deliver it to Meltorrrrr... urrrgghhh!"

With a final clamp from the giant ant's deathly grip, Rathek's head followed the same fate as the cable and was severed with a scissor-like action. Bradley watched in horror as the nobleman's limp body was tossed against the tunnel wall by the giant creature. The eternal chosen one was enraged and conjured up a bounty of selfless courage, as he instinctively charged passed Musgrove. He snatched the starter handle out of his friend's trembling hand and launched himself at the huge creature.

Bradley landed on its back and wielded the metal bar aloft. With a single strike, he penetrated the insect's eye socket and a stream of yellow fluid squirted out of the horrific wound. Bradley then wrapped his legs around the creature's neck and clung on tightly to its feelers, as if he was riding a rodeo bull at a fairground. The giant ant collapsed in a crumpled heap with its legs still twitching, as Bradley somersaulted across the floor to complete his heroic maneuver.

More giant ants scurried down the narrow tunnel and Bradley gave the signal to Musgrove and the Mauled Miner to move back. The ghost stood still and then pointed upwards to a ledge. Bradley looked up and directed his light at the narrow shelf in the strata. He moved his head slowly and followed the ledge along the side of the tunnel. It appeared to lead to a series of steps. "Go with the Mauled Miner, Muzzy... I think he's telling us there's another way out of here - I'll be with you in a few minutes."

"You're crazy, Brad... those things will kill you!" cried Musgrove, as he moved closer to his brave friend. "I'm not leaving you!"

Bradley afforded Musgrove an admirable look and handed him the starter handle. "Okay, here... wave this around in front of them, while I remove Rathek's heart!"

"Are you serious, Brad... you're not really going to take his heart out - are you?" asked Musgrove, as he struck another of the creatures with the metal bar.

Bradley did not answer and quickly removed the Swiss army knife, as he extracted the longest blade. He ripped open the nobleman's upper clothing to reveal Rathek's blood stained chest and without hesitation performed the surgery needed to extract the Devonian's heart. "Forgive me, Rathek... I know Meltor will benefit but I'm so sorry you had to die!"

Musgrove urged Bradley to hurry, as the angry insects struck out their long barbed legs. "Come on, Brad... let's lift him up to the ledge!" he shouted and struck another one of the creatures.

The giant ant screeched and lowered its head to snap the sharp pincers at Musgrove's arm. Bradley kicked the creatures head and knocked its killing jaws against the tunnel wall.

"Muzzy, we have to leave his body... it's too heavy!" shouted Bradley, as a second incensed creature tried to clamber over the first.

"We can't just leave his body here for those things!" pleaded Musgrove. "They're savages... they will tear him to shreds!"

Bradley repeated his request. "We have no choice, Muzzy... let's climb up to the ledge before the next one strikes out at us - Rathek's job is done!" he explained. "We have his heart and the Mauled Miner will lead us the rest of the way!"

The faceless ghost had already started to climb up the side of the tunnel, as the ravenous insects tried to squeeze through. He reached down to pull Musgrove to safety and Bradley quickly followed. They reached the sanctuary of the steps and witnessed Rathek's body being ripped apart by the merciless creatures below.

"What are those things?" asked Musgrove.

"Troglobites!" replied Bradley, as he passed Rathek's warm heart to the Mauled Miner and wiped his blood stained hand on his overalls. He calmly closed the sharp blade back into the outer casing of the Swiss army knife and then removed the map from the leather pouch. "Here... look at the map - there are pictures of the insects sketched alongside the tunnel."

Musgrove looked at Bradley and admired his composure. He smiled at his friend and then studied the map, as the commotion below them ensued.

Musgrove stared down, as one of the insects collected Rathek's severed head in its pincers and reared up onto four of its back legs, as a show of defiance to show off its trophy. Two more of the insect predators fought over the remains of the Devonian's body and they continued to squabble with the limp torso, as they dragged it back out of the narrow tunnel.

Musgrove placed his hands on his head and scrunched his blond mop of hair, as the frightened teenager looked at Bradley. He pulled a sympathetic face and sighed. "That was horrific, Brad... poor Rathek!"

"Come away from the edge, Muzzy... there's nothing we can do for him now," encouraged Bradley, as he pulled on the sleeve of his bewildered friend.

With the remains of Rathek's body taken by the Troglobites, Musgrove looked away and closed his eyes for a moment. "He didn't deserve to die like that - I feel so helpless up here, Brad."

Bradley consoled his friend and put his arm around his neck, as the Mauled Miner stood motionless with Rathek's pumping heart in the palm of his open hand. "There's no time to feel guilty, Muzzy... you can see on the map we have another task ahead of us - we still have to find our way through the Maze of Death!"

Musgrove faced his friend with the faint glow of his dipped cap lamp creating a halo around Bradley's eyes. "You were very brave down there, Brad... Rathek would have been proud of your actions."

"It's the least I could have done... the rate at which that creature was tearing at his body - I had to act fast or we wouldn't have stood a chance," replied Bradley in a humble tone, as he ripped one of the sleeves from his overalls. He then broke a hanging stalagmite into small pieces and placed the cold crystals onto the clean side of the material. Bradley gently took the heart from the Mauled Miner and lowered it onto the ice crystals. The protection of the precious organ was complete and he made sure the crystals had completely covered it before proceeding to use the cloth as a bandage.

"Well... it was a fearless thing to do - we wouldn't be alive if it wasn't for you, Brad!" exclaimed Musgrove," as he watched Bradley place the vital organ inside a canvass bag. "It was a brave request from Rathek and there's also something else that's been playing on my mind... he said something really strange just after the Mauled Miner grabbed you - it was as if he knew the identity of our ghost friend."

Bradley secured the piece of hessian to his belt then turned and looked into the Mauled Miner's empty face. "Tell us the truth... did you know Rathek?"

The ghost nodded confidently and then turned away, as he started to climb the steps.

"Well, we got our answer," stated Bradley, as he got to his feet. "I guess we'd better follow him... he hasn't got any facial features so he can hardly speak - I don't think we're gonna find out much from him."

Musgrove agreed. "I'm sure there'll be an explanation for all of this when we eventually get into Pathylon... that's if we ever get there!"

The Mauled Miner led Bradley and Musgrove up the steps and into a cave-like chamber. The small cavern shaped room was dimly lit by crystallised pieces of strata that hung down from the roof like organic chandeliers.

The ghost pointed to a painted emblem near an exit point. Bradley approached the drawing, which depicted a square-shaped maze just like the one on the map. "This must be the way to the Maze of Death," he announced, as Musgrove peered over his shoulder.

"I think you might be right there... *Sherlock*," agreed Musgrove. "Do you think faceless here will show us the way?"

The Mauled Miner made a groaning sound and made his way over to Musgrove. The ghost-like figure clenched his fist and made the boy aware of his disapproval by holding it next to his trembling face.

Bradley pushed the ghost's arm away. "He meant nothing by that... your face intrigues us both - Muzzy didn't mean to upset you."

Musgrove let out a sigh of relief, as the disgruntled coal miner backed away. "Thanks Brad... I thought I was done for then!"

"Put your brain in gear Muzzy... with Rathek gone, we really need this guys help - now don't go upsetting him again," suggested Bradley to his older friend. "If Sereny was here she'd be having a field day with you... now pull yourself together and try to get on with the poor fella - we need him whether you like it or not."

"I'm sorry Brad... it's just - I can't stop thinking of what those insects did to Rathek," explained Musgrove, as he banged the base of his clenched fist against the cavern wall.

Bradley tried to console his friend. "We have to move on, Muzzy... it's what Rathek would have wanted - there's still lot's to do."

To the surprise of both boys, the Mauled Miner re-approached them and placed a hand on each of their young shoulders. He nodded in agreement with Bradley's last comment and urged them to move forward in the direction of the exit.

The ghost reached above their heads and lifted an old *Davy Lamp* from a small niche below one of the hanging crystals. He pulled out a metal striker from the base of the lamp and quickly pushed it back in again, as a small flame appeared inside the glass housing. He adjusted the height of the flame and the cavern was suddenly filled with more light. The new intensity of the flame revealed the full emptiness of the faceless man. The boys stared into the darkness of his head, as the ghost turned and then moved towards the exit. The two boys remained speechless and followed the ghost out of the chamber.

The exit led another long tunnel, which was quite low and they all crouched, as they made their way along the hundred or so metres. Eventually they reached another small chamber, which contained a pair of wooden doors at the far end.

The Mauled Miner rested his lamp on a table-shaped boulder adjacent the doors. He reached into his pocket and pulled out a large brass key and then inserted it in to the keyhole. He tried to turn the key but it did not move.

"Here, let me try opening it with this," suggested Musgrove, as he passed the end of the starter handle through the eye of the key. "We can use this to lever the key round."

"It's come in pretty useful... that metal bar," commented Bradley. "Glad you brought it along, Muzzy."

Musgrove smiled and proceeded push against the bar with his midriff. The key started to turn and there was a loud click, as the lock released. "What's behind these doors?" he asked, as he indicated to Bradley to check the map.

Before Bradley could reach into the leather pouch, the Mauled Miner pointed to a simple drawing on the wall to left of the doors. It was a picture of a maze and in the centre there was a skull with two horns sticking out from either side.

"I guess that gives it away a bit!" exclaimed Musgrove, as he pulled the starter handle out of the key. "You can put the map back in your wallet, Brad... I think we're about to enter the Maze of Death!"

Bradley took a closer look at the drawing on the wall and asked the Mauled Miner if the skull bared any significance.

"Does this represent another creature... and if so - is it in there?"

The ghost nodded and held his arms out wide. The speechless miner then animated the charging of a bull by pointing two fingers and held them above the two empty black holes that represented his disfigured eye sockets.

Musgrove looked at the doors and gave Bradley another one of his *'I can't believe this'* looks. "We really do get the rough end of the deal... looks like we've got another monster to slay - when's it ever going to end, Brad?"

Bradley smiled and moved over to the doors. He placed his hand on one of the large hooped handles and pulled the door ajar. A swirl of grey smoke passed through into the chamber, as he swung the door open fully to reveal an impressive site.

The boys stared open-mouthed at the magnificent landscape. The huge cavern was at least two hundred or so metres high and a series of monumental rocks sprouted up like a mountain range that encircled a series of stone passageways below.

"This is fantastic... how could such a beautiful location be left undiscovered like this?" gasped Musgrove.

Bradley surmised. "I think our friend here may have something to do with that... the fact that he had a large brass key would suggest that he is a Gatekeeper - just like Turpol."

The Mauled Miner nodded, as Musgrove walked towards the entrance of the maze. "There's no way to see over this thing... the height of those rocks must be at least ten metres - we have no option but to go through it!"

"Okay... let's do it - we've come this far and we know the entrance to the vortex lies at the other side - we have no choice!" rallied Bradley, as he led the way into the maze. "But we must stay together!"

They journeyed deeper and deeper into the maze, as waistline smog carried them towards the centre. Eerie noises echoed around the damp rocks and the sound of screeching bats could be heard high above their heads.

The Mauled Miner stopped and held up his lamp. Bradley and Musgrove waited for the ghost to indicate something and they did not have to wait long, as the sound of a raging beast thundered through the maze.

"What was that?" screamed Musgrove, as he clung tightly to the starter handle.

Bradley moved towards the Mauled Miner to catch a glimpse of his face. The ghost turned and allowed Bradley to stare into the emptiness again. It was if the ghost was smiling at the boy and Bradley felt himself falling into some sort of trance. He quickly shook his head to cast off the spell and took a step backwards then stumbled.

Musgrove anticipated his friend's fall and reached out to grab his arm. "You okay, Brad?"

"Yes, I'm fine... err, thanks Muzzy," replied Bradley calmly.

Bradley had recognised something deep within the Mauled Miner's empty face but he couldn't understand what he had witnessed. The answer would become clear eventually but the boy hero had to quickly refocus his attention on the next task. "Musgrove get ready... I think we are about to meet our next challenge!"

Bradley was right, as a large horned creature appeared in front of them. The beast stood on four hoofed legs and its bull-shaped head boasted two gigantic curved horns.

"My god... look at the size of that thing, Brad!" exclaimed Musgrove. "It looks like a Hoffen... but much bigger!"

Musgrove was right, the beast was indeed a breed of Hoffen, but this particular creature had been cross-bred with a Krogon Koezard by the Mece to stop any intruders from passing through the maze.

Bradley agreed with his friend, as the creature circled all the three of them. "It does have the look of a Hoffen but take a look at its teeth... this thing is definitely carnivorous and we're not made of grass!"

"Well I think he wants to graze on us... what do you suggest we do next, Brad?" asked Musgrove, as he tightened his grip on the metal bar. "I don't think this thing will be much use this time!"

Saliva dripped from the creature's mouth and its nostrils flared violently, as it moved nearer. Bradley was desperate for a way to avoid an imminent death and he looked around for some inspiration. The Mauled Miner held out his Davy Lamp and turned the brass knob to increase the height of the naked flame inside. He then twisted the bottom of the unit to release the flammable gas contained in the base unit.

Bradley recognised what the ghost's intentions were and he grabbed the starter handle from Musgrove. "Stand back, Muzzy... looks this thing's gonna have its uses again after all!" declared Bradley, as the snorting creature scraped one of its front hoofs repeatedly on the floor and then pounced forward. "Okay... throw it now!"

The ghost launched the old miner's lamp at the beast and Bradley timed his throw to perfection, as the metal bar collided with the oil lamp in mid air. Splinters of glass shot out of the lamp, as the gas ignited. A ball of fire engulfed around the horned beast's head and it reeled backwards. The smell of burning hair and flesh filled the confined centre of the maze and Bradley recognised an opportunity to escape.

"Come on you two... this is our chance to get round this thing!"

Musgrove and the Mauled Miner ran past the burning creature, as it cried out in pain and followed Bradley along the exit route. Several twists and turns later, they heard the dying cries of the beast, as the noise echoed inside the vaulted ceiling of the cavern. The noise disturbed the wildlife above, as hundreds of bats flew in a spiral formation and screeched above the maze.

They stopped to take a breath and Bradley congratulated the Mauled Miner on his quick thinking. "I thought we were as good as dead in there... thank goodness for that blinking starter handle again - I've lost count how many times that thing has saved our bacon!"

Musgrove exclaimed. "Oh no, the starter handle... we left it in the centre of the maze - we must go back and get it!"

"Forget it, Muzzy... it's not worth it'" replied Bradley. "We may get lost in there if we go back... we've got this far and it can't be long now to the other side of the maze - anyhow that creature may still be alive."

Just then the charred beast reappeared behind Bradley and Musgrove shouted out a warning to his friend. "Look out, Brad!"

The blinded creature hooked one of its burnt forearms around Bradley's neck and smothered his face with a shovel-like hand. Musgrove and the Mauled Miner rallied around to assist their friend but the beast kicked out at the frustrated helpers.

Bradley's line of sight was temporarily obstructed by the creature's grip around his face and he was struggling to breath. The pressure of the beast's grip sent a rush of blood to his eye sockets that created dancing images within his impaired vision. For a split second the face of his grandfather appeared and he remembered the birthday gift bequeathed to him, as he reached into his pocket to pull out the Swiss army knife. He instinctively threw it into the air for one of his friends to catch it and Musgrove confidently obliged. The teenager pulled out the same blade that had extracted Rathek's heart and lunged forward to plunge the weapon into the blackened arm that was gripping Bradley's neck. The creature released its grip immediately and reeled backwards, as it held on to the open wound.

Bradley shouted to his startled friend. "Throw the knife back to me, Muzzy!"

Musgrove instinctively closed the blade and tossed the weapon to his friend. Bradley quickly reopened the knife, as he leapt on top of the beast to penetrate the blade into its neck several times to cause its deathly fall to the ground.

"Wow!" exclaimed Musgrove. "That was close... you okay, Brad!"

"Yes... thanks to you, Muzzy - I owe you one!" replied Bradley, as he closed the knife and placed it back in his pocket.

Musgrove shrugged his shoulders. "Ah... it was nothing - faceless here did his bit as well!"

The Mauled Miner did not respond and Bradley placed his hands on both their shoulders. "Thanks, you guys... you saved my life - now let's move on shall we?"

"What about the starter handle?" asked Musgrove. "Surely it's safe to go back in and get it now?"

Bradley shook his head. "Leave it Muzzy... we don't have time."

Musgrove shrugged his shoulders again and reluctantly accepted the loss of his trusty weapon, as the Mauled Miner nodded his approval and waited for Bradley to pass by. Without the old Davy Lamp, the ghost would have to rely on the light from the eternal chosen one's cap lamp to guide them.

The boy hero would now lead the rest of the way to ensure they escaped the maze to face their next daunting challenge - locating the Vortex of Silvermoor and coming face-to-face with the strange creatures that guarded its entrance.

24

Another Skeloyd Encounter

Norsk and his ice-submarine crew were nearing the shores of Freytor. They had successfully negotiated the long journey across the Red Ocean and had also managed to monitor the fully laden ice-cloud's safe passage in the skies above.

The Admiral barked his next order to the quartermaster. "Not too close... we don't want to alert the attention of my brother - the same blood line may run through our veins but I feel he would not hesitate to attack our ship in order to save his beloved senate!"

The crew on the command bridge pressed all the control buttons necessary to secure the ship's position and rested the ice-craft gently onto the sea bed in readiness for the next part of their mission.

Admiral Norsk watched intently on one of the ship's monitors, as the ice-cloud drifted effortlessly over the capital city of Frey. "It would appear that the cloud is in position!" he roared. "Now, get ready for my instructions... we just need to wait for my powers to recharge so I can send the bolt of electricity that's needed for the cloud to release the kratennium!"

The quartermaster approached the Admiral. "Sir.. how long do you anticipate before you are ready?"

Norsk afforded the crewmember a disapproving scowl and lashed out. "Do not question how long... you pathetic insubordinate!" he retorted and smashed his great white paw across the cowering sailor's head. "Now... let that be a message to all of you!" shouted the angry Freytorian, as the quartermaster reeled in pain and rolled on command deck floor. "We will attack when *I* am ready!"

Meanwhile back in Silvermoor the Maze of Death had been successfully negotiated, as Bradley led the group around the next bend in the tunnel and ordered everyone to crouch down. He noticed some movement in the distance. "I think we're nearly there... I can see a light up ahead and I'm sure I can see someone moving around," he whispered. "It has to be the vortex... according to the map, the roadway we've just travelled down had a double twist in it - so the entrance should be located about a hundred metres ahead of us."

Muzzy repositioned his dipped cap lamp and directed the faint beam of light at the map in Bradley's hand, as he confirmed Bradley's deduction. "You're right Brad, looking back at the bend in this tunnel... I would say you're pretty spot on, mate."

The Mauled Miner placed his blackened hand on the shoulder of Muzzy and pointed at a skeletal figure on the map. The skull-like emblem was positioned adjacent the entrance to the vortex and the ghost placed his forefinger to his throat then sliced across with the action of a knife blade.

"I do wish you could talk... I guess with no face - it's a bit difficult," Musgrove joked, as Bradley gave him another stern look to remind him not to keep making fun of the ghost. "What do you think he's trying to tell us, Brad?"

"Not sure," replied Bradley, as he pointed to the skull and asked the Mauled Miner to elaborate. "Can you mime a bit more and explain what the skull means?"

The disfigured ghost was growing tired of Musgrove's quips but chose to ignore him again and leant over, as he pulled a pencil out of the top pocket in Bradley's overalls. The boys pointed their dipped cap lamps at the map, as the Mauled Miner started to write.

Musgrove placed his hand on the pencil to stop the ghost. "Are you sure it's a good idea to write on the map... isn't it supposed to be sacred?"

Bradley pushed his friend's hand away. "It's only a pencil and it will rub out... let him carry on - this must be important," he insisted. "Anyhow, the Mauled Miner should know what lies ahead of us... he's been down here long enough."

The ghost nodded at Bradley to acknowledge his statement and then started to write on the map next to the skull. *'Skeloyds!'*

Bradley and Musgrove immediately recognised the written word and both slumped backwards simultaneously, as the Mauled Miner handed the pencil back.

"We are going to have to be very careful," exclaimed Bradley, as he placed the pencil back in his top pocket. "Turpol told us about an unfriendly group of Skeloyds that guarded the Vortex of Souls back in Pathylon - we know we won't receive a hospitable welcome from them if what he told us they all had to go through back then was true."

Musgrove acknowledged his friend's remark. "We have every reason to believe what the dwarf said... so I guess we're in for tough time."

The Mauled Miner pulled out a small handcrafted knife from his utility belt and made a gesture to indicate that he was ready to fight the flesh-eaten beings.

"Thank you," acknowledged Bradley, as he placed his finger on top of the ghost's rustic blade and pushed it downwards. "If what you have written on the map is true... I think it's going to take more than that to beat them - not even my trusty army knife is going to help us in this particular situation."

"Hey Brad... remind us - what did Turpol actually say about the Skeloyds back in Pathylon?" insisted Musgrove.

"Well according to the little Gatekeeper, they were half-dead creatures that were employed by the ancient High Priesthood of Pathylon as tunnel workers," explained Bradley. "You may recall, Turpol told us... that before they became Skeloyd creatures - their original form was that of Devonian labourers who had been punished because a small section of the workers had attempted to travel out of Pathylon, whilst the Vortex of Souls was being installed."

"So what happened to them... before you're Dad and my Brother killed them?" asked Musgrove.

Bradley tried to recall what Turpol had said. "Well, if I remember correctly... they didn't have the necessary authorisation from the High Priesthood to make the journey, so the vortex ripped out their souls whilst they were being transported and only their half-dead skeletal bodies reached the other side," continued Bradley. "Instead of facing an instant execution, the Skeloyds were entrusted with just enough life to enable them to guard the Vortex of Souls against any intruders that may stumble across it from the outside world – they say that..."

Before Bradley could conclude, a loud rumble shook through the rocky tunnels, which suddenly interrupted his explanation. It was if the same situation was repeating itself... just like back when the search party had approached the Vortex of Souls. This time it was Bradley and Musgrove's turn to face the Skeloyds that guarded the Vortex of Silvermoor.

The ground affected a series of tremors beneath their feet and Musgrove held onto the Mauled Miner for support. "What was that!" he shouted, as his fingertips tightened around the faceless figure's clothing.

The ghost reciprocated and held the boy tightly to reassure him that no harm would come to him.

"It felt like an earthquake," said Bradley, repeating his father's words and steadying himself against the tunnel wall. He then explained. "According to Turpol, the ground only shook in that way when a vortex was being used as transportation... someone must have travelled through the vortex - there can't be any other explanation," concluded the Bradley. "I wonder... do you think it might have been Sereny?"

"I sincerely hope you're right, Brad!" replied Musgrove.

"Well, if it was Sereny... we definitely have to get back into Pathylon - we have no choice," insisted Musgrove," as he released his grip on the ghost and clambered to his feet. "We have to deal with the Skeloyds... it's our only chance of finding the amulet before Basjoo Ma-otz destroys the kingdom."

216

Bradley stood next to the Mauled Miner and thought back to what Rathek had said before he was brutally murdered by the Troglobite creature. "Remember his last words... once inside the vortex - we must remember to take the right fork."

"That's all well and good, Brad... but we have to get past the Skeloyds first!" exclaimed Musgrove, as the Mauled Miner brushed past to lead the way.

"Well, I guess we're about to face our next challenge, mate," said Bradley. "Our friend here is keen to test out his trusty blade!"

Musgrove pulled at Bradley's arm. "I hate to admit this Brad, but I'm scared," he trembled. "The three of us are no match for these creatures and if what Turpol said is true... they are a savage bunch - we don't stand a chance, mate!"

Bradley held onto his friend's trembling hand to offer his assurance. Even though he was two years younger than Musgrove, he yet again displayed great courage in the face of danger. "We have to do this Muzzy, not just to save Pathylon... but to avenge Rathek's death and don't forget if that was Sereny entering the vortex we have to save her as well - as far as we know she has already travelled through to the other side."

"My god... I do hope Sereny is okay!" exclaimed Musgrove. "What if that wasn't her entering the vortex... do you think the chamber below the blue light... leads to Pathylon?"

"Let's just hope the noise we just heard was Sereny jumping into the vortex," assumed Bradley. "Come on Muzzy, the Mauled Miner is walking towards the light... we have to go through with this - so much depends on our bravery," he insisted and tugged at his friend's hand. "Now.... let's go!"

The boys caught up with the ghost and it did not take them long to reach a small sub-station about twenty metres short of the entrance to the vortex.

"They must be our Skeloyd friends, then?" surmised Musgrove, as two skeletal figures moved back and forth in front of the entrance. "They look quite scary and by the look of those sabres they're holding, we're in for a tough fight."

Bradley made an observation, as he pulled his Swiss army knife out of his pocket again. He drew the same lucky blade used to kill the maze-beast and smeared the creature's blood on either side of his face using the blunt edge of the blade to complete the effect of war-paint. "There only appears to be two of them... we may not need our weapons if we can cause a distraction - we stand a good chance of jumping into the vortex without having to fight."

"Are you really going to use that?" asked Musgrove and stared at the red parallel markings on Bradley's cheeks.

"If I have to... and if we fail to distract them - the Mauled Miner can't fight them alone," replied Bradley.

"Hey look Brad, our friend here is pointing to the left," replied Musgrove. "I can see the heads of another three of them behind some kind of control panel... you might need to use your knife after all!"

"Ah, yes... I see them - this is going to more difficult than I thought," declared Bradley, as he tapped on the Mauled Miner's back. "Can you create a diversion for me and Muzzy?"

The ghost nodded and reached into his utility belt again to draw out his knife. He ushered the boys to the bank of the metal switch housings at the end of the sub-station and then gave a sign, as if to tell the boys to wait for his signal. The

Mauled Miner then crouched behind a section-switch before disappearing from view.

"What do you think he's going to do?" asked Musgrove.

"Not sure, Muzzy... but whatever it is - we had better be ready," insisted Bradley, as the Mauled Miner raised his arm to indicate his intentions. "Here we go... get ready, Muzzy!"

Within seconds the ghost mysteriously appeared behind the three Skeloyds that were positioned at the control panel. Before they had chance to turn around the Mauled Miner carved them down with three swift actions from his knife. The two Skeloyds at the vortex did not hear the felling of their colleagues and continued to march in front of each other, as they passed the swirling kaleidoscopic entrance.

Bradley watched in amazement, as the ghost disappeared again only to reappear behind one of the Skeloyds guarding the vortex. "Come on Muzzy... it's time to help our friend - looks like it's us that will have to create the diversion!"

The two boys leapt out from behind the sub-station and ran towards the two guards, as they shouted out a tirade of obscenities. They waved their arms in the air, as the two Skeloyds looked over to the approaching threat and held their sabres aloft.

"Arrrrrrrrrghhhhhh!" shouted the boys with simultaneous effect, as they ran to within a metre of the Skeloyds.

"Now!" yelled Bradley. He shouted at the top of his voice, as he held his weapon aloft in one hand and secured the bag containing Rathek's with the other.

"Help us kill them, you plonker!" shouted Musgrove, as he looked over to the Mauled Miner and then launched himself towards the startled guards.

The ghost miner stood still and did nothing, as the two boys pounced at the Skeloyds. They had no option but to raise their right legs into a marshal arts position to counter the sabres of the creatures. The two Skeloyds were forced to the ground by the force of the boys steel toe-capped boots and with a swift follow up action both of the guards were knocked unconscious by simultaneous blows from the right fist of each boy hero.

It all happened within seconds and Bradley looked at Musgrove, as the two Skeloyds lay motionless in the stone dust. "Wow... what a rush, Muzzy - glad I didn't need to use my knife!"

"Rush... rush - I'll give you rush!" exclaimed Musgrove, as he aimed a barrage of abuse at the Mauled Miner. "Why didn't you do something... we could have been killed, you idiot!"

The disfigured miner stood motionless and calmly placed his knife back into his utility belt. Musgrove's words did not faze the faceless ghost and he turned towards the entrance to the vortex then held out his arm to direct the boys.

Bradley returned his open blade into the knife's housing and placed it carefully back in his pocket. He held onto Musgrove's arm. "Don't be too hard on him, Muzzy... he did his bit and we did ours - now let's get a move on!"

"Why didn't he kill them when he had the chance?" shouted Musgrove, as he struggled to release his friend's grip.

"He couldn't kill them... the last two guards had to survive - they are unconscious and that's all that matters," explained Bradley, as he let go of Musgrove's arm. "Think about it... we need the vortex to get back - if we had killed the last two Skeloyds then there wouldn't have been anyone left here to keep the vortex working!"

"Oh... so we just let these two flesh-eaten creatures survive to kill us when we get back then!" exclaimed Musgrove.

Bradley replied in a calm voice. "Better to cross that bridge than no bridge at all... I'm sure we'll be more than ready for them - at least we know what to expect now, so let's concentrate on the task in hand?"

"I guess you're right, Brad... as always." Musgrove acknowledged his friends calming influence and brushed past the Mauled Miner towards the entrance to the vortex. "Okay, let's go face-ache!"

"Don't be too hasty, Muzzy... remember what Rathek said," insisted Bradley. "Once inside... we have to take the right hand fork!"

"Yeah... you already said that ten minutes ago!" replied Musgrove, as he rolled his eyes in a nonchalant manner.

Bradley ignored Musgrove and he felt a damp patch on his thigh, as he looked down to feel the sodden leather pouch that was hanging from his belt. The ice pack protecting Rathek's heart was starting to melt and the cold water seeped out of the bag onto his bright orange overalls. He held on tightly to the hessian sack, in the knowledge that Meltor's life depended on the safe delivery of the vital organ to the ailing High Priest.

The ghost stood between the two nervous boys, as they joined hands and stared into the swirling gateway. Musgrove took a deep breath and gripped the Mauled Miners cold hand, as he prepared for the unknown.

Bradley continued to hold the pouch and concentrated his thoughts on their next move, as he calmly declared. "No use hanging around… we've got a job to do – let's do it!"

Without hesitation all three jumped into the Vortex of Silvermoor, as a series of flashing lightning strikes arced between the metal entrance and their steel toe-capped boots. The self-rescuers on their belts glowed like embers, as a multitude of coloured lights exploded into a crescendo of mini-explosions.

A final explosion projected firework-like sparks and yellow stars in all directions, as the entrance was filled with a bright white glow. Within seconds they were sent spinning into the infinite swirling spiral and disappeared from view.

25

The Battle for Trad

Back inside the cave below Mount Pero, Basjoo Ma-otz stood over the deceased Krogon. Harg was dead and the Hartopian had to decide whether to turn back or carry on through one of the tunnels that lead to the Mece village.

Before his untimely death, the Krogon had led Ma-otz to believe the middle tunnel was the safe way through but now the skeptical Hartopian doubted the old warrior's integrity. For all he knew, the middle tunnel could contain a dangerous hazard and the Krogon may have sub-consciously influenced him to take the wrong route.

Basjoo Ma-otz approached the junction in the cave where the three entrances to the tunnels met. He paused for a moment then looked back at the felled Krogon, as he muttered to himself. "Are you that intelligent to come up with a plan to send me to my death, Harg?" he then looked back at the choice ahead of him. "I think not... anyhow, I am not going back - so what have I got to lose?"

The Hartopian looked round again and took one last glance at the motionless corpse. "Let's see if you were right,

Krogon!" He surmised and let out a loud roar before heading into the middle tunnel.

The echo of his roar filled the tunnel, as he jumped occasionally to avoid any potential loose stones that could activate a trap door. His fears were overcome by his hapless fall and he soon realised his fate, as he landed awkwardly. He rolled forward about five metres before hitting the side of the tunnel wall and there was a loud explosion, as the floor started to shake. Basjoo Ma-otz looked back down the tunnel and witnessed the floor starting to fall away, as the continuous effect of the quake worked its way towards the terrified Hartopian.

Meanwhile back in the Devonian region, Varuna and his new army of Tree Elves marched on relentlessly towards the Royal City of Trad. The Hartopian sat proudly atop his newly claimed Koezard mount and assessed the horizon for the first sight of the cityscape. His traitor accomplice Flaglan rode close behind with her head lowered, as she slumped back in the saddle.

Varuna's authoritative approach had secured the backing of Flaglan's people and his lead role in the partnership was making a demeaning impression on the deflated sorceress. Flaglan was powerless to stop the Hartopian taking sole control of the Pathylian throne should they successfully defeat the noblemen in Trad.

The High Priestess lifted her head, as she urged her Koezard forward to ride by Varuna's side. "You think you have won, don't you?'

Varuna looked across to Flaglan and offered her a surprised look. "What are talking about, my dear... won what exactly?"

"You know what I mean, Varuna... you think you have control of my people - but they will see through your devious ways soon enough!" scorned the sorceress. "I know what you're like... I have witnessed your selfless acts before - as soon as we defeat the Devonians, you will have what you

224

want!" she revealed and cast the smirking Hartopian a disrespectful stare. "My people are not stupid and will see you for what you really are... a coward!"

Varuna continued to smile at the flustered female's rant and kicked his heels in to Shatar, as he rode on confidently. The Hartopian straightened his back and winked at the sorceress. "Flaglan, you worry too much about my impending treatment of your people... they will share our victory and reap the rewards that success brings - and I am pleased to hear you're confident about us defeating the Devonians," he declared and roared a stream of laughter, as he kicked harder to drive the reluctant Koezard forward.

Flaglan pulled a disbelieving face and tugged on the reigns to guide her mount away from the pompous Hartopian and muttered under her breath. "I'll have the last laugh, Varuna... you'll see!"

Sereny watched the spat between the two Pathylians with amusement from the cage. "Look at them, Turpol... they really don't get on with each other - do they?"

The dwarf smiled and nodded. "You'd have thought Flaglan would have learnt her lesson by now... she should know what Varuna is like - he is selfish, greedy and so obsessed with his intent to reign over Pathylon," explained Turpol. "King Luccese forgave her once for her treacherous behaviour during the last attempt to dethrone him... but this time he will show no mercy."

Sereny stopped herself from falling and held on to the bars of the cage, as the cart's wheels mounted a hump in the road. She asked her fellow prisoner a question, in a worried tone. "What will happen to us, Turpol... are they going to kill us?"

"I doubt it, little Miss... whilst Bradley is out there, Varuna will not harm you - should he be successful in taking control of the capital and resuming his false reign over the kingdom, you would be his insurance against any attack," replied the confident dwarf. "He will most likely keep you in the Royal Palace... as for me - I'm not so sure."

"What do you mean... why would he hurt you?" asked Sereny, as she raised her voice. "You pose no threat to him!"

"Shhhhhhhh," whispered the cautious Gatekeeper. "They will here you... now let's stay quiet - we must not attract attention to ourselves."

Sereny nodded, as the entourage suddenly came to a halt. The City of Trad could be seen in the distance and Varuna had commanded the first battalion of archers to make their way to the right and across a large open field that led to the eastern side of the city. The Hartopian waved his arm and directed a second battalion to make there way to the left along side the River Klomus.

The remaining Tree Elves moved forward along the road led by Varuna, as Flaglan held her flag standard steady. She looked up at the Haldon Forest emblem blazoned on the brightly coloured canvass, as it fluttered graciously in the breeze and glared into the back of Hartopian's head. "I do this for the freedom of the great forest... not for you, Varuna!"

The Tree Elves steering the cart cracked their reigns and the Hoffen moved off slowly and tracked the sorceress some twenty metres behind. Turpol held Sereny tightly and offered the frightened girl some words of assurance. "Stay behind me at all times... and whatever happens - keep your head down."

The command was given and the battalions of Tree Elves charged forward. The Hoffen pulling the cart galloped behind Flaglan's Koezard and Varuna led the army ahead, as Shatar twisted his large lizard-like head in response to the cruel lashing from the Hartopians whip. The army of traitors covered the ground to Trad in no time, as Varuna held up his arm and gave the order to stop.

The first two battalions of archers knelt down in precise lines and tilted backwards to point their bows into the air. Varuna pulled his arm down by his side, as thousands of bowstrings were pulled back. On his second command, the tension on the strings was released and a hail of arrows flew in the direction of the city. The deathly slithers of wood flew over the city walls and landed with killing precision, as many Devonian noblemen fell under the first attack.

As the second hail of arrows penetrated deep into the torsos of the embattled Devonian's, they scattered like a dysfunctional unit without any leadership. Without their High Priest Pavsik and their King, who languished in Freytorian exile, they were soon overcome and Varuna's army surged forward to take the city with ease.

The beaten Devonian's lowered their heads and cowered, as the Tree Elves chorused out a jubilant cheer. The surviving noblemen had to endure the sight of the victorious Hartopian entering the city gates of Trad, whilst their King was stranded far away in a foreign land.

Varuna was followed by closely Flaglan and the cart carrying the two prisoners, as the entourage circled around the courtyard in front of the royal palace. The victory precession finally came to a halt at the palace gates and the cart was ushered by ten Tree Elves into a cordoned off area.

Inside the cage, Turpol had laid over Sereny to offer her protection throughout the battle and she was now struggling to breath. "Come on Turpol... I think it's safe to get up now - you're squashing me." The girl prodded the dwarf's fat belly to get him to move but the Gatekeeper stayed motionless.

The cage door was unlocked and two grim faced Tree Elves climbed in. One of them lifted Turpol's body and the other pulled Sereny out from beneath the limp dwarf. Sereny cried out, as she was dragged kicking and screaming from the cage. "Turpol... no!"

The sight of the dead dwarf sickened Sereny, as the archers pulled the limp body out of the cage and threw him on the dusty ground. The Gatekeeper had eleven arrows sticking out of his body, as one of the Tree Elves started to laugh and pulled them out one by one. "Looks like the old fella got struck by a few stray ones!"

Sereny released herself from the grip of the other Tree Elf and rushed over to Turpol. "Get off him... and leave him alone you animals!" Cried the distressed girl. "Give him some respect... you horrible evil creatures!"

A group of Tree Elves pulled Sereny way from the stricken dwarf, as Flaglan approached. "What's all the fuss about?"

A Tree Elf soldier replied. "The girl went all hysterical on us because the little fella got killed, my lady!"

Flaglan laughed and her voice croaked, as she failed to control her delight at the sight of the dead dwarf. "Some High Priest of Krogonia you turned out to be, Turpol!" She teased and kicked Turpol's defenseless midriff.

Sereny released herself from Tree Elves hold again and ran over to Flaglan. The girl lunged forward and dug her finger nails into the sorceresses face. "Take this... you evil witch!"

"Arrrrrghhhh!" Screamed Flaglan and reacted by pushing the possessed girl to the floor, as she reached up to feel blood streaming from her cheeks. She instantly reached down and detached a jewelled pouch from her slender waist band. Inside the pouch was a mirror and the High Priestess inspected the parallel cuts to her beautiful face. "Take the little harlot into the palace... I will deal with her later!"

"What about the dwarf, my lady?" asked one of the Elves.

"Burn him!" replied the bitter sorceress.

"No!" cried Sereny.

"Silence you pathetic human!" exclaimed Flaglan, as she pointed to the cart. "Show her and these defeated Devonian imbeciles what happens when anyone attacks my beautiful face!"

Sereny watched helplessly, as a group of Tree Elves lifted Turpol's body back into the cage on top of the cart. The Gatekeeper's body lay motionless in the straw, as flaming torches were lit and thrown onto the makeshift funeral pyre. The Hoffen tethered to the cart reared and then bolted forward, as the blazing cortege was pulled out of the palace grounds.

Varuna arrived just in time to witness the inferno that destroyed the dwarf's body and Sereny wept uncontrollably as the lazing cart disappeared into the distance. The

228

Hartopian approached the tearful girl. "This is what happens when you meddle in business that does not concern you!" he roared, as he looked at Flaglan's blood stained face. "And look what you have done to my future Queen!"

Sereny responded by staring momentarily at Flaglan and then at the raging Hartopian. "You are both evil and cruel... you're not fit to be King and Queen - why did you have to burn his body?"

Flaglan grabbed Sereny's hair and pulled her head back. "You haven't seen anything yet, young female... just wait till you see what we are going to do with your precious Bradley Baker - once he hears you are our prisoner, he's bound to make an attempt to save you and we'll be waiting to kill him!"

Varuna put his arm around Flaglan, as he instructed the Tree Elves to place the girl within a secure bed chamber inside the royal quarters of the palace. "Make sure you put a round the clock guard on the girl's door... I don't want anything to happen to our precious bait!" growled the Hartopian, as he guided the wounded sorceress towards the main palace doors. "Now come with me, my dear... let's get those nasty cuts looked at - we'll have you looking perfect again in no time."

Flaglan looked into the devious red eyes of the Hartopian. "As soon as my archers had taken control of Trad, I was going to seek revenge on you, Varuna... for taking control of my army - but that girl's action has changed my mind."

"That's good news," replied Varuna, as he moved a stray lock of fallen hair away from the sorceresses deep green eyes. "I meant what I said... I'd be honoured if you would be my Queen and together we can rule over this land for many years!" he declared. "We will produce many siblings and they will continue our blood line to secure the realm forever... Luccese will never regain control of Pathylon again!"

Flaglan flinched slightly and held her hand over her face, as the wound inflicted by Sereny sent a sharp pain through her cheek. "I would be happy to be your Queen... I think we are going to work well together - Pathylon is ours now and its time to wreak havoc throughout this kingdom for eternity!"

"Excellent, my dear... if only you knew how happy that makes me feel!" replied the beaming Hartopian.

Flaglan changed the subject of conversation, as she recognised another challenge that they would have to prepare for. "You do realise that when Luccese and Meltor hear of our victory... they will send word to the Galetians and your fellow Hartopians in the Blacklands to challenge our rule."

"Let's not worry ourselves about that right now, my dear... anyhow, the Hartopians would not dare to challenge me and as for the Galetians - we'll deal with them when the time comes!"

"Should we not tell our army to prepare?" pleaded Flaglan, as her chest heaved nervously in anticipation of the Hartopian's advances.

"The Galetians will not make a move without their beloved Meltor leading them... it will be some time before they can launch an attack on Trad - now let us make use of the respite and spend some quality time together."

Flaglan knew there was no going back now and she nodded, as Varuna took hold of her slender arm and pulled her close to his battle robes. His face glowed with anticipation of finally consummating his feelings for the voluptuous lady of the forest and he escorted her into the palace.

In the knowledge that Sereny was locked away safely, they made their way along the ornate corridors of the residential area of the palace and discussed how to stop Basjoo Ma-otz from ruining their new found status. The Hartopian and the High Priestess continued their discussions, as they entered the King's bed chamber. Varuna was impatient and did not want to talk any more, as Flaglan made one last attempt to repel Varuna's advances but her lust for control over Pathylon made her open to his groping.

The two hearts inside Varuna's chest pounded with anticipation and his bad breath filled the air, as saliva dripped from his yellow fangs. He bit into Flaglan's shoulder and she pulled her body back to take one last look at the Hartopian's severed wrist, as she closed her eyes to ignore the repulsiveness of the injury inflicted by Harg during their last encounter.

The two traitor's evil partnership was now official and they had to hope that Bradley Baker would defeat Ma-otz and then come after the girl. The new King and Queen of Pathylon would have to wait and see whether their reign would be short lived, but in the meantime they focused on each other's personal needs.

26

The Klomus Hawk

Bradley and Musgrove held on to each other's arms like a pair of skydivers, as they twisted and turned inside the Vortex of Silvermoor. Their heads crashed together and Musgrove's cap lamp dislodged, as it swung by its cable like a yoyo. Bradley reached out to prevent the light from smashing into their faces and managed to attach it back to his friend's helmet in a single swinging action.

The two boy's continued to spin aggressively, as the kaleidoscope effect of the swirling lights inside the time portal made it difficult for them to focus through the tubular vortex ahead.

The Mauled Miner followed in close pursuit but he was beginning to fall back, as his ghostly form span like a boomerang out of control. The boys were unaware of his failure to keep up with them, as the fork that Rathek had predicted appeared in the distance.

Bradley managed to pull Musgrove closer and they linked their arms around each other, as the light from their lamps bounced off the walls of the vortex like laser beams. The fork was now within a few metres and the boys maneuvered their bodies to the right, as a multitude of shooting stars flew out in all directions around the Y-shaped junction in the vortex.

"Hold on tight, Muzzy... we have to make sure we take the right fork!" shouted Bradley. "Get ready to move quickly in the same direction!"

"Okay, Brad... here we go!" exclaimed Musgrove, as they curved their bodies in parallel to ensure the motion of the portal pulled them down the correct path.

They successfully negotiated the acute turn in the vortex but the ferocity of the bend split the two friends' apart and they span out of control. The boys collided with each other several times and bounced off the side of the vortex, as the colours within the portal changed dramatically. The light from their cap lamps dulled considerably, as more stars and explosions erupted repeatedly around the time travellers.

Bradley steadied his flight path and held his arms out to simulate an airplane preparing to land. He looked across to Musgrove who had copied his aviation procedure and they smiled at each other in encouragement.

Bradley called to his friend, as they flew in tandem. "This is so cool, Muzzy!"

Musgrove laughed and then displayed a confident flight simulation maneuver, as he twisted his body to perform a complete three hundred and sixty degree turn. "Try that one, Brad!"

"You're mad, Muzzy!" shouted Bradley in an excited tone. "I'll give it a go... but watch this one first!" he declared and pulled is knees towards his chest thcn tipped his head downwards.

Bradley started to spin forward with a rapid motion within the fast current of the vortex and then lifted his head again to stop the tumbling action. He then held out his arms to regain his composure. "What did you think of that one?"

"Not bad!" replied Musgrove and he turned to see if the Mauled Miner was watching their antics. "Hey, Brad... he's gone!"

Before Bradley had chance to reply, the exit from the vortex appeared and the two boys were tossed out of the spiral. They were airborne for a few seconds then landed hard with a thud, as their helpless bodies rolled across the sandy ground until they collided with a row of shrubs.

A combination of legs and arms became entangled in the course foliage, as their excited body language turned into disgruntled groans. Bradley lifted one of his legs out of the shrubbery and managed to flip himself on to his stomach. "Ouch, that hurt... are you okay, Muzzy?"

No reply came back from Musgrove and Bradley called out again. There was still no answer from his friend, as the thorns cut through his overalls and into his legs. Blood started to seep through his clothing and he finally managed to crawl out of the bushes. He sat upright and could just make out one of Musgrove's boots but the rest of his friend's body was hidden in the prickly shrub.

There was a slight groan from the bush. "Errrrghhh."

"Muzzy... are you alright?" shouted Bradley, as he silently suffered the pain and managed to stand up at last.

"Errrrghhh," repeated Musgrove and attempted to release himself from the tangled foliage. "Get me out of here!"

Bradley rubbed his legs to numb the pain from the cuts and made his way around the bush to witness Musgrove in an upside down position with only his legs sticking out of the shrub. "You remind me of when I fell in some brambles when I was kid!" replied Bradley, as he chuckled to himself. "I was stuck there for ages until my Grandfather pulled me out!"

Musgrove reacted by wiggling his legs about in the air. The pain in Bradley's legs quickly diminished at the sight of the stricken teenager and he could not stop himself from laughing, as he placed his hand over his mouth to prevent his friend from hearing his outburst.

Bradley need not have been concerned about his friend's feelings because Musgrove could not hear anything. As well as being stuck in the bush, he had also managed to land head first into some warm soggy substance. Unbeknown to the boys, the shrub was also home to a native flax, which had been sick only a few minutes previous. Musgrove's head was now partially submerged in the wild animal's vomit.

Bradley tried to stop sniggering and took hold of his friend's boots. He readied himself to pull Musgrove free, who was now starting to get anxious. The trapped boy mumbled a few more words of frustration and his head was finally released from the regurgitated food.

Some of the foliage clung to the thick gung, which moved slowly down Musgrove's long blond hair. He scrunched his nose and pulled a disgusted face, as the smell of the dark brown slime intensified. "This stuff stinks!" he exclaimed and started to wipe his face with his sleeve.

"You smell like a sewer, mate," insisted Bradley, as he pulled some dry grass out of the ground. "Here... use this to wipe it off."

Musgrove replied. "It's gonna take more than that... we need to find a stream or something - there's gotta be water nearby."

As the boys scanned their surroundings, they realised the magnificence of the landscape around them. Bradley and Musgrove stared open mouthed at the snow-capped mountains that towered into the clouds on the horizon.

"Wow!" exclaimed Musgrove, as he clenched the dried grass in his hand. "This place is amazing... it reminds me of the school skiing holiday last year, when we went to *Pinzolo* in Italy - but these mountains seem much taller."

Bradley acknowledged Musgrove's description of the mountain range. "We must be in the Unknown Land... and these magnificent peaks must be the Peronto Alps."

"Well... at least we've arrived in the right place," replied Musgrove, as both he and Bradley continued to survey the alpine landscape.

Bradley's attention was interrupted by a large bird that circled above. He followed its elegant decent, as it flew down and landed on the dead branches of a nearby felled tree. The underbelly of the bird was magnificent and it's orange and yellow plumage shone like gold. It had unusual striking features, which made the creature incredibly intimidating. The vibrant red headdress matched its breast that extended to six legs, each with extremely sharp talons that clung tightly to the branch.

Bradley whispered to Musgrove. "Hey, Muzzy... take a look at that bird - it's got six legs."

Musgrove stopped his admiration of the mountain range and looked over to the eagle-like creature, as it cleaned one of its outspread wings with its blue beak. "It's beautiful... I've never seen anything like that before - look at the colour of its feathers."

The huge bird seemed unconcerned with the boys' presence and continued to inspect its plumage. Bradley's attention was distracted away from the bird and he noticed a cave-like opening in the rocks near to where the creature had landed. "That must be the time portal's entrance... we had better mark this spot so we can find it easily when we get back."

"I don't think we need to mark anything, Brad... I'm not likely to forget that bush where we landed in a hurry!" replied Musgrove and laughed at his own expense.

"Hey, Muzzy... I've just realised something'" declared Bradley, as he walked over to the vortex entrance. "We've been so wrapped up in the beautiful landscape and the colour of the bird's feathers... we've forgotten about our friend - where's the Mauled Miner?"

The bird fluttered its wings and edged its way along the branch using all six claws, as Musgrove joined Bradley at the entrance and peered into the void.

Musgrove reassured the frightened bird. "Steady my friend... we won't hurt you," he said in a calm voice, then looked inside the gap in the rock. "The poor fella obviously didn't make it... let's check inside - in case he's lying in there."

"No... don't go back in, Muzzy," insisted Bradley and pulled at his friend's arm to stop him moving forward. "It's too dangerous... you might get sucked back into Silvermoor!"

"I guess you're right... we'll just have to leave without faceless then," agreed Musgrove and he turned to look at the bird again, which was now more relaxed in their presence. "I think it likes me, Brad."

"I'm sure you two would get on famously, but we'd better get a move on, Muzzy," suggested Bradley and walked away from the portal's entrance. "We also have to find Sereny... if it was her that travelled through the vortex - we need to know if she's okay before we start looking for the Mece."

At that moment the bird fluttered its wings again and to their astonishment, it spoke gently with a slight croak in its voice. "I have travelled from the Forest of Haldon... I was told of your impending arrival by the bird-whistler and I am here to inform you of the current situation in Pathylon."

Bradley and Musgrove could not believe what they were hearing and their jaws dropped, as they stared at the magnificent creature. The bird jumped down from the branch and waddled awkwardly over to the two boys. "Don't be alarmed... my name is Ploom and I am a rare breed of Klomus Hawk - there are only three of my kind left in Pathylon," explained the bird, as the boys closed there mouths simultaneously. "We live in the great forest... near to the River Klomus and our identity is protected by the royal congress - we only serve the King of Pathylon in extreme circumstances and I have been summoned to deliver a very important message to you."

"Nice to meet you, Ploom!" replied Bradley and asked the bird. "Why are there only three of you left?"

The bird dropped its head forward and paused to regain its composure. "There was a mysterious disease that spread though the forest some years ago... almost all the Klomus Hawks died - leaving just three surviving females, including me."

"So there are no males left to breed with?" replied Musgrove.

"No... we survived the disease because we happened to be part of the King's private collection and therefore avoided coming into contact with the virus," explained the bird. "As soon as it was declared safe again, the King set us free to live out the rest of our lives in the forest but we still work for the Luccese occasionally as messengers - but only on specific missions of great importance."

"So that's why you are so far away from your home and the safety of the forest," declared Bradley, as he stroked the creature's headdress.

Ploom shook her head to realign the plumage then fluttered her wings again and explained. "Yes, I am very far from my home but I have to inform you that the Shallock Tower has been destroyed, Varuna has escaped and Flaglan has joined forces with him... and to make matters even worse, a Freytorian Sea Commander by the name of Norsk has deployed an ice-cloud, so the threat to Pathylon is no longer just about Basjoo Ma-otz and the Amulet - there are now three strains of evil attacking the kingdom from all directions."

The boys listened intently to the clear explanation provided by the tame Klomus Hawk. They were now fully informed of the difficult tasks that lay ahead of them, as they took a few moments to reflect and digest the information. As the boys contemplated their next move, the bird spoke again. "I heard you mention a name... Sereny - is it a young girl you speak of?"

Bradley confirmed with no hesitation. "Yes... have you seen her, Ploom?"

"I haven't seen her but I have heard she is alive... the girl was captured in Krogonia by Varuna and Flaglan," replied the Hawk. "As far as I know, she is being kept prisoner inside the palace."

Bradley surmised. "If Sereny was captured in Krogonia... she must have travelled there via another time portal - there's no way she could have come through the Vortex of Silvermoor and travelled so far on foot."

"Maybe the trap door under the blue light leads direct to Krogonia?" suggested Musgrove.

Bradley nodded. "Yes... so it couldn't have been Sereny, who travelled through the Vortex of Silvermoor!"

"Then who was it?" asked Musgrove.

"I'm sure we'll find out soon enough!" replied Bradley in reassuring tone. "At least we know Sereny is alive!"

The Klomus Hawk interrupted the two boys and spoke again. "My task here is complete and I have made you both aware of the situation back in Pathylon... I must now return to the forest but before I go - I must direct you to the Mece village," insisted Ploom. "Just follow the stream to the base of Mount Pero and then the take the pathway that leads to the skull."

"The skull?" exclaimed Bradley.

"You'll know what I mean when you get there... it's obvious - there's a large vertical rock face shaped like a kalmogs head and it looks like a skull!" replied the bird. "It was carved into the rock by the Mece to ward off intruders and marks the spot where the entrance to a cave that leads to the Mece village," she explained. "Oh... and one more thing - when you enter the cave you will have to choose from three tunnels."

"What will happen if we choose the wrong one?" asked Bradley.

Ploom ruffled her feathers again in readiness for her long journey. "Well... let's put it this way," she crowed. "It's a long drop if you pick the wrong one... so be very careful - now, if there is nothing else - I must get going!"

Musgrove afforded Bradley a glancing look and pointed to the canvass pouch on his utility belt. "What about Rathek's heart... Ploom could deliver it for us."

Bradley smiled and nodded. "Brilliant idea, Muzzy... I'd forgotten about Rathek's heart - I'd better check to make sure it isn't damaged," he continued and carefully removed the canvass bag from his belt.

"A heart you say?" enquired the bird. "For whom is it intended?"

"Meltor!" replied Bradley, as he opened the protective covering to reveal the crystals that secured the living organ. "Phew... thank goodness - it's okay."

Ploom stared at the precious cargo and asked. "I'll do what I can to help... what do you suggest?"

Bradley answered. "Would your strong wings be able to carry Rathek's heart as far as the island of Freytor?"

The bird paused for a moment and puffed out her red breast. "That's a big ask... but I am sure I can manage the journey - Meltor is great leader and I'll do everything I can to ensure he receives the heart as fast as my wings can get me there."

"Then I need you to take it to the medical centre, which is located in the island's capital Frey and ensure Rathek's final request is honoured... Meltor will need a life-saving operation if he is to survive - I'll also attach a note to inform them of Rathek's wishes," insisted Bradley and he started to scribble a message onto the back of the map.

"You're defacing that sacred piece of paper again, Brad!" exclaimed Musgrove. "Are you sure you should be doing that?"

Bradley replied, as he continued to write. "Well, we don't need it anymore... we know our way back - so I don't think anyone will mind me using it as note paper."

Musgrove hunched his shoulders and took the map from his determined friend then secured the note and canvass pouch to one of the bird's legs. "Thank you for doing this, Ploom... Meltor will really appreciate your help!"

The Klomus Hawk puffed out its vibrant multi-coloured plumage again and replied. "It's an honour... as I said, Meltor is a great High Priest and I'll make sure the package is delivered to Frey in good time!"

Without any further hesitation, the bird spread its impressive wingspan, as all six legs launched its muscular frame into the air. The Klomus Hawk took flight and the strength of its wings helped it to soar up into the clouds with great speed, as it disappeared from sight within seconds.

Bradley thought for a moment then reiterated that they must now use the time effectively to stop Basjoo Ma-otz placing the Amulet of Silvermoor back on to the sacred ledge of Mount Pero. "We are here to help save Pathylon and we have some difficult tasks ahead of us, Muzzy," he insisted.

Musgrove suggested that they discard some of their equipment. "We should leave our hard-hats and self rescuers near the entrance to the vortex... we're not going to need them any more - it looks like a long walk to Mount Pero and we need to lose as much weight as possible."

Bradley agreed. "Do you agree we should take the cap lamps though?"

"Yeah, definitely... they weigh quite a bit but they could prove useful - especially when we get into the mountains," replied Musgrove, as he discarded the self rescuer from his belt. "Looking at the sun's current position in the sky, it's going to be nightfall soon... we'd better get a move on - and I'd like to dip my head in the stream as well, to get rid of this slime in my hair."

Bradley smiled and nodded. "Not a bad idea, Muzzy... you do whiff a bit," he agreed, as he covered their helmets and safety equipment with some loose foliage. "I'm gonna take my mobile phone though," he stated and attempted to turn the power on. "It's still not working... but you never know!"

"You and that blinking mobile phone... you're inseparable - take the damn thing if it makes you happy!" replied Musgrove and he commented on their overalls. "Anyhow, more importantly... we hardly fit in with these orange clothes - do we?"

Bradley discarded the plastic shower cap that had protected the telephone and placed the device back in his pocket, as he replied. "It's not like last time, Muzzy... everyone knows we are making this particular journey - I don't think it's going to make any difference to the Mece or anyone else *for-that-matter* what we are wearing." He concluded and checked his other pocket to make sure the Swiss army knife was still secure.

Musgrove shrugged his shoulders again and accepted his friend's explanation, as he rolled up his sleeves. Bradley encouraged him to move on, as they set off in the direction of the stream that led to the base of Mount Pero.

27

The Mece

A frightened and desperate Basjoo Ma-otz clung tightly to a stone ledge, which had been formed by the crumbling rocks inside the cave at the base of Mount Pero. The tunnel floor had completely disappeared and he was stranded above a gaping precipice that echoed to the sound of falling stones. The Hartopian tried to climb upwards, as the leather straps on his footwear slipped on the tough granite. He finally managed to get a foot hold to secure a temporary position but his attempts to escape the abyss were proving fruitless.

Basjoo Ma-otz clung perilously to the ledge, which was positioned some ten metres and more down from the original floor level. The desperate half-bread carefully turned his head and looked upwards, as he shouted. "Can anyone hear me... is there anybody up there?"

The helpless Hartopian was exhausted and he stopped calling out, as he rested his head for a few moments against the rough surface of the solid granite. With his weasel-like ear pressed uncomfortably against the cold stone, he heard a scraping sound emanating from the rock just below his feet. He looked down and witnessed a metal spike shoot out of the wall, which looked like a large tooth biting through a piece of flesh. The sharp object disappeared and left a clean hole in the rock and within seconds it reappeared again. This continued until a large gap had been created that was big enough to fit a body through it.

The Hartopian clung even tighter to the ledge, as a white fury creature appeared out of the hole. The strange species turned its face upwards to face Ma-otz and its jet black eyes shone like two round balls of polished ebony.

Basjoo Ma-otz slipped and he grasped the rock to regain his footing, as he called down. "Are you here to help me?"

The creature did not answer and disappeared back into the hole. The Hartopian groaned and waited a few seconds before shouting down again. "Please help me... my hands are aching and I am losing my grip!"

Suddenly, an arm appeared from the gap in the rock and threw a rope up towards the startled Ma-otz. He reached out instinctively and grabbed it at the first attempt. Without hesitation he released his hold on the stone ledge and grabbed the rope with both paws, as he placed his faith in the unknown rescuer. The Hartopian fell into the darkness and regretted his decision, as he continued to fall into the abyss at rapid speed. There was a sudden jolt when the length of the rope reached its limit and the weight of the trusting Hartopian hung like a lead weight. He held on tightly and sighed, as he was hoisted back towards the hole.

It did not take long for Basjoo Ma-otz to reach the gap in the wall, as the same white fury arm reached out to grab his paw and pulled him to safety. The Hartopian held on tightly to the rope until he had reached the safety of the hole. He looked ahead and was faced with the soles of the creature's feet, as it crawled away on all fours along the narrow tunnel.

Basjoo Ma-otz did not attempt to make conversation and followed the creature along the tunnel until they reached daylight at the other end. The Hartopian adjusted his eyes to the outside light and focussed on the strange looking being. It's long snout and flax-like ears reminded him of his own kind but the creature was covered in white fur and its stance was slightly hunched. It wore animal skin clothing that had been stitched together crudely with what looked like lengths of reed. It was a very primitive looking creature and displayed no intentions of opening a dialogue with the Hartopian.

Basjoo Ma-otz mirrored the creature's silence and then suddenly realised that his sacred staff was missing. He dropped to his knees and put his head in his hands. "It's all been a waste of time... without the staff, I am powerless - why did I bother?"

The creature finally broke its silence and spoke calmly. "Is that the Staff of Evil you speak of?" it declared and pointed to a wooden walk bridge that spanned a narrow gorge separating the base of Mount Pero from the Mece village.

The long wooden pole was balancing tentatively on the rungs of the rope handled walk bridge. A gentle breeze swung the bridge and it creaked as the staff tipped slightly. Ma-otz got to his feet and made his way over to the bridge. "Is this thing safe to cross?" he asked.

The creature nodded and approached the Hartopian. "Let me get it for you... I do not want you to fall - my people have been waiting a long time for this moment."

Basjoo Ma-otz stepped back to let the creature pass. "Then you must be from the Mece tribe!"

"Yes, I am one of the Mece... but there are very few of us left - the Troglobites come every day to take our elderly and weak," replicd the creature. "Let me save this thing you call the *Staff of Evil* and I will meet you at the other side... there is much to talk about but I will let my Father explain what you need to do next," it insisted. "Wait here till I reach the other side... this bridge cannot take the weight of two."

"What is your name?" ask the Hartopian.

"My name is Wuku... I am the Chief's daughter - my Father is called Kuma." she replied.

"Oh... you're a female!" exclaimed Ma-otz.

"You sound surprised!" replied Wuku, as she took the first delicate steps across the bridge.

At last she reached the centre of the bridge, as it swayed uncontrollably. The staff teetered on the edge and Ma-otz called out, as it started to tilt. "Do not lose the sacred staff... please do not let it fall!"

The bridge swayed too much and the staff started to fall, as Wuku dived forward. She caught her foot in the runners, as she fell off the edge and reached out to grab the staff. The Mece creature held on to the staff with one hand and pulled herself back up with the other in what seemed like a well rehearsed action.

Basjoo Ma-otz jumped up and punched the air with his clenched fist. "Yessss... well done, my friend - great catch, Wuku!"

The Mece female ran over to the other side and encouraged the Hartopian to follow her lead. Basjoo Ma-otz checked his pouch for the Amulet and once he was satisfied it was secure, he ran across the bridge to join Wuku.

"Now... I will take you to see my Father," she exclaimed and they ran into the village, which was made up of twenty or so mud huts erected on wooden stilts with straw covered roofs.

They arrived at the largest hut in the centre of the village and set of wooden steps led up to the entrance. Wuku shouted up to attract the attention of its inhabitants. "Father... the visitor we have been waiting for from Pathylon - he has arrived!"

Basjoo Ma-otz waited in anticipation, as a mature and rather portly Mece creature appeared at the doorway. "Is that your Father?"

"No... that is my older brother - Rama," she replied and shouted up again in a determined tone. "Rama... please ask our Father to come outside - you can tell him it's safe!"

Rama turned to face the doorway and then called back down to his sister. "Father asks... does the stranger bring with him the blue light of Mount Pero?"

The Hartopian stepped forward and reached into the pouch on his belt. He pulled out the Amulet and held it up. "Is this what to you are talking about... is this the blue light?"

Wuku's black eyes glistened at the sight of the sacred jewel that wad sparkling at the centre of the ornate necklace and exclaimed. "At last we are saved... Rama, tell Father to come outside - quick!"

Meanwhile, Bradley and Musgrove had passed the carved skull and were entering the cave. They moved forward tentatively and it wasn't long before they stumbled across the old Krogons corpse.

Bradley crouched down and recognised him immediately. "Oh my god... I don't believe it, Muzzy - it's Harg!"

"Is he dead?" asked Musgrove.

"As a dodo... but he's still warm - it must have happened quite recently," replied Bradley. "I've a feeling Basjoo Ma-otz has something to do with this... look at the marks on Hargs body - it looks like some electrical bolt has hit him and the only thing I can think of that would leave a mark like that is the Staff of Evil!"

Musgrove knelt down next to his friend and felt Hargs body. "You're right, Brad... he is still warm - that means we can't be too far behind the Hartopian."

The expression on Bradley's face changed to surprise and got to his feet, as he felt the mobile phone in his pocket vibrate. "What the eck!" he exclaimed, as the high-pitched ring tone pinged out. He pulled the device from his pocket and looked at the screen. "Look at that, Muzzy!"

Musgrove stared at the dazzling blue gemstone on the screen, as it flashed continuously. "Well whadda ya know... the blinking phone does work over here!"

"It did the same thing on my birthday... just before the embarrassing candle blowing routine - look at the name under the network signal, *TECO*!"

"Never heard of that network... maybe it has something to do with Pathylon," suggested Musgrove. "The blue crystal on the screen could be receiving a signal from the Amulet... see if you can bypass the sapphire by inputting a pass code!"

Bradley paused for a moment and then pressed a few buttons on the handset. "I'm going to try something... now - let's see if this works!" he exclaimed, as he pressed the letters and then read them out one by one. "P, A, T, H, Y, L, O, N !"

"Anything happened?" asked Musgrove.

"No... damn - I thought that would work!" exclaimed Bradley in a disappointing tone.

Musgrove took the phone. "Let me try!" he insisted and pressed both his thumbs on the keypad, as he read out another set of letters. "S, I, L, V, E, R, M, O, O, R !"

Still nothing happened and the crystal continued to flash. Bradley insisted that Musgrove hand him the phone and as he did so, the device bleeped. Musgrove looked at his friend for a reaction and asked. "Did it work?"

"Yep... the blue gem has finally disappeared from the screen and it looks like some sort of satellite navigation system has booted up - this is really weird!" declared Bradley and a location search icon appeared on the screen. "It's just like Dad's *Sat-Nav* in his car... it's starting to search for our location!"

The boys watched in amazement as a map appeared on the screen and an animated pin-head fell to mark the spot. Bradley observed. "It's doing the same sort of thing that a Sat-Nav would do... the pin has located Mount Pero - it's marked our location!"

Before Musgrove could concur, the phone's screen went blank and the device shut down. Bradley pressed the on/off button several times but the phone would not restart. "I don't believe this... the blinking battery must be flat - now what do we do?"

Musgrove moved away from his friend and focussed his attention on the tunnel entrances. "Maybe we should forget about your mobile phone for the moment and concentrate on how we're gonna get through to the other side," he said

248

calmly and walked over to the junction of the three arches. "Come over here, Brad and take a look at this."

Bradley joined the teenager and peered into the middle tunnel, as he placed the lifeless phone back in his pocket. Musgrove declared. "There's no floor... but plenty of dust flying around in that one."

"Well observed, Muzzy... Basjoo Ma-otz must have gone through there but I've got a feeling he might not have make it - but we'd better continue," insisted Bradley. "We have to try one of the other tunnels!"

"Which one?" asked Musgrove, as he shone the full beam from his cap lamp down the first tunnel. "This one looks clear."

"I trust your judgement," replied Bradley. "Let's go for it... we don't have time to delay - if Basjoo Ma-otz did survive, he will have reached the Mece by now!"

The two boys ignored the risk and ran into the first tunnel. Bradley led the way and called out to Musgrove. "Whatever happens, Muzzy... keep running as fast as you can!"

"Okay!" panted Musgrove, as a slight tremor rumbled beneath their feet. "Something's happening, Brad... the floor is moving!"

Both boys picked up their pace and sprinted faster, as the floor behind Musgrove started to crumble away. Every time he lifted his feet the floor disintegrated into dust, as the light at the end of the tunnel appeared in the distance.

"Keep going, Brad!" shouted Musgrove, as his foot slipped into the crumbling rock. "Don't think I'm gonna make it... but keep going!"

Bradley continued to run towards the daylight and managed to turn his head, as Musgrove stumbled. He continued to run and pulled the cap lamp from his belt, as he through it back. The lamp head reached its limit and the cable tensioned, as it extended its maximum length. "Grab it, Muzzy!"

Musgrove reached out but failed to grasp the lamp head. With only a few metres left till he reached solid ground, the floor beneath the stricken boy gave way completely and he began to fall. Bradley retrieved the cable to create a lasso around his head and released it again in a final attempt to save his friend.

Musgrove reached up instinctively, as the cable wrapped around one of his wrists and his head struck the side of the rock face. He was knocked unconscious and swung helplessly, as the cable tightened to secure his fall.

The ground beneath Bradley's feet crumbled and he dove forward on to the solid, as he landed safely outside the tunnel exit. The cable stretched to breaking point, as the weight of Musgrove's body pulled on Bradley's utility belt. The belt looped over his bottom and down to his legs, as he instinctively bent his knees to stop it slipping any further. "Arrrrrghhhh!" he cried, as the leather strap dug into his overalls and the excruciating pain penetrated the back of both legs. He felt himself being pulled into the tunnel, as Musgrove's limp body slipped further into the abyss.

"Arrrrrgggghhhhh!" cried Bradley again, as he tried to ignore the open wounds that had been cut by the belt through his clothing. "Hang on, Muzzy!"

Musgrove was still unconscious and offered no reply, as his weight pulled heavily on Bradley's legs. The brave hero did not know whether his friend was still alive but with the pain running through his legs, he certainly knew he was still attached to the cable. Bradley reached out to take hold of protruding rock and placed both hands around the stone, as he clasped the rough surface. The skin on his fingers peeled away like the zest of a lemon and he cried out in more pain. "Arrrrrrgggggghhhh!" he cried, as the warm feeling of blood ran down his arms. "I'm not going to lose you... we've come this far and you aren't falling down that hole - not on my watch!" he shouted and thought beyond the pain, as he started to haul himself forward.

Bradley conjured an image in his mind and thought back to his last adventure in Pathylon. He visualised Meltor, as they were saying their goodbyes. Meltor's words echoed in his head; *'You are the eternal chosen one, Bradley Baker... never misuse your powers and always put them to good use!'*

Bradley shook the thought out of his head and focussed on the blood stained stone, as he summoned all his strength. "Arrrrrgggghhhhh!" he screamed again and pulled his body towards his hands until his torso rested on top of the stone. He twisted his body so his bottom rested behind the stone and then sat upright. He started to pull the cable and both his bloody hands slipped, as the cable squelched in his raw grip.

Bradley continued to pull on the cable and Musgrove's wrists appeared at the edge of the hole. He quickened his pace and placed his foot behind the stone, as the last reserves of energy dissipated from his upper body. The cable started to fray, as it rubbed against the sand-like surface. Bradley could see that the cable was about to snap so he quickly double-wrapped it around his lower arm. He leant back and exerted one final pull, as Musgrove's body was dragged onto solid ground. The exhausted boy fell backwards and his chest rose up and down violently. He breathed heavily and every muscle in his aching body pumped like a beating heart, as he covered his face to shield his eyes from the brightness of the sky.

Musgrove regained consciousness and let out a huge groan, as he moved his head. The teenager turned to face the soles of Bradley's boots, as his brave friend lay still. He reached over and grabbed the toe cap of his boot, as he shook Bradley's foot. "Hey, Brad... you okay!"

Bradley lifted his head off the floor and sat upright to look at Musgrove, as he smiled bravely through the pain. "Thank goodness you're okay... thought for a minute there, I was going to lose you!"

Musgrove started to laugh. "You should see your face, Brad... ha-ha - that's funny!"

Bradley clenched his sore hands and examined his face with the tips of fingers. "What's wrong with my face?"

Musgrove was referring to the two hand prints left by the blood. "You look like some Red Indian from a cowboy

251

movie!" exclaimed the grateful boy. "Seriously though, Brad... thank you for saving my life - that must have taken enormous strength."

Bradley continued to nurse his wounds and touched the backs of his knees. "You can thank Meltor... when I was about to lose you, I thought about the words he said to me back along - it seemed to summon an inner strength that I didn't realise had!"

"Well, whatever or whoever did that... it certainly worked - maybe this is something you can use in the future?" surmised Musgrove.

Bradley had finally realised the inner power he held. "Yeah, you're right, Muzzy... whenever I come across an opportunity for good to rise above evil - I now know I have the power to influence it."

Musgrove sat next to his friend and put his arm around his shoulder. "You've always been so humble, Brad... it's time you realised you do have special powers and you are most definitely the *eternal chosen one* - I for one am eternally indebted to you for saving my life!"

Bradley smiled and acknowledged the compliment, as he rubbed the backs of his legs again. "Well, I'm feeling a lot better now... these cuts seemed to have stopped bleeding so we'd better get ourselves across that bridge," he declared. "We need to know if Ma-otz survived the tunnel... and if he did - we've still got a heck a task to complete!"

28

Betrayed Again

Back on the island of Freytor, King Luccese marched back and forth with his hands clasped tightly behind his back. His heavy robes dragged on the floor, as he twisted his regal body to face the same direction to that from which he just strode.

Queen Vash approached her distressed husband and offered him some words of comfort. "There's nothing you could have done to stop them... how were you to know that Flaglan would betray you again?"

"I should have known better... I should have banished that sorceress to the Unknown Land with Harg when I had the chance - how could I have been so stupid?" stated Luccese, as he pulled the Pathylian crown from his head. "I'm not worthy of this... I have let my people down again - I'll never forgive myself for allowing Varuna to slaughter the people of Aedis and Trad!"

The King's wife pushed her arms beneath her husband's robe and wrapped her tiny hands around his muscular bicep. She pleaded with him to stop punishing himself. "You are not to blame for those that perished during the onslaught... Varuna and Flaglan are evil - and they will pay for what they did, my love."

The King accepted the Queen's sympathy but gently shrugged her affections away and walked towards the window. He stared out at the ice-caps and pushed his heavy robes outward with his elbows, as he placed his hands on his hips. "We are stuck here on this godforsaken island, when we should be back in Trad... defending our homeland - instead we have put our own safety before our people and we should have been there to help them in their hour of need!"

The Queen approached her husband again. "Luccese, you must stop this... it's not doing any good - we have no alternative but to wait and bide our time," explained Vash in a calm voice. "We have to hope and pray that Bradley Baker retrieves the Amulet... Pathylon must be made safe before we can return - then and only then can we challenge Varuna and reclaim our kingdom."

Luccese turned to face his adoring wife and held out his arms. "You're right, my dear... but then you always are - what would I do without you?"

At that moment Pavsik entered the room. "Sire... one of the Klomus Hawks has arrived in Frey - it is Ploom and she is waiting to address you."

The King rushed over to the doorway. "Good... hopefully she has news of Bradley Baker and Rathek - let's go down to see what she has to say," exclaimed Luccese, as he turned to his Queen and smiled. "Maybe there is an alternative after all!"

They all made their way out of the senate building and the royal couple followed Pavsik down the icy steps that led to the harbour side to find the great bird resting her weary wings.

"Ploom!" shouted Luccese. "How are you feeling?"

"Your majesty," replied the tired bird and bowed before the King. "I am quite well... considering the long journey and I bring you tidings - both good and sad."

"Oh... then I would prefer that you tell me the sad news first," shuddered Luccese, as he encouraged the bird to follow them back inside. "But first, let us get back into the warmth of the senate building... it's freezing out here!"

The Klomus Hawk agreed and waddled by Pavsik's side, as they followed the royal couple back up the steps. Pavsik continued to make polite conversation, as they completed the ascent and finally made their way into the King's temporary quarters. "Err... ermm!" interrupted the King and asked Ploom to reveal the sad news. "I do hope it is nothing too serious."

The Klomus Hawk paused for a moment then untied the pouch that was attached to one of her legs. "Here, your majesty... Bradley baker has sent you this - he has also included a note for Meltor."

Queen Vash and Pavsik gathered round, as Luccese untied the pouch to reveal the crystals. He gently moved them aside to display the vital organ. "This looks like a Devonian heart... oh no - please don't tell me this belongs to Rathek!"

Whilst the King stared at the precious cargo, Pavsik read the note to himself. "I'm afraid it is, sire... Bradley explains in his message that it was Rathek's last request for his heart to breath new life into Meltor."

The Queen carefully took the parcel from her husband. "It's no good just looking at it... heaven knows it may already be damaged - let me take it over to Meltor's surgeon inside the health pod."

Pavsik handed Queen Vash the note. "You'd better take this as well, ma'am... it is intended for Meltor's eyes - he'll need to know what Rathek and Bradley have done for him when he wakes from the operation.

The Queen left the room, as Pavsik looked out of the window and spoke to the King with an underlying tone of concern in his voice. "The ice-cloud hangs heavy and looks very daunting, your majesty... why do you think it has arrived here?"

Luccese joined Pavsik and stared at the grey nebula, as it floated threateningly in the Freytorian skies. "I'm not sure... it seems strange that it has stopped above the city," replied the King and turned the Klomus Hawk. "Ploom... can you shed any light on this?"

The bird waddled over to look up at the cloud. "Your majesty... all I know is that a Freytorian sea commander used his powers to send lightning bolts from the Kaikane Idol to charge the cloud - rumours are spreading throughout the lands that he then extracted kratennium from the Flaclom Straits to feed the ice-cloud - that is all I know."

Pavsik looked worried and gasped. "Oh no!" he cried. "Norsk intends to destroy Frey... if the kratennium is released from the ice-cloud - the pure Pathylian water will melt the ice-cap!"

"What are you saying, Pavsik... what will happen to us?" demanded the King.

The Devonian High Priest rushed over to the door. "Your majesty... we have to leave immediately and evacuate the Freytorian Senate - I believe General Eidar's brother wants to destroy the political system!" urged Pavsik. "Think about it... with the senate destroyed - Norsk will be able to lead the Freytorians back to their pillaging ways!"

The King asked Pavsik to warn the Queen. "We must get as far away from Frey as possible... please ask General Eidar to arrange for the Queen to be transported to the city of Tor at the far side of the island - I will stay here with Meltor!"

"But Sire, you can't stay here... it is not safe!" declared Pavsik. "I cannot allow you to put yourself in danger!"

"I have made up my mind... anyhow, I have an idea - now go, Pavsik!" ordered the King, as the reluctant Devonian left the room and slammed the door behind him. Luccese approached the Klomus Hawk. "Ploom... I know you are tired - but this is what I want you to do for me."

Meanwhile, the ice-submarine still rested on the sea bed and Norsk was growing impatient. The powers he needed to release the kratennium from the ice-cloud were taking far too long to develop. Without any warning, he tested the energy within his body by casting his arm in the direction of one his crewmen. A bolt of crimson lightning trickled from the tips of his claws and the Freytorian sailor was thrown back against the control desk. The stunned crewman shook his head, as Norsk roared out his frustration. "How much longer must I wait... the Freytorian Senate must be destroyed so I can rule over Freytor and wreak havoc on the world!"

The quartermaster tried to calm his Admiral. "Please, Sir... if you keep doing that - you will waste your powers."

"Silence, you meddling fool... don't tell me what I can and cannot do!" roared Norsk, as he pointed his outstretched claw at the quivering Freytorian. "Do you want to be next?"

The crewman shook his head and moved away from the angry sea commander. Norsk checked one of the monitors on the command desk. The ice-cloud was still hovering over Frey and he used the telescopic lever to pan in to the ice-windows of the senate building below. The Admiral roared with laughter at the sight of King Luccese. "Well, well... a double whammy - I get to kill the King of Pathylon as well!" he cited. "This is going to be so much fun!"

Norsk made is way across the control bridge. "I'll be in my quarters... I need to connect my body to the ship's capacitors and rest - the energy I need will manifest much quicker if I sleep and then the city of Frey will feel the deadly force of my powers!"

The crewmembers on the bridge parted one by one, as the muscular Admiral passed through them and they all chorused with a nervous acknowledgement. "Aye... aye, Sir!"

Back inside the senate building, Ploom prepared herself for another long flight across the Red Ocean. The King had explained what he wanted her to do and the bird was ready to follow his command. Luccese approached the trusted Klomus Hawk. "I am very grateful to you, Ploom... now fly back the Forest of Haldon and find the other two females of your kind - you know what you need to do!"

Ploom nodded and the bright red feathers in her head plumage shook. "I will fly as fast as my wings can carry me, sire... and don't worry, I will find my fellow Klomus Hawks - Flute and Harp will be more than happy to help us to complete this very important task!"

Luccese opened the window and the huge bird hopped gracefully onto the sill. "Now go... and bring back what we need!"

Meanwhile, back in the Royal Palace Sereny lay on the soft mattress that adorned an ornate bed inside her makeshift prison chamber. She stared up at the gilded drapes that hung down majestically from the four poster bed. "I feel so helpless," she mumbled to herself, as the handle of the bedroom door started to turn.

The frightened girl sat upright and shuffled off the side of the bed to pick up a candlestick from the dresser. She ran over to hide behind the door and held the silver weapon against her chest.

The hinges creaked and the door swung open, as Sereny lifted the candlestick above her head in readiness to strike the uninvited guest. A tiny wrinkled hand appeared around the edge of the door and pushed it back gently. The door closed slowly to reveal a short hooded figure and Sereny prepared herself to issue a fatal blow to the intruder. As she lowered the candlestick, the dwarf-like creature revealed his face. "Turpol!" she exclaimed and quickly retracted the weapon. "I don't understand... you're supposed to be dead - I saw them burn your body!"

The Gatekeeper winked and scurried to the middle of the bed chamber. "Close the door and I'll explain," he insisted and jumped onto the bed. The dwarf swung his tiny legs and dangled them over the side of the high mattress and proceeded to tell Sereny how he had tricked everyone to believe he had been killed. "I did not intend to upset or mislead you, Sereny... but I had to - it was the only way I could escape."

"This is a joke, right... you're gonna take off your mask any second and reveal yourself as *Derren Brown*!" replied the girl, with a slight laughing undertone to her voice.

The dwarf looked puzzled. "Derren who?"

"Oh never mind!" replied Sereny. "So come on... tell me how you did it!"

Turpol smiled and tried to disguise the smugness of his body language, as he sat on his hands and continued to swing his stubby legs. "Do you remember the sack in the corner of the cage?"

Sereny pondered for a few seconds and recalled the tatty cloth bag. "Ermm, yes... I think so - it was full of corn wasn't it?"

"Well, that's what I wanted everyone to think... the fact is there wasn't any corn in the sack - there was something else inside," teased the dwarf.

Sereny put her hands on her hips and tapped her foot, as she waited whilst the Gatekeeper paused. "Are you going to tell me what was in the sack or not?"

"Me!" replied the dwarf and sniggered cheekily.

"Yes... you!" insisted Sereny.

"No... I mean - *me*!" giggled Turpol. "I was in the sack!"

"How could *you* have been in the sack... *you* were protecting *me* - in the cage?" quizzed the girl.

"Easy!" replied Turpol. "There was two of *me*!"

Sereny shrugged her shoulders and afforded the dwarf a blank look. "You're not making any sense, Turpol!"

The dwarf put her out of her misery. "Okay... I'll stop playing with you - one of the *me's* wasn't really *me*," declared the Gatekeeper. "The *me* protecting *you* was a dummy, which I smuggled into the cage before we left the Flaclom Straits... I had intended to use it as a decoy - should the opportunity arise for us to escape."

"Ah... very clever," replied Sereny and she smiled at the dwarf. "You're full of tricks aren't you... you could give *Derren Brown* a run for his money!"

"Who's this *Derren Brown* you speak of?" asked the curious dwarf. "Is he from Pathylon?"

"Don't worry about *Derren Brown*... and no he's not from Pathylon - just tell me why you felt you had to smuggle another *you* into the cart?"

"I needed some insurance... I knew Varuna would not harm you because he needed to use you as bait to lure Bradley Baker," explained Turpol, as he jumped down from the bed. "*Me*... on the other hand *was* dispensable - as you witnessed Flaglan did not hesitate to burn what *she* thought was my body," continued the dwarf. "She didn't even check to see if I was breathing!"

"So how did you escape from the burning cage?" asked Sereny.

"I wasn't in the cage!" replied the dwarf. "I sneaked out while you were all making a fuss over my body double," he laughed and made his way over to the door. "Now... explanation over - we have to get out of the palace before Varuna and Flaglan have finished their nuptials!"

Sereny pulled a disgusting face. "That's repulsive... I don't even want to think about that - those two at it, errrrrrgh!"

Turpol laughed, as he wrapped his grey wrinkled fingers around the handle and pulled the bed chamber door ajar. The gap was just wide enough for him to peep through and he signalled to Sereny with a waving arm that it was safe to leave. "Let's go... the coast is clear."

29

Double Dose of Death

The summit of Mount Pero cast an intimidating shadow, as Bradley made his way steadily across the wooden walk bridge. Musgrove waited for his friend to reach the other side before stepping onto the flimsy runners. The bridge continued to sway from side to side, as the cautious teenager reached the midway point and stopped. Bradley shouted to his friend. "Come on Muzzy, its quite safe!"

"That's easy for you to say... you're smaller and lighter than me - this things swinging like a pendulum!" replied Musgrove, as he held on tightly to the two lengths of twisted vine that acted as rope hand rails.

The two friends continued to debate the nervous boy's hesitation until they were interrupted by a loud buzzing noise. Bradley looked around to see where the sound was coming from, as Musgrove shouted a warning call. "Watch out, Brad... duck!"

Bradley reacted to his friend's advice and dropped like a lead weight, as he crashed to the floor. It was perfect timing, as a huge flying insect passed over his body. Musgrove's nerves dissipated into a heroic charge across the walk bridge and he picked up a rock, as he somersaulted across to where Bradley was lying.

The giant flying ant turned in the air and dove back down to attack them again, as Musgrove threw the rock. The stone bounced off the insect's head and had no effect, as the buzzing from its flapping wings grew more intense.

"It looks a Troglobite!" shouted Musgrove. "And this one can fly!"

The giant insect dived at the boys again and snapped it's pincers at them, as it narrowly missed their outstretched arms. The insect disappeared from sight but intense buzzing sound of its wings could be heard in the distance and informed the boys that it was about to make another run at them.

"Nice one, Muzzy... that's a great observation - now let's head for those bushes before that thing comes back again!" suggested Bradley, as he dragged his aching body off the floor and ran for cover.

"I don't think the bushes are going to save us!" declared Musgrove. "We need to find somewhere more substantial to hide!"

Bradley spotted a hole in the side of the rock face. "Over there... quick - follow me, Muzzy!"

"I'm right with you, Brad... lead the way!" replied Musgrove, as they dashed across the open ground towards the bolt hole.

Musgrove's long legs took him past his younger friend and he dived inside the gap in the rock. Bradley was lagging a few metres behind but he soon caught up and followed his friend. As he took flight, the Troglobites pincers hooked into his trouser leg and lifted the startled boy into the air. "Arrrrrggghhhh!" shouted Bradley, as the insect soared higher and his arms dangled down helplessly.

Musgrove reappeared from the safety of the hole and watched in disbelief as Bradley was carried away. "Oh no... I don't believe this - I've got to stop that thing!" he shouted and started to run in the direction of the insect.

Bradley tried to twist his body upright but the backs of his knees were still in so much pain. He looked down and could see Musgrove running after them. "Muzzy, run to the left... I can see a small village over the next hill - that must be where the Mece live!"

Musgrove continued to run and was nearly out of breath, as he shouted up to his friend. "Use your knife!"

Bradley, who was still hanging upside down, responded immediately and pulled out the Swiss army knife from his pocket. The insect was flying from side to side, which made it difficult for Bradley to focus on extending one of the blades. He ended up pulling out a corkscrew bottle opener but thought out loud. "This will do!"

The blood was rushing to Bradley's head and he had to act quickly. He noticed some tree tops coming into view and timed the execution of the corkscrew with great precision. He used all the energy he could muster and levered his body into a position where he came eye to very large eye contact with the Troglobite.

Musgrove stopped running and watched in amazement, as Bradley pulled back his arm and thrust the corkscrew attachment into the insect's eye. The giant ant's pincers immediately opened and Bradley fell into the tree tops below. Crash, crash, crash went the sound of each branch, as he tumbled through the foliage and eventually landed in a bush at the base of the cretyre tree.

"Bradley!" shouted Musgrove, as he ran over to help his friend. "Bradley... are you okay?"

"Errrrrrgggghhh!" groaned the acrobatic hero, as he lifted his head out of the bush and rubbed his bottom. "What a ride... ouch - my bum's killing me!"

"Never mind your bum!" exclaimed Musgrove, as he pulled his friend out of the foliage. "That giant insect is circling us again... it doesn't give up - does it?" he declared and dragged Bradley to the base of the tree. "Wait there, Brad... I'll see this thing off - once and for all!"

Bradley shouted. "Musgrove, don't... the creature's badly wounded and it's angry - it will kill you!"

Musgrove ignored his friend's advice and ran out into the open ground. "Come on you big ugly bug.... I mean err, bugs - oh dear!" He screamed and turned to run back in the direction of the cretyre tree, as a swarm of twenty or so Troglobites appeared from behind the rock face of Mount Pero.

The injured giant ant still had the Swiss army knife sticking out of its eye, as yellow puss poured from the wound. The angry insect led the flying Troglobites towards the tree, where Musgrove had now returned to the side of his injured friend. "Okay... we have to move fast - we're not safe here, Brad," insisted Musgrove. "We have to make a run for the village... hopefully we'll get the help there we need to fight these things."

"Sounds like a plan, Muzzy... let's go!" agreed Bradley, as he was helped to his feet. "You ready?"

"Yep!" replied Musgrove. "Let's go, mate!"

As soon as the boys emerged from the shelter of the tree, the swarm sensed their movement and headed down a well-rehearsed formation. Bradley and Musgrove ran for their lives and headed straight into the village. The Mece had heard the commotion and were ready, as the boys ran under the stilts that supported one of their huts.

The whole tribe wielded primitive weapons above their heads to ward off the flying creatures, as one by one they were picked off by the insects. Their sharp pincers penetrated the unprotected white fur of the mouse-like creatures.

Basjoo Ma-otz appeared at the doorway of the chief Mece's hut and muttered to himself, as he wielded his staff in the air. "Pathetic... weak creatures - let me show you how to defend your territory."

The Hartopian muttered a series of unpronounceable words and circled the staff above his head, as piercing bolts of lightening shot in all directions. The Troglobites started to fall from the air, as the electrical strikes sliced through their bodies.

The only insect left flying was the one wounded by Bradley's knife and it was being held in a tracer-like beam affected by the staff's power source. Basjoo Ma-otz moved the staff around and the insect remained locked in the beam. "This is what you call power!" roared the Hartopian, as he addressed the surviving Mece, who by now had gathered in the village square below.

Bradley and Musgrove reappeared from under one of the huts and Basjoo Ma-otz kept his Staff of Evil locked on the disorientated insect, as he watched the two boys walk towards the Mece. The Hartopian let out a loud roar of laughter and shouted down. "Well, well... the famous Bradley Baker - to what do I owe the honour?"

"Ma-otz, let the creature down... it can't do us any harm now - I need to talk to you!" reasoned Bradley, as he stepped forward in front of the small crowd of onlookers. "I need you to hand over the Amulet of Silvermoor!"

Before Basjoo Ma-otz could reply, the Mece chief and his son Rama appeared on the decking beside the Hartopian. The chief spoke in an authoritative voice. "I am Kuma... who are you that demands the Light of Mount Pero be taken away again?"

Bradley took another step forward. "My name is Bradley Baker!" he shouted, as the noise from the wounded insect's wings continued to buzz loudly. "If you let Ma-otz place the Amulet back on the sacred ledge... you will destroy Pathylon - do you want that to happen?"

The chief's daughter appeared next to her father. Wuku was uncomfortable with Basjoo Ma-otz presence in the village and tried to support Bradley's request. "Father, please do not let the Hartopian serve his death warrant on Pathylon... why should we harm a world that leaves us in peace?"

The chief looked at the menacing Hartopian half-breed, as he continued to wield his staff and hold the insect in his control. "My daughter and the Baker boy are right... as much as I would like to see the Light of Mount Pero back in its rightful place - I do not want this at the expense of many innocent people across the mountains being killed unlawfully!"

Bradley confronted the Hartopian again. "Ma-otz, you heard Chief Kuma... please get down from the insect and hand over the Amulet!"

Basjoo Ma-otz sensed a coup against his demands and turned to face Kuma. "I thought we had come to an agreement... you have betrayed my trust and now you will pay for your indecisiveness!"

The chief's son could see an immediate danger to his father and rushed to seize the Hartopian's staff. Ma-otz was too quick and he retracted the beam holding the insect and turned it on the advancing Rama. It took a single bolt of electricity to fell the chief's son and he collapsed in a fatal heap.

Bradley seized his opportunity and ran up the steps that led to the decking. The Hartopian caught sight of the boy in the corner of his eye and turned the staff in Bradley's direction. Wuku dived on top of Ma-otz and she punched him as hard as she could in the snout. A stream of Hartopian blood spurted out of Ma-otz's nose and flickers of yellow fluid splattered on the chief's face, as he was knocked backwards into the side of the hut.

Wuku continued to lay punch after punch into the Hartopian's body, as Bradley took hold of the staff and shouted at the relentless female Mece. "Stop... that's enough, Wuku - he's unconscious!"

Wuku ignored Bradley's request and continued to punch the motionless body of the Hartopian. She shouted her dead brother's name each time she landed another blow onto Ma-otz's blood-stained face.

Chief Kuma got to his feet and held his arms around his daughter's shoulders in an attempt to control her relentless onslaught. Wuku finally stopped her revengeful attack and broke down crying, as she placed her head on her father's chest. The chief looked up at Bradley, who was standing by holding the staff in his right hand. He knelt down to console the distraught father and daughter. "I'm so sorry this has happened to you and your people... but unfortunately, it was inevitable - Ma-otz was always going to double-cross you."

Wuku lifted her head and spoke gently. "I knew he was trouble the first time I laid my eyes on him... I should have trusted my instinct and let him to fall into the abyss."

Bradley sympathised. "I know the death of your brother is a high price to pay... but if you had let him fall into the abyss - we would have lost the Amulet forever."

Musgrove arrived on the scene and interjected. "Speaking of the Amulet... where is it?"

Basjoo Ma-otz opened a blood-shot eye and took his opportunity. The Hartopian was quick to shrug Wuku off his body and he sprang to his feet. His reflexes were at lightning speed and before Bradley could do anything, Ma-otz grabbed the staff from him.

The Hartopian jumped off the decking and landed on the floor with ease, as he somersaulted his way over to the injured Troglobite. As the surviving crowd of Mece approached to confront him, he moved his staff in a rotating manner to ward them off. Basjoo Ma-otz reached into his pouch and pulled out the pendant. "Is this what you're looking for?"

Musgrove jumped down from the decking and shouted over to the Hartopian. "Give it back, Ma-otz... we'll let you go if you hand it over!"

"Ha, ha, ha, ha!" roared Basjoo Ma-otz. "You idiot... I intend to fulfill my task and destroy Pathylon - and none of you are going to stop me!"

Bradley followed his friend's trajectory and leapt from the balcony to confront the Hartopian. "Hand it over Ma-otz!" But the determined traitor did not grace Bradley with a reply and he walked backwards carefully, whilst still pointing his staff in front. He rounded the stunned Troglobite and kicked its back to waken its consciousness, as the insect started to

267

flap its wings again. Ma-otz carefully mounted the insect and kept eye contact with the approaching crowd.

Bradley called out again. "Don't do anything stupid, Ma-otz!"

The Hartopian snarled and kicked his heals into the flying insect. He roared out another scream of venomous laughter. "Ha, ha, ha, ha, ha... fools - the lot of you!

Wuku jumped down from the decking and charged the Hartopian just as the insect prepared to take off. But Ma-otz aimed a fatal bolt of energy and pierced the middle of her chest, as the floored Mece creature reeled in agony. Chief Kuma raced down the steps to his dying daughter, as the Troglobite took to the air and flew upwards to the heights of Mount Pero's rocky face.

The crowd below was left with a feeling of total devastation caused by the Hartopian and the Mece Chief knelt down beside Wuku's limp body. "So much death and destruction has been bestowed upon our village... I have lost my son and my daughter is dying - now that maniac is going destroy Pathylon."

Bradley touched Kuma on the shoulder and Wuku's head fell sideways, as she passed away peacefully. "Oh, Chief Kuma... I am so sorry for your loss - I can assure you that it will not be in vain," he stated and turned to his friend. "It's not over yet, Muzzy... we have to get to the sacred ledge of Mount Pero before Ma-otz."

"We don't stand a chance... that flying ant will transport him there within minutes - it will take us hours to climb that mountain!" exclaimed Musgrove.

Before Bradley could muster a reply, there was a series of loud screeching noises in the sky above. A group of large birds flew above their heads and the enormous wing spans of three creatures stretched out elegantly, as they circled above. Their familiar red breasts stood out against the golden orange and yellow feathers and Bradley let out a cry of delight. "Well whadda ya know... its Ploom... and look she's brought the other two Klomus Hawks with her!"

The three birds landed on the decking and hopped down to join Bradley and Musgrove, as Chief Kuma continued to mourn his daughter.

"Hello Bradley... nice to meet you again," said Ploom. "Let me introduce you to my friends... Harp and Flute!"

Bradley made the birds aware of the chief's loss and then asked. "Why did you come back?"

Ploom told Bradley and Musgrove about the ice-cloud hovering over Frey and that Luccese had asked her to collect the other Klomus Hawks and fly back to help. "Luccese wanted to make sure you accomplished your task here and then we are to take you back to Freytor to dispel the threat from the ice-cloud," explained Ploom. "Did you stop Basjoo Ma-otz and do you have the Amulet?"

Bradley dropped his head slightly. "I'm afraid you're too late and the answer to both questions is no!"

Musgrove continued. "You've just missed the fight... Ma-otz has caused chaos in the Mece village and has killed both the chief's offspring - the Hartopian flew off on a giant ant about five minutes ago with the Amulet."

Ploom wrapped her wing around Bradley and asked. "Have you ever ridden bare back on a Klomus Hawk," she smiled and performed a little shimmy with all six claws.

Bradley smiled and replied with excitement. "No... but I've got a feeling I'm about to!"

Ploom lowered her wing. "Come on... jump on - let's find that Hartopian!"

Bradley climbed onto Ploom's back and Musgrove chose Flute as his ride, as Kuma stood up. The chief wiped away his tears and spoke gently. "I will ride with you... I owe it to Wuku and Rama - but when we find Ma-otz, please let *me* kill him!"

"Deal!" shouted Musgrove, as Harp lowered her wings to allow the Mece chief onto her back.

Within moments the three Klomus Hawks soared into the air and headed for the top of Mount Pero in search of the Hartopian. Bradley held on tight, as the wind blew through

269

his thick brown hair. He shouted over to Musgrove. "If only they could see this back home... it's a shame we can't tell them about it!"

Musgrove lifted his hand and stuck up his thumb. "Never mind whether we can tell anyone... we gotta get back home yet!" he declared, as they disappeared into the clouds that covered the top of the mountain.

Bradley placed his head down to aid the aerodynamic performance of Ploom's incredible speed, as the icy cold air bit into his face. "There's no wonder you got to Freytor and back in such a quick time... you fly incredibly fast!"

The bird smiled and continued to climb upwards, as she shouted her response above the noise of the wind. "We Klomus Hawks are the fastest birds in the whole of Pathylon... that is why the King employs us to carry out the most arduous tasks for him!"

Bradley stroked Ploom's head to acknowledge his admiration of her speed, as he clung tightly to her neck. "Did you manage to deliver Rathek's heart?"

"Yes!" replied Ploom, as she twisted around the rock face of Mount Pero. "Rathek's heart was delivered safely to King Luccese and the Queen hand-delivered it to Meltor's health pod!"

"Good... I just hope we've done enough to save him!" shouted Bradley, as they neared the summit. He scanned the mountain's side and immediately spotted the Hartopian. "Look, Ploom... over there - it's Basjoo Ma-otz!"

The Troglobite carrying the Hartopian was still circling around the top of the mountain and the thick clouds made it difficult to keep them in constant view. Bradley ordered Ploom to dive into the clouds to try and intercept the insect and dislodge Ma-otz from his mount. The Klomus Hawk obeyed his command and pulled back her wings back to create the maximum amount of speed needed to catch up with the Troglobite.

The two flying creatures clashed and their limbs tangled in the heat of the battle, as Bradley grabbed hold of Ma-otz's staff. The boy desperately clung on to Ploom's back with his legs, as he wrestled with the Hartopian in mid-air. "Let go, Ma-otz!" shouted Bradley, as the Hartopian held on to the staff. "We'll both fall if you don't let go!"

Basjoo Ma-otz maintained a stubborn grip on the staff, as Bradley gave once last tug. The Hartopian released his hold on the giant insect so as not to lose the staff and he fell to one side, as the Troglobite sensed its chance to escape. Bradley's knife was still lodged in the insect's eye and the giant ant flew away into the dense clouds.

The screaming Hartopian was left dangling beneath Ploom and his grip on the staff started to weaken. Bradley made every effort to pull him up to safety but he was too heavy. "It's no good human... I can't hang on any longer - you either let go of the staff or I fall! He shouted. "Either way... the Amulet will be lost forever!" warned Ma-otz and Bradley watched in horror, as the Hartopian's his paws slipped further down the shaft.

30

Clash at the Summit

The crew of the ice-submarine waited patiently for their commander to return to the command bridge, as the ship lay still on the sea bed just off the Freytorian coastline.

Admiral Norsk woke from his deep sleep feeling fully energised. He sat upright on his bunk and stretched out his arm's, as tiny flickers of crimson electricity arced between the ends of his claws. "I am ready," he snarled to himself and unclipped the suckers that connected the coloured wires to the ship's capacitors. "The energy form the Kaikane Idol has finally recharged my body and the ice-cloud can now be powered up!" he raged and swung his huge frame off the bed. "The kratennium will fall on Frey and I will rule the senate."

The excited Freytorian made his way down to the command bridge and was received with a rapturous applause, as he positioned himself at the helm. The clapping faded away and he addressed his crew. "My powers have been restored and I have the energy reserves I need to activate the ice-cloud... soon Freytor will be ours and we can return to our pillaging ways!"

A great cheer chorused around the command bridge and the order was given to raise the ship to the surface so that Norsk could perform his dangerous task.

Meanwhile the dramatic events at the top of Mount Pero continued to develop, as Basjoo Ma-otz slipped further down the shaft. Musgrove arrived on his Klomus Hawk and guided Flute beneath the Hartopian. Chief Kuma followed close behind on Harp and they each grabbed one of the Hartopian's legs.

Basjoo Ma-otz released his hold and fell forward, as the Amulet of Silvermoor slipped out of the pouch attached to the his belt. The chain securing the pendant caught around the Hartopian's long snout and he grabbed it with both claws. Bradley shouted to his friend. "Muzzy, get the Amulet!"

"I'll try, Brad!" replied Musgrove and reached out to wrestle the pendant from the Hartopian's grasp.

Basjoo Ma-otz defended himself and punched Musgrove in the stomach, as he straddled across the backs of both Klomus Hawks. "You won't stop me!" threatened the Hartopian and he wriggled free from Chief Kuma's grip, as Musgrove held his painful torso with both hands. Ma-otz rolled over and shouted. "Prepare for Pathylon to be destroyed!"

The Hartopian kept hold of the Amulet and fell about twenty metres, as he hit the snow covered rocks on the summit of Mount Pero. Bradley watched on helplessly, as Ma-otz somersaulted several times and recovered almost immediately. "Muzzy... he's going for the sacred ledge - I can see it from here!" he screamed and turned Ploom's head to send her into another dive. "I have to stop him!"

Musgrove pulled Flutes head and followed Bradley's lead, as his Klomus Hark charged like a remote controlled tomahawk missile hunting down its target. "I'm coming to help you, Brad!"

Basjoo Ma-otz allowed the weight of the Amulet to lengthen the chain and it dropped by his side. He then proceeded to twirl the pendant above his head like a lasso, as he struggled to walk through the deep snow. He approached the sacred ledge and stopped spinning the Amulet, as he removed the splendid blue jewel from the pendant. He scanned the ledge and looked for the matching shape in the rock to lock the sapphire in place. He was only a few centimetres away from fulfilling his task and reached out with the sparkling gem clasped tightly in his paw.

Bradley urged Ploom to go faster and shouted. "He's nearly there!"

The bird responded but struggled to gain any more down force. "If I go any faster we will smash into the rocks... we will both die?"

"It's a price we may have to pay, Ploom... now keep going!" replied Bradley, as they came within a few metres of the Hartopian.

Bradley kept hold of the staff in one hand and reached out to grab the Amulet with the other, but it was too late. Basjoo Ma-otz placed the jewel onto the ledge and it locked into it's housing with an eerie clunk. The mountain top shuddered and a blinding blue light beamed out from the centre of the sapphire, as a series of cracks started to appear in the rock face.

The Hartopian let out a deathly scream, as he disappeared into a crevice caused by the quake and clung on desperately to the side of the rock face. Bradley stared into the evil creature's red eyes and witnessed the final moments of Ma-otz's life, as the Hartopian disappeared into the gaping hole in the snow.

The death of Basjoo Ma-otz caused the mountain to celebrate and it shuddered again, as streams of airborne lava shot out of the cracks on the summit. The bright red volcanic liquid fired out in all directions, as Bradley pulled Ploom out of the dive and back up to the safety of the clouds.

Back in Ravenswood, the light at the top of the cenotaph burst into life and the street where Bradley lived was illuminated with a cold blue glow. Inquisitive neighbours appeared from their homes one by one and gathered on to the street, as they stared at the flickering bright light.

Patrick Baker looked at the clock on the dashboard of his car and spoke to his reflection in the rear view mirror. "Damn... I'm late - I should have been home hours ago to cook the kid's tea."

Back at the top of Mount Pero the action continued, as Musgrove and Flute flew around the summit and made a second turn. They joined Bradley and the two birds flapped their wings in a reverse spiral motion, as they hovered over the disruption below. Chief Kuma had been watching from a distance and instructed Harp to fly down to join her fellow Klomus Hawks.

Bradley kept a secure hold on to the staff and looked down solemnly. "We have failed... Pathylon is doomed - we have to do something!"

Ploom continued to flap her wings in a circular motion and turned her bright blue beak to face the disillusioned boy. "Bradley, there's nothing more you can do to stop the chain reaction deep inside the mountain... King Luccese sent us here to help you prevent Ma-otz from placing the Amulet on the sacred ledge and we have failed in that respect - Mount Pero has been detonated!" explained Ploom. "But there is something else you must do!" she revealed and leveled her wings to circle the top of the mountain. "I know we have failed to stop the Hartopian but the King told me to make sure you retrieve the Amulet and take it back to Frey at any cost... removing the Amulet from the ledge won't stop the atomic explosion but we can still use the jewel to great affect - now, you must retrieve the Amulet from the ledge and we have to make our way to Freytor as quickly as possible!"

Bradley was confused about what the Amulet could do to help the situation back in Freytor, but he agreed to retrieve it and asked Ploom to fly down so he could jump onto the summit. The bird did not hesitate, as she swooped down through the volcanic eruptions and darted between the flying lava. As she neared the ice-covered peak, she tipped her body and the heroic boy slid off her back. Bradley landed in the deep snow adjacent to the wide chasse that had earlier claimed Basjoo Ma-otz body.

A blizzard of molten ash blew inside a series of mini tornados cast up by the melting ice, as Flute flew down with Musgrove and hovered near to where Bradley was standing. "Be careful where you tread, Brad... the rocks could give way at any point and it's a long way down - don't want you following Ma-otz!"

Bradley heeded his friend's advice and moved slowly, as he felt the heat from the molten lava burning his face. He took a few more tentative steps and carefully strode over the crack in the mountain top, as he finally reached the sacred ledge. The exhausted boy carefully lifted the shining sapphire out of its housing. "Got it!" he shouted, as Ploom swooped down again and hooked two of her claws into his overalls. She lifted Bradley by his shoulders and clear of the dangerous mountain, as he held the Amulet tightly in his cold hands. The bright blue colour of the gemstone started to dim and the sparkling brightness faded, as Ploom lifted them away from the mountain.

In Ravenswood, the light at the top of cenotaph reciprocated the shining Amulet of Silvermoor and it started to flash intermittently, as the village onlookers stared at each other in a confused manner.

Patrick Baker entered the housing estate and swerved his car, as the flashing blue light caught his attention. He slammed on the brakes and climbed out of the vehicle, as one of his neighbours approached. "It's just started doing that... you'd better put your electrician's hat back on, Patrick - I think the bulb's on it's way out!"

Bradley's father laughed to appease his annoying neighbour and replied. "No... I don't think it's the bulb, Larry - it's probably just a dirty connection!"

There was a slight tremor beneath the street and both men stood opened mouthed, as the light shined brightly and steadily for a few more seconds before distinguishing. The neighbour chirped. "Told you it was the bulb... and I'd better call the council to sort these drains out!"

Patrick watched the tubby old man walk back to his front gate and he got back into his car. He completed his arrival back in Ravenswood by parking the car on his drive and then made his way in to the house. "Bradley?" he shouted. "I'm home!"

There was no reply and he looked up the staircase and shouted again. "Bradley... are you up there?" There was still no reply, so he ran up the stairs and proceeded to inspect each bedroom to see if the children were hiding. He entered the bathroom and noticed the picture on the floor and spoke out loud. "What's Bradley been up to and why has he taken my picture of Silvermoor Colliery out of the frame?"

Patrick looked around the bathroom and noticed that the bath tub had dirty marks on the bottom and the remnants of a tide mark where the water had been. "What have they been up to... the bath is filthy - his Mum will kill me if she sees this when she gets back tomorrow!"

Bradley's father ventured into unfamiliar territory and set about cleaning the bath tub as best he could. "There... that will have to do - just wait till I get hold of him!" he exclaimed, as he turned away. The grobite in the plughole started to glow but Patrick had failed to notice it and he made is way out of the bathroom.

Patrick scurried back downstairs then entered the kitchen and muttered to himself, as he opened the fridge door. "They must be playing in the woods... never mind - I might as well go down the pub," he thought and removed the top from a milk carton. "Right... that's the last straw!" he shouted.

"Blumming kids... no milk - now I'll have to drive down to the blinking shops first!"

Back on the side of Mount Pero, a loud rumbling sound emanated from within the rock face and a multitude of small avalanches started to descend from the summit. The first stages of the atomic explosion had started and streams of energy conducted out of the mountain, as spurts of larva oozed out of the cracks that had been formed by the initial blast.

The three Klomus Hawks flew away from the spitting larva and made their way back down to the Mece village. They landed safely in front of Chief Kuma's hut, as the surviving Mece tribe members gathered round. Bradley, Musgrove and Kuma dismounted from the exhausted birds and paid their final sympathies to villagers.

Bradley turned to the Chief and expressed his regrets. "We are so sorry that you and your people have endured so much torment from the Troglobites... I sincerely hope that they will now leave you in peace," he sympathised.

Chief Kuma nodded respectfully and replied. "Thank you for your help Bradley... you and your friend's have been very brave and I am glad that the Hartopian met his demise - I wish it was me that had killed him but I now feel the death of Wuku and Rama has been avenged."

Musgrove added. "What Ma-otz did to them was unforgivable... I wish we could have done more to help."

"You did all you could," replied the Mece Chief. "We bought into what Basjoo Ma-otz told us about the Amulet and we thought by letting him place it back on the sacred ledge... our village would be safe again - alas that was not the case and the Hartopian tricked us."

Bradley held the staff over his raised thigh and concluded. "Well he is dead now and we have managed to retain his Staff of Evil... so he won't be able to inflict any more dastardly deeds - I will destroy this thing."

"No!" exclaimed Ploom, as she pushed in front of Musgrove and Harp to stop Bradley from breaking the staff over his knee. "You are going to need that thing... trust me - it will now be used to bring good!"

Bradley stopped his actions and afforded the bird a puzzled look. Ploom did not react and chose not to reveal what the staff would be used for but instead she insisted that they all say there farewells to the Mece.

Bradley obliged and Kuma waved at the two boys, as they walked away with the trio of Klomus Hawks to the edge of the village to plan their next moves. The Chief was left to mourn the loss of his children and the Mece tribe gathered around him to start their planning their rebuild of the depleted populous.

Bradley and his weary group stood in front of the walk bridge at the base of mount Pero and with the obligatory goodbyes to the Mece villagers over, he asked Ploom if she or her fellow Klomus Hawks had spotted a human girl on their travels. "Her name is Sereny and we haven't heard anything from her - do you know if she is okay?"

Ploom replied. "Harp may have some news for you."

The shy Klomus Hawk stepped forward and nodded, as she spoke in a very quiet tone. "I have heard that Varuna is keeping a small girl prisoner in the Royal Palace - this could be the one you speak of."

Musgrove interrupted. "Have you seen her?

"No," replied Harp nervously. "But I have heard whispers within the great forest that she has bunches in her light coloured hair... and they are tied with ribbons."

Bradley interjected. "That's sounds like Sereny, alright... I can't imagine many girls in Pathylon with bunches and ribbons!"

"Well we can't just leave her there... we should at least try and rescue her on our way to Freytor!" insisted Musgrove. "Ploom will be carrying Bradley and I will fly with Flute... so we if we can locate Sereny - she can ride with Harp!"

Bradley agreed. "Muzzy does have a point, Ploom... but do we have time?"

"I don't see why not," replied Ploom, as she turned to Harp. "Will you fly ahead to Trad and check out the palace... see if you can find out where they are keeping the girl?"

The elegant bird bowed her crested head and walked backwards. Harp then turned, as she fluttered her wings to steady her take off and flew up into the smoke filled skies. Ploom shouted after her. "We'll catch up with you as soon as we can... you have no passenger so you will fly much quicker than us - see you in Trad!"

Bradley tore a piece of cloth from his other sleeve to wrap the gemstone and then tied the Amulet onto his belt, as he clung to Ploom's back. "Okay... Trad it is then - let's go!" he declared, as Musgrove positioned himself on Harp.

The ground started to tremble again and the two Klomus Hawks held on to each other for support. Small cracks started to appear in the ground beneath their claws and they averted the danger by lifting their legs, as they hovered. A quick glance in each other's eyes and they flew upwards at speed before gliding around the side of Mount Pero. They climbed above the black smog created by the spewing lava and focussed on the landscape ahead. The view became much clearer and they flew off in tandem towards the Peronto Alps. Bradley called over to Musgrove. "With the incredible speed of these hawks... we should reach Trad before the hour is up!"

Sereny and Turpol had managed to elude the Tree Elves that were guarding the corridor out side the bed chamber. The dwarf had discovered a series of passageways behind the walls that acted as air ducts. There was a maze of theses small tunnels running throughout the Royal Palace and they successfully negotiated their way out into a small courtyard adjacent the palace kitchens.

Turpol whispered. "If we can create a diversion... all we have to do is get past those Tree Elves at the end of the courtyard - we can then make our way to the river, which is not far away."

Sereny added. "If we can get to the river and into the Forest of Haldon... I know where Grog's cabin is - we could hide in there till the coast is clear."

"That's sounds like a very good idea... now what can we do to create a diversion?" asked the Gatekeeper.

"I don't think we need to create a diversion," suggested Sereny. "Do you see that container over there?" she observed, as she pointed to a large whicker basket positioned next to the kitchen's rear entrance door.

"Yes... I see it," replied Turpol. "What do you propose we do with it?"

"Well, whilst we've been crouched here... I've seen three other containers being carried outside the courtyard gates - I think they may be filling them with rubbish from the kitchen," whispered Sereny. "If we can get inside the last container without being noticed... we should get out of here - it's worth a try but we'll have to wait for that kitchen worker to go back inside."

Turpol and Sereny made their way over to the refuge bin and waited for the kitchen porter to finish his break. The Devonian servant was in no hurry and Sereny took the opportunity to ask Turpol a question that had been playing on her mind since their first adventure back in the summer holidays. She tapped him on the shoulder and whispered. "Turpol... why are you the only dwarf in Pathylon?"

The Gatekeeper smiled and whispered back. "I wondered how long it would take before one of you asked me that question... it's a long story but I'll keep it simple," he replied. "A long time ago my parents travelled from a land across the Red Ocean called Rekab... they escaped from Crystal City where all the dwarves live – soon after their arrival in Pathylon they were killed by a group of Hartopians and I ended up as an orphan."

Sereny sighed and offered Turpol an affectionate squeeze. "Sorry to hear about your parents... but how did you become the Gatekeeper of Pathylon?"

Before Turpol could answer, the servant got to his feet and went back into the palace kitchen. The dwarf whispered. "We can continue this conversation another time... right now - I think we should make our move."

Sereny nodded and as soon as the door to the kitchen closed, she jumped up and grabbed the side of the container. Turpol tried to climb up after her but he was too short. Sereny chuckled, as she grabbed his arms and pulled him over, as they both fell head first in to the smelly bin.

"Shhhhhhhh," whispered the dwarf, as he placed one of his hairy fingers over his lips. "I'm glad you think it's funny you cheeky minx."

Sereny stopped sniggering, as they shuffled into their seating positions and started to cover themselves with fruit peelings. "Not sure if this was such a good idea," she gasped, as the smell of putrid food aired the container.

Turpol pinched his nose and chose not to reply, as they both lay still and waited for the bin to be collected.

Meanwhile, the ice-submarine moved steadily across the surface of the water towards the harbour port of Frey. Norsk peered through the periscope at the line of Harpoon wielding Freytorians on the harbour wall. He focussed the lens at a small tower on the nearside harbour wall. "Well, well... if it isn't my brother Eidar - nice of him to come out to play," he sniggered and slammed the periscope handles shut. "This should be interesting!" Norsk then ordered his quartermaster to open the hatch that led to the viewing gallery. "I am ready to unleash my powers... prepare the submarine for submersion, as soon as I return - as soon as I have charged the ice-cloud, we will need move away at speed to avoid the kratennium melting the ship!"

"Aye-aye, sir!" replied the quartermaster, as he set the submarines co-ordinates in readiness for a swift get away.

The confident Admiral climbed the metal ladders and emerged onto the viewing gallery to the sound of jeers from the harbour side. Norsk ignored the unpopular reception and made his way along the deck to secure a clear view of the ice-cloud.

Luccese joined General Eidar at the top of the harbour tower and he stared at the unhappy Freytorian. The King paused for a moment to consider the delivery of his next order, as he finally broke the uncomfortable silence. "Are you alright, General?"

Eidar shook his head and replied. "No, your majesty... I'm not alright - I'm about to give the order to my fellow Freytorians to fire upon my own Brother!"

"I cannot to begin to understand how that might feel, General... but you have to do what is right - there are many lives at risk here!" sympathised the King. "Now, do what you have to do!"

Eidar nodded and breathed out a huge sigh before turning to face the waiting army of ice bears on the harbour wall. He raised his arm and roared a defiant order. "Grrrrrrrggggghhhh... fire at will!"

The hundred and more Freytorians released the triggers on their harpoons and a multitude of spears shot across towards the ice-submarine. The vessel was too far away and the missiles fell short of their target, as they pierced through the surface of the water.

The General gave the order to reload the weapons and make the necessary adjustments to the trajectory, as he turned to King Luccese. "Norsk is too far away, your majesty... the harpoons cannot reach him - my Brother will have allowed for this and he has positioned himself just outside the target perimeter," he stated, as the next round of spears soared across the harbour.

The King approached the frustrated Freytorian. "Well... at least you do not have to take responsibility for the demise of your own Brother - let's just hope the Klomus Hawks can help us!"

General Eidar sighed again, as he turned to face the ice-submarine and lifted his telescope to his eye. "Norsk is preparing to unleash his powers... I will use mine to keep him at bay until the birds' return - that's if they do!"

"How long can you hold him off?" asked the King.

"Not long... he will have extracted a huge amount of energy from the Kaikane Idol and his powers will be much stronger than mine!" explained the General.

"Can you give me an idea of time?" asked Luccese.

"I'd say an hour at the most... let's hope your back up plan works!" replied Eidar, as he prepared himself for a battle with his twin brother.

31

Back to Freytor

Bradley secured the Staff of Evil through his belt and clung on tightly to the feathers around Ploom's neck, as the bird's lightning speed carried them over the Galetis Empire. Flute maintained a close distance behind her fellow Klomus Hawk but she was finding it difficult to keep up with the extra weight she was carrying, as Musgrove hung on awkwardly.

The two magnificent birds cast out their huge wing spans occasionally to gather the extra momentum needed to maintain their high velocity, as they rushed through the clouds. Bradley looked down at the dessert landscape and the City of Kasol whizzed in an instant. "Wow... this is so fast, Ploom - your speed is incredible - we should reach Freytor in no time!"

The Forest of Haldon came into view and Musgrove shouted ahead. "Bradley... I'm feeling a little queasy - I think I'm going to be sick!"

Bradley turned to respond but before he had chance, Flute turned her head and glared at the ashen-faced teenager. "Don't even think about it!"

"Try and hang in there, Muzzy... it won't be long now - look, there's the river ahead!" shouted Bradley, as Ploom picked up more speed to reach the edge of the River Klomus.

Musgrove looked down and screamed out with glee, as the sight of Harp's wingspan in silhouette with the water. This took his mind off his rolling stomach for a moment and he exclaimed. "Look, Brad... it's the other Klomus Hawk - and look who's hitching a ride!"

"Sereny!" exclaimed Bradley, as the bird flew towards them and he noticed a pair of stubby arms wrapped around the girl's waist. "And who's that sat behind you?"

Harp turned to fly by their side and the little dwarf came in to view. "Hello Bradley... good to see you again!"

Bradley lost concentration for a second, as he shrieked with delight. He steadied himself and regained his composure, as Ploom managed to maintain the same flight path to allow them to continue their reunion. "It's great to see you both alive and well!" shouted Bradley. "We've been so worried about you... especially you, Sereny!"

"Harp tells us that we need to get to Freytor!" declared the pretty girl, as she admired the confident way that Bradley rode the bird's back. "Why do we have to go there?"

"Not quite sure... Ploom says that King Luccese needs the sapphire from the Amulet but I'm not sure what he wants it for - Mount Pero will explode soon so I guess it must have something to do with that!"

Ploom couldn't help but over hear the conversation and felt it necessary to intervene. "The King will explain when we get to Freytor... now, stop talking and let's concentrate on getting there as fast as we can!"

Turpol concurred and added. "I think I know what Luccese needs the Amulet for... but Ploom is right - we'll get a full explanation when we arrive in Frey!"

With that Bradley scrunched his shoulders and smiled at Sereny, as Musgrove continued to struggle to balance his heavier frame on Flute. The girl laughed at his antics and cast another admiring glance at the eternal chosen one, as the three birds pinned back their wings again to launch themselves forward. Sereny screamed with delight, as the air rushed through her hair. The wind blew so hard that the ribbons holding her bunches were swept away.

"Yee ha!" shouted Bradley and he crouched forward to improve the aerodynamics, as Ploom responded to his yell and carried out a perfect three hundred and sixty degree roll.

"Show off!" screeched Sereny and pulled on Harp's neck feathers to encourage her to repeat the maneuver. The bird did not respond and Turpol breathed a sigh of relief. The Gatekeeper was hanging on the girl's waist for dear life and he patted the bird's wing to offer his thanks.

The coastal shores of Devonia approached and the horizon depicted the Kaikane Idol standing proud on the Island of Restak. With the fun over, the serious task of reaching Frey within the hour was set, as the three Klomus Hawks flew in super fast formation over the Red Ocean with their heads straight and their wings pinned back.

Back on the viewing gallery of the ice-submarine, Norsk was ready to start his power surge into the ice-cloud. The Freytorian lifted his arms in the air and tilted his head backwards, as he closed his eyes.

A hole appeared in the cloud that was large enough to accept the energy stream and the swirls within the cloud started to turn. The nebula twisted, as the Admiral's claws began to twitch and a series of red coloured lightning bolts shot out from his claws. The power source penetrated the cloud and struck the kratennium, as the colour of the ice-cloud turned to a crimson glow. The electrical energy arced violently and the melting process began, as small droplets of pure kratennium started to form on the edge of the cloud.

Norsk roared out a statement of content. "The Freytorian Senate will soon experience the wrath of my powers and the true pirates of Freytor will be free to pillage the world again!"

More bolts of lightning emanated from the Admiral's claws, as the cloud absorbed the energy and increased in size. The kratennium deep inside its core was now at boiling point and it would not be long before the droplets started to rain down on the ice caps below.

The cheeks on Bradley's weathered face were shuddering, as the force caused by the rushing air passed over his body. The Klomus Hawk carrying him was flying just above the surface of the ocean and she continued to propel her bullet-shaped frame. From above the three birds flight path simulated the shape of an arrowhead, as Ploom led the other two birds in close formation.

Musgrove was clinging tightly to his mount and shouted ahead to Bradley. "How far do you think it is, to Freytor?"

"Not sure, Muzzy... hang on a minute - I'll ask Ploom!" replied the wind struck boy.

Sereny interrupted and joined the conversation. "He's hanging on alright... for his dear life - ha-ha!" She laughed, as Musgrove fought to stay upright on the super fast bird.

Bradley turned to see what all the fuss was about and chuckled to himself. He knew Musgrove wasn't in any danger from falling off but he was loving the fact that Sereny was tormenting his friend. He turned back to face the beautiful ocean ahead and asked Ploom how far it was to Freytor.

Ploom cleared her throat and croaked, as the air entered her beak. "About another twenty miles or so... you can just make out the headland of Freytor on the landscape - the ice-cloud is quite visible from here!"

"Oh yes... I see it now!" exclaimed Bradley, as the faint glow of the cloud with its crimson aura floated above the headland.

Ploom continued. "We should be there in about ten minutes... the cloud has turned red in colour - that means Norsk has started to charge the kratennium!"

Bradley turned again and answered Musgrove's question. "Ploom says about ten minutes and we'll be there... prepare yourselves for the worst - we might be too late looking at the colour of that cloud!"

288

Sereny checked that the Gatekeeper's hands were st gripping her thin waist. She felt the coarse hairs on the bac of his chubby fingers and asked. "You okay back there, Turpol?"

"Yes, Sereny... I don't mean to be quite but I have been trying to work out why King Luccese would want the Amulet back in Freytor - and I think I know the answer!" he shouted and issued a request to the exhausted Klomus Hawk that was carrying them. "Harp... can you fly next to Ploom - I need to join Bradley!"

The bird sighed with relief and did not hesitate to take advantage of the dwarf's request. Carrying the heavier load had tired her and she flew parallel with Ploom, as the Gatekeeper released his hold on Sereny. Turpol jumped onto the other bird's back and steadied himself, as he adjusted his seating position.

Bradley was taken by surprise as the dwarf held on to his orange overalls and the Gatekeeper apologised. "Sorry to alarm you Bradley but I need to speak with you before we reach the ice-cloud... I've been giving some thought as to why Luccese would want you to deliver the Amulet to Freytor and I think I've worked it out - there's something very important that the King will need you to do!"

"What is it, Turpol?" asked the excited boy. "You always seem to presume correctly... so tell me - is it dangerous?"

The Gatekeeper paused for a second and then sighed deeply. "Very dangerous!"

Bradley scrunched his face and lifted his shoulders. "It can't be any more risky than what we had to go through back on Mount Pero... so let me have the information - tell me what I have to do!"

Turpol put his head close to Bradley's ear and explained his thoughts. The boy nodded, as the dwarf continued to deliver his presumption of the King's plan. Bradley acknowledged the Gatekeeper's tome and agreed to carry out the task, as he shouted over to Musgrove and Sereny. "I have to get close to the ice-cloud and I will need you two to distract Norsk!"

Sereny replied in a concerned tone. "Why?"

"No time to explain right now... Turpol has told me what he thinks the King will need me to do - just keep General Eidar's brother busy and don't worry about me!" explained Bradley, as he gently kicked into Ploom's side. "Can you go any faster?"

Ploom did not answer but pulled back her wings and accelerated forward, as Turpol grabbed Bradley's waist. Harp and Flute followed her lead and the three Klomus Hawks shot like bullets across the top of the ocean waves.

Meanwhile back in the harbour, Eidar continued to order his Freytorian squadron to fire their harpoons at his twin brother's ship. King Luccese was standing close by to ensure the General did not waiver in his attempts to stop Admiral Norsk.

The King approached the General. "This isn't working... you must launch your landing crafts and get nearer to the submarine!"

"Your Majesty... please let me do my job - it will take too long to arrange for the landing crafts to be deployed!" roared Eidar in retaliation the Pathylian King's suggestion. "The trajectory of my soldier's harpoons are getting closer to the correct co-ordinates... my brother's ship will be hit quite soon and the threat he imposes upon us will be over!"

Luccese afforded the Freytorian commander a look of disbelief, as he witnessed the continuous thread of lightning bolts being emitted from Norsk's claws. "You better get your trajectory right soon, Eidar... the kratennium is starting to fall on the city - this whole ice cap will melt in minutes!"

Eidar was about to launch another verbal abuse to assure the King that his troops would be able to secure Norsk's demise when the sound of whooshing air interrupted his tirade, as the three Klomus Hawks sped past above their heads. They looked up and both punched the air, as the sight of Bradley Baker warmed their confidence.

Ploom circled, as Bradley shouted down. "Good to see you again, your majesty... and you General!"

Luccese applauded and replied. "It's so good to see you too, Bradley... now I need you to - !"

Bradley interrupted. "I know what to do... Turpol has worked it out - leave it to me, Sire!"

The King smiled and waved at them, as the lightning bolts continued to crash into the ice-cloud. "Good luck, Bradley!"

The boy kicked his heals into Ploom once more and the bird launched upwards in the direction of the cloud. Bradley waved his arms to instruct Musgrove and Sereny to head for the submarine. They both acknowledged by saluting their brows, as Harp and Flute spread their wings to glide down towards Norsk.

Bradley nudged Turpol in the belly and asked him to remove the chord around his tubby waist. "I'm going to need something to secure the Amulet!"

The Gatekeeper did not hesitate and started to pull at the chord. "What are you going to attach it to?"

"This!" replied Bradley, as he reached into his pocket and pulled out his mobile phone.

"What is that?" asked the dwarf.

"This, my friend... is the device that will stop Norsk from destroying Frey and hopefully save Pathylon from destruction!" shouted Bradley, as he powered up the phone and keyed in the password.

The flashing blue gem displayed its brilliant glow on the screen again and the network signal reappeared. "See this?" asked Bradley as he pointed to the word below the signal strength indicator. "I still can't work out why my phone works in your world... but *TECO* appears every time I switch it on - so I guess it must be your local network!"

Turpol laughed and held on to Bradley, as Ploom ascended at a steep angle. "Network... I think not - this world does not have such things," he explained. "The only method of communication is by telepathy!"

"So what does it mean?" asked Bradley, as he tied the chord around the phone and inserted the blue gem back into the metal-linked necklace. "Why does *TECO* appear on the screen?"

The Gatekeeper sighed, as the Klomus Hawk adjusted her wing span and straightened her flight path. The dwarf laughed slightly again and placed his rough palm on Bradley's hand, as he tied the Amulet to the mobile phone for him. "My dear boy... you are *the eternal chosen one*!"

Bradley paused then smiled and declared. "The Eternal Chosen One... TECO!"

The dwarf patted him on the back, as Ploom dodged the bolts of crimson lighting and headed into the cloud. As they entered the nebula, Bradley said a few more sincere words to Turpol. "If we don't get out of this thing alive... I'd just like to say - it's been a pleasure flying with you."

Turpol replied. "You too, Master Bradley - you too!"

32

The Depths of the Cloud

Admiral Norsk was unaware of the impending threat around him and kept his eyes tightly closed to maintain full concentration, as he stood rigid at the front of the viewing gallery. The energy continued to pour out of his charred claws and the long arcs of electricity connected to the ice-cloud like a stream of dancing lasers.

Harp and Flute flew in close to the ice-submarine, as Sereny and Musgrove planned their next moves. They guided the birds to within metres of Norsk and simultaneously launched their attack on the deranged Freytorian.

The two Klomus Hawks revealed their sharp talons and aimed twelve sets of razor sharp claws at the Admiral. Norsk opened his eyes, as the birds dived to disrupt his concentration. The Freytorian shifted his arms in front to defend himself, as the energy beams shot in all directions.

Sereny pulled at Flutes neck and dodged a stray lightning bolt, as the bird recomposed her flight path and aimed her talons at the Freytorians head. The Admiral waved his arm and crashed his fist into Flutes beak, sending her and Sereny crashing down onto the ship's deck.

Musgrove steered Harp at the Freytorian and again the Admiral reacted swiftly by knocking the bird sideways into the ice covered railings attached to the submarine's viewing platform. Feathers splayed everywhere and the ice-bars snapped, as Harp collided with brittle structure. Norsk reacted angrily and roared, as the diffused bolts of lightning from his claws crackled and sparked. "You stupid imbeciles... how dare you interrupt my moment of Glory - you will pay for this with your deaths!"

Sereny managed to crawl away from Flute, as the bird lay motionless on the deck. She noticed a detached harpoon that was leant upright against the viewing platform and she dived towards it. The Admiral noticed her actions and quickly threw his heavy frame in the same direction. The girl managed to retrieve the weapon but Norsk was quick to grab hold of her arm, as they both slid along the icy decking.

Musgrove dismounted Harp, as the bird took flight again and flew directly above his head. They dived from different angles at the Freytorian who was squeezing his strong paw around Sereny's slender throat.

"Urrrrrrgghh!" she choked, as the Admiral straddled her tiny body.

Musgrove jumped on the Freytorians back and wrapped his arm around Norsk's neck. "Get off her... you great white bully!"

The Admiral drove his sharp claws into the deck and pinned Sereny down, as he threw his muscular arm back to fend off the boy. Harp outstretched all six legs and sunk her talons into the Freytorians back, as Musgrove dived out of the way.

Norsk reeled upright in agony, as the Klomus Hawk sank her talons deeper into the Admirals flesh. Musgrove seized the opportunity to grab Sereny and pull her to safety, as the Freytorian released his grip to defend himself against the fierce attack from the enraged bird. Harp was not going to let go and disappeared under the great bear's frame, as he rolled over to squash his attacker.

"Arrrrrrggghhhh!" squawked Harp, as Norsk crushed her body into the cold decking.

Norsk rose to his feet with the dead bird attached to his back and her talons still embedded. He tried to reach behind to remove the dead weight but to no avail. Sereny spotted another opportunity to use the harpoon and without hesitation picked it up, as she ran towards the injured Admiral who had now managed to detach Harp's limp body from his back.

Musgrove cried out. "Sereny, be careful!"

"Don't worry, Muzzy... this bear is going down!" she replied and jumped into the air, as she crashed the harpoon spear into the Freytorians skull.

Norsk had no time to react and the sharp metal rod pierced his armoured headgear. The cracking of bone could be heard, as he fell heavily onto the deck. Sereny landed on top of the ice-bear and steadied herself, as she looked around at the two dead Klomus Hawks.

The commotion had alerted the crew below and the quartermaster led some of them onto the viewing gallery. "Get them!" he shouted, as a group of Freytorians started to descend the ladders that led down to the decking.

Sereny jumped down from the felled Admiral and ran over to Musgrove. "We've got to get off this ship before they kill us!"

"Wait... look - they've stopped!" declared Musgrove, as the quartermaster recalled his crew members.

"Why have they stopped?" asked Sereny.

"There's your answer!" declared Musgrove. "Look!"

Sereny followed Musgrove's pointing finger and noticed a fleet of landing crafts approaching the ice-submarine. General Eidar had finally succumbed to King Luccese request and deployed the small vessels.

The quartermaster instructed his crew to return to the confines of the ship, as General Eidar and King Luccese boarded the submarine. The King approached the two children and applauded their bravery. "Well done... you have stopped Norsk and I thank you both."

Musgrove looked at Sereny adoringly and replied to the King. "It's Sereny you need to thank, Sire... she was the one who killed Norsk!"

General Eidar knelt down by his dead brother and placed his paw on Norsk's blood-stained face to close his staring eyes. He turned to the children and issued his thanks. "I heard what you just said and I too applaud your bravery... I am saddened by my brother's death but you did what you had to do - today was the day he was meant to die!"

Sereny walked over to approach Eidar and she spoke nervously. "I am truly sorry, General... but he was trying to kill us."

General Eidar rose to his feet and placed his large furry paw on the young girl's shoulder. "As I said, my dear... you had no choice - now, what about the ice-cloud!"

The King stared up and observed. "The kratennium rain is still falling upon Frey... I'm not sure if Bradley and Turpol are going to manage it!"

Musgrove stood by the King's side and asked. "Manage what, Sire?"

The King explained. "I have tasked Bradley to deploy the Amulet of Silvermoor into the centre of the cloud... this will freeze the kratennium for a short period - hopefully giving us enough time for the southerly winds to build up and blow the cloud away from Freytor."

Sereny asked. "But what will happen to the ice-cloud if Bradley manages to deploy the Amulet?"

"The winds should take it out into the red ocean and the natural process of dissipation should be enough to disperse the cloud and release the kratennium into the sea," replied Luccese.

Musgrove intervened and offered his thoughts. "Well, if I know Bradley... he won't settle for saving Frey - I think he's up to something else!"

Sereny asked. "What to mean?"

"Do you remember when we were flying away from Mount Pero... he wouldn't tell us something?"

"Yes!" replied Sereny.

"Well, I think he's got plans to send the cloud back to Mount Pero!" retorted Musgrove.

King Luccese stepped forward. "What makes you say that, Muzzy?"

Musgrove explained to the King that Bradley had a mobile communication device that could be used to navigate. He continued. "Bradley set the GPS system on his mobile phone and entered the co-ordinates for Mount Pero... now why would he do that?"

Sereny screamed. "Because he is a very bright boy... I think you're right, Muzzy - Bradley could use his mobile phone to send the cloud to Mount Pero!"

King Luccese smiled. "Very clever... if what you both say is true and Bradley manages to deploy the Amulet into the ice-cloud and uses this mobile phone you speak of to the send the cloud to Mount Pero - then the kratennium could be released onto the mountain to stop the atomic explosion."

Sereny asked. "Do you mean Bradley could save Pathylon?"

"Yes, my dear... it does - Bradley Baker could certainly save Pathylon!" declared the King and they all looked up in hope at the cloud, as the boiling kratennium within it sparkled brightly.

Ploom flew deeper into the nebula, as Bradley ensured that his mobile phone was securely attached to the Amulet. Turpol's eyes squinted, as he focussed on the multi-coloured swirls within the cloud. "We are nearing the centre... you will need to throw the Amulet soon - but you must ensure it is imbedded in the kratennium for your plan to work!"

"Okay!" replied Bradley, as the Klomus Hawk steadied her flight. "I had better set the phone's GPS system!" He then pressed the necessary buttons to access the memory on the handset and set the coordinates for Mount Pero. "Right... it's ready - head for the kratennium, Ploom!"

The Klomus Hawk dived deeper into the cloud, as the rich red vein appeared through the crackling lines of electricity. Turpol shouted. "There... just ahead to the right - there's the kratennium!"

Ploom reacted and flew towards the clear crimson liquid, as Bradley prepared himself to throw the Amulet and mobile phone. "My Mum will kill me for losing this!" he shouted and stood up on the bird's back. "Here goes!" he declared and threw the device.

Turpol held his breath, as the object disappeared into the pool of kratennium. He groaned, as the Amulet reappeared and floated helplessly in the cloud's structure. "This isn't going to work!"

Ploom flew over to retrieve the device and explained. "It's too light, Bradley... you need to weight it down with something heavy."

Turpol interjected. "But we don't have time to go back and get anything else!"

"Wait!" declared Bradley and handed the Amulet and phone to the dwarf. "Here... hold this Turpol - I've got another idea!"

Bradley handed the Staff of Evil to Turpol and removed the belt from his waist and slid off the cap lamp battery. He then wrapped the battery around the device using the cable that attached the lamp. He tied it securely and replaced the belt around his waist. "Okay give me back the staff and let's try this!" he declared and lifted his arm in readiness to throw the consortium of electrical technology back into the kratennium.

"Let me try," declared Turpol, as Bradley nodded and handed the dwarf the handmade device. The Gatekeeper then took aim and launched the object.

Ploom, Turpol and Bradley waited for a few minutes and there was no sign of the object. Ploom croaked. "I think you've done it, Turpol!"

298

Bradley sighed. "No you haven't... see over there - it's come back out of the kratennium again."

The dwarf was beside himself and placed his hands on his grey hairless head. "Damn... this isn't going to work - it's still too light!"

Bradley whispered in Ploom's ear and the bird croaked again defiantly. Turpol asked what they were planning but no answer came and Ploom dived down to retrieve the device, as Bradley jumped from her back and grabbed the Amulet.

Turpol shouted. "Bradley... what are you doing?"

The eternal chosen one smiled and fell into the kratennium, as Ploom spread her wings and lifted the Gatekeeper to safety. The dwarf looked down to see Bradley disappear into the liquid and dragged the Amulet down with one hand and he held the Staff of Evil aloft with the other, as his arm gently sunk into the kratennium.

"Why did you let him do that?" insisted Turpol, as he pulled hard on Ploom's neck feathers.

"He insisted... I'm sorry, Turpol - it was a very brave thing for Bradley to do," replied Ploom, in a consoling tone. "Now we have to get out of the cloud before we are also dragged to Mount Pero!"

The landing crafts ferried everyone from the ice-submarine and they berthed safely in Frey Harbour. The kratennium rain had stopped falling from the ice-cloud and the glowing nebula had begun to move away slowly.

Sereny and Musgrove looked up in search of the last Klomus Hawk, as General Eidar escorted them off the landing craft and on to the icy steps of the harbour side. King Luccese was greeted by Pavsik and Queen Vash and they all made their way across to the harbour master's office.

General Eidar announced. "We can wait here for your friends to return... it looks like they have been successful - the ice-cloud is moving away."

King Luccese put his arm around his wife and agreed, as he spoke to the worried looking children. "Now that Bradley has dealt with the ice-cloud... let's hope that he has managed to secure the mobile device you spoke of, Muzzy."

Musgrove walked over to the window and stared up towards the sky. "Still no sign of Ploom... I hope they made it out of that thing okay."

Sereny stood by the teenager and gazed through the icy glass and then screamed. "Ahhhhhhh... there they are - look its Ploom!"

Everyone rushed to get a glimpse of the weary Klomus Hawk circling above their heads. They all made their way out of the harbour master's office and the King led them down to the quayside, as Ploom descended gracefully. The great bird glided down closer and then the realisation hit home, as Sereny held her hand over her open mouth.

Ploom held out her six clawed feet and flapped her wings in a propelling motion, as she landed gently by Musgrove's side. Turpol noticed the shocked look on the boy's face and held his hand out to him, as he stepped down from the hawk's back. The distraught dwarf took a firm grip on Musgrove's arm and offered a consoling hug, as they sat down on the icy harbour side.

Sereny approached the Gatekeeper and flung her arms around his neck. Her embrace was short lived and she pulled out of the embrace to confront the dwarf, as she spoke tearfully. "Where is he... where's Bradley?"

Turpol acknowledged the sadness in the girl's eyes and lifted his sleeve to wipe away the tears, which were cascading down her rosy cheeks. "He just took the responsibility of dealing with the cloud into his own hands... the Amulet wasn't heavy enough to sink into the kratennium - even though we laden it with lot's of equipment."

Sereny tried to enquire further but her voice was too tearful. Musgrove pulled her away from the Gatekeeper and held her tight. "Come on... he maybe okay for all we know!"

Turpol shook his head. "I don't want you to build your hopes up, Muzzy... I saw Bradley disappear into the centre of the cloud and the kratennium was at boiling point - I doubt anyone could have survived those temperatures!" he exclaimed. "Anyhow, if he did survive... we might never see him again - the cloud is on its way to Mount Pero!"

King Luccese thanked Turpol for his assumptive response and spoke gently, as he looked at Musgrove. "It seems your explanation was correct, Muzzy... Bradley did set the coordinates of the mobile device as you said - he is a very brave boy and a true hero."

The dwarf nodded and confirmed the King's summation. "That is correct, your majesty... when the cloud reaches Mount Pero the kratennium will melt again and the Amulet will be released - the mountain will be frozen and hopefully the disaster will be averted."

Pavsik commented. "Then Bradley's brave actions have saved Pathylon once again... but this time his has taken his own life."

Everyone fell silent and they had not noticed Ploom, who had walked slowly over to two canvas sheets that were covering the bodies of his dead colleagues. Queen Vash ran over to console the bird and the others looked away briefly to witness the ice-cloud disappear into the horizon.

Sereny spoke softly and choked. "Goodbye Bradley."

33

Retrieval of the Knife

Back in Trad, Varuna was troubled by the disappearance of the young female and the loud rumblings that had quaked beneath the royal palace earlier. Flaglan dressed for dinner and the Hartopian watched the curvaceous figure of his new love move elegantly around the bed chamber. Although he had enjoyed her company, he was angry with himself for allowing his lust for the sorceress to override his watchful eye on the girl. As well wanting to know how the girl had managed to escape, he was also concerned that the quakes were caused by the Amulet's return to Mount Pero.

Flaglan sat in front of her dressing mirror and let the Hartopian pace back and forth across the bed chamber. "My dear Varuna, you will wear out the floorboards if you persist in troubling yourself with such petty circumstances... the girl has gone - so what?"

Varuna frowned and growled under his breath. "She was no threat, I know... it's just the thought of her escaping that infuriates me - anyhow, it's the rumblings in the ground that I'm more concerned about!"

"Come along... get yourself ready for dinner - we have a big day ahead of us tomorrow," insisted Flaglan. "The coronation will secure our control over Pathylon... we are to be King and Queen of this wonderful kingdom - you have what you have always wanted and that stupid old Luccese is stuck on the cold island of Freytor with his ugly wife!"

Varuna scowled and asked. "Did you not feel the quakes and have you not given any thought that they may have been caused by an explosion on Mount Pero... it means that Maotz must have secured the Amulet - Pathylon is doomed and we have to get out of here!"

Flaglan approached the Hartopian, who was not aware of the situation with the ice-cloud and was sweating profusely. She stroked his pointed snout with the back of her slender fingers and kissed his nose sweetly. "Let us have dinner and wait to see what happens in the morning... if the tremors stop then we hold our coronation and rule the land - if the quakes persist then we can leave for Rekab."

The Hartopian snarled a disapproving growl and grabbed the sorceress. "Rekab is for witches and werewolves... I am not leaving Pathylon for anything or anyone - anyhow, let's forget about having dinner... it's you I want!" he snarled and threw Flaglan onto the bed.

Back at the base of Mount Pero, the Mece people were silent, as the funeral cortege moved slowly through the village to the nearby burial grounds. The mountain continued to spit out streams of hot lava, as the structure shook with a raging quest to destroy the worlds that bordered the unknown land.

The ceremony was about to begin and the Mece chief stood at the head of the cortege, as it came to a halt. The bodies of his two offspring were laid in the ground, as he recited the ritual prayers. The proceedings were interrupted by a darkness that filled the sky. The chief looked up to the top of Mount Pero and saw the ice-cloud appear. "They have done it... the Amulet has returned - our village is now safe from our enemies!"

The chief continued to preach to the Mece people, as the cloud began to disperse the kratennium over the mountain. The lava stopped leaking out of the cracks in the mountain side and the kratennium reacted with the snow caps to form an icy barrier at the summit.

A swarm of Troglobites had been watching the funeral procession and they flew into the air. The giant flying ants started to hover above the Mece just as the Amulet detached itself from Bradley's mobile phone. It fell from the cloud onto the sacred shelf and lodged itself perfectly back into its rightful place at the top of Mount Pero.

The Mece Chief lifted his arms, as he pointed to the Troglobites and uttered. "Be gone with you... no more shall you threaten our village!"

The huge insects scattered immediately and flew up the mountain side to the summit to witness the structure being covered with more kratennium to seal the huge ice-cap blanket. One of the Troglobites still had the Swiss army knife sticking out of its eye and it circled the mountain top in anger, as it focussed on the blue gemstone that was now sparkling deep beneath the thick ice cover.

The creature was taken by surprise, as a heavy object landed on its back. It turned to see what had fallen and was faced with a familiar figure. "Hello ugly!" shouted the boy, as he smashed the staff of Evil across the insects head. "And I'll have that back... thank you very much!" retorted Bradley and pulled the knife out of the creature's eye, as yellow puss gushed out of the wound.

The Troglobite squealed in pain and tried to dismount its agile rider by bucking its rear end. Bradley increased his grip by tensioning his thigh muscles and placed the knife between his teeth, as he multi-tasked by slinging his belt around the insect's neck. "Not a chance, mate... I'm going nowhere - in fact you're coming with me!"

The Mece people below were watching the boy's acrobatic actions and the events at the top of the mountain were received with a chorus of cheers below, as Bradley waved to acknowledge their support. He controlled the creature and flew down to pass over the burial site, as a final mark of respect.

Chief Kuma smiled and waved, as Bradley used his belt to guide the insect back up the mountain side. "Okay, you giant cockroach... let's get the hell out of here - I've got some friend's back in Freytor waiting for me and some insecticide waiting for you!" he exclaimed and kicked his hard toe-capped boots into the side of the insect.

Meanwhile back in Trad, Flaglan and Varuna continued to celebrate their illegal rule over Pathylon. The Hartopian stopped petting with the sorceress and sat upright. "Can you hear that?"

"Hear what?" replied Flaglan.

"Exactly!" roared the Hartopian. "I can't hear or feel any tremors... Mount Pero must have been secured - Pathylon is ours to rule!"

Flaglan afforded her new partner a smug look. "I told you everything would turn out okay... now we need to make plans for our coronation tomorrow - our people will be expecting a party!"

Varuna roared out an aggressive laugh and pulled the sorceress back towards him. "You are going to be a very wicked Queen!"

"And you are going to be a very evil King!" she replied, as they both burst into uncontrollable laughter.

Word had been sent to Freytor that the ice-cloud had successfully reached Mount Pero and the tremors in Pathylon had ceased. Now that Pathylon was safe, King Luccese was making plans with General Eidar for an attack on Devonia, but it would be some time before a fleet of ice-submarines were ready to make the journey and make a serious bid to remove Varuna from the Pathylian capital.

Whilst the hierarchy made their plans, Sereny sat in the waiting room of the health pod with Musgrove, as they waited for Meltor to recover from his operation. The old Galetian had undergone the complicated heart operation and was still under the effects of the anesthetic. He wasn't expected to wake for a few hours and Queen Vash sat with the two children, as the atmosphere remained solemn for some time.

Pavsik walked into the room and announced that the Freytorian time-machine had been prepared to take the children back home to the outside world. "Are you both ready to leave... the locomotive is ready when you are?"

Sereny stayed silent, as Musgrove got out of his chair. "Come on, Sereny... there's nothing more for us to do here - it will be some while yet before Meltor wakes." He explained. "Bradley is gone and we need to get back to Ravenswood to explain everything to his parents."

The girl did not reply and stood up with her head still bowed. She walked in a dream-like state over to the waiting room door, which was being held ajar by Pavsik. Sereny dragged her feet and carried on walking under the High Priest's outstretched arm, as her ruffled blonde hair brushed on the heavy hanging cloth from his sleeve.

Musgrove followed and Pavsik moved out of the way to let the tall teenager pass. Queen Vash pulled on Musgrove's overalls. "Will you two be okay, Muzzy... I am concerned about Sereny?"

The boy turned to face the Queen. "Don't worry ma'am, I'll look after her... but we will miss Bradley - he was a good mate and a real hero."

Pavsik nodded and announced. "As the High Priest of Devonia... I declare that Bradley Baker will go down in Pathylian history as a brave hero," he stated and bowed, as her royal highness passed through the doorway.

Queen Vash led the group away from the health pod and Pavsik escorted the forlorn children to the ice shed where the locomotive was waiting to take them home. As they entered the huge hanger, the sound and smell of industrial steam filled the air. The engine puffed out clouds of coal-fired smoke from its bright red chimney and the loco's brakes strained, as they fought to be released from their hold.

Musgrove put his arm around Sereny, who was still walking with very little awareness of what was going on around her. He spoke softly. "Come on Sereny... we have to board the train now - we are going home."

Sereny lifted her head and looked at Musgrove's kind face. "What are we going to say to Bradley's Mum and Dad?"

"We just have to tell them the truth... that their Son was a very courageous fella and that he gave his life to save a wonderful kingdom," replied Musgrove, as he wiped away a stray tear from the girl's cheek. "Come on, Sereny... let's get back."

King Luccese and General Eidar arrived on the platform, followed by Turpol. The King stood next to Queen Vash and the dwarf approached the children, as they turned to board the engine. The Gatekeeper did not speak and simply offered them both a sympathetic look. The dwarf held up his short arm and waved to acknowledge their departure.

More steam bellowed out from the engine and covered the platform, as the children stepped onto the locomotive. Sereny turned and waved to the Queen but Vash was preoccupied, as the inquisitive girl followed the direction of her stare. She noticed the silhouette of a large shaped figure hovering above the platform and it was moving in the smoke at the far end of the hanger.

The steam swirled as the strange shadow approached and the giant flying insect appeared out of the smoke. Sereny let out a frightened scream, as the Troglobite flew towards them and the Queen shouted. "Sereny... it's Bradley!"

Sereny's screams turned to cries of delight, as the eternal chosen one pulled on the insect's head and turned it to reveal his confident riding position. He yelled down at his friends and laughed. "Hi there... have you missed me!"

Musgrove and Sereny jumped back on to the platform and ran over to the others, as they waited for Bradley to control the resistant Troglobite. Sereny wrapped her arms around the

Queen's waist and squeezed her tightly. Vash reciprocated and exclaimed. "How wonderful... he's back - I am so pleased for you, Sereny!"

"I can't believe it!" cried Sereny. "Bradley did it... he saved Pathylon - I can't wait to speak to him and find out what he did!"

The weary Troglobite became tired of fighting the boy's controlling influence and landed on the platform, as Bradley tapped it on the head with the Staff of Evil to ensure the insect obeyed his command. The boy climbed down from the ant's back and twirled the staff in his hand before throwing it over to the Gatekeeper. "Here you go Turpol... keep it safe!"

Sereny released her grip on the Queen and ran over to Bradley. She pounded her fists on his cheats and exclaimed. "We thought you were dead... we were just about to leave and tell your parents!"

"Well, I'm back and everything is okay," replied Bradley calmly, as he held his opened hand out to Musgrove. "Good to see you again, Muzzy."

The teenager smiled and offered his hand in return, as they gripped their handshake firmly. "Good to know you are okay, Brad... great to have you back - and that's a pretty firm handshake you've got there, Brad!"

"Must be something to do with the kratennium... I feel so much stronger!" replied Bradley, as he explained what happened inside the ice-cloud and how he managed to secure the Amulet back on Mount Pero.

King Luccese had been listening intently to the three friends and approached to offer his thanks. "We owe you so much, Bradley Baker... we will never forget what you have done for Pathylon."

"Your majesty, I did what I had to do!" replied Bradley. "The task set by Meltor and the message on the grobite called for my help... it was my duty as the eternal chosen one - I hope the task is now complete and we can return home!"

The King explained that Varuna had taken control of the Devonian capital and he was imposing himself as the new ruler of Pathylon again. "There is still plenty to do and we are working with General Eidar to launch an attack on Varuna's army of Tree Elves... he has teamed up with Flaglan - when Meltor wakes we will try to get in touch with the Galetis Empire to seek their help."

"How is Meltor... did the operation go okay?" asked Bradley.

Pavsik intervened. "He hasn't woken from the anesthetic yet... so we do not know whether the operation was a success - but because of your quick thinking and Rathek's bravery, he has a good chance of making a full recovery."

Bradley nodded and looked at his friend's then offered his support. "Do you need us to stay and help?"

The King shook his head. "No, Bradley... we can take it from here - you three need to get back to your own world before your parents start suspecting your absence."

The Gatekeeper escorted the children back over to the locomotive, which was still exhuming smoke from its enormous chimney. The noise of the engine over-powered any further conversation, as the children boarded the time machine.

Sereny and Musgrove disappeared inside one of the carriages and Bradley turned to offer one last wave, as he shouted to King Luccese. "Please give Meltor my best wishes... and remember - do not hesitate to contact me if you need any help with Varuna!"

Luccese lifted his arm to acknowledge the boy's comment and the locomotive started to move along the tracks. Turpol ran by the side of the engine and shouted up to Bradley. "One last thing... if you are called back to Pathylon again - avoid the Pyramids of Blood!"

A puzzled look appeared on Bradley's face. "Okay... but why?"

The Gatekeeper could see the platform coming to an end and he tried to conclude. "The kratennium has definitely made you stronger... but if you enter the Pyramids of Blood - you will be transformed you into something else!"

"What?" shouted Bradley.

"You would become a w...!" Turpol did not have time to finish his sentence, as the screeching of locomotive's wheels ground on the tracks and the engine lifted into the air.

Sereny and Musgrove reappeared to join their confused looking friend, as the three children waved at the entourage on the platform.

A loud bang erupted from the coal-fired engine and the spinning of the locomotive's wheels screeched again, as the Freytorpian time machine shot away at lightning speed. Luccese, Vash, Pavsik, Eidar and Turpol stood on the platform waving, as it lifted into the air and left the hanger with a gulf of swirling steam in its wake.

34

Brothers in Armchairs

Back in Ravenswood, Margaret and Frannie had returned from their shopping trip in Leeds. Bradley's mother left the lounge and made her way into the kitchen to prepare dinner, she called back to her husband. "Have you seen Bradley since you got back from work, Patrick?"

"No dear... I had to go down the shops to get some milk - I haven't been back in the house that long!" replied Patrick, as he winked at the strange figure that was sat comfortably in one of the fireside chairs.

Margaret reappeared in the lounge and heard the front door burst open. "That must be them, now!"

The three exhausted children entered the house and made their way into the lounge. Bradley was uncomfortably aware of the attention being paid to his dirty orange clothing, as he assessed the audience. He paid particular attention to the well-groomed man sitting in the chair, whose face looked strangely familiar. Sereny and Musgrove followed their friend into the crowded room and waited for a predictable comment from one of Bradley's parents.

Immediately, Patrick Baker approached his weary-looking son and placed a welcoming hand on his shoulder. "Welcome home, Bradley... we've been worried about you - when I got home from work earlier I searched everywhere for you!" he exclaimed. "I even tidied up the bathroom after you... your Mum was well impressed."

Margaret laughed and agreed. "Yes... I think that's a first - I shall have to get your father doing the house work more regularly!" she exclaimed, as Patrick cast his wife a disapproving stare.

Bradley's father changed the subject and commented. "Your Uncle Henley has travelled over from Sheffield to visit for the day and has been asking after you... tell him what you've been up to - by the look of your clothes I think you'll have lot's to say!"

Bradley afforded his father a puzzled look and cast his attention back to the eerie figure in the chair, who was wearing a flat cap and who now wore a broad smile across his face. "Are you really my Uncle... and why are you wearing your cap indoors?"

Patrick squeezed his son's shoulder and Bradley turned to face his father again. "Of course he is your Uncle and as well you know he always wears a flat cap indoors you cheeky devil... he never takes it off and he's been waiting all morning to see you - now introduce your friends to Uncle Henley and tell him what you three have been up to during half term."

Sereny leant over and muttered to Musgrove. "Surely this can't be... Bradley told us his Uncle was killed at the coal face down Silvermoor Colliery in 1975."

"Yeah... you're right," replied Musgrove. "But I guess anything is possible... remember back in the summer when my father mysteriously reappeared after all those years - it must have something to do with the coin!"

"I still haven't got over that incident... you must have so many questions to ask your Dad - it must be so frustrating for you," declared Sereny.

Yeah, it's difficult but I can't reveal the secret of the coin and Pathylon - anyhow, let's see what Bradley has to say," insisted Musgrove, as Patrick waited for his son to explain himself.

There was an uncomfortable silence in the room, as Bradley's parents and uncle waited for his response. The tension in the room was suddenly transferred to Frannie, as she ran into the lounge and tripped over one of K2's plastic bones. The toy squeaked, as the four year old fell forward and hit her head on the toe of Uncle Henley's left shoe. Now all the attention was focussed on the little red head, as she lay sobbing with her head face down in the carpet pile.

Frannie's body became rigid and she refused to move, as Margaret placed her hands either side of the girl's rib cage. She struggled to pick up her distraught daughter. Patrick and Henley rallied to help Margaret, as the brothers-in-arms planned the best way to lift the sulking child off the floor without causing her any further embarrassment.

The unnecessary over-acting from Frannie caused the three adults to enter into a debate and this was Bradley's opportunity to make a hasty retreat. He turned to leave and brushed by his friends. "Come on you two... she'll be okay - let's get out of here while they calm her down!"

Musgrove and Sereny took a glancing look to assess the recovery operation of Frannie and did not hesitate, as they followed Bradley out of the room and into the kitchen.

"What did you make of that?" asked Bradley, as he approached the kitchen sink.

"Well... your little sister did over react!" replied Musgrove.

"I don't think Bradley was referring to Frannie's little incident!" surmised Sereny, as Bradley filled a glass with water from the cold tap and proceeded to consume the contents in one attempt.

Musgrove waited for his friend to finish quenching his thirst. "Right, yeah... Sereny and me were just talking about it," he hesitated, as his face coloured a little and he looked to Sereny for support. "Meeting your Uncle Henley like that... it was a very similar situation to when my Dad was sat in your Aunt Vera's lounge in the summer - following his mysterious disappearance."

Bradley surmised. "I'll tell you what I think... something I've suspected for some time - I think my Uncle Henley is the *Mauled Miner*!"

"What makes you think that?" asked Sereny.

"It was the smile on his face," replied Bradley.

Musgrove commented. "Don't be daft... the mauled miner didn't have a face, so you couldn't have seen him smile!"

"You're right Muzzy... however, when we met the mauled miner I took some time to study the emptiness beneath his pit helmet - I looked beyond the blackness and I saw the same smile deep within his head!" explained Bradley. "You are looking at me as if I'm talking a load of rubbish and I know it sounds weird... but you have to trust me on this one - I felt it when my so-called Uncle smiled at me in the lounge just now."

Sereny sympathised with her charming young friend. "I don't think Muzzy disbelieves what you're saying Bradley and neither do I... we all know that anything is possible after what we have been through - if your Uncle Henley is the mauled miner then surely that is a good thing."

"Sereny is right... I've accepted my Father's return and you should be pleased that your Dad has his long lost brother back in his life," agreed Musgrove.

Bradley acknowledged his friends. "Thanks guys... but that's the whole point - my Dad doesn't know any different. As far as he is concerned Uncle Henley has never been away!"

"Well you are just going to have to do what I did," replied Musgrove. "Just accept it and celebrate all the good that has come out of it... after all - it's better to have your Uncle in your life rather than think of him wandering through a disused mine or the Vortex of Silvermoor with no face for all eternity."

The three children continued to debate the situation and the impact it would have on Bradley's life. Their discussions were interrupted as Uncle Henley appeared in the kitchen. The conversation froze, as the handsome man approached and offered his hand to Musgrove.

"Hello... my name is Henley - and you are?" he asked, as Musgrove felt the strong clench of the man's handshake.

"Errr... errr - Muzzy!" replied Musgrove in a very shaky tone and confirmed nervously. "Err, well... Musgrove actually - but everyone calls me Muzzy."

"Well it's great to meet you again, Muzzy!" replied Bradley's uncle and then corrected his comment. "I mean... it's a pleasure to meet you."

Sereny interjected and offered her petite hand, as she smiled. "Hello, Mr. Baker... my name is Sereny Ugbrooke and it's a pleasure to meet *you* at last - the boys have told me all about you!"

Bradley nudged Sereny gently and offered her a frowned look. "What are you doing?"

"Oh come on, Bradley... your Uncle knows!" she replied, as the broad smile appeared on Henley's face again. "Look at your Uncle... see that smile - he knows alright!"

Henley Baker released the gentle hold on Sereny's hand and turned to Bradley. "She's right lad... I know everything."

"I knew it was him!" declared Bradley, as he afforded his friends a smug look.

Uncle Henley acknowledged his nephew's observation. "I had no doubt you would recognise me quickly, Bradley... after all you are the *eternal chosen one* - and your powers are much greater now than you could ever imagine!"

"You said you know everything," said Sereny.

Bradley intervened. "So what exactly do you know?"

"Well, as we have already established... I was the mauled miner!" replied Henley, as he reciprocated his brother's action and placed his hand on Bradley's shoulder. "When you, me and Muzzy jumped into the Vortex of Silvermoor together... I tried to keep up with you both," he explained.

"But you were travelling a lot faster than me and I could not keep up with you... when I eventually reached the other side my facial features had returned - I was no longer a ghost."

"Okay... assuming what you are saying is true" acknowledged Bradley. "How did you get out of Pathylon?"

Henley gripped his nephew's shoulder and guided him towards the large kitchen table. "Let's all sit down... I have a lot to explain - Frannie is being consoled by her Mum and Dad in the lounge so we have some time to talk before they come back in here."

Musgrove and Sereny followed the man's suggestion and took their seating positions around the large oak table, as Bradley stared into his uncle's persuasive eyes. "Please sit down Bradley and I will begin," insisted Henley, as he gentled pushed down on his nephew's shoulder.

"This is weird," said Bradley, as he acknowledged his uncle's request and his bottom touched the seat of the chair. "So... come on Uncle, tell us - how did you get out of Pathylon?

Henley took a few seconds to gather his thoughts and then started to offer his explanation to the three bemused children. "I never entered the world of Pathylon... when we all jumped into the Vortex of Silvermoor... I could see you and Muzzy swirling ahead of me and I shouted out to you both - but neither of you could hear me."

"Well... it was pretty loud and scary inside that thing!" replied Bradley. "So why were you shouting at us?"

"I could see the junction ahead... it was the fork in the vortex and I wanted to make sure we all took the correct route - as it happened it did not make any difference to me."

Sereny asked in an inquisitive tone. "What do you mean?"

"Well... Bradley and Muzzy were taken down the right fork that led to Pathylon and even though I tried to follow them - I was pulled in the opposite direction and I had no choice in the matter," continued Henley. "As you know... Bradley and Muzzy entered the Unknown Land but I eventually ended up in a darkened room - it was as if I was meant to be sent there on purpose."

"So where was the room located?" asked Musgrove.

"At the end of Bradley's road!" replied Henley, as he stood up from his seat and looked out of the kitchen window. "Just over there." He pointed.

All three children stood up and followed the direction of the man's finger. Henley indicated his attention to the war memorial that stood at the entrance to the housing estate.

Bradley exclaimed. "The Old Blue Light!"

"Yes," replied his uncle.

"But how did you get there?" asked Sereny.

"It must have been the same way you entered Silvermoor... via the trap door in the chamber" replied Bradley.

Henley approached the table and took his seat again. "What do mean, Bradley - so you already know about the hidden chamber?"

"Yes... when Rathek came here - we were transported into the chamber beneath the old blue light and that's when Sereny disappeared," explained Bradley, as they all sat down in turn.

Musgrove stared at the centre of the kitchen table. "It's as if all this was pre-rehearsed... I feel we're all in some sort of trance."

Henley reassured Musgrove. "It's not pre-rehearsed, Muzzy - the events that have taken place recently were created by your intervention and the sacred coin that Bradley possesses will always ensure that Pathylon is protected."

"So apart from seeing your family again... why is your return from Silvermoor so important?" asked Sereny.

Bradley's uncle chose not to answer the girl's question directly and proceeded to tell the children more about the hidden room located beneath the cenotaph. He went on to explain that this was the entrance to another shaft that used to allow men to access the Silvermoor mine to pump water out of the two main shafts.

Bradley interrupted. "My Dad used to tell me about this... they used to call it *the Well* - he was one of the electricians that used to go down and maintain the pumping equipment at the bottom of the well shaft."

"That's right Bradley... and the well shaft is located midway between the East and West Pit shafts," explained Henley.

"So why did the Vortex of Silvermoor send you there?" asked Musgrove.

"Not sure... I guess that's a mystery I cannot explain - but for future reference at least you know there is another way into the strange world of Pathylon and as we know, it's right outside your front door!" exclaimed Henley, as he cast his nephew an encouraging look.

Bradley thought about what Turpol had told him about the Pyramids of Blood, but he didn't comment and decided to smile in an approving manner. His uncle's detailed explanation and that last look he gave him was all he needed to be convinced that the truth was being told about their last visit to Pathylon. "Will you promise to keep Pathylon a secret - Uncle Henley?"

"Of course I will, Bradley... you have my word!" he replied. "And I have a vested interest in keeping it a secret... I don't want to be the mauled miner again - anyhow, there's another important thing that I haven't told you yet."

The children waited with baited breath as Henley stood up again and started to pace the kitchen floor. He cast another longing stare at his nephew and paused for a few seconds.

"Come on Uncle Henley," insisted Bradley, as he pounded his clenched fist on the table. "What is it that you haven't told us yet... the others will be coming in to see what we're all up to in a minute?"

Bradley was right and the tension in the room was interrupted, as the kitchen door swung open with an animated announcement from Frannie. "Hello everyone... I just thought you'd be pleased to hear that I'm fine now - so what are you lot talking about?"

Bradley replied with utter annoyance. "Get lost Frannie... you're a real pain - we were having a private conversation with Uncle Henley!"

"Chill out, Bradders!" Frannie replied cheekily. "He's my Uncle as well as yours," she teased. "Anyhow, you love me the most... don't you Uncle Henley?"

Henley smiled at his niece then sat back down again and Bradley, Musgrove and Sereny looked at each other in frustration. The little girl had interrupted the conversation at a crucial climax and there was no way they could continue now. Bradley glared at his sister for calling him Bradders and then responded gratefully to a gentle nudge from Sereny, who offered him an affectionate glance.

Bradley's brief moment of intimacy was interrupted by his father, who entered the kitchen and immediately focussed his attention on his son. "Well it's great to see you have spent some time with your Uncle Henley... under slightly bizarre circumstances I hasten to add, with your sister taking a little knock and all that - but I hope you've had a chance to catch up and tell him what you've been up to this week."

Bradley's uncle interjected. "Yes Patrick... Bradley and is friends have told me all about there adventures this week - especially the bit about playing in Silvermoor Woods," he explained and winked at Bradley.

"Oh... errr yeah - playing hide and seek in the woods was especially fun but as you can see we found these old clothes got them a bit mucky," he improvised.

Patrick asked. "Where did you get them... they look likc National Coal Board issued overalls?"

Sereny thought quickly and offered an explanation. "We found them in a basement in an old shop down the road - Bradley and Muzzy thought it would be fun to dress up!"

Patrick knew the girl was referring to the old lamp room cellar where he had found the old photograph. He decided not top pursue his line of questioning for fear that Margaret would suspect his illegal entry into the premises some days previous.

Margaret overheard their comments and reacted to the words *'dirt and clothes'*, as she entered the kitchen. "Don't worry Bradley... I'm putting a load in the washing machine tomorrow morning - just make sure you leave your dirty clothes in the laundry room tonight after you've all had a bath."

Henley looked at the three children. "Just make sure you have separate baths!"

Bradley, Musgrove and Sereny all laughed, as Margaret replied to her brother-in-law. "I should hope at their age they will be taking separate baths Henley... you really need to be careful what you say - isn't that right children?"

Before any of the children had a chance to reply, Henley commented. "Oh I'm sure they all know what I mean... don't you kids?"

All three children nodded. They knew exactly what Henley was referring too. Jumping in the bath together meant only one thing to them; more amazing adventures down the plughole.

Bradley's attention wandered, as he remembered the grobite and disappeared out of the kitchen with an excuse to use the toilet. He made his way upstairs and entered the bathroom. "Phewww!" he exclaimed and reached in to the bath to retrieve the gold coin.

35

Delivering the Bad News

Back in Freytor, Meltor slept soundly in his hospital bed, as General Eidar waited in the health pod reception area. The Freytorian was keen to be the first to deliver the good news to the ailing High Priest. Now that Pathylon was safe from the evil threat of his brother, he felt it necessary to apologise personally for the upheaval that Norsk had created.

One of the health pod care assistants rushed into the reception and approached the General, holding a feather quill in her white paw. "Sir... if I may hold your attention - the Galetian patient has woken and he wishes to speak with you."

"Thank you, nurse... please tell Lord Meltor I will be with him shortly," replied Eidar, as he shuffled some paperwork on the reception desk. "I just need to finish this report."

"Of course General... I'll let the patient know," replied the health pod care assistant, as she ticked a box on her computer pad and then adjusted the broad purple belt around her thin waste.

General Eidar watched the female ice-bear as she inserted the quill into the top pocket of her white coat and held the computer pad close to her chest. She then turned with the precision of a regimental guard and quickly made her way across the reception area. The General waited for the pretty nurse to disappear before turning to look at his paperwork. Eidar did not really have a report to finish; he just needed some time to compose himself. The Freytorian was not looking forward to telling Meltor about the loss of his young protégé. He was certain the Galetian High Priest would blame himself for Rathek's death.

Eidar muttered to himself. "Had Meltor not fallen ill Rathek would not have ventured into the outside world... the old fool will not be able to forgive himself."

The young health pod care assistant reappeared and showed her concern that the General was taking so long. "Sir... the patient is asking for you!"

Eidar's patience grew thin and he let out a gentle roar. "Young nurse... please remember who you are addressing - I said I would be through shortly!"

The health pod care assistant cowered and replied in a nervous tone. "Forgive me, General... I will leave you alone - my sincere apologies?"

"No... no please don't go - it is I who should apologise my dear," insisted Eidar, as he approached the nurse. "It's been a stressful few weeks and I'm very tired... I did not mean to shout at you - please lead me to Lord Meltor."

"That's alright, Sir... I understand and I am sorry to hear about the death of your brother - I can't imagine what you must be going through," commiserated the health pod care assistant. "Each and every Freytorians thoughts are with you and I hope you don't feel that anyone thinks the same about you... although your brother's intentions were honourable - they were wrong and it is the strength of your leadership, which has saved us from being disowned by the rest of the world."

The General was stunned by the brave words coming from the nurse and he afforded her a caring smile. "You speak courageously on behalf of our people my dear and your words are wise... thank you - now please lead me to our Pathylian friend."

Meltor was now sat upright and eating a meal that had been delivered from the health pod canteen. He pierced a piece of the raw freyfish on his plate and scooped some kind of Freytorian sauce over its silver scales. "This looks very appetising... not!"

As the Galetian High Priest put the food to his mouth, General Eidar walked into the room. This was a good excuse for Meltor to put the food back on the plate and he pushed the tray to one side.

"How are you my old friend?" asked Eidar. "I hope they're feeding you well!"

Meltor removed the napkin ring and pretended to wipe his mouth. "Mmmm.... yes - delicious!" he lied and held out his hand to the General. "I am feeling much better... now please tell me - has the threat of Ma-otz been repelled?"

Eidar was pleased to avoid telling Meltor of Rathek's death and relayed the news of Basjoo Ma-otz demise. "Oh yes... he fell to his death on Mount Pero."

"That is excellent news... and the Amulet of Silvermoor - has it been retrieved?" asked Meltor.

The General sat on the end of the bed and assured the High Priest. "Well, sort of... it was retrieved and lost and is now secure again - I'll fill you in with all the details later but I have to inform you that Varuna has eluded us and..."

"Varuna... eluded us - what do you mean?" exclaimed Meltor, as he moved the meal tray out of the way and attempted to get out of the bed. "Arrrrgh!"

General Eidar leaned forward and the nurse rushed into the room. Together they helped the High Priest back onto the bed. Meltor held his chest tightly and breathed in sharply.

"You must rest," insisted the health pod care assistant. "Your new heart is still weak - you have to give your body time to accept it."

"New heart!" queried Meltor, as he looked for an explanation from the anxious General. "What's going on, Eidar?"

"I think I had better start from the beginning," explained the Freytorian, as he sat back on the bed and held the Galetian's lower arm.

The nurse checked that the intravenous drip was secure and left the room, as Eidar proceeded to tell Meltor about what had happened and the High Priest stayed silent, as he started his explanation of events.

Over an hour had past before the nurse returned to check on Meltor. General Eidar had finished talking about the capture of Basjoo Ma-otz and the safe return of the Amulet to Mount Pero. He had also told Meltor about the death of his brother and how Varuna had escaped from the crumbled Shallock Tower and was now in control of Trad. He also told of Bradley Baker's double heroics and how he had saved Pathylon by stopping Norsk's deathly plans, as the ice-cloud was diverted to Mount Pero.

"So my young friend Bradley not only saved Pathylon... he also saved Freytor too - I am so pleased to hear everything went to plan," said Meltor. "Thank you for explaining everything to me... well, almost everything - what about my heart?"

"Ah... yes, well errr - you may have to brace yourself for the next bit," insisted Eidar. "What I am about to tell you will cause you great sorrow my friend and I am concerned that you will react badly... your heart is still weak and I am concerned for you!"

Meltor grabbed the General's seal-skin cloak and gave him the assurance needed. "Eidar... I have to know - now please tell me."

"Very well... Rathek was killed by one of the giant ant creatures that frequent the Silvermoor mine - he insisted that before the creature killed him, your friend Bradley Baker was to extract his heart and give it to you," explained Eidar, as the High Priest dropped his head. "Bradley did indeed perform the task... he was successful in salvaging the vital organ from the remains of Rathek's body - and it's a good job he did!"

"That is terrible news... if I had not fallen ill - Rathek would not have been put in danger," replied Meltor. "And what do you mean... it's a good job he did?"

"I knew you would blame yourself for his death," replied Eidar. "It wasn't your fault Meltor... Rathek travelled to the outside world to find Bradley Baker of his own accord and he was successful in his mission - his death played a major part in the future of Pathylon by securing the Amulet, which without that the ice-cloud would have most certainly destroyed Freytor and Pathylon would have been obliterated."

"It's difficult to accept that such a brave young Devonian has sacrificed his life for the cause and especially when it should have been me who travelled to the outside world," declared Meltor. "And this feeling of life within me is being supplied by Rathek's beating heart inside my chest."

The Galetian completed his expression of grief and broke down in floods of tears, as General Eidar moved next to him to hold the High Priest as he wept. "Yes... you have Rathek's heart - as I said, it was the last thing he requested before he died."

Meltor sobbed inconsolably and he managed to regain his composure to explain his feelings. "What a brave thing to do... what a brave young Devonian - I am very proud to carry his heart and I can feel Rathek's soul inside me."

"I'm sure that is what he would have wanted you to feel... Bradley Baker was very adamant that Rathek's final request was carried out," explained the General and handed the High Priest a note. "Here... Queen Vash gave me this to give to you - according to the Klomus Hawk; Bradley wanted you to have this."

Meltor wiped the tears from his eyes and took the note from Eidar. He opened it and noticed it was written on the back of a map. He started to read Bradley's words out loud;

'Meltor,

Apologies for the quality of the paper this message is written on but it's all we had. At time of writing, Muzzy and I have just arrived in the Unknown Land through the Vortex of Silvermoor.

I sincerely hope you are reading this letter, because if you are it means that the operation to replace your weakened heart has been successful. I just wanted to let you know that Rathek fought well against the Troglobites and his last request was for you to have his heart to make you better.

He died with his final thoughts of you in my mind and wished you well... you are a proud Galetian but I know you will be even more proud to have a Devonian heart.

Check out the back of this note... it's an old map of Silvermoor that my Dad found and should give you an idea of what we've gone through to get this far.

I hope to catch up with you soon, but first we have to retrieve the Amulet and stop Basjoo Ma-otz. The Klomus Hawk also told us about Norsk and the ice-cloud, which I believe is heading your way and must be destroyed.

As far as I know Sereny is with Turpol and I just hope they are okay. I just hope that when you read this note we have all been successful.

> *Best wishes,*
> *Bradley Baker'*

Meltor appreciated Eidar's support and the Freytorian moved aside, as the High Priest held the note to his chest. "Thank you for letting me read this... it is a lovely letter and I appreciate Bradley's words - I will make Rathek proud and I accept his heart in the knowledge that he died to help the people of Pathylon live!"

"Hopefully you will be able to thank Bradley in person one day... but for now I think you should rest old man," said Eidar, as he summoned the nurse to his side.

The health pod care assistant asked Meltor to get some sleep and the Galetian lay back still clutching the letter. "Would you like me to take that?" she asked and reached out for the note.

"No... err, no thank you - I'll keep it for now," replied Meltor, as he closed his weary eyes and drifted off to sleep.

General Eidar reached out and touched the High Priest in a gesture of solidarity. He knew it was always going to be difficult telling Meltor about Rathek and he was glad the conversation was over. Before leaving, the General lifted the covers over the Galetian's chest to keep him warm. He then escorted the nurse out of the room, leaving the tormented old man to rest for a while.

36

The Beacon of Hope

Back in the Baker household, the sacred gold coin was in Bradley's possession again and the relieved boy had now rejoined his friends in the kitchen. They waited patiently for the adults to finish their conversation so they could discover what else Henley had to say.

Margaret suggested that Bradley's uncle stay for dinner and he agreed. Patrick asked Frannie to go upstairs and wash her hands then suggested to his brother that they retire to the lounge to watch some of the rugby highlights on the television.

Henley acknowledged his brother's request but proposed something different. "Actually Bro... I'd quite like to take K2 for a walk and I was wondering if Bradley wanted to come with me - and his friends too, if they want?"

"That sounds like a good idea... I might come with you," replied Patrick, as the children simultaneously shrugged their shoulders and looked to Henley for his response.

Without realising it, Margaret came to their rescue and told Patrick he could help her prepare tea. "You're going nowhere, Patrick Baker... you can clear those dishes for a start - we'll need most of them to set the table for dinner."

Patrick sighed and vented his response. "Well... that's me sorted then - Bradley, you'd better call K2 in from the garden."

Bradley smiled at his friends and made is way over to the pantry. "Sereny, you call K2 and I'll get the dog's lead... Uncle Henley - I'll meet you outside with Musgrove and Sereny.

There was no need for Sereny to make the call, as the clinking sound of the lead being taken off the hook alerted K2's attention from the bottom of the garden. The large hound came bounding into the kitchen and Margaret laughed. "It's amazing what dogs can hear... when it suits," she said. "Especially when it's walkies time... off you go then you lot - we'll have dinner ready for when you get back!"

K2 was pleased to have received the unplanned exercise and he ran through Silvermoor woods ahead of the group. He sniffed around a few trees than scampered off into the undergrowth in search of some woodland wildlife to torment.

Henley and the three children walked at a slow pace through the woods and it wasn't long before Bradley's uncle brought up the subject of Pathylon again. "So was the mission as successful as you had hoped, Bradley?"

Bradley paused for a moment to reflect on the exciting events over the past few days. "Yes... we managed to save the day and Pathylon is safe again... for now - Varuna is still free but I'm sure King Luccese will regain control again once Meltor's is well enough to lead the Galetian army," replied Bradley, as he kicked at the autumn leaves. "It's just a shame Rathek didn't make it... he didn't stand a chance against the Troglobites - but then you were the mauled miner so you witnessed that horrific scene and I'm sure neither of us want to talk about it any more."

Bradley's uncle put his arm around his nephew. "Rathek's death fills me with great sorrow... but there are some other things I need to tell you - it is very important that you all hear what I have to say."

Sereny had an idea she knew what one of the things Bradley's uncle was referring to and interrupted to make an assumption. "Well... Mr. Baker - at least you're back safe and sound..."

Henley responded before she had the chance to relay her thoughts. "Please, Sereny... call me Henley - not sure about the Mr. Baker thing."

"Okay," replied the girl. Her cheeks coloured with embarrassment, as she decided not to reveal her thoughts and instead asked. "So are you going to tell us about the other important things?"

"Yes... of course," replied Henley, as he surveyed the woods for a place to rest. "Shall we all sit over there on those logs?"

Musgrove ran ahead towards the felled tree stumps. "Sounds like a good idea to me!" he shouted.

The group sat down and Henley paused for a moment, as he removed the flat cap from his head. He parted his thick hair to reveal two short horns. "I am not just Bradley's Uncle... I am also Rathek's second cousin - I am a Devonian from Pathylon!"

Musgrove held his head in his hands and directed his forehead towards his knees, as he spoke into his blood-stained overalls. "I can't take much more of this... now I'm totally confused!"

Bradley smiled, as Musgrove lifted his head again. "I get it... if you are Rathek's second cousin and also my Uncle - for my Father to recognise you as his brother, you must have previously travelled from Pathylon into our world some time ago."

"That's right... I used to travel in and out of Pathylon with Meltor - as you know, he used the alias Old Mac back then," recalled Henley. "That's when I first met your Aunt Vera!"

"You met my Aunt Vera?" confirmed Bradley.

"Yes... she was only seventeen when I first met her and very attractive," replied Henley.

"I can't imagine your Aunt Vera ever being attractive!" exclaimed Musgrove. "No offence, mate!"

Sereny interrupted. "So how did you end up as a coal miner at Silvermoor Colliery?"

Henley smiled at the inquisitive girl. "I fell in love with Bradley's Aunt... she was visiting Sandmouth on holiday and I was in a strange world away from family in Pathylon," he explained. "Against Meltor's advice, I decided to follow Vera back to Yorkshire... but it was to no avail - it just didn't work out between us!"

Bradley asked. "So how did you end up being my Uncle if you are really a Devonian from Pathylon?"

"Good question and one I am happy to answer," replied Henley. "When your Aunt Vera moved from Yorkshire to live in Sandmouth... I took board and lodgings with your Dad's family - so you see I'm not your real Uncle but I grew very close to your Grandparents and they adopted me as their own."

Bradley acknowledged Henley's explanation. "So you followed my Grandfather Baker down the mines and ended up getting yourself killed in the process... getting your face torn off must have been a horrendous experience."

Henley replied. "Yes... it was an horrific accident and it meant I had to roam the underground passages as a ghost for some time until someone linked to Pathylon and the outside world found me - those people were my second cousin Rathek and you!" he stated. "But... I have to say - it is you I have to thank the most, Bradley for leading me out of Silvermoor!"

Musgrove offered his condolences. "I am really sorry that Rathek lost his life fighting to those giant ant creatures."

"Thank you, Muzzy... Rathek knew that travelling out of Pathylon to find me and Bradley would be dangerous - but his loyalty to the kingdom of Pathylon and his family was too strong," replied Henley. "He paid the price with his life and I am grateful for his brave actions!"

"Bradley smiled at Henley."Well... I'm sure Rathek too would have been very proud of your actions in Silvermoor too - I'm certainly proud to have you as my Uncle!"

Henley nodded in appreciation and continued to explain why he had decided to suggest they go for a walk in the woods. "Being here in the forest is very appropriate for what I am about to say next and it could mean that your help is needed again."

"What do you mean, Uncle Henley?" asked Bradley.

"Well, when I was pulled into the left hand fork of the vortex... I met someone - someone you know," revealed Henley. "Actually... someone you know very well indeed."

Sereny was sure she knew who Henley was referring to but probed a little more just in case she was wrong. She adopted a puzzled look and asked. "You mentioned that the forest was appropriate... so, who did you see?"

Henley paused for a moment then decided to explain in more detail the circumstances in which the children could help rather than reveal the person's identity immediately. "Before I tell you who I saw... I want you all to promise me that you won't go running off now to help him - it is important that you listen to everything I have to say."

Sereny smiled and her body was filled with a warm sensation, as the three children chorused their reply. "We promise!"

Bradley asked his uncle the reason for him not revealing who the person was first and Henley explained that the Vortex of Silvermoor holds the keys.

"Keys to what?" asked Musgrove.

"The keys to reincarnation!" replied Henley.

"Is that why you came back to life?" asked Sereny.

"Yes... I collected one of the keys inside the Vortex of Silvermoor and unlocked a door that led me to the chamber beneath the cenotaph," explained Henley. "The person I met in the vortex was a ghost like I was... his soul was not at rest and he was trying to find his way back."

"To where?" asked Bradley.

"It turns out that the left side of the vortex is carrying any lost souls that have been killed against their will and are trying to return to their mortal world... I'm not an expert - but as I said, I collected a key and found my way home," replied Henley. "Now this is my plan... I want to return the favour and I need your help you to find this person so he can claim another key - then he too can return home!"

Musgrove scratched his head and said. "I'm still trying to think who you are talking about... the only dead people we know are already back with us - Bomber, Tank, and Muzzy's Dad!"

Sereny afforded Bradley's uncle a knowing look, as if to inform the Devonian that she knew who he was talking about.

Henley acknowledged the girl's gesture then watched the two boys' debate and he smiled in amusement. Bradley mentioned the two Klomus Hawks and Musgrove replied back with the names of many others that had been killed during their last adventure. Henley interrupted the boy's. "I believe Sereny has worked it out... so shall I tell you now and do you promise not to go rushing off?"

Before they could answer, Musgrove piped in. "You don't need to... I can beat Sereny to it because I know who it is - it's Rathek!" he exclaimed confidently.

Bradley responded. "Don't be daft... how can it be Rathek - we saw his body being carried away by the Troglobites?"

"That's true," said Sereny, in a smug manner. "Bradley's right."

Musgrove was disappointed with himself. He had shown himself up again in front of Sereny and Bradley who had once again been made out to be the hero of the hour. "Okay, I got it wrong... let's see if *Miss Know-it-All* here is right - come on then, put us out of our misery!" he exclaimed.

Henley made one last comment. "I said that this woodland setting was appropriate... one last guess anyone - Bradley?"

Bradley paused for a moment then he smiled with excitement. "It can't be... I hope it's - the big fat tangerine man?"

Sereny screamed out at the top of her voice. "Yes, I was right... Grog!"

Henley burst out laughing and all three children jumped off their tree stumps and started hugging each other. Bradley caught his uncle's eye and put his thumb in the air. "So what do you think about that then?" asked Henley, as the children calmed there excitement.

"Brilliant!" replied Musgrove.

"Fantastic!" exclaimed Sereny. "When I passed through his tomb and his body had gone... I had a feeling something magical would happen to him!"

Henley congratulated Sereny. "Well, you can certainly take full responsibility for Grog's journey through the vortex... if you hadn't fallen through the trap door beneath the blue light - the gate to his tomb would never have been opened and he would still be lying in his crypt."

Sereny smiled and hugged Bradley, as the eternal chosen one declared. "We need to start our next adventure right now... we have to find Grog?" he exclaimed.

"Not so fast... the time is not right and I'm glad you all kept your promise - it's important we stay calm about this," insisted Henley. "The only way to help your Krogon friend is to be patient... he is aware of the situation and he knows that I would be meeting with you."

"So what do we do next?" asked Bradley, as he picked up a stick and waved it at K2. He through it in to the undergrowth to keep the dog preoccupied.

Henley responded to his nephew's question. "Whilst Grog and I travelled through the Vortex of Silvermoor... he told me about the keys - and that a special release key only becomes available every time there is a full moon."

"So how come you got a key and he didn't?" asked Sereny.

334

"Good question," replied Henley, as he took the next turn to throw the stick for K2. "Grog did collect a release key inside the vortex but he insisted that I take it."

"Why?" asked Musgrove.

"I can answer that," interrupted Bradley. "Because Grog isn't stupid or selfish... he knew that if my Uncle Henley made it out of the vortex alive then he would be able to tell us about it - if Grog had taken the key we would have never known about my Uncle."

"Well done, Bradley... that was a great summation," stated Henley. "And you're right... that is why Grog insisted I take the key and I promised him I would go back for him - but there's one problem!"

"And what's that?" asked Musgrove.

Bradley interrupted again. "Sorry guys... I think I know the answer to that as well," he said, as Musgrove dropped his shoulders again. "None of us can enter the left fork of the vortex because we aren't dead!"

"Correctomundo Master Baker... well worked out," praised Henley and he afforded his nephew an admiring look. "So we'll have to try and work out a plan and we won't be able to do it till Christmas... the next full moon isn't till December 25th!"

"I can see lot's of things affecting these rescue plans," suggested Sereny. "Firstly... Muzzy and I will be in Sandmouth at Christmas time and secondly - who do we know who is dead with a lost soul?"

"Kill me," said Bradley calmly.

"Don't be daft... that's insane!" exclaimed Sereny, as she held on to Bradley's arm.

"It's the only way... at least I can control where I go if I entered the Vortex of Silvermoor again - we know that there is an entrance below the old blue light," insisted Bradley, as he acknowledged Sereny's affectionate hold.

Henley intervened. "Sereny is right, Bradley... that is not an option - anyhow we have plenty of time to think of something before Christmas."

The conversation within the group continued for a little while longer and they debated the various options, as they walked through Silvermoor Woods. With no real plan to conclude their discussions, they all agreed to return to Bradley's house.

It did not take long to reach the end of Braithwaite Road and their pace quickened, as they approached the cenotaph. The blue light shone brightly; as they stood side by side and all looked up at the shining beacon.

Bradley broke the silence. "I'm going to rename it... instead of the old blue light - it will be known as the *beacon of hope*!"

"Nice one, Bradley... that's a great title," replied his uncle. "Now... we'd better go back to the house... your Mum and Dad will be wondering where we are."

Musgrove suggested one last thing before they headed back inside. "Do you remember after our last adventure... we toasted our friend Grog - can I suggest we do it again but this time in the hope that we will see him again soon?"

"Good idea, Muzzy," agreed Sereny and smiled. "But we don't have any Dandelion and Burdock!"

Bradley laughed and explained to his uncle about when they said there goodbyes after their summer holiday adventure. "We don't have any plastic cups either!"

Henley noticed a bottle of milk on the doorstep of one of the neighbour's houses. He ran over to collect it and then quickly ran back. "Here you go... let's all take a swig from this - Sereny, ladies first."

"That's very naughty of you... stealing!" said Sereny, as she took hold of the bottle.

Bradley supported his uncle's suggestion. "It's alright Sereny... that's the Brocklesby's house - they don't get back from holiday till next Tuesday."

"Well, I guess it's alright to drink it then... anyhow - it will have gone off by then," laughed Sereny, as she removed the foil top and raised the bottle in the air towards the blue light. "To Grog!"

336

Musgrove took the next slurp and repeated the toast. "To Grog!"

Bradley insisted that his uncle make the next toast but Henley refused and insisted that the three children should be the only ones to honour their long lost friend. So Bradley took the bottle of milk from Musgrove and held it up to the cenotaph then waited.

"What's the matter Bradley?" asked Sereny, as Bradley moved sideways a little.

"Bear with me everyone... I'm just waiting for the clouds to move," explained Bradley, as he focussed on the dark sky beyond the blue light.

"Why?" asked Musgrove.

"Because it's almost a full moon tonight and as my uncle said... there won't be another full moon till Christmas day," replied Bradley, as the clouds shifted and the cenotaph became a silhouette in front of the lunar planet. "Here we go... perfect - I propose a toast to Grog and the beacon of hope!"

"Here... here!" everyone shouted, as Bradley glugged at the milk and then turned to face them with a white moustache that shimmered from the blue light's reflection.

Musgrove joked. "You've got a look of General Eidar, about you, Brad!" he giggled and they all burst into to laughter, as Bradley wiped his mouth with what was left of his orange sleeve.

The group continued to celebrate their last adventure and spoke enthusiastically about the opportunity of meeting Grog again. Frustration was evident on the children's faces and their wait till the next full moon at Christmas seemed like a life time away.

Bradley detached himself from the conversation, as his mind started to wander and he thought about what Turpol had told him on the platform in Freytor. If they were to enter the Vortex of Silvermoor again in December, would the journey eventually lead them back into Pathylon.

Bradley stopped to let the others walk ahead of him and he turned to face the cenotaph. The Gatekeeper's words were still very clear in the boy hero's mind and the *Pyramids of Blood* could reveal a dark secret that will change his life forever. Since he had returned from Pathylon, an aching inside his chest was growing more painful and it felt as though the skeletal form throughout his whole body was changing.

Bradley would have to wait to find out what the long term effects from absorbing the kratennium within the ice-cloud would have on his well-being. But for now he tried to ignore the pain and refocused on the group celebrations ahead, as the others turned and waved their arms at him.

Bradley acknowledged their attention and waved back. "I'll be right with you!" he shouted and took one last look at the blue light before running off towards his friends.

....

Look out for the third book in the amazing
adventures series...

BRADLEY BAKER

and the Pyramids of Blood

The kratennium absorbed from the ice-cloud is taking its effect on Bradley Baker. The boy hero will have to face his greatest challenge yet to overcome the evil strain that is growing inside his young body.

The eternal chosen one will find it hard to differentiate between friend and foe, as he battles with the Shadow Druid to stave off the power induced by the magic potion...

Sneak preview of the first chapter...

1

The Shadow Druid

The power of the storm intensified and the rain hailed down like a shower of bullets, as the waves crashed up against the curved rocky structure. The bottom of a small wooden boat scraped on the shingles, as a tall hooded figure dragged the craft to the safety of a cave at the base of the solitary rock. The strange being had used the small rowing boat to ferry himself across from an ice-ship, which was anchored just north of Hooked Point.

The mysterious figure had made the windswept journey across the Red Ocean from Freytor with the help of a skeleton crew. Together they had managed to maneuver the icy vessel along the coastline of Rekab before securing it the shallow ocean floor. He was here to make a special collection and his task was to seek protection against an impending threat that lurked on the outside world. The mysterious individual was looking for an old spinster, who lived in the stone cottage that was perched a few hundred metres above on the side of the crooked rock.

The stranger made his way over to the base of the three hundred or so rickety steps that ascended to the cottage and he looked upwards to assess the climb. The waves continued smash against the surrounding rocks and the rebounding spray drenched his dark cloak. Smoke rose from the chimney of the cottage and he could see a flickering light from one of the windows. The stranger groaned in anticipation of reaching the rickety house and placed his foot on the first step, as he held on to the mollusk exposed hand rail to begin the long climb up the slippery steps.

Inside the cottage, the old lady moved slowly across the stone floor of the parlour and reached over to take a tall jar of salt from the dresser. She wrapped her long bony fingers around the glass container and held it close to her chest, as she made her way to the sturdy oak kitchen table in the centre of the room.

The spinster supported her arched back, as she positioned the jar next to three other glass containers of differing heights and colours. The combined ingredients would be added to the bubbling water in the cauldron next to the open fire. Then the salt would be added later for seasoning but first the deformed woman picked up the second jar and emptied the contents into the iron cask. The thick white wolf fur fizzled when it hit the scolding liquid and soon disappeared beneath the surface, as the old lady stirred the mixture with a large wooden ladle.

A scabby black cat purred, as it rubbed its body against the spinster's leg and she bent down to pick up the hungry feline. "Ready for your supper are you my little friend?" cackled the witch. "I won't be long, Truffles... just a few more ingredients to add and I'll be done preparing my new potion - it will need to boil for at least an hour before I can store it and I still need to include the most important ingredient."

The cat purred again and jumped out of the witch's arms, as she struggled to lift the third jar off the table. The sparkling contents were heavy and she put her hand inside the jar to pull out three round gleaming objects. "Ah... my favourites - gemstones from the Emerald Caves inside the Mountains of Rekab," exclaimed the witch, as she held one of the glistening stones out in front of her hoary face. The dancing flames from the fire sparkled through the pure green crystals and she smiled an evil grin, as she cast them one-by-one into the cauldron.

The emeralds made distinct plopping sounds as they hit the water and a haze of green smoke steamed up from the surface of the bubbling liquid and she added two more gems. "Five of those beauties should be enough," declared the old lady, as she stirred the liquid again and then replaced the lid back on the jar.

The cat purred again and rubbed against the witches leg once more, as the old lady delayed adding the contents of the forth container. "Very well, Truffles... you win - anything to please you my precious little fluffykins," stated the witch and placed the cat's bowl on the floor. "There you are... freshly caught flax meat - nothing but the best for my little darling!"

The aged spinster picked up the fourth jar and carefully opened the lid. A strong stale smell of rotten eggs filled the room and the fur on the cat's back stood on end, as it devoured the raw flesh in its bowl. The old lady picked up a spoon and scooped out the smelly contents from the glass container. The paste was dark brown in colour and was made up of crushed Troglobite eggs, powdered Krogon bones and mixed with Hoffen urine to bind the stock. "Now... I have to be careful not to add too much of this particular ingredient - one level spoonful will be sufficient!"

The witch tapped the spoon on the side of the cauldron and the sticky paste dropped into the melting pot. The bubbles grew larger and more intense, as she rinsed the remains of the stock off the spoon and continued to stir the liquid at the same time. The potent smell wafted up under her large hooked nose and she closed her eyes to enjoy the smell, as the odour was drawn into her flaring nostrils. "Beautiful... now, just a little salt and we can leave it to boil," mumbled the witch, as she took the first jar and emptied all the contents into the mixture. "You can't have enough salt... that's what I say!"

The witch stirred the potion for a few more minutes until the paste had thickened the mixture. She then placed the ladle on the hearth and made her way over to the parlour window. Her dark clothing and wrinkled skin made her look a lot older than her fifty five years, as her scrawny silhouette stood hunched in front of the moon lit window panes. "Tomorrow night will bring a full moon and my potion will be ready for the final ingredient... but first I will need to venture out to collect it!" she exclaimed and looked over to the mainland at the twinkling lights scattered like dust over the Crystal City.

The view from the window looked out across the water to the mainland of Rekab, which was a mystical world full of haunted forests and horror torn cities. The witch only ventured from Hooked Point and across the narrow water inlet to the mainland during daylight hours. At night some of the habitual creatures of Rekab would prey on any unsuspecting strangers that were brave enough to travel across the open territory of the treacherous landscape.

The cat had finished its food and jumped on to the window sill to join the witch, as she continued to stare out to the mainland. "Did you enjoy your flax, my dear?" asked the witch and gently stroked the cats head, as she described the view to the uninterested animal. "Look out there, Truffles... to the north live the Were beasts, a species of wolf-like predators who hunt in packs and protect their crudely built homes in a place called Wolf Town - further inland, on the edge of the town there is a thick woodland setting called Yeldarb Forest where a strange scurry of black squirrels hide and cohabit with the Wood Ogres," explained the deranged old lady.

The witch was fully aware that the cat did not understand a word she was saying but she continued to describe the dark landscape despite a lack of response from the nonchalant pet.

The moonlight illuminated the horizon and the witch pointed her finger, as her nail scraped on the window glass. "Now... you see the mountains in the distance?" she asked, as the cat continued to ignore her and lick its fur. "That's where I found my beautiful gemstones... inside the Emerald Caves," continued the witch. "And let's not forget those magnificent specimens that crown the centre ground of Rekab and attract so many unwanted visitors to our land... the Pyramids of Blood!"

The three pyramids stood south of the Yeldarb Forest and were worshipped daily by the dwarfish inhabitants of Crystal City. Every time a creature from the city died, a grand ceremony would take place and the deceased dwarf would be buried in front of the tallest pyramid, which was named *Talum* because of its aluminum tipped apex. The collective name for the pyramids was associated with blood because of the underground river that flowed beneath the structures. Before a dwarf was buried, it would have its head removed to prevent the body returning to back to mortality. The blood from the dead dwarf would run into the river below the pyramids and thus the name for the great landmarks was derived from the ceremonial acts.

The witch looked away and walked across the parlour. She placed the cat on the table and then approached the cauldron again. A quick stir with the ladle and the potion was ready to cool. The light in the room dimmed considerably, as she doused the embers of the fire and left the contents of the cauldron to simmer back. "Come along, Truffles... it's time for bed and we have to set off early in the morning - we have to catch the tide when it's out."

The cat obviously understood this particular topic of conversation and leapt off the table straight into the old lady's arms, as the witch picked up a rusty oil lamp from the dresser. The witch cast another look out of the kitchen window and observed the incessant activity across the water. "It's nearly midnight and the lights in Crystal City are still shining," she observed and struck the lamp to ignite the flame. "That can only mean one thing... another dwarf has perished today and it's just what we'll need to finish our project - the *Shadow Druid* is due to arrive tomorrow evening and he will be very pleased with this particular potion!" she exclaimed in an excited and croaky voice. "It is tradition that the dwarfs bury their dead before the next sunrise so there has to be a burial ceremony tonight... we need to collect fresh blood from the river and we'll have to get to the pyramids and back before nightfall tomorrow - we don't want to be late for the *Master's* arrival and the blood has to be warm when we collect it," she explained and concluded the self appraisal. "There has to be a full moon when we add the dwarf's blood to the mixture!"

Everything was in place and the timings were perfect for the witch, as she closed the door behind her and left the parlour. With the cat still purring in her arms, the old lady made her way upstairs to the only bedroom in the cottage. "Sleepy time for Truffles," she whispered and entered the room.

Suddenly, the stifled sound of crashing waves against the rocky isle was eclipsed by a loud banging noise that emanated from the front door of the cottage. The witch placed the cat carefully on the mattress and made her way to the top of the landing, as the persistent thudding continued to pound at the door. "Alright, alright... I'm coming - wait a minute!" she shouted and held on tightly to the hand rail, as she climbed down the narrow staircase sideways.

The thumping on the door continued and was briefly interrupted by intermittent lightning bolts that lit up the hallway through the tiny round windows. The ugly facial features of the witch were highlighted and the flashing strikes were quickly followed by the deep rumbling of thunder.

The witch pushed the metal spy-hole cover aside and peered through at the strange hooded figure that was waiting impatiently on the doorstep. The stranger had his arms folded and both were hidden by the sleeves of his dark cloak, as the

347

frightened old lady bent down and shouted through the keyhole. "What do you want?" she cackled and took a step back from the door.

No reply came, as she approached the door again and peered through the spy-hole. The witch focused her line of sight, as another bolt of lightning lit up the porch area. The hooded figure had disappeared from view. "Where are you?" shouted the old lady and proceeded to slowly turn the latch. "Who would be visiting me at this time of night... and on such a stormy evening?"

Before she had chance to answer her own question the door burst open and the dark figure stood with his arms still permanently folded, as the sheets of rain poured down over his heavy cloak. The shadowy figure's head was bowed to shield his face and the witch was transfixed by the powerful presence of the ghost-like being.

The uninvited guest took a few steps forward and entered the cottage, as the old lady took a few steps back. The hinges on the door creaked, as it slammed shut and the whistling noise of the storm ceased. An eerie quietness filled the hallway and the muffled silence was interrupted by the slow dripping of water from the stranger's cloak. The witch lowered her head and focussed her attention on the droplets of water, which formed miniature rivers that trickled through the dust on the worn oak floorboards. She was momentarily transfixed by the movement of the salty water, as the streams merged into one large puddle.

The old spinster shook her head to clear the momentary trance and looked up again to face the stranger, as another flash of lightening lit the hallway. She finally plucked up enough courage to ask the mysterious visitor to reveal his identity and was interrupted by the cat, as it meowed from the top flight of the stairs. "Be quiet Truffles!" she shouted and turned her attention back to the hooded figure. "Who are you and want do you want?" she asked in a nervous tone, as the cat leapt down the staircase and brushed up against the stranger's wet cloak. The rain water caused the cat's fur to stand up like electrical spikes, as it meowed softly again to welcome the hallowed guest and the witch commented. "It would appear that Truffles likes you… she is normally very particular about who to approach!" she exclaimed, as the shadowy figure lifted his hands out of the rain-sodden cloak sleeves.

The stranger lifted his arms and held the side of the hood that shielded his face. The old woman watched in anticipation, as he pulled the hood back to reveal his identity. She placed her wart covered hands across her mouth and drew a sharp intake of breath, as she screeched out a shocking revelation. "It's you!"

···········•

Follow the Author

DAVID LAWRENCE JONES

http://www.facebook.com/davlawjones

twitter: @DavLawJones

Discover more about General Eidar (pictured) and all the
other characters in the Amazing Adventures series;

http://www.bradley-baker.com